The Last Raider

It's 1994 and a downed Navy pilot is held captive by a ruthless Serbian colonel. The White House will not authorize a rescue mission. The young pilot's grandfather Carl Bridger and three of his WW II bomber crew must fly Carl's restored and modified B-25 into enemy territory in a desperate all-out attempt to rescue his grandson.

Reader Comments:

Wonderful, well-written story on par with any Clancy, Griffin, or Coonts titles. — Stanton Pratt

Not just a military book but very entertaining on many levels! Great job! Really keeps your interest. — Randy Zenk

A good read cover to cover. I was amazed at the detail and accuracy. This story is real page-turner. The author puts you right in the scenes especially in the plane. — Anon

Excellent story! I feel like I've met these guys at one time or another. The characters were well developed and believable. — Joseph Gordon

An excellent read for any and all! — Anita Lhue

I couldn't put it down! The story pulled me in from the first page. — Gerry Jones

The Last Raider

A Novel by

Spencer Anderson

Synergy Books Publishing, USA

Text copyright © 2014 by Spencer Anderson

Cover Art © 2014 by Spencer Anderson

All rights reserved. Published in the United States by

Synergy Books Publishing, USA.

First Edition —

— First Printing, February, 2015

— Second Printing, July, 2015

Visit us on the web at: www.synergy-books.com

ISBN Hard Bound: 978-1-936434-67-1
ISBN Soft Bound: 978-1-936434-68-8
ISBN E-Book: 978-1-936434-69-5
ISBN Audio Book: 978-1-936434-71-8

tographic evidence of what the Serbs are up to, if anything. That is your next mission: to fly a photo recon sortie into the area. You two get the short straw on this one ... questions?" Messner offered.

Cody cleared his throat. "Yes sir. It looks like we'll be violating the no-fly zone in order to get what we need. Will we have air cover?"

"Negative, Lieutenant. We can't afford to create an incident by sending in an entire flight of armed aircraft. You'll be on your own. Your target is this area outside Sarajevo," Messner pointed to a red circle on the map. "The details are in your mission packet. You'll want to get in and out fast, gentlemen. Two armed Tomcats will be orbiting here, just inside friendly airspace, to escort you back to the Roosevelt. Wheels up at 0840, gentlemen."

Cody and Perry stood as Messner left the room. The two walked out of the briefing room and headed to the ready room to don their G-suits and other gear for the mission.

"I don't like this, Archer. We don't have any backup in case we meet hostiles up there. We're going inside enemy territory with no teeth. What if we're engaged by MiGs?" Perry wanted some reassurance, or maybe some expression of concern from Cody that matched the unpleasant sour taste of fear in his mouth. He swallowed hard and pushed the feeling to the back of his mind.

"Relax, Per. Five minutes in and five minutes out. Our guys will be orbiting on the edge of the no-fly zone. All we have to do is make it clear of Serbian airspace and we're home free," Cody replied.

Forty minutes later the two friends climbed the ladders to the open cockpit of their F-14 Fighter/Reconnaissance jet. The Low Altitude Navigation and Targeting Infrared for Night (LANTIRN) system had been swapped out for a photo-recon mission employing the Tactical Airborne Reconnaissance Pod System (TARPS). They were tasked to locate and photograph military strongholds of the

Serbian forces of the Republika Sprska in and around Sarajevo.

The jet catapulted from the deck of CVN-71 and climbed to 3,000 feet before turning toward the eastern coastline of the Adriatic Sea. Ten minutes later, the F-14 began orbiting on-station over a predetermined point in Serbian-controlled airspace approximately seven-thousand feet above and twelve miles east of Sarajevo. Intelligence reported the buildup of a Serbian Army outpost near the city and the presence of Serbian MiG-21s in the area in direct violation of the U.N. no-fly zone.

"Okay, Per, keep your eyes out for bogeys and light up the cameras. Coming up on target in 3 ... 2 ... 1."

The RIO captured the targeted locations, one after the other as Cody flew the Tomcat on a predetermined grid pattern.

"That's the last one, Archer. Let's get the hell out of here."

"Roger that. I'll feel a lot better once we're back on-board the Roosevelt." He hadn't been able to calm his uneasy sense of something going wrong that began in the briefing room.

No MiGs had made their presence known, and they got some good photos of the Serbian encampment that would keep the intelligence people busy. The F-14 turned back toward the carrier.

"Another routine sortie, Per, let's head for home," Cody said with more confidence than he felt.

"Roger that, Archer. We got some good pics of the Serbian base. I can't be sure, but I think they're setting up a mobile missile site. I can't wait to get our recon photos back to the Roosevelt."

"Yeah, well I hope it was worth the trip. NATO must have thought it was important enough to violate its own no-fly rule." Cody banked the fighter west toward the Adriatic Sea and home.

The ten-inch screen of Lt. Judd's Programmable Tactical Information Display (PTID) lit up.

"Bogeys inbound. One...no, two SAMs." Perry called out. Cody saw them at the same time and immediately went to full military power while he pulled sharply back on the control stick and put the fighter into a high-G climb. Pulling between 8 and 10 Gs, Cody   released a bloom of hot burning magnesium flares and banked hard right to draw-off the bogey. The lead SAM took the bait and exploded harmlessly below and behind them. Cody rolled the fighter over and pulled the power all the way back, banking hard at a ninety-degree plane to the remaining inbound missile's path. As he completed his turn, he applied after-burner and held his bank angle while he released another bloom of flares, but the missile had already jinked toward them. The explosion rocked the jet and alarms blared in the cockpit. His port engine failed.

"Damn! Port engine out!"

With his heart pounding in his chest, Cody expertly manip-ulated ailerons, rudder, elevator, and throttle against the F-14's ten-dency to drop out of controlled flight after high-G turns. His airspeed suddenly dropped by 200 knots because of the drag on the airframe caused by the maneuvers and loss of one engine. "Archer" brought the F-14 out of the flat spin and advanced the throttle on the remaining good engine.

"We're still good, Per. Let's grab some altitude." Cody couldn't suppress a nervous break in his voice. The missile hit had shaken him badly, but his training took over and he suppressed his growing urge to panic. He soon brought his heart rate and his emo-tions under control. *Thank you, Lord,* he thought as he applied af-terburner to the good engine, and put the Tomcat into a steep climb.

"Roger that, Archer. That was too close." the RIO said shakily.

At that moment the compressor on the right TF30 turbofan engine failed, and the light went out on the remaining engine.

"Alarm! Starboard engine flameout!" Cody's trained eyes scanned the Multi-function display and engine parameters. He immediately noted the compressor problem. *Dammit!* His mind shouted.

With no power and at an altitude of only three-thousand feet above the surface, Cody knew he didn't have enough altitude to attempt a windmill restart of his only good engine. They could not hope to make it to safety.

"Eject! Eject! Eject! Cody commanded as he rolled the plane back to level flight, popped the canopy and pushed his head against the contoured seatback. First his RIO pulled his ejection lever, followed a fraction of a second later by Lieutenant Bridger. Seven seconds after the flameout two bright trails of rocket flame propelled the airmen up and away from the crippled jet.

CHAPTER II

Carl Bridger pushed back the brim of his sweat-stained Justin hat and, with the palm of his hand, shaded his face from the bright afternoon sun. His ice-blue eyes scanned the expanse of sun-bleached prairie grass waving gently in the mountain breeze, causing amber swells to undulate in a lulling rhythm that spoke peace to his heart. A lover of the outdoors, he cherished the open range of the north central part of the state. He and Annie rode these same rolling hills often after they moved on to the ranch in 1978 following the passing of his father Gifford Bridger. Carl retired early from the CIA and took ownership of the Rocking Double-B Ranch per his father's wishes.

"I miss you, Annie." His wife had been gone, dead from cancer, for twelve years. The thought of her pushed him deep into a reverie of those times they rode together. Their years on the ranch provided many compelling memories, mostly heartwarming, and a few heartbreaking. The latter thought brought a pang of loneliness to his heart. *Stop it, Bridger. She wouldn't like the self pity,* he admonished himself.

"C'mon, Two-bit, … H'yah!" Carl nudged the animal into an easy canter, and headed toward a ridge, on the other side of which his foreman and several of the ranch hands were engaged in counting a group of the 17,000 head of cattle carrying the Rocking Double-B brand.

Carl grew up on the 22,000 acre ranch northeast of Cascade, Montana and learned the cattle business under the watchful eye of his father. Giff taught him to ride when he was four, and gave the boy his first horse for his eighth birthday on August 17th, 1931. He learned to handle a lasso at eight, and at ten his father trained him to rope and tie a steer for branding. Carl won the Montana State Fair Junior Team- Roping Championship when he was twelve and was handling full ranch hand duties from then on. The boy thought he'd never leave the ranch...never wanted to, either. He loved it here.

All of that changed on December 7th, 1941 when the combined air and sea forces of the Empire of Japan attacked and all but destroyed the American 7th fleet at Pearl Harbor. Carl was eighteen-years old. Being the only son of a cattle rancher he was granted a waiver from the draft. Beef and leather goods quickly became high demand military items. The Rocking Double-B brand contracted with the government for eighty percent of its cattle.

By the end of 1944, Carl had a need to scratch a severe case of "red-ass," best described as that righteous urge to answer the call to duty his father drilled into him through the years: *A patriot never knows he's a patriot until he fights for his country. It's a man's duty, son.* Carl entered the Army Air Corps and was found possessed of that unique set of skills which qualified him for pilot training. Within a few weeks after boot camp he was sitting behind the controls of a B-25 twin-engine medium bomber at Maxwell Field's Advanced Pilot Training School in Montgomery, Alabama.

The blaring ring-tone of his cell phone caused Carl to reign in Two-bit. He reached into the saddle bag and withdrew the device. He was thankful for the new technology that allowed him to talk to someone hundreds of miles away while sitting astride Two-bit, high in the summer range on the Double-B.

"Yeah, Carl here," he drawled.

"Pop, this is Giff." Carl's only son, named after his grandfather, spoke with an edge to his voice that suggested trouble.

"Giff ... haven't talked to you since you called on Father's Day, son. When are you and Alisa comin' up to the ranch? It's been too long." Carl knew his son was busy trying to juggle family and his responsibilities as President and C.E.O. of the high-tech company InterDyn Corporation, a weapons design and manufacturer of cutting- edge human interfaced defense systems based in Utah.

"Pop, I ... I have some bad news. Cody's F-14 got hit by a missile over Serbia. He's down, Pop." Cody Bridger was Gifford's oldest child and Carl's only grandson.

Carl's heart sank, and his breath caught in his throat. "When, son? Has the Navy sent out Search and Rescue? Do they know where he is?" he choked out.

"He's been missing for ten days, Pop. I only just heard about it yesterday. The Navy put a lid on the incident for 'national security' reasons, or so they say. To be honest, I'm pissed off, Dad. I called the Pentagon and ..." his voice trembled "... talked to my contact in USNORTHCOM. SECNAV has ordered the USS Theodore Roosevelt to stand-down from any attempt to send a recovery team to the area."

"Why the hell not, Giff? What national security reasons?" Carl couldn't believe what he was hearing.

"That's all I know. I need to do something, but I don't know where to begin."

"I bet Alisa and Rachel are beside themselves. I'm so sorry, son." Carl's mind searched for anything he might do to help lighten Gifford's and Alisa's load. "I want to help. Is there anything I can do?

"They're as upset and angry as I am. The Pentagon is being stone quiet about this, Pop. I've called every contact I know in the Department of the Navy and even a member of the House Armed Services Committee that has pushed a couple of InterDyn's contracts through committee. They're either playing dumb, or they don't know anything. I was hoping you could help; maybe call someone. Do you still have any contact with the CIA?"

Gifford's mention of the Central Intelligence Agency ratcheted up Carl's caution meter. He hadn't talked to any of the old guard at the Agency since '82, the year breast cancer took Annie from him; no one, that is, except his old friend and one time protégé Mac Aldrin.

Carl's career took an unexpected turn in '47 as a result of two signatures by President Harry S. Truman. One was the bill creating a new branch of the military, the United States Air Force. The other was Truman's signing into law the National Security Act. For Carl, those actions meant a career change: either become a pilot-instructor for the U.S.A.F or muster out of active duty altogether. He loved flying, but the thought of being a non-mission-related pilot trainer didn't hold much appeal.

Like a fastball pitch right at his strike zone, the answer came in the form of a suited, be-speckled intelligence officer from D.C. His assignment was to recruit into the newly formed Central Intelligence Agency the brightest and best of soldiers, sailors, and airmen who had distinguished themselves in the war. Carl's two Distinguished Flying Cross citations placed his dossier at the top of the pile of prospective CIA field agents. Carl's mastery of Russian helped as well. He learned the basics of Russian in high school. Later, with help from his former B-25 co-pilot, Alexandre Chekov, he became proficient, mastering a Ukraine dialect in the process. Alex, as he preferred to be called, was born in the U.S. after his parents emigrated from Russia following the revolution by the Lenin-led Communist Rebellion.

Carl and Annie packed up and moved themselves and baby Gifford to Virginia where Carl began his CIA field training at the "Farm" in Quantico.

"McKenzie Aldrin is still there. Mac came to me as a new field agent when I was Station Chief in Budapest. He's Deputy Director of Covert Operations now. I'll call him, Giff, but I don't think he'll tell me much even if he knows something. I'll get back to you."

Carl collapsed the antenna and put the brick-sized phone back into the saddle bag.

"This can't be happening. Not to Cody. I won't let it happen!" He yelled, tapping his right boot heel on Two-bit's flank. The big bay-roan quarter horse spun to the right. He kicked Two-bit into a full gallop toward the main house.

Two days had passed since Carl's third call to Quantico and his conversation with Giff. He had left messages on Mac's phone and with his aide. The message stated simply, "Mac, I need to talk to you about my grandson." Mac would make the connection, no problem. The Deputy DCI of Covert Operations and Carl had kept in touch, albeit sporadically, over the years.

Carl figured ... hoped ... Mac was working off the book on his request, which would explain the reason Carl hadn't heard back from his friend. Phone conversations in and out of the Agency were notoriously un-secure.

At 6:30 a.m. Carl checked with his ranch foreman, Clete Plunkett, and briefed him on the day's work, then drove into town for his favorite breakfast of eggs, biscuits smothered in sausage gravy, toast, coffee, and orange juice.

The Wagonwheel Motel and Restaurant had the best food in town; the main reason being that the diner was the only eatery in Cascade. Another, and more personal reason for Carl's driving to town, came in the form of Beth Thomlinson.

Beth stayed on to run the Wagonwheel after her husband Garret passed away in '83. The Thomlinsons were close friends to Annie and Carl. They stood at Carl's side when Annie died. Carl returned the favor by comforting Beth when Garret passed suddenly from a heart attack a year later. Beth had found Garret in the middle of his wheat field still sitting in the cab of his Massey Ferguson tractor.

"Hey there tall, grey and wrinkled, it's been a while." Beth's jibe brought a grin to Carl's face.

"Hi ya, gorgeous. Figured I'd punish myself with one of your famous cholesterol specials. It's nice to see ya, Bethy. Business good?" Carl didn't need the menu, and Beth knew his order by heart. She was the balm his heart needed to salve the pain of his family's recent troubles. He could feel his heart lifting from the doldrums.

"Business is always good during summer and fall. Workin' on a landscape of the Grand Tetons. It's a period piece with Indian tepees and horses. Startin' to get some tourist traffic comin' and goin' between Yellowstone and Great Falls. Got a couple of fellas pulled in about an hour ago in a black SUV. They checked in for an overnight stay."

"Oh, yeah? Hmmm, most likely tourists, like you said. Hey, why don't you join me for breakfast? I'd like to catch up." Carl offered a smile that wasn't missed by Beth. He had developed an unvoiced yen for this artist-entrepreneur.

"Sure thing. Back in a jiffy." Five minutes later Beth returned with their meals and a fresh pot of coffee. She eased her still youthful body onto the bench across from Carl. "So what keeps you busy out on the Double-B these days?"

"Checkin' on the herd in the high range. In a few weeks, it'll be time to bring the cattle down to pasture. Mostly, though, the Plunkett boys do the heavy lifting. Clete and the other hands will handle the drive, so I can take as much time as I want to work on *Annie*." Carl took a generous bite of the gravy-covered biscuit.

"Now Carl, you've been working on that monstrosity since you and Annie moved in. Are you ever going to get it off the ground?"

"Yes, indeed. Pretty soon, actually. Getting the '25 back from China was the hardest part; a genuine diplomatic pain in the ass. If the plane hadn't been in the way of a government housing project in the area, she probably wouldn't have been found at all. They were glad to let me haul her away and get a fist full of cash in return. I'm into the restoration too far to quit now. The *Annie* will fly. She's almost ready for her maiden flight. What about you, Beth? You keepin' up with your painting? You're the best artist to come along in these parts since Charles Russell."

Beth blushed at the compliment. "That's pretty high praise, but thank you, kind sir."

Carl had learned over the years that Beth's painting was a big reason for Garret's and her move to the area. After Garret passed, Beth sold the acreage and kept the house. She bought the bedraggled motel for a song and designed a total remodel of the place.

"It's true, though. I love your work. You did a great job on the remodel of the old motel, too, Bethy. The upgrades you added, the remodel of the diner and changing the name really work. 'The Wagonwheel Motel and Restaurant' fits the area much better than the old 'Bailey Motel' did. I'm happy that things have worked out well for you."

"Thanks, hon ... oh, by the way, I sold three paintings on consignment last week. It looks like my stuff is starting to get some recognition in the western art market. I'm a lot like you, Carl: comfortable, healthy, and not beholding to anybody. Life is good; lonely at times, but good. The State Fair's around the corner. I'm thinking about entering a few of my newer landscapes. I've been asked to do a show at the Helena Fine Arts gallery to kick off the fair. The curator called me back in March, so I've been painting up a storm ever since."

He found himself in want of her effervescent optimism and humor. They liked each other...very much.

"That's great news, Beth. Hey, I have an idea. What do you say we get together for dinner and a movie Friday night, and you can tell me all about it." Carl wanted very much to hear more about Beth's success with her painting. He also desperately needed to tell her about Cody's situation, and to feel her support.

"Are you asking me to go on a date, Mister Bridger? My, my, what will people say?" Beth batted her eyelashes at Carl for added effect which brought a laugh from the old rancher.

Carl left the Wagonwheel with a full stomach and a peaceful glow in his heart. As he walked to his truck, he noticed a shiny black Suburban SUV parked in front of one of the units. The Montana plate was not of the typical blue-on-white emblazoned with "Big Sky Country" seen on most civilian vehicles. The Suburban's tag was clearly marked "U.S. Government" in blue letters. *Mac,* he thought. *If I'm right, I'll let him come to me.*

    Carl parked his truck in front of the main house and walked to the barn. He fumbled with his keys and found the one he wanted. Removing the padlock from the hasp, he pushed the huge door back on its tracks and entered the oversized barn containing six horse stalls, a tack room, a hay loft, a blacksmith shop for doing his own horse shoeing ... and a Billy Mitchell B-25 medium bomber.

    Two weeks earlier he had finished the last of the painting of the fuselage and wings. The World War II blue star with a red circle in the middle on a white chevron shined in sharp contrast to the olive-green over sky blue belly. The original serial-number plate had been replaced by a shiny replica and screwed into the instrument panel; 40-2236, one of the original Doolittle Raiders that flew from the deck of the USS Hornet on a one-way mission into the history books. It had been a daring bombing raid at the heart of Tokyo on April 18, 1942, just four months after Pearl Harbor. One of the last of 16 bombers to fly off the Hornet, 2236, flying on fumes, reached the China coast where she attempted a controlled wheels-up landing in the heavy jungle near a friendly Chinese fishing village. She almost made it, except for a long abandoned shrine in the path of the '25. She ran out of fuel and had to set down. The pilot couldn't stop her from plowing into a massive stone wall, crushing the Plexiglas nose and killing both of the guys in the cockpit. Carl's subsequent investigation was stalled by Communist red tape, and he never found out what happened to the rest of the crew.

He only knew that one body had been recovered. First Lieutenant Stanley Crane, U.S. Army Air Corps, 1918-1942 can be found in Arlington National Cemetery.

The last four numbers of the bomber's serial number shone proudly emblazoned in yellow on the vertical stabilizers. Carl stenciled his name for the bomber in bright red script on both sides of the fuselage below the Plexiglas cockpit ... *Annie*.

Carl backed his Case IH-4694 tractor up to the front of the '25and hooked the tow bar onto a sturdy yoke connecting chains to the main gear struts. He didn't want to risk damaging the nose wheel by placing the heavy load on the front strut alone.

For the first time in forty-nine years, the powerful lines of the beautiful skin of 40-2236 glistened in the sun, looking like she did when she came off the line at North American Aviation back in February, 1942.

Carl parked the tractor and removed the chains. He started his walk-around preflight inspection when he noticed a black SUV exit the state road onto his property. He recognized the Suburban as the same one he saw at the Wagonwheel earlier. He walked toward the main house as the government car pulled into the gravel drive and stopped.

Two men climbed out of the Suburban. One wore a dark suit and expensive looking sunglasses. The other, an older man, was dressed in casual denim jeans, a sensible cotton shirt and light tan wind-breaker. His feet sported black lace-up Doc Martens.

"Mac ... is that you?" Carl walked up to the two men with hand extended.

"None other, old friend. How the hell are you, Carl?" Mac Aldrin took his hand in a warm, firm handshake. "It's been too long. I'm only sorry it has to be under such dower circumstances."

"I'm mighty glad you're here, Mac. I wasn't sure you got my message. Who is this dapper young man?" Carl nodded toward the "suit."

"Sheldon Macvie, Mister Bridger. I'm honored to meet you, sir. You're a legend at the Agency." The youthful looking agent held a straight face as he shook Carl's hand.

Carl took note of Macvie's eyes flitting about as if he were taking note of every detail of his surroundings from behind the amber lenses of his Foster Grants. *He's all business, this one,* Carl thought, and stored his first impression of the young agent for future reference.

Mac kept looking over Carl's shoulder at the *Annie.*

"What have you got going here, Carl? My gosh, she looks brand new. You told me back in '82 you negotiated a deal with Beijing to recover an original Doolittle Raider. You claimed her as a national treasure, didn't you?"

"It was the only way I could cut through the red tape; that, plus a nice bundle of cash in the hands of the Chinese Industrial Bank of Beijing. They were funding a major housing project in the province where the '25 was found. It's easier doing business with a bank than with the government of The People's Republic of China. The CIB arranged for the plane to be moved, loaded on to a Hong Kong-bound freighter, and from there I brought her to the States. I was just about to take her up for a test flight. You want to come?"

Carl seized the opportunity to talk privately to his old friend about his grandson, preferably out of ear-shot of Sheldon Macvie. Apparently, Mac was on the same page, because he didn't hesitate.

"Hell yes, I do." Mac was a good private pilot in his own right. He was certified IFR and had his multi-engine rating. "Shel, hang out here at the house. I'll be back in a jiff."

"Roger that, boss."

19

Shel Macvie would make good use of his time. The young agent sensed something was about to happen outside the established boundaries of Agency protocol. Being constantly on the watch for opportunities to advance his career, Macvie was a ferret where it came to sniffing out irregularities such as these; *just visiting an old friend...really, Boss?* He thought. That was Mac's story. Sheldon knew about Cody Bridger's relationship to Carl. He also knew about the shoot down and subsequent capture of the pilot and his RIO. So, he insisted on joining Mac on the Montana trip. Mac couldn't refuse Sheldon's request without drawing suspicion to himself. The young agent would conduct a thorough recon of the house for clues as to the real reason behind the visit.

"I leveled and compacted 2,000 feet of the alfalfa field and fenced it off to keep animals out. I mowed the strip three days ago, so we're good to go. Climb on in, Mac. I'm itching to get airborne." Carl led the way up the steel ladder into the belly of the plane, and helped get Mac settled in the right seat of the cockpit. He pulled the ladder up behind them and closed the crew-access hatch.

Once inside, Carl buckled himself into the pilot's seat. He felt the rush of adrenalin as he began the engine-start sequence; first the ignition switch to the "on" position, followed by the booster switch and the primer. He noted the satisfactory "click-click-click" of the fuel filling the primer line. The moment of truth arrived. He held down the energizer, primer, and engager switches. The starboard propeller began to turn as Carl moved the mixture lever to the full-rich position. The Wright 2600 14-cylinder power plant belched a puff of smoke and fired up. He adjusted the throttle to idle at 1,200 rpm while he repeated the sequence for the left engine. It, too, started without a problem.

With both engines idling smoothly, Carl did a quick sweep

of the engine instruments. All the gauges were in the green. The excitement he felt was intense. He was about to take a B-25 up for the first time in forty-nine years, and he was as hyped as a race horse on Derby day.

"Here, put on your headset so we can talk to each other!" Carl yelled over the noise from the engine. Both men pulled their headsets over their ears and adjusted their microphones.

"Can you hear me alright, Mac?"

"I hear you, Carl. My gosh, this is exciting!"

Carl released the brakes and eased the throttles forward until *Annie* began to roll. He taxied out to the end of the grass strip and performed the engine run-up sequence. He smiled, the engines and instruments performing without a hitch. He reset the propeller pitch to 1600 rpm. "Ready, Mac?"

Mac looked at Carl and grinned as he raised his thumb in a "good to go" gesture. "Man, listen to those engines. I never realized the '25 was so loud. I'm glad we have our headsets on."

"Roger that. Back in the day we stuffed our ears with cotton. Quite a few guys suffered hearing loss and got grounded."

Carl lowered the flaps half-way and eased the throttles forward as *Annie* began her take-off roll. Satisfied the bomber's nose was centered on the dirt strip, he pushed the throttles firmly forward to maximum power. At 80 mph, he applied a little back pressure on the control yoke to lessen the strain on the nose wheel. At 100 mph, the cool morning Montana air caressed the bomber's wings and lifted her from the ground. Carl brought up the gear and flaps. When the airspeed indicator reached 120 mph he raised *Annie's* nose above the horizon and began a smooth climb, banking the ship to the left. He set his course for the Wagonwheel, planning to give Beth a little surprise. He knew the town sheriff well enough to know he wouldn't call the FAA if he flew below the minimum five-hundred feet above the buildings of the small town. At two-hundred feet above the ground, Carl set his airspeed at 180 mph.

At 1:00 p.m. the lunch regulars talked quietly in their usual booths at the Wagonwheel restaurant. Beth was cheerfully serving up burgers and fries, salads, French dip sandwiches, pie and coffee to her customers. A faint droning sound came to her ears. At first she thought it was the air conditioner acting up; but, then the sound got louder ... and louder still. Before anyone could say a word, the B-25 roared overhead.

"What in the Lord's name was that?" Chester Gibbons was not one to profane, but when he jumped up from the booth and spilled his coffee in his lap he gave in to the moment. "Oh, shit!" He blushed and apologized to his dining partner who was belly-laughing at his friend's plight.

The restaurant emptied into the street, including Beth, and all nine people turned their eyes skyward. The '25 was completing a tight bank and headed back to the diner. This time, *Annie* waggled her wings when she roared overhead.

"Oh my ..." Beth uttered softly, as she raised her hands to her breast. "… He's done it!"

Carl took *Annie* up to one-two-thousand feet and set the auto pilot on a course toward Yellowstone. He set the radio to the Common Traffic Advisory Frequency (CTAF) and announced his position for the benefit of any local air traffic.

Army four-zero-two-two-three-six is type B-25, altitude one-two-thousand on a heading of two-four-zero degrees, one- zero miles south of Helena.

"I hope you're licensed to fly this thing. You're likely to hear from the FAA about that low pass." Mac Aldrin grinned over at Carl.

"No problem. I fly a few hours every month down at the

Helena Municipal Airport to keep my license current. A friend of mine owns a Beech Baron he lets me take up whenever I need to. I'll tell you, Mac, this is the most fun I've had in long time. Ya gotta love this!" Carl was enjoying the adrenalin rush of the decade.

It's time to get down to business, Carl thought. He glanced over at his friend. "What do you have for me, Mac?"

"The Agency has a deep cover operative in the Serbian Republika Sprska. He knew about the downed F-14 before I contacted him. It caused a lot of excitement among the Serbs. They sighted two parachutes about six clicks outside Sarajevo. Serbian forces located and captured both men and it's our operative's best intel they're being held in a fenced and guarded compound somewhere in the forest near the '84 Winter Olympic site. The CIA has asked NASA to position a satellite over the area. We should know more in a few days."

"Does the Defense Department and SECNAV know about this?" Carl was beginning to suspect some political spin, but needed more information.

"Navy Intelligence and SECNAV were briefed by Defense. All I can tell you is the White House has put a lid on the whole thing. D.C. is in negotiations with N.A.T.O to put together some kind of intervention to end the Bosnian-Serbian war. If the President were to acknowledge the overflying of Serbian airspace by American fighters it would set back the talks with N.A.T.O., and maybe ruin the negotiations all-together. We're not supposed to be overflying Serbian airspace. I'm sorry, Carl. That's all I know for now. Do I need to state the obvious here?" Mac looked at his old boss. His career depended on Carl's discretion.

"No, no you don't. We never had this conversation. Will you keep me informed of any changes?" He understood the political pecking order in D.C. Feathers could get ruffled if someone broke protocol and started casting too wide of a net without going through channels. He understood Mac's delicate position.

"Look, Mac, I don't want my grandson to be just another sacrificial lamb for the cause of political expediency. I want no part of attending Cody's funeral, not if I can do something to prevent that from happening."

He was in desperate need of a plan. *What plan, old man? What can YOU possibly do to save Cody?* His thoughts echoed the helplessness he felt.

"Of course, Boss. I don't like this any better than you do. We'll need to get you an encrypted phone with instructions for its use. Don't attempt to use it until I call you on it. Understood?"

"Roger that. We need to get *Annie* turned around and headed back to the barn." Carl busied himself with the controls and began his descent back to the ranch. Thoughts of his grandson filled his mind: *How am I going to get you back home, Cody...how?*

The grass runway was laid out in the direction of the prevailing winds which were generally from the southeast at zero-one-three degrees. He approached straight in and centered the plane over runway 13 making his approach at one-hundred-twenty mph. At an easy 100 miles per hour, just as he flared, he pulled the throttles to idle and the mains touched down followed by the nose wheel which dropped gently on to the grass. Carl raised the flaps and taxied to the barn. He shut down the engines and the two men climbed down to the ground.

"Wow, Mac. It's like the last forty-nine years never happened. All of the old skills are back! *Annie* flies like an angel!" For a while, Carl was twenty-two again without a care in the world. "Thanks for coming along for the ride. I can't tell you how much I needed this." He clapped his hand on Mac Aldrin's shoulder.

"I wouldn't have missed it, my friend." Mac smiled back at his old mentor.

Sheldon Macvie approached them from the main house.

"Here comes Shel. We'd better play it cool. I don't trust him."

24

CHAPTER III

Captive

Cody and Perry Judd made it to a small barn in a village not far from Sarajevo following their successful ejection from the crippled F-14. Cody mostly carried his injured friend after Perry broke his leg when his chute carried him into a pile of boulders. The going had been slow. Despite their efforts, a Serbian patrol found them inside the barn and took them to an encampment somewhere high in the mountains; high enough that even the late summer air had a chill to it.

The cold seeped into Cody's bones. The damp wood-planked floor of the locked windowless shed he and Perry were imprisoned in sucked whatever warmth was left from his aching body. When he moved, every joint and muscle yelped with pain. Beatings and torture had been the daily fare since their capture in the Serbian highlands twelve days earlier.

Cody's Navy flight suit provided little warmth and the only thing preventing hypothermia was a tattered and dirty wool blanket, and the warmth of his friend.

"Hey, Per, you awake?"

"Yeah, Archer, I'm still with you, partner." He moaned, turning to face the young pilot. "It's been almost two weeks. What do they want from us?" Before Cody could respond, the steel door to their concrete cell screeched on its hinges and swung open. A giant of a man entered with his AK-47 assault rifle at the ready.

"You come with me now." The man spoke with a strong Serbian accent.

Cody wrapped Perry in the blanket. "I'll be right back. Hang in, brother." He stood reluctantly and followed the man out into the chilly cloudless morning, wondering what the anticipated interrogation would bring: a bullet to the head, or, maybe just another beating. The Serb jabbed the barrel of the AK into Cody's back and pushed him toward the door of another shed where pain awaited.

For the last twelve days, his captors fed him a breakfast of barbed wire handcuffs, glaring lights that made it impossible to discern his interrogator's face, water-boarding, bruising punches and a variety of pain-inducing instruments from pliers to knives, painful clamps to bend and pull his joints to near breaking, and the gun ... always the gun with its cold muzzle pressed hard against his temple when the questions came:

"Why did you invade our airspace?"

... pain.

"What were you doing?"

... pain again ... wire tearing at my wrist.

"What aircraft carrier did you launch from?"

... blind-side punches ... vision blurring ... God this hurts!

"Who gave you the orders to come here?"

... sudden burning across my throat ... the knife!

"Why is the United States involved in our civil war? Who is your government working with?"

... more pain ... wire taken off my wrist s... hang in, Bridger ... almost over ... oh no! Not the table! ... drowning! ... can't breathe!

Cody's thoughts formed the lyrics of a macabre aria of pain; an anthem of Hades accompanied by a symphony of torture rising in swells and crashing upon his mind in crescendos of relentless agony. The torture and interrogation went on for two hours.

Every once in a while, Cody was allowed to sit without the hand cuffs. He could hear his interrogator's voice behind the glare of the lamp when the man offered him a cup of hot coffee. It was a gentle voice spoken with impeccable English, clearly the voice of an educated man. In stark contrast to the man's professorial demeanor, a black ski mask hid his face.

Colonel Stefan Radic, late of the Yugoslavian People's Army, was indeed an educated man. An Oxford graduate, he held a Doctorate degree in Geopolitics. The son of a Soviet party member and Politburo minister, he had been on the fast track to the Kremlin before the dissolution of the Soviet Union for which he blamed the United States. His hatred for America cut deep. At present, he took pleasure in handling the interrogation of this American himself.

"We do not enjoy doing this to you, you understand? It is better for you to answer our questions. We will find out, anyway. Besides, anything you tell us will not change the outcome of what will happen in my country, so why not end this unpleasantness for both of us. Good food and a warm bunk await you and the other officer. He will receive medical attention for his leg."

Cody poured the coffee on the floor in defiance as he glared at Radic's faint form out of his one good eye. His left eye had swollen shut. The whole left side of his face throbbed from the bludgeoning he had received. Blood from his cut throat oozed down over his flight suit. The cut was superficial, but painful. Both of his legs burned and throbbed from being repeatedly struck by the big guy wielding a two-by-four. He coughed out a mouthful of blood, looked at the man and smiled. "Bridger, Cody G. 513490065, Lieutenant, United States Navy."

Radic bristled and stood up. "You Americans are weak. We will do this every day until you tell us what we want to know. Take him back to his boyfriend."

Cody felt himself being lifted from the chair and dragged back to his cell where the two-by-four wielding giant dumped him like a sack of flour onto the floor. He crawled over to his friend who wrapped him in the blanket. "Hey, buddy. You're okay. I've got you." Perry cradled the pilot's trembling body..."I've got you."

Three days passed. Cody could see out of his left eye a little between his swollen eye-lids. The pain in his legs had diminished considerably; although, after the day's visit to the torture shed, his right leg flared when he tried to bear weight on it. He gingerly probed his leg and when he pressed on the tibia four inches below his knee, the bone shifted and Cody released a yelp of pain.

"Dammit!" He exclaimed. "He broke it! It looks like we're both absent a leg to stand on, Per'." They had a good laugh at the joke. For a couple of minutes, the two Navy airmen forgot about their plight. Thankfully, the cut on his throat did not require stitches. Cody had bandaged the wound with cotton strips torn from his tee shirt. The bandage was bloody, but seemed to be doing the job.

"We have to keep ourselves in shape, Per. C'mon, partner. A few laps around the room will get your blood going." Cody's leg fracture was not a compound one and the bones appeared to be aligned properly. He had been given two wooden slats and some tattered strips of cloth with which he fashioned a serviceable splint. He handed Perry the crude crutch provided by their captors, and they began to limp around the inside perimeter of their cell, making as many circuits as they were able until Perry's strength faltered. He was stricken with a fit of coughing, and had to sit down. He wiped his mouth on the sleeve of his dirty flight suit and the RIO noticed a light smear of blood on his sleeve.

Their meager rations, albeit lacking variety and flavor, sustained them at least. Twice each day a single tin plate of boiled potatoes, cooked meat resembling venison, and a chunk of stale bread accompanied a flask of water divided into the two metal mugs which they were allowed to keep. They ate with their fingers.

The door to their cell opened and sunlight streamed into the dark space. Once more the gun-toting giant ordered Cody to stand. "You bring other man. We go."

Cody helped Perry to his feet, and they limped across the compound to the shed. "Here we go again, partner, only this time they're inviting you to the party as well."

"Let 'em do their best. We're a team, Archer. I'm up for this."

Perry straightened his back and stepped into the room that had been the place of so much pain for his friend. *Maybe they'll go easier on Cody if I can get them to focus on me,* he thought.

"Please, sit gentlemen," the interrogator spoke with a cordial tone. "Coffee?"

"Just get started. We're not going to tell you anything, asshole, so cut the phony concierge voice." Perry goaded.

"You misunderstand, Lieutenant JG Perry Judd from Akron, Ohio. Let's see now..." The man ruffled some papers and photographs. Perry recognized them from the F-14: pictures of his family and a couple of letters from his fiancé and his parents. He always carried them with him in a pouch stuffed in the back of his seat. "Oh yes ... my, oh my, such an attractive young woman, your betrothed." He put the photo on the table with the rest of the items.

"You must understand, gentlemen, that we have recovered what was left of the cockpit recorder and these belongings from your aircraft. We now have all of the information we need about the USS Theodore Roosevelt, of how you violated orders by diverting from your flight plan to photograph our troop positions. You were never ordered to violate our airspace at all, were you? Tsk...tsk...tsk...such foolishness, and all for nothing."

"Okay. So why not negotiate our return? It would count in your favor with the press. 'Serbian rebels return two rogue U.S. Navy pilots to the U.S. military.' You guys have been practicing genocide; 'ethnic cleansing' the press calls it. Our release can only shed a more favorable light on your cause in the world's eyes, don't you think?" Perry offered with a strong note of sarcasm.

"A tempting thought, but, no. I have a much simpler solution in mind. In fact ..." the masked man turned to Cody. "... a simpler and much more profitable idea, indeed."

Radic glanced at the documents in front of him. "Cody G. Bridger, son of Gifford Bridger, President and CEO of InterDyn Corporation, specializing in the design and manufacture of the latest generation of human interfaced weapons systems. You will be happy to know, Lieutenant Bridger that the unpleasantness of the last two weeks is behind us. I'm certain you will find your new accommodations much more to your liking. As for the young, soon to wed Lieutenant Judd, I regret to say ... there will be no ceremony."

He nodded to a similarly masked man standing behind Perry. The big guard nodded back to Radic, put the barrel of his automatic pistol to the back of Perry's head and fired.

Cody was paralyzed in wide-eyed shock by the sudden and unexpected act. He never had the chance to launch an attack on the murderer. A burning furnace of anger swelled within him. He clenched his fists and the muscles in his legs tensed. He launched himself at his interrogator in a blind, screaming rage.

"I'll kill you, you cold-blooded bastard!"

He would have, too, if not for the two Serbian terrorists who stood by his side and brutally jerked him back down to his seat. They probably saved his life, because the arrogant Oxford man on the other side of the desk had leveled the muzzle of his 9x18 mm Makarov pistol at a point somewhere between Cody's eyes. As it was, Cody was treated to an instant nap courtesy of the same 2x4 usually reserved for his shins and knees. The plank wielder was the same big man whose penchant for brutality expanded his horizons to the back of Cody's head.

"Lieutenant Bridger. Lieutenant Bridger, wake up!" The interrogator yelled.

The words came from a thousand miles away. Cody fought to rise above the fog. When a bucket of cold water was thrown in his face, awareness suddenly filled his mind. He coughed and drew in a deep, gasping breath of air. The fog cleared and was immediately replaced by skull-splitting pain.

"Okay, okay"... (cough) ..."I'm awake" He coughed again and tried to raise his hands to his throbbing head, but handcuffs pinned his arms to a chair. A pair of high-intensity flood lights blinded him from seeing the man silhouetted in front of him. The voice came from beyond the glare, but he knew the voice well.

Cody hated him and vowed to kill Radic if ... *no, when ... I get the chance,* he thought. He took note of the two men who flanked the sadistic terrorist on either side, both armed with AK-47 assault rifles. *I'll wait for the time being ... for the opportune moment.* He allowed his head to drop down until his chin rested on his chest. *Tired ... need to sleep.* Cody held back a sudden wave of nausea.

"Take his hand cuffs off." The man on Cody's left removed his restraints and resumed his position. "Hold this newspaper in front of you." The guard dropped a copy of the Washington Post on his lap. The paper was dated the previous day; Wednesday, August 3rd, 1993, but it would do. "Now, I am going to turn on a camera. You will not speak until I tell you to, and then you will read aloud precisely what is written on this paper."

The man placed a sheet of paper on Cody's lap. "Say nothing else, Lieutenant ... only what you are told. Any deviation will be to your detriment, I assure you." Radic nodded to the camera operator. The "Record" light flared red.

CHAPTER IV

Carl held his blue and white Ford F-250 steady at 80 mph on the I-15. The pickup's tires hummed along smoothly to the enchanting voice of Whitney Houston's "I will Always Love You." The old rancher reached for the radio.

"Oh, don't change it, hon. I love this song. I can't believe her vocal range and control." Beth took Carl's right hand and squeezed gently. "Can I ask you something, Carl?"

"Sure." He smiled.

"What's going on with you and those government guys who were here earlier this week?"

He wasn't sure he could talk about Cody without losing control of his emotions. *Pull yourself together ... she deserves an answer.*

"My grandson's plane got shot down over Serbia two weeks ago." *There, it's out. I may as well tell her the whole story.* He felt a knot of anxiety in his stomach.

"Oh, no! Cody's a Navy pilot, isn't he? Is he...is he ...

"Dead? No ... well, we don't know for sure, yet. Mac ... my friend Mackenzie Aldrin, who works for 'The Company' ... is checking on it for me, but he thinks Cody is being held by the

Serbs." Carl drove on while Whitney belted out ... *and I-yee-I will always love you* ...

"So that was the CIA at the Wagonwheel? My gosh, Carl, I had no idea. What are you going to do?"

He shrugged his shoulders. "That's the million dollar question. Until we find out more, we're stuck for now."

"I'm so sorry, hon. I imagine your boy Gifford is beside himself." She held tight to Carl's free hand.

"He's the one who told me about Cody. I called in a big marker by asking Mac to put his ear to the wall for me. He's trying to gather some details on the sly. Bethy, if any other strangers show up at the Wagonwheel, will you call me? If anyone you don't know asks you anything at all ..."

"I have no idea what you're talking about, hon. I'm only a country bumpkin waiting tables for a living. They'll have to ask someone else." She grinned and chuckled.

Beth understood him so well. Carl relaxed a bit, knowing he had an ally in her. "Enough soap opera stuff. Steaks await us at the Angus Grill and after dinner, 'The Fugitive.' What do you say?"

"I love Harrison Ford almost as much as I love you, flyboy."

Carl went dumb quiet at Beth's declaration. *What do I say? Do I dare tell her?* His mind flooded with a confusion of memory and new found ... *What? Love? Yes ... love.* He hadn't loved anyone but Annie, or the memory of Annie for the first ten years after her death; but, when Beth began to occupy a greater place of prominence in life; his loss of Annie became gradually less painful. For the last three years his friendship with Beth had grown to that of best-friend status. Carl came to realize he could never commit to another relationship at the cost of losing Beth. Love just sort of sneaked up behind him and took hold of his heart.

He pulled off onto the shoulder of the road and put the gear shift in Park. He turned to Beth and met her gaze; their eyes locked.

She didn't look away ... just waited.

"I love you too, Beth. I reckon I've been feeling this way for quite a while." They fell into each other's arms and kissed long and thirstily, drinking in each other's love. The tension of the moment was replaced by a flood of excitement that settled into a calming reassurance that the dark waters of loneliness they had both been adrift in had at last been bridged.

Half way through dinner, Carl's cell phone sounded its familiar ring-tone.

"I need to take this. It's probably Giff." As he walked across the dining room to the men's room, Carl lifted the phone from his jacket pocket, and pushed *Talk*.

"Carl here," he whispered.

"It's Giff, Pop. I got a manila envelope from FedEx. It's them." He started to say more, but Carl stopped him.

"Get yourself out to the ranch, Giff. This connection leaks like a sieve ... not secure. Answer me this first; is anyone doing anything about it?"

"No, two weeks and nothing but a big stone wall."

"I need you here ASAP, son. I'll pick you up at Helena Municipal Airport. Let me know your ETA." He pocketed the cell phone and returned to the table. His gestating plan kicked at his mind. It was showing signs of life. *It's time to birth the baby.*

"What's happening, Carl? I gather someone has contacted Gifford?" Beth had dropped her voice to a whisper.

"Cody is alive ... for now. We're on a short clock, though. We've got to do something. I need to make another quick call." He punched in the number to Mac's personal un-secure phone. It rang only twice.

"Mac here."

"The fox is in the hen house and the rooster is alive for now. I need animal control." Carl knew Mac would understand.

"On my way; figure on 5:00 a.m. Mountain time." Mac hung up.

Beth looked across at Carl. "Wow! That sounded cryptic. Do we need to get back to town, Bridge?"

Carl smiled back at Beth. "Heck no. I'm lookin' forward to holding your hand and eating popcorn. Harrison Ford awaits, darlin'."

The rest of the evening was a welcome respite from the problems at hand, a chance to sit together quietly and tune out the thoughts running up and down the corridors of his mind. Carl found himself relaxing and drawn to the warm and gentle caress of Beth's hand in his. She was equally content to let the subject of Carl's grandson rest on the back burner for now.

The drive back to Cascade was subdued and quiet. They both had some thinking to do about where their new relationship was headed. Carl swung the pickup into Beth's driveway and shut off the engine.

"Can we do this again, Bethy?" He met her gaze with his eyes.

"Absolutely, Bridge. There's no going back now." They both laughed. Beth's use of the nickname "Bridge" settled pleasantly with him and elicited a smile.

"I need to take care of the Cody business. Can I call you in a couple of days?"

"Yes, of course." She was okay with the lack of details and trusted Carl would keep her informed as events unfolded. They kissed warmly on her front porch before Carl drove back to the Double-B.

Carl walked into his den, and for the rest of that night and well into the morning, he crafted a rough plan of action. He fished out a stack of old aeronautical charts from a box in the top of his closet, some as much as five-years old. At one time he had thought of flying the '25 to various air shows around the world after he finished the re-build. Now, the idea re-emerged in a more serious context. He rummaged around for Aeronautical Charts for Europe. *I need to call Aviano,* he thought, and picked up the phone. He recalled an air show being planned at the big American/N.A.T.O. air base.

"Aviano Air Base, how may I help you?" the base operator asked.

"I'm calling from the United States about the air show at Aviano. Can you give me any information about it?" Carl inquired.

"One moment, sir, I'll connect you," the operator said. A few audible *clicks* later and a man's voice came on the line.

"Base Operations, Lieutenant Shaw speaking."

"Lieutenant, I'm interested in the air show coming up at Aviano in a couple of weeks. Is it still being planned?" Carl crossed his fingers.

"Oh, yes sir. The Air Force is sponsoring the fly-in as part of a good will effort for the N.A.T.O. member countries stationed here. Where are you calling from?"

"I'm calling from Montana in the States. I own a B-25 Mitchell, and I'm interested in flying her to your air show." He mentally crossed his fingers, hoping he could get the okay.

"Yes, sir. You may be a bit late to enter your plane in any of the events, but I'm sure you'd be welcome to put your bomber on display. I can give you a contact person at Malmstrom Air Force Base in Montana, if you'd like. Maybe they can expedite your registration."

"Thank you, Lieutenant, I'd like that." Carl wrote down the information and hung up. *Good. This is a start.* He smiled and went to the fridge to pop the top off a beer.

At 4:00 a.m., after not quite two hours of sleep, Carl's alarm clock nudged him awake to the electronic reproduction of wind chimes. He reached over to his night-stand, tapped the "off" button and lowered his feet to the carpeted floor.

Twenty minutes later he was rolling down the I-15 toward the Helena Municipal Airport. An old leather brief case lay on the seat beside him and a mug of hot coffee rested in the cup holder of the center console. As he drove, he thought of Cody and a chill ran down his spine at the image of what the Serbs must be doing to his grandson. Visions of torture filled his thoughts. He shook the images from his mind and concentrated for a moment on Beth. Almost missing the turn-off to state road 280/Airport Road, he had to brake hard and skidded on the soft shoulder onto Exit 12. He got the pickup under control and headed toward the rotating green and amber beacon which identified the Helena Regional Airport.

"Stay awake, old man; you almost screwed the pooch there." He admonished himself.

Ten minutes later, Carl walked through the terminal door just as the G-5 Gulfstream touched down. He waited for Mac and, when the CIA Deputy Director entered the passenger lounge, greeted him with a warm handshake. "Thanks for coming, Mac. I hope this little meeting isn't going to raise any eyebrows at the shop."

"No sweat, I scheduled a few days off for some R and R. I haven't taken a vacation in eight years. At some point I'll have to check in on some company business with the Great Falls office. Our liaison officer there is due for a de-briefing session, so I was able to finagle the G-5 on the government's dime for the trip. To be honest, I'm hoping to catch another ride in the '25, maybe even take the controls for a couple of seconds." He grinned broadly at Carl, knowing his friend would jump at the opportunity to show her off again.

"We need to do that, for sure. Let's get out of here and head back to the ranch so we can talk." Carl led the way out to the pickup.

He drove to where the I-15 crosses the Missouri River at Tower Rock State Park. Exiting at a rest stop and scenic overlook, he found a spot out of the direct glow of the halogen lights which illuminated most of the parking lot. Satisfied they were alone, he released the catches on the briefcase. Inside were numerous aeronautical charts and a stack of papers with what appeared to be navigational information, weight and moment figures, fuel consumption, and a bunch of other calculations. "What's all of this, Carl? You recreating Lindbergh's flight?"

"You're not far off, Mac. I'm going a bit farther than The Spirit of St. Louis, though. Before we get into it, I need you to brief me on any new intel about the Serbian camp and the Navy's position on my grandson's rescue."

Mac looked at Carl as though his friend and former boss had gone seriously senile. "Okay — so far, the Navy's been ordered to stand down. There's nothing coming out of D.C. to indicate any change in what I told you earlier. Are you planning to do what I think you are?"

"If I have no other choice than to go after my grandson myself, then ... yes." Carl waited for the impending eruption of his temperamental friend.

"You're insane! What are you thinking, Carl? You don't stand a rat's chance of pulling off a stunt like that. Do you think they're simply going to give you a visitor's Visa so you can walk up to the Serbian thugs and ask them to please release your grandson?"

"Don't patronize me, Mac! I know it's a desperate idea. I haven't thought the whole thing out. I'm just gathering information for right now.

Were you able to get any intel on where Cody's being held?"

"Alright, Boss. I'll play along for now ... for the sake of our friendship. I've got satellite photos of the compound outside of Sarajevo with GPS coordinates. Our operative inside has pin-pointed the building where Cody is being held. Carl, I'm not going to ask how you intend to accomplish a rescue operation without violating a hell of a lot of international laws, but even if you reach their compound before you get blown out of the sky, there's no place to land for a rescue."

"Let me worry about the details. I figure I can do as much damage to them as I need to in order to create a diversion for your extraction team to get Cody safely out and to the LZ. ... here." Carl tapped a red "X" marking the extraction site.

"Extraction team? What extraction team? Are you out of your mind? This is nuts! You're asking the CIA to do what SEC-NAV, the Secretary of State, and the Defense Department were expressly ordered by the White House not to do!"

Mac got out of the pickup and walked over to a picnic table and sat. He stood after a few seconds and circled a tree, twice, like a mutt looking for a place to pee. Finally, he returned to the truck. He didn't get in the cab right away, choosing, instead, to lean against the hood shaking his head.

Carl waited as Mac argued with himself, arms and hands waving about like some Italian waiter describing the best entrée on the menu. Finally, back in the truck, Mac fixed his eyes on Carl ... staring at him intensely. Carl felt uneasy, and blurted,

"Say something, will you? I'm starting to think you've gone into some kind of seizure, Mac."

"Well, hell, man. Why not? We're both going down the rabbit hole, so tell me the whole plan," Mac raised his hands in resignation.

"Okay, this is how I've got it figured: In two weeks, Aviano Air Base is staging a fly-in of the largest display of World War II warbirds in one place in over twenty years."

Carl unfolded one aeronautical chart after another and laid out his flight plan to Aviano, Italy. "The *Annie* will fit right in. I'll fly her to Italy, refueling here...here...here...and here." He pointed to places marked in red pencil along his intended flight path.

"After the show, the plan will be to take the '25 from Aviano, down the Italian coast to San Marino, turn east to Sarajevo, and pick up Cody at a point to be determined. Your extraction team will neutralize any guards there may be and remove Cody to the LZ before we get there. We'll take off and head down toward Albania until I'm out of Serbian airspace. I'll fly back to Naples, refuel, and fly north to Berne, Switzerland.

Carl took a deep breath and plunged on. "The rest will be up to you, Mac. I'll need to get the press on my side ... raise a big enough ruckus the government won't be able to resist taking credit for the rescue, which I'm more than happy to let them do. They can throw me in the can for the rest of my life. I don't care. I want my grandson home with all his body parts working ... not in a body bag."

The CIA Covert Operations Director sat silently weighing all of the ifs, ands, and buts of his friend's desperate plan.

"This harebrained idea of yours has more holes in it than the Bay of Pigs fiasco, Carl. But ... okay, let's assume, if by some miracle, you can get Cody safely aboard the plane. We're still left with a potential international crisis. Somebody's going to take a big fall, and I don't want that for either one of us."

Carl considered his friend's position. He wondered if he had any right to ask him or anyone to be a part of his selfish plan to rescue his grandson. "I get that, Mac. If you can't risk doing this, then don't. I'll take you back to the airport right now and will still count you as my good friend. You have a family to consider. You've done enough already. I'll understand if you go home now."

"Let me think things over. I'll give you my answer after

we've both had some sleep." Mac rested his left hand on Carl's shoulder and squeezed. "Either way, my friend, I pray that you can pull this off."

Carl and Mac were finishing "breakfast" at two in the afternoon when the sound of a car door slamming shut announced a visitor. Carl stood and walked toward the foyer as Gifford entered.

"Giff, what the heck? I thought you were going to call me." Carl hugged his son, happy to see him.

"I know, Pop. I've been on the move since we talked yesterday ... no time for phone calls. The Gulfstream landed in Great Falls about an hour ago. I came straight here." Gifford eyed the platter of eggs and bacon. "Hey, you got some of those eggs for me? I'm starving." He dropped his bag on the kitchen floor and pulled up a chair next to Mac.

"You must be Mac Aldrin. Pop told me all about you." He extended his hand. "I'm Giff Bridger."

Mac smiled and took Gifford's hand. "President and CEO of InterDyn, one of the big dogs in the military weapons development industry. You're work with AI and weapons integration is cutting edge. You are about to reveal your new IVOTACS system. Your wife is Alisa; two children, Cody and a daughter Rachel, right?"

"Wow! You've done your homework, Mister Aldrin. No one is supposed to know about IVOTACS." Gifford couldn't hide his surprise.

"I'm Mac to you, Giff, and don't be surprised. It's what we do at Langley." He winked at Carl. "You're Dad was the best in the Agency back in the day."

Carl and Mac briefed Gifford on the plan. Together, the three refined some of the logistics and, using Mac's satellite photos, began to map an approach alley where, flying low, the *Annie* wouldn't be seen until she was on top of the Serbian camp.

Then, Gifford spotted something interesting.

"What's this, Mac?" Giff asked. His finger hovered over a long bare swath cut through the trees less than two kilometers from the compound.

"A ski slope would be my guess, but it's too flat for any downhill event; probably left over from the Olympics. I could use a calculator if you own one." Carl walked to his desk in the den and returned, handing the calculator, along with a protractor and a geometry compass, to Mac.

"What's on your mind, Mac? Are you thinking what I'm thinking?" Carl moved closer to get a better view of the satellite photos.

Mac ran his finger along the top edge of the photo. "These numbers and markings are GPS coordinates and scale ratios. I think we're looking at a cross-country ski trail about two kilometers from the Serbian compound. I'm not sure, but my guess is that the last time anyone groomed the trail was for the '91-'92 ski season. It appears to be clear of much growth, probably mountain grass for the most part. I doubt anyone has touched the slopes since the siege of Sarajevo began in April of '92." His eyes met Carl's.

Carl traced his finger along the grassy strip, tapped the map as if to assure himself the old cross-country trail was the correct choice. He nodded and smiled at Giff and Mac.

"Alright then, I'll land the *Annie* here, on the longest straight stretch of the course. How long is the clearing, Mac?"

Mac did some measuring and crunched a few easy numbers. "Roughly twenty-three hundred feet ... just under half of a mile. Carl, there won't be time for a fly over. The Serbs are going to regroup and try to stop you from taking off. You'll have maybe five minutes to grab Cody and get airborne."

"Can we land and take off in that distance, Pop?" Gifford's tone was presumptive.

"Uh...what do you mean 'we', son? You're not going. I won't risk losing you and then trying to explain to Alisa and Rachel why they've lost Cody and you both."

"Pop, Cody's my son. If you think I'm going to sit home while you're risking your life, you need to think again. Anyway, I think you'll change your mind after what I show you."

Gifford retrieved his laptop from his bag. He pressed the "On" button and the screen lit up. The InterDyn logo glowed amber against a blue background. He withdrew a number of floppy discs from a small metal case and placed them next to the computer. He selected the disc he wanted and inserted it into the disc-drive. The monitor screen filled with a different version of the InterDyn Corp logo. Giff keyed in a password and a menu popped up showing choices of what appeared to be access ports to weapons systems in the InterDyn R&D arsenal. He brought up the first schematic which filled the screen.

"You're looking at a 20mm Vulcan M61A1 cannon capable of firing six thousand rounds per minute. The Air Force currently deploys this weapon in its F-16s. The Gatling-style cannons are typically tied to a Low Altitude Safety Targeting Enhancement system which is a laser designated target acquisition and firing platform. InterDyn has developed a faster human integrated version of the LASTE system we call IVOTACS, for Integrated Voice and Optical Targeting and Command System. It's faster than the LASTE from target acquisition to deployment. When the cannon is mounted on a fully articulated cradle, it can be directed to sweep from one point to another during deployment; elevation, swivel left and right, all done with eye movement." Giff could see from their faces that he had their complete attention.

He continued while he had their full attention. "Additional improvements on the cannons have reduced the weight of each from approximately 206 pounds to 185 pounds. Streamlining the breech assemblies and thinning the barrels by using a stronger and lighter heat resistant alloy developed at InterDyn made it possible. The whole assembly is only 72 inches long; sweet, huh? A simple menu of voice commands will activate the IVOTACS system and the helmet, as well as fire control. The Fire Control Officer visually acquires the target, the Vulcans lock-on and he fires … that simple. Of course, the manual override provides a more hands-on experience."

Mac released a whistle of amazement. "Wow! Where did you come up with this? It's generations ahead of anything being used by the military."

"The IVOTACS is my baby. I did the preliminary math and created the initial design model. R&D and Engineering refined my design and built the prototype. It's only been field tested from a stationary ground-based platform, but this is one deadly accurate system. You see this helmet in the specs? It links the IVOTACS to the pilot or Fire Control Officer. It's a heads-up display and requires no manual operation to slow the process. This thing will lock-on and fire literally as fast as you can think."

Carl looked at Giff as though he was an arms dealer finishing a sales pitch. Giff caught his father's expression, then looked at Mac who looked back at Carl in a similar look of dumbfounded awe.

Carl broke the silence. "How many of these do you have?"

"The original prototype, a second one with some minor changes in the cradle, and one more that can be ready in less than a week." I can bring it all here in seven days.

"We'll need to modify the *Annie* before we can mount the guns. You're the engineer, son; any suggestions?"

"I can tell you for sure after I get into the front turret area and bomb-bay to do some measuring, but I believe we can squeeze the cannons in with some minor modifications. The M61A1 cannon is designed to fit into the F-16 above the wing just behind the pilot. We can shorten the nose gunner's bubble and enclose it. We'll build out two 'blisters' to accommodate the cannons. Removing all of the nose gunner's hardware will compensate for most of the weight of the two cannons. That plus shortening the nose by a couple of feet should keep the center of gravity within tolerance." Gifford paused to let Carl digest the barrage of data he was throwing at him.

After running the information around in his head, Carl nodded. "Okay, but it seems as though we're still going to have a couple of hundred more pounds up front after you add in the weight of the ammo. The *Annie* will still be a little nose heavy, don't you think?"

"Yes ... a little bit. I did my homework on the engines, Dad. We'll increase the '25s power by swapping out your Wright 2600 fourteen-cylinder engines with the larger Pratt and Whitney R2800 Double-Wasp 18 cylinder engines. We can square-off the wing tips and add a foot to the ailerons. This will give you better roll stability and increase the wing area for more lift. The Army Air corps tried this in 1943 on a project called the NA-98X. A modified B-25 was designed for low-strafing missions using the modifications I described, and it worked." Gifford waited for his father's reaction.

"Yeah, it worked fine until it didn't. Major Perry Richie's NA-98X disintegrated during a high-speed run over the runway. That story was part of our pilot training in '44," Carl retorted.

"True, but he flew the plane repeatedly at speeds and G-forces far in excess of the design limits. I read the logs, Pop. He was warned to stay inside the performance envelope. He didn't and he paid the price. Besides, with the new stronger and lighter aluminum alloys, we can make the *Annie* much safer than Richie's plane."

Carl considered all Gifford had said. "Okay, I'll buy it for now. Go ahead on."

"Alright. We'll mount twin fifty-cals in the tail gunner's position and use the third Vulcan on the ground for training your gunners. The *Annie* is long enough and, with the 'blisters', will be wide enough to accommodate two couches for the Vulcan gunners.

We won't be carrying any bombs to take up space. I want to fit a couple of SRAAMS into the bomb-bay with drop-down racks. You might need them. They're only good at short range against a predator like a MiG-29."

Carl considered the workarounds and modification needed for the '25. "Seems like a lot to do in the nine days before we leave. I'll need to get someone to man the rear fifty-cals, and I think I know the right guy."

"One more thing, Pop, what those guys are demanding will likely swing the tide of the war in their favor. They want our latest tank busters and SAM technology. Once they get them the Serbs will wreak havoc on the Bosnian Air Force as well as being capable of forcing back the Bosnian ground forces. The result would be the fall of Sarajevo, and it would give the Serbs the upper hand in the region. They've given me three days to agree to their terms or they'll kill Cody. There are a lot of people I need to get moving on this ASAP."

"Whoa! Slow down." Carl's mind was reeling under the barrage of information. What had begun as a tickle in the back of his mind had grown into The Hulk in less than three days. "So far, the three of us are the only ones who know what's going on in this room." Carl felt something unknown in his experience ... uncertainty and hesitation.

"Are we saying that we're actually going to do this?"

"You tell us, Boss. This is your Frankenstein monster. Want to throw the switch and give it life?" Mac looked at Carl with his characteristic fixed stare.

Carl hesitated only for a moment. "Yes. Let's get our crew together. How about it, Giff? Can you stall the Serbs?"

"I'll come up with something. Maybe I can buy us an extra day or two. The logistics of smuggling a secret shipment of arms to a foreign military power, particularly one that's not friendly to U.S. interests, are ... shall we say ... complicated?"

Mac rose to his feet. "Well, I think you two crusaders have things pretty well figured out. As for me, I'm getting back to business as usual. I don't want to attract any curious eyes by breaking routine. I'll keep you updated on the intelligence end and let our op' in Sarajevo know when and where the extraction will take place." He pulled his sunglasses from his pocket.

"If you need to call me, use this phone. It's on a secure dedicated line. This is new, more compact technology with a digital 2-inch screen. Just flip open the clamshell cover and you're good to go." Mac handed the cell phone to Carl. "We'll talk again soon." With a nod and a hand shake, Mac turned to leave, and then stopped. He turned back to face the two men with a sheepish grin on his face. "I forgot. I need a ride to the airport."

Carl fished the keys to the pickup from his pocket. "Take the pickup. Just lock the keys in the glove box. I can use my spare set. I'll get Beth to drive me down to Helena tomorrow." He tossed the keys to Mac, who nodded his thanks, and left.

Carl and Gifford talked long into the night, filling sheaves of papers with plans for modifying the former Doolittle Raider into a wholly different kind of raider. When they had enough to involve the electrical and mechanical engineers at InterDyn, Gifford started getting people out of bed. After a couple of hours he had a team of people working on all of the supply-chain issues including everything they would need to modify and refit the *Annie*.

Justification for the unorthodox scheme was provided by the cover story of using the '25 as a test platform for the IVOTACS. Gifford even supplied his team with specs for the modifications needed on the bomber. He explained to them he wanted the project to be "off the books" for security reasons. He assured them, further, that the Air Force would provide a representative on-site to oversee the project. Now all he had to do was get an Air Force officer, preferably one with Command Pilot wings to make it appear official. It didn't matter if the guy was retired; only that he had the uniform. He made one more call.

Buckminster Rogers, Brigadier General, U.S.A.F. (Ret.), former test pilot and Apollo astronaut, snatched the phone from the nightstand. "It's after three in the morning, who dares wake the great and mighty Oz?"

"Bucky, Giff Bridger. Sorry to wake you, but I'm in need of your particular brand of magic to solve a dire situation." Gifford waited for a response.

"Well, gee, Giff. Don't keep me guessing. Excuse me while I pull on some shorts and take this in the living room." A few seconds later, sporting a pair of khaki boxers, the General came back on the phone. "Okay, I'm all yours, Gifford. What's got your tighty-whities in a knot at this hellish hour?"

Gifford told him about Cody and of the government's inaction. Then, he laid out the events of the last few days; about his dad and the *Annie*, and the rescue plan. He deliberately left out any mention of Mac and the CIA. When he finished the story, he drew in a deep breath and waited. Either Bucky would laugh himself silly before hanging up in Giff's ear, or he would be on the next flight out of Miami International.

"So you want me to dust off my 'blues' and look official for your team and, I assume, for any local law enforcement whose ears might perk up a bit. Sounds fun, but I have one requirement."

"Anything, Bucky. You name it," Giff said.

"I want to fly right seat next to your dad. That's my deal, take it or leave it." The General waited for Gifford to wrap his mind around the request.

"Okay ... done deal. How soon can you get here?" Gifford had no idea how his father was going to take the news.

The plan was in motion with all of the logistics in place. Gifford would be staying at the ranch until the job was done. He was officially on remote location for the purpose of testing the new IVOTACS system.

The day the semi-tractor trailer was scheduled to arrive, Gifford rose early. He walked into the kitchen where he found Carl standing in front of a hot stove. The smell of bacon and fresh-brewed coffee made his mouth water.

"Throw a couple of slices of bread in the toaster, will you, Giff? I think we're going to have a very busy day today. No time for lunch breaks, so we'd better fill up now. Oh, by the way, you never told me if you got your Air Force contact on board." Carl flipped a half-dozen eggs over on the grill.

"Yes, I did. I, uh ... had to make a deal with him, Pop."

"Deal? What kind of deal ? We need to keep this operation on the down low, son." Carl put the eggs on a plate and placed them on the table. "What did you do?"

"Nothing much, Pop. I just had to add another member of the crew, that's all." Giff waited for Carl's reaction.

"What the hell, Giff! This isn't going to be a pleasure trip. I sure as hell don't need to babysit some tourist up there. What is he, some bureaucrat pencil pusher from the Pentagon?"

"No, Pop, he's a former test pilot. You may have even heard of him — General Buckminster Rogers?" Gifford couldn't suppress a smile at the dumbfounded expression on his father's face.

"Buck ... Rogers? *The* Buckminster Rogers? Holy crap, son, when you said you knew someone, I had no idea ... well, HELL YES he can join the crew!" Carl couldn't believe what he was hearing.

"I'm glad you agree, Pop, because he's going to be flying

right seat."

"Say what?" Carl paused and thought it out. "Oh ... what the hell. The man has probably flown everything with and without wings *but* a B-25. A couple of touch and goes and he should be good to go. Harry Osborne will be star struck when I tell him the news."

"Who's Harry Osborne?" The name tickled the far recesses of Gifford's mind; *maybe someone Pop knew in the war.*

"You told me yesterday to get someone who has a huge pair of cajones and isn't afraid of big guns, right? I called Harry and he jumped at the chance. I told you about him when you were just a kid. Harry was my radioman and top turret-gunner; the best damned gunner in the Army Air Corps back in the day. He had three kills on a single mission. All three were zeros; part of a flight of a dozen or so ganging up on us and four other '25s off the coast of Formosa."

Carl brought a large platter of eggs and hash browns over to the table.

"He can do the job, Giff. I called 'Doc' Henreid, also. He was a medical corpsman before he took the flight mechanic's exam and joined the crew near the end of the war. After the armistice Doc went to med school and was Chief of Surgery at the VA hospital in Atlanta. He retired in '85. I figure we may need a medic on board. Adding Doc gives us a five man crew. With Cody, that'll make six. We have our crew. Now, let's eat before your people get here." Carl poured the coffee, and father and son dug in. Carl ate fast. He needed to ask Beth to take him to the airport to get his pickup. His sense of urgency was matched by his concern over Beth's likely reaction to the rescue plan.

Beth and Carl headed out of town toward Helena. Carl placed his hand on her right thigh and patted her gently. "Sorry I never called yesterday. With Mac and Giff at the ranch there was just a ton of stuff we had to get figured out."

Beth glanced over at him for a second, and returned her eyes to the road. "I guess that means you're going to do something about Cody on your own, huh? Is the government still sitting on their thumbs?"

"So it seems. Mac's keeping an eye on Washington. The Agency would be among the first to know if a rescue operation was being planned. I seriously doubt the Navy will do anything. It's up to us. You want to hear the plan?" Carl watched a tear slide down Beth's cheek.

"I always do better when I know the whole story. I tend to assume the worst if I'm left to my imagination." She withdrew a tissue from the small box on the dash board.

Carl outlined the plan. He left out the technical stuff about the re-fitting of the *Annie* and the IVOTACS system. "I'll be fine, Beth. I've got a good crew, and ..." Beth interrupted him.

"Don't you dare try to sugar coat this for me, Carl Bridger, DON'T YOU DARE! You're going to be breaking enough international laws you'll be lucky if you don't start a war between whatever governments want the first crack at shooting you down. Even if you do make it back alive, you'll probably spend the rest of your life in prison. What about us, Carl? What about me? Friday night I thought we had started something."

"We did, Bethy. I promise you ..." Carl tried to console her.

"Just ... don't say anything, Carl. I need to think. I'll drop you off at the airport. We can talk more tomorrow." They sat in silence until she pulled up next to Carl's pickup.

She waited for him to start the truck. When she saw him pull out of the parking space, she put her Explorer in gear and drove away in a spray of gravel.

CHAPTER V

One of the less well known jobs of the Domestic Operations Department of the CIA is monitoring the flow of communications to and from the heartland of the American industrial complex. In particular, certain corporate entities who deal with sensitive issues such as the defense and aerospace industries were closely monitored by the CIA, NSA, and FBI. Corporations working in partnership with foreign companies in countries unfriendly to American interests: China, former Soviet satellite states, Iran, and Iraq, were of particular interest.

In this instance, one such company, and the one which Communications Analyst Ted VanPatton was currently monitoring, was InterDyn, the cutting-edge weapons engineering and development firm contracting for a dozen or more projects for the three military services under the Joint Chiefs of Staff.

A young, be-speckled man of 26, Ted was an unassuming

fellow. To pass him on the street one would never guess he spoke five languages fluently and possessed PhD's in International Politics and Social Psychology. At the moment, bent over his console festooned with dials, switches, and computer screens, he sat suddenly erect. Adjusting his headset and pushing the record button on his console, he waited until the conversation which caught his interest ended.

Ted withdrew the recording disc from the computer's drive and placed it in a sealed envelope marked "SENSITIVE" in red letters. He placed the envelope in the pick-up tray for his boss, Richard Hicks, the Communications Director, and pushed another button which rang a phone on his boss's desk.

The Director of Domestic Affairs, Willard Helms, was expecting his Communications Director and had a carafe of hot coffee ready for him by the time his secretary stuck her head in the door. "Director, Mister Hicks is here."

"Send him in, please." Helms stood and walked around his desk when Director of Communications entered.

"We've got something interesting here, Will ... thought I ought to bring it to your attention and see if you wanted to follow up on it." Hicks' eye caught the tray holding the carafe. The tantalizing aroma drew him toward the table. "Ah, coffee. May I help myself?" Hicks poured himself a cup and one, as well, for his boss.

Will Helms sat on the sofa and placed his cup on a coaster on the colonial style walnut table in front of him. "What have you got?"

"Activity at InterDyn. They're moving some heavy fire power for testing and they seem to be in a hurry."

"So, what's the problem, Dick? Sounds pretty routine." The DODA sipped his coffee and set the cup on its saucer..

"What got our attention is the location of where they're setting up the testing. Normally they would do that kind of stuff inside a controlled Military Operation Area, like the west desert in Utah or someplace where security could be monitored by the military. This time they're setting up in Montana."

The DOD Director raised his eyebrow. "Montana? Do we have any MOA's in Montana?"

"There's only one. The Hays MOA, but that facility is not set up for weapons testing; only pilot combat training. So far as we know, there has been no live-fire testing in the area."

"Thank you, Dick. I'll assign someone to look into it. It's probably nothing."

Will returned to his desk as the Communications Director exited the office. He considered calling the FBI or the NSA, but decided to keep the matter of InterDyn in-house for now. He picked up the phone and called the Deputy Director of Covert Operations, Mac Aldrin.

"Director, how are things in Domestic Affairs? All quiet on the home front, I hope."

"Mac, I need someone to check on some movement out of InterDyn. Come on up to my office and I'll brief you."

"On my way, sir. There in five." Mac figured this call would come eventually, and he was prepared for it. He took the elevator to the fifth floor and walked down the powder blue carpeted floor to the DODA offices.

After being briefed by Director Helms on the InterDyn movement, Mac needed to appear to be handling the situation with the intention of keeping Domestic Affairs placated and at the same time preventing an escalation of the investigation. He planned to make two phone calls: the first to Wesley Steed, his man in Great Falls. This call would be made over a standard non-secure land line. He wanted to give the communications people every reason to believe the matter was being taken seriously and was being handled at the highest level.

The second call would be made over the scrambled cell phone that was linked to the phone he gave Carl. It would be untraceable and completely safe ... for now, at least.

Mac left the building to take an early lunch. He climbed into his black BMW 750i and drove out of the parking lot to Ferrilli's Italian Bistro. He was seated in an out-of-the-way booth. At 11:25 A.M. the lunch crowd was still a half hour from filling the popular lunch stop. He ordered Cannelloni stuffed with Italian sausage, spinach and ricotta cheese with a side of bread sticks and a Coka-Cola®. When the waitress finished taking his order he flipped open his phone and punched in the code for Carl's phone.

Carl's voice answered. "I'm here."

"You will have a guest within the hour. Is your staff ready to give him the VIP treatment?" Mac asked quietly.

"His accommodations are ready." Carl hung up. The cryptic message told him the CIA resident agent in Great Falls was on his way.

Mac returned to his office to find Sheldon Macvie waiting for him. He thought it odd that his subordinate stood behind, rather than in front of his desk. Shel faced the office window supposedly admiring the view of the Potomac River.

"Hi, Shel, keeping my seat warm, were you?" Mac asked with a deliberate chuckle as he traded places with his assistant. Mac's visual perceptual skills had been sharpened to a fine edge over the years, and he took note of some of the documents on his desk. A few had been moved around; not by much, but enough. It wasn't the view from the window which captured the young man's attention. *He's been nosing around the same way he did when he was left alone at Carl's ranch the day we took Annie up for her maiden flight.*

"Just enjoying the view, boss. My only view is of a photo of the President and a reproduction of *Washington Crossing the Delaware.*"

The CIA covert operations agent sat in a chair across from Mac's desk. "Boss, I've had something on my mind that's caused an itch that needs scratching."

"Oh? What's up, Shel?" Mac feigned an oblivious attitude, but he understood why Macvie was in his office; *snooping,* he thought. He would let the less experienced man take the lead in the conversation; *all the better to find out how much he knows.*

"I've been thinking about our visit with Mister Bridger. To be frank, I'm certain you were not merely connecting with an old friend. What's going on up in Montana? Is there something you're not telling me, Boss?"

"Why would you think anything is going on, Shel?"

"Alright, I'll tell you what I know; one, Mister Bridger's grandson is MIA in Serbia; two, Gifford Bridger is his son; three, InterDyn is Gifford's company and I know the business they're in. What I don't know is why the Director of Covert Affairs of the CIA flew up to Montana on a whim."

"Okay, I'll tell you, but then I'll need for you to not involve yourself any further, Shel. I flew to Montana to meet with my old friend. He told me about his grandson and asked if I could use my clout with the Agency to find out if his grandson was alive, and if so, where he was being held. I told him I'd ask around. I also told him to not expect much. Now, Shel, have we sufficiently scratched that itch of yours?"

"Fair enough." Macvie rose from his chair. "Oh ... one more thing, sir. Why did you go back to Montana later?"

Mac didn't like having to explain himself to Macvie, and the hair on the back of his neck bristled. "Shel, you're starting to piss me off. Carl Bridger is my friend. I had a few days of R-and-R coming, and I worked it out to spend a couple of days at his ranch for some fishing and to get another ride in the *Annie* ... OKAY?"

"Sure, Boss. I'm sorry if I've intruded into your personal

life. By the way, are you aware of anything unusual going on with InterDyn?"

Mac returned his subordinates fixed gaze. *He's fishing ... time to put him in his place.*

"I sure am, Shel. As a matter of fact I had a conversation with Will Helms about it earlier this morning. Now, unless you are planning on becoming the Director of Central Intelligence in the next few seconds, I'll invite you to get the hell out of my office." He glared at Macvie, who turned to leave. Mac waited for his snoopy assistant to get as far as the door before stopping him.

"And Shel ... just so you know; if I ever catch you going through my desk again, you'll be lucky to find a job enforcing cruelty to animal statutes in Nome, Alaska. Are we clear?" Mac scowled at the agent until he turned and left.

The big Peterbilt semi-tractor towing two trailers swung onto the dirt road leading up to the Double-B's barn. The boxes bore no corporate markings to announce InterDyn's presence. A private trucking company, "Interstate Hauling, Inc." out of Provo, Utah, leased the semi to InterDyn.

"Back it up to the barn. We'll unload everything there," Carl directed.

Earlier, he had moved the *Annie* out of the barn, and parked her under a tent-like structure of the kind used for carnival displays, backyard wedding receptions and the like. The rear trailer contained all of the materials and equipment needed to re-fit the '25, from reframing the forward fuselage and applying the new skin to installing the cradles for the two M61A1 Vulcan cannons. Miles of wiring and boxes of electronic devices were carefully stacked inside the barn. Work benches, portable generators, welding equipment, computer terminals and monitors were unpacked and technicians began powering everything up.

After the team finished unloading the rear trailer, the driver pulled the empty box forward and backed the rig up to the side of the barn where he uncoupled it. In less than five minutes the forward trailer was in position to be unloaded. The team offloaded three ten-foot long crates and carried them to the rear of the barn. Plastic-sheeted frames holding the cradles for the cannons were taken off the trailer as well. Finally, less than one hour after driving through the gate of the Double-B, the truck left, leaving the two trailers parked next to the barn.

Carl never wavered from his decision to move forward with his plan to rescue his grandson. In fact, the presence of the new weaponry and the InterDyn team of engineers strengthened his resolve to see his plan through. Transforming the B-25 into a modern warbird was in Gifford's hands. Until now, Carl always had something demanding his direct attention; decisions that only he could make. Now, there was nothing to be done but to leave *Annie* in InterDyn's care.

As his thoughts turned to Beth, his heart yearned for her. He picked up the phone from the end table in his den and dialed the number. One ... two ... three rings. "C'mon, Beth, pick up," he whispered as he stood and walked across the room.

... Hi, this is Beth. Sorry I missed your call. Leave a message, and I'll get back to you. The beep sounded and Carl started to say something, then changed his mind. He put down the receiver and headed out the door to his pickup.

Carl pulled into a parking place in front of the Wagonwheel and all but ran to the restaurant's door. He stepped inside and scanned the room for Beth.

"Hi, Carl. If you're looking for Beth, she didn't come in

this morning." Ruth stood alone in the dining area wiping down a table.

Carl's thoughts shifted from his urgent need to be with her, to concern for her welfare. "Is Beth okay? Have you talked to her?" "Oh, I think she's fine. She called me last night and asked me to come in early so she could go see a friend of hers who's in the hospital in Great Falls. Rebecca Lawson; do you know her? She had a fall and broke her hip. They had to ambulance her to Great Falls Regional yesterday. She's pushing eighty. I guess Beth decided she needed the extra help. Shall I tell her you dropped by, Carl?"

"No ... no thanks, Ruth. I'll check on her later." Carl turned and walked back out to his truck .

He drove out of the parking lot, snapped on his left turn signal and started his turn back to the ranch. He stopped almost immediately.

"No you don't, Beth. I'm not going to end this day without settling things." He swung the wheel to the right and headed south for Great Falls.

Beth was waiting in the Surgery Visitor's Lounge for word from the surgeon doing the hip replacement for her friend. Finally, when the physician pushed open the double doors to the O.R. Beth stood up and smiled tiredly at him. "How is she, Doctor?'

"She came through the operation just fine, Mrs. Thomlinson. She has remarkably good bone density for her age and we were able to give her the new hip with no complications. She's in recovery now, but you can wait for her in her room if you want to."

"Thank you, Doctor, maybe I'll do that." Beth checked her watch: *10:00 a.m.. I need to get back.*

She walked to the gift shop and bought a bouquet of fresh flowers and a card which she took up to the third floor orthopedic wing. She asked the charge nurse which room Mrs. Lawson would be brought to, and then walked into room 307. She placed the flowers on the window sill and pulled a pen from her purse. She wrote a note on the card wishing her friend a sincere "Get Well" and promised to visit her in two days. Sitting in a chair next to the empty bed, her thoughts went to Carl. *I can't do this ... going about things and pretending nothing's wrong. I miss him. Even if he doesn't come back we still have now.* "I can't let him leave without telling him I love him," she said out loud. She stood and walked briskly to the elevators.

The skyline of Great Falls appeared in the fading afternoon light five miles ahead. Traffic had picked up a little forcing Carl to slow to 55 when a familiar merlot-colored Explorer sped past in the opposite direction.

"Beth," he said as his heart jumped. He pulled on to the shoulder of the highway, checked his mirrors and swerved hard left down the embankment of the grass divider and up the other side onto the northbound lane. He punched the Ford F250 truck up to 80 miles per hour and soon spotted Beth's Explorer only three cars ahead. He was waiting for a passing opportunity, but Beth exited into a rest stop. Carl followed and parked next to her car.

Beth walked over to a small garden in the middle of a picnic area and waited for Carl to climb out of his truck. Approaching her with a cautious smile, he took her left hand in his and turned her to face him. "Bethy. I'm so sorry I've brought this trouble to us. I love you; more than I care about anything. I'm feeling so ... torn. If Cody ..." Carl let his sentence trail off. He was at a complete loss for words.

"Shhh ... it's alright. I love you, too, Bridge. If I can't stand by you at a time like this ... well, I wouldn't be much of a woman, would I? You do what you need to do, my love, and come back home to me. Until then, I want us to spend as much time as we can together until you leave."

She pulled Carl's face toward hers and, standing on her tip toes, kissed him long and with passion. They talked for the next hour, strolling hand-in-hand around the rest area, renewing each other with the sheer power of the content of their hearts. Finally, they walked back to their vehicles. Beth let go of his hand reluctantly.

"It's almost two o'clock, hon. I need to get back and relieve Ruth. Will you come over to my place later tonight?"

Carl nodded and smiled. "How about I bring some groceries and we'll have a late dinner? I make a mean stroganoff. I'll bring the wine, too. The Double-B is going to be a bit crowded for the next few days."

"Good idea. I'll make the salad. I'll close the diner early and meet you at my place at eight-thirty. Does that work for you, Cowboy?"

"That's perfect, Bethy. I'll even put a clean shirt on." Carl chuckled.

He followed Beth's car back to Cascade, then turned onto the dirt road leading up to the main house, feeling much happier than when he'd left the Double-B earlier.

Carl climbed out of the truck and immediately saw the blue-white light of an arc welder coming from the barn. He walked over to the big white tent where the *Annie* was parked and entered the makeshift hangar. He gasped at the sight before his eyes. The entire front of the fuselage beneath and in front of the flight deck was missing. From the ground, the inside of the cockpit was completely exposed. A mass of wires dangled from behind what used to be the instrument panel. The throttle quadrant had been severed from the engines and flight instruments. The entire superstructure was cut away: Plexiglas cockpit and forward gunner enclosure ... gone. While he was looking at the carnage, Gifford walked up behind him and placed a hand on his father's shoulder.

"It's like heart surgery, Pop. Cracking open the chest of a human being is ugly business. Once the ribs have been spread wide with clamps, the miracle can ..."

"Geez, son. Could you be more morbid? Yuck! I get it. You guys are going to make the *Annie* newer, stronger, faster, and more powerful than ever before. Sounds like the old T.V. show, but I hope this won't cost me six million dollars." Carl shook his head.

"More like two, Pop. InterDyn is writing a chunk off to R&D." Gifford beamed with pride. "Come into the barn, I want to give you a glimpse at what the *Annie* will look like four days from now. And, by the way, there are some folks here you'll want to meet."

Inside the barn, white-jacketed men were working on avionics and the IVOTACS command system. One engineer wore a helmet, and turned toward Carl. A Vulcan 20mm cannon swiveled in its cradle and pointed its six barrels directly at him. Carl froze in his tracks and turned pale.

"Don't worry, sir," the engineer said, pulling off her helmet. "She isn't loaded."

"Pop, this is Doctor Lauren Dupree. Lauren is our lead design engineer and head of InterDyn's IVOTACS development team. Lauren this is my dad, Carl Bridger."

With a smile that would melt titanium, the attractive and brainy brunette took Carl's offered hand in a firm grip and shook it confidently. "I'm very pleased to meet you, Mister Bridger. So, you're the reason we're all here, eh?"

"I suppose I am. I take it Giff has filled you in on the ... uh, test he wants to run on your IVOTACS system?" *I don't know what story Gifford told his team. Best to not say too much.*

"Indeed he has, and I must say this is quite unorthodox, sir. But, as is usually the case, Gifford is way ahead of the rest of us. This test platform and the location allow us to accurately test, not only the IVOTACS, but on-the-fly maintenance, repair, and field fabrication of the components as well. This all-in-one operation will save the military and InterDyn millions in future design and upgrade expenses for the next generation of the IVOTACS."

"I'm sure it will, Doctor Dupree." Carl nodded, and the scientist returned to her duties.

"Are they all as focused as she is?" He scanned the crowded room. Everyone appeared to be working at a fever pitch.

"They know we're in a time crunch. They'll get the job done. Come over here, Pop."

Giff led his father to the rear of the barn, the source of the welding glare Carl had seen earlier. Standing upright in a supported cradle was the assembled superstructure of the B-25's cockpit and nose assembly. "We started working on this in sections back at InterDyn from the original old North American Aviation specs. We had to run them down, but we found a set in good shape at the Air Museum in Fairfax, Kansas. This is what I wanted to show you."

Gifford pulled a tarp off the new 'skin' for the '25's nose. Carl ran his hand over the flawless surface.

"You're touching a carbon fiber/aluminum alloy; thirty-percent lighter than the aluminum sheeting used back in the day. Plus, it's more pliable and can withstand a hundred-seventy percent of the G-force stress the old skin could.

"Notice the build-out on both sides. These blisters allow for the installation of the cannons. Your gunner will have a one-hundred-eighty degree view of the terrain through his heads-up display.

"You saw Doctor Dupree demonstrate the helmet. There are six cameras, which feed a virtual three-dimensional panoramic view into the HUD on the helmet's visor. The display is infra-red capable and can paint a target from over two miles away, lock on and fire a missile before the enemy can hear the sound of your engines. Of course, you'll be using the Vulcans from much closer in."

"Impressive. *Scary* impressive, Gifford." Carl noted the absence of the Plexiglas nose-gunner enclosure. The new stubbier nose was fully enclosed. He began to feel out of his league here. *It's best to leave the technical stuff to these folks.* "You said you had someone else for me to meet?"

Carl and Gifford walked over to the main house and entered by the front door. The air in the room was redolent with the aroma of cherry-blend pipe smoke. It curled up in puffs from Carl's leather recliner which faced the fireplace. A hand reached over to the end-table and placed the pipe in an ash tray. The pipe, Carl's favorite, was hand-crafted out of hickory ... ornately carved in a relief of trees, an elk and a fish tail dancing at the end of a hook; all highly polished.

His brow furrowed into a frown. Carl was protective of his privacy, and the hair on the back of his neck began to bristle. He opened his mouth to speak, but the man in the recliner stood and turned to face the perplexed rancher. He approached Carl with hand extended, wearing a grin as big as that of Alice's Cheshire cat spread across his face.

"Aw! You're Carl Bridger! Damned happy to meet you, sir, damned happy indeed! Buck Rogers ... and no wise cracks, Mister Bridger. I've heard all of the wise cracks you could possibly think of ... used to cause trouble in my school days. I always thought it was the wise-ass remarks from my classmates that motivated me to get away from it all and go to the moon." He bellowed out a string of har-dee-har-hars and fell silent.

"Carl Bridger, General. Welcome to my home ... and my chair, and ... my pipe. May I offer you a beer, or a snifter of my best brandy?" The 'brandy' remark was meant as a friendly jab at the General's presumptiveness.

"Please forgive me, Carl. Gifford invited me to make myself at home, and I always take a man at his word." Buck released a loud guffaw, seemingly pleased with his own sharpness of wit. "A beer would be just grand, sir. The bottle is fine."

Carl brought three beers out from the kitchen. The 'General' and Gifford sat on the leather sofa across from Carl's recliner, which he sat in after placing the beers on the coffee table. He gazed squarely into the face of Buckminster Rogers and got straight to the point:

"So, you and I are going to fly halfway around the world, pick up my grandson, and try to get him to safety. We can expect armed aircraft from every country in the region ... some friendly and others not ... all trying to knock us out of the sky. So, let me ask you, Buck. Why would you want to place so much on the line for a kid you've never met?"

The General seemed to consider the question. "That's a fair question, Carl. Back in '69 NASA slated me for the Apollo Fourteen moon shot. I came down with the flu ten days before the mission and Chuck Conrad replaced me as Mission Commander. I ended up on the ground as the sim backup in case the crew got into trouble. Anyway, I became completely absorbed by all the pre-launch work. The intricacies ... no room for mistakes.

"Well, one day I was going over the specs and procedures for the emergency escape protocol and came up with something I thought could present a problem for the crew in the event they needed to get out in a hurry in the Pacific Ocean after splash down. A series of explosive bolts was designed to blow the hatch off and away from the module in the event of a breach in the hull. A three-step sequence was needed to trigger the charges. The first step was to arm the bolts by punching a five-digit code into the emergency exit panel. Next, two of the crew had to simultaneously turn two keys to fire the charges.

"I noticed one of the servos operated by turning the key at the Mission Commanders station had a different part number than the part number listed for the other servos in the on-board system. I brought this to the attention of the Flight Director. I heard back from him that the servo came from a different manufacturer, but met all the specifications. Well, to make a long story short, when the mission returned, the capsule was brought back to the Johnson Space Center. I had the opportunity of removing the servo and testing it in the simulator. I could not blow the hatch.

"As it turned out, the mission worked out fine, but only because the emergency-evac protocol never had to be used. We lost three brave men in the Apollo One fire because of short cuts. I vowed then and there I would never take a man's word again about something if I smelled a rat. Your grandson is being used as a pawn by Washington in the current situation. He's been deemed expendable for the sake of political expediency. Carl, I smell a rat."

"I like the way you think, Buck." Carl had made a new friend.

"As soon as the *Annie* is ready for a test flight, we'll start your training. Until then, General, make yourself comfortable. The fridge is stocked with plenty of beer. Lots of goodies in the pantry, too. Oh, by the way, do you ride?" Carl asked.

Another Cheshire smile appeared on the General's face. "Sure do. My butt's gotten used to cushioned chairs, but I rode quite a bit down in South Dakota where I grew up."

Carl nodded his approval. "Tomorrow morning, you and I will head up to the summer range. I need to check on my cattle and it'll give me a chance to read you in on the flight plan and mission strategy ... and to pick your brain for some ideas, if you don't mind."

"The man has a plan." Buck chuckled. "I may just have an idea or two up my sleeve." They shook hands and Buck walked toward the front door on his way to the barn.

"I'll check with you later, Carl. I want to familiarize myself with every aspect of *Annie's* refit. I intend to be ready when I get my first shot at the controls."

Carl turned to his son. "I like him. Despite his gruff and flamboyant exterior, there's a sharp mind under that grey hair. What's your impression, Giff?" Carl's assessment of the General relied heavily on Gifford's experience working with Buck professionally in his collaboration with the Air Force. Carl was looking for his son's professional opinion.

Gifford nodded. "He's no nonsense where work is involved. He's meticulous in his research and tough as nails as a negotiator at the bargaining table. Anything he doesn't know he makes a point of finding out, and he's a mighty fast learner. He even has an F-16 assigned to him down at Ellsworth which he flies regularly to keep his command pilot certification active. The Air Force takes care of its own. Besides, Buck makes for good press for the military."

For Carl, much of the rest of the afternoon was spent watching the buildup of the bomber's forward fuselage and flight deck. The assembly team prepared to install the new skin to the geodesic aluminum/carbon-fiber tubing skeleton while four InterDyn avionics systems engineers busied themselves assembling the instrument panel with its array of upgraded digitized telemetry: radar, transponder, automatic direction finder, and GPS. Other instruments such as the pressurized altimeter, airspeed indicator, and engine instruments were left unchanged and were relegated to the function of backup for the digital Primary Flight Display. A new Master Flight Display containing altitude, indicated airspeed, compass, distance to destination, aircraft attitude, armament and targeting information would be contained in a Heads Up Display (HUD) which would be projected on the windscreen of the '25

At 7:00 p.m., Carl left the barn and returned to the main house where he stripped off his clothes and turned on the shower. Grabbing his shaving gear, he stepped into the shower, placing his razor and a can of shaving cream in the shower caddy suction cupped to the wall. Ten minutes later, he walked into the bedroom while he toweled off his hair.

He fished out a Pendleton plaid shirt from the closet and a clean pair of Wrangler jeans. Dressed, he pulled on his Justin boots ... the ones for dressing-up (the scuffed ranch-worn boots he left on the floor by the bed), and donned his "for goin' out" saddle-tan Stetson hat. He even splashed on some after-shave from a two-year-old bottle of Old Spice. Ready to head for town, Carl picked up a grocery bag of ingredients for the stroganoff from the kitchen counter and headed out the door. He was about to climb into the cab of his pickup when his phone rang. Opening the truck's door he dropped the groceries on the seat then retrieved the cell phone from his jacket pocket.

"Carl Bridger here." He settled behind the wheel and pulled the door closed.

"Harry Osborne, Skipper."

"Hey, Gunner! Are you on your way here? I have some crazy serious stuff you need to see." Carl didn't want to use words like 'weapons' or 'firepower' that might perk up prying ears.

"I got a call from Doc Henreid about an hour ago, Skipper. We worked it so we'll arrive in Great Falls tomorrow by 1:00 p.m.. I'll actually get there a little before Doc and I've arranged a rental car, so we should be at your place around two-thirty or shortly after. Can you hook us up with a room?"

"Sure thing, pal. I'll arrange it tonight. I have an in at the Inn, so to speak. I know the owner of the place. Call me when you land, Gunner. I'll give you the directions."

"Roger that, Skipper," Harry acknowledged and hung up.

Carl started the pickup and headed for Beth's place. His mind shifted from the mission to his "Bethy." The thought of spending the evening with her pushed up the chiseled lines on his face in what could only be described as a smile.

Beth dabbed at her lips and put her napkin down. "I'm learning a lot about you I didn't know, hon. You know your way around a stove. The stroganoff was perfect. I may have to add your recipe to the menu. The dinner crowd will think I've hired a new chef."

She stood and began to clear the table. Carl started to carry his plate to the kitchen. "No you don't! Now, you take the glasses and the rest of the wine and make yourself comfortable in front of the fireplace. I won't be a minute." She headed into the kitchen before he could say anything.

Carl poured two glasses of a fruity merlot from the half empty bottle and placed them on the coffee table. He relaxed on the sofa and took in the decor of the living room. The fireplace was of massive stone cut from the old Welch Spur granite quarry outside of Butte. Cedar-planked boards with barn-wood accents covered the walls which were complemented by deep-red Italian cherry-wood floors. The furniture was rough-cut Hickory; clearly handmade and stained dark to compliment the floor. Indian blankets, throws, and pillows in a western motif made for a comfortable and relaxing ambiance. Her paintings, though; that's what held his eye.

Landscapes of the majestic Glacier National Park, the Upper Yellowstone Valley, the Grand Tetons in Wyoming, and the Great Basin Wilderness area pulled at his senses. Beth's use of light streaming from behind trees and reflecting off the water and mountain peaks, added a three-dimensional quality and warmth to her work.

Beth walked up behind Carl and wrapped her arms around his waist. "I love the upper Yellowstone. It's one of my favorite places. We should go up there sometime ... take a long scenic road trip."

"Sounds good. Maybe even in early October this year. I'll bet the fall colors will be spectacular because of the wet summer we're having."

"Hmmm ... " Beth cooed softly. "Carl, I'm going to suggest something, but don't feel obligated to go along, alright?"

Carl's gaze met Beth's eyes. She was as fidgety as a kitten on catnip. "What, Beth? What are you thinking?"

"I'm thinking I want to spend as much time with you as I can before you ... fly off. I'm thinking I don't want you to go back to the ranch tonight." She found herself holding her breath.

Carl pulled Beth to him and kissed her in a long and warm embrace. "I would like that, Beth ... more than anything I can think of."

Carl pushed himself up and leaned on his right elbow. Reaching over he gently brushed Beth's hair away from her eyes and whispered.

"Hey, are you awake, Bethy?"

Her eyes opened and she smiled up at him. "I'm awake." She pulled his face toward her and kissed him lightly. "How 'bout you follow me down to the Wagonwheel and let Bert cook you up your special breakfast? Then, it's off you go back to the ranch."

"The breakfast sounds wonderful. Leaving you while I go back home ... not so good." Carl chortled. "But, you're right. There's a lot of work to do. Which reminds me; two friends of mine, Doc Henreid and Harry Osborne are coming into town around two-thirty this afternoon. Will you fix them up with two of your finest rooms? Put it on my tab."

"Sure. You're in luck. I have three vacancies. I'll reserve the two ground floor rooms for your friends. I'll take good care of them, not to worry." She eased out of bed and padded across the carpet to the bathroom to ready herself for the day, while Carl looked on with a lustful smile, grateful she'd left her bathrobe behind. He finally pulled on his clothes and headed for the kitchen. A cup of coffee and a slice of toast with Beth's peach marmalade later, they were off to the Wagonwheel.

After breakfast at the diner, Carl got up to leave. Beth was taking an order from a young couple who had pulled off the interstate for a bite to eat. Carl didn't want to disturb her and was about to head for the door when she glanced over at him. He winked and said goodbye with a subtle wave of his hand. She winked back and returned to the business of taking care of her customers. Carl paused long enough to write a note on a napkin, left a generous tip on it, then walked out into a crystal clear sunlit morning to the tinkle of the door chime.

Beth retrieved the tip Carl had left and noticed some writing on the napkin. She opened the folds of paper and read: "Today, tomorrow, and all of the tomorrows after that ... I will love you more with each passing day — Carl." She folded the napkin and tucked it into her apron pocket.

Carl headed out onto the main highway leading to the turn off to the ranch. He glanced in his rearview mirror and caught a black sedan pulling out from behind a billboard in a hurry. *Tail,* he thought. He reached the dirt road and swung to the right beneath the log entry with the "Rocking Double-B" brand placard hanging from the cross beam. The sedan drove slightly past, then slowed and turned back toward town. Carl punched in Beth's number on his cell phone.

"Beth, hi sweetheart. Don't say anything, but I spotted a black Crown Vic following me. He's headed back in your direction. If he stops, will you get his plate number? I'll follow up with you later."

"Alright, but are you okay? Who do you think it is, Carl?" Beth asked.

"Probably a Fed ... FBI or NSA. Maybe even the Agency, I don't know. Call me if you find out anything, will you?"

"Of course. You take care of yourself, my love. Promise?" Beth's concern added an edge to her voice.

"I will. Don't risk trying to get too much out of this guy. I don't want his attention to be drawn to you. I love you." Carl pushed "End," and returned the phone to its dashboard-mounted clip.

He drove to the ranch with no further sign of the black sedan. Carl parked the pickup and headed straight for the barn. The big red doors hung open and his tractor was pulling out into the sunlight. Perched on the flatbed he used for hauling hay and fencing materials, rested the B-25's new nose job. Sleek, beautiful, and as intimidating as hell. The business-end of the two blisters sported empty holes for now, but by the middle of the next day, *Annie* would be showing her teeth.

Carl walked alongside as the trailer skillfully backed up to the nose wheel of the bomber. The cavity of the missing airframe stood directly above the new assembly. The tent had been taken away for now, and in its place was a twenty-foot tall log tripod with a block and tackle dangling from the apex of the structure. Carl made a mental note to have the crew reposition the device behind the barn below the hay loft when they finished with it.

Gifford jumped down from the cab and walked over to Carl.

"Hi, Pop, you want to lend a hand? I need a spotter on the far side. I'll take this side. Together, we'll guide the nose assembly into position. Come with me so I can show you what to look for."

Gifford walked his father around to the left side of the '25. "Do you see the guides we've welded into the original bulkheads? Okay, now locate the corresponding spars on the new nose section. You'll find three of them on your side and three more on my side. Each spar is four feet long and needs to be lined up with the matching slots in the guides. Once in place, the bulkheads should match

73

up perfectly, and we can weld everything up. You'll need a steady hand to guide the spars into their slots. We don't want to throw off the alignment so much as a millimeter. Okay?"

Carl nodded. "Alright then, let's do this."

They took their positions on either side of the assembly and Gifford issued the command for InterDyn mechanic Kyle Breckenridge to raise it from the flatbed trailer.

Gifford called out."Raise her up, Kyle ... slowly ... slowly. Stop! Now, we need to come down about three inches. Stop. That should do. How are we on your side, Pop?"

"I'm about an inch low over here. I think the *Annie* is a little higher on the port side."

"Okay. We need to either level the plane or rig another block and tackle to lift the left side of the assembly. Ideas...anybody?" He got no response. "C'mon you guys, you're all engineers."

"I've got just the tool for the job." Buck Rogers approached from the main house and walked over to the left side of the plane, picking up a screw driver from a nearby work bench. He dropped to his knees beside the bomber's port side landing gear. "Tell me when, Carl." He stuck the tip of the screw driver into the valve stem on the tire and was rewarded with a whistle of air. The tire began to flatten slightly.

"More ... a little more ...," Carl coaxed as the spars slowly came into alignment with their corresponding slots. "Stop! That's perfect."

Two men brought the welding tanks alongside and set to the task of joining the new to the old. The skin was spot-welded to the bulkheads from the inside. Finished, the men stood back and admired their work. There was not so much as a hair's width between the old aluminum skin and the new stronger and lighter skin. By one o'clock in the afternoon, the engineers were well into installing the upgraded instrument panel and the web of wires and fiber optics which would bring it to life.

While the flight deck and forward fuselage were showing signs of progress, the wings and engine nacelles were a fright to behold. Both Wright 2600 14-cylinder engines sat on the floor in the barn. A team of engineers and welders were making the wing modifications Gifford described earlier. Already, the squared-off wing tips and the aileron extensions were taking shape. Two shiny refurbished Pratt and Whitney R-2800-51 18-cylinder engines sat on the ground beneath plastic wrap coverings waiting to be installed while the engine nacelles were being rebuilt to accommodate the larger engines with their 4-bladed propellers and bright aluminum hubs.

Carl took Buck aside. "You ready for the ride we talked about, Buck?"

"Sure enough, Mr. B. Put me on a gentle one, will you?" The General was a game old warrior.

They walked out to the corral where a tack shed stood at one end. Carl opened the padlock. Inside, the air was heavy with the smell of leather, musty horse blankets and saddle soap. Four saddles lay slung over a log. "Pick one out, Buck. Grab a blanket and let's head out to the corral. The bridles are hanging by the door. My horses are used to a bosal hackamore. I don't like using a snaffle bit except sometimes if I'm cutting. Don't do much of that these days ... leave that stuff to the younger hands. Your saddle is single-rigged. Most likely what you're used to. Need some help?"

"Nope; not right away, anyhow. Which one is mine?" Four horses were lolling about the corral. Carl put two fingers to his lips and blew a single sharp whistle. Two-bit lifted his head, turned and trotted up to the fence.

"Yours is the big Appaloosa. Name's 'Lucy'. Don't let her fool you, Buck. She's plenty of horse. Call her name and whistle. She'll come a-runnin'." Carl watched to see how Buck handled being out of his element.

"Lucy!" Buck called out and released a shrill whistle from between his teeth. Lucy perked up her ears, spun around and trotted over to Buck. The General put his face up to Lucy's and pulled both her ears downward until her head dropped and they were eye to eye. "I'm Buck. You and I are going to be good friends. You're a good girl. Good girl!" He patted Lucy's neck and slipped the bridle over her ears and adjusted the bosal on her nose. Then, he climbed over the fence and threw the blanket over her back as if he'd done it all his life. Next, came the saddle. Reaching under Lucy's belly, Buck drew the cinch up as Lucy sucked in a lung full of air. Buck kneed her firmly in the gut and Lucy released a gust of air while he pulled up the cinch another notch. Once done, the former astronaut gracefully swung himself up into the saddle.

"Now this feels good ... mighty good. Come on, girl," Buck clicked his tongue twice and tapped Lucy's left flank with his heel. She followed Two-bit out of the Corral. After Carl closed the gate he spurred Two-bit into a gallop. Buck took the challenge and Lucy practically leaped out from beneath him. He was ready for the sudden surge and quickly pulled alongside Carl.

CHAPTER VI

After hanging up following her phone conversation with Carl, Beth walked over to the left of the entry door and pulled back the chintz curtains. The two-inch wide shutters shaded the small lobby from the afternoon sun. She peeked between the vinyl slats into the Wagonwheel Restaurant's parking lot. A black sedan pulled into a parking space. A man wearing khaki slacks, a blue denim shirt and a matching light windbreaker climbed out. He appeared as any vacationer passing through who decided to stop for a bite to eat. *Something is off,* she thought . Maybe Beth's discerning artist's eye for detail caused her to reassess her initial impression. *He's no vacationer.*

The man was a little too buttoned-down and well put to-gether for a vacationer. He wore brown expensive-looking lace-up shoes rather than the casual footwear of a tourist. Most vacationers wore shoes for hiking the countless trails in the wilderness areas nearby. The slacks were pressed and his hair ... high and tight and squared off at the back. He was alone. No wife and no kids. Beth returned to the counter with its eight swivel stools sporting the '50s motif of shiny chrome and red vinyl seats. The man with the polished shoes entered the diner. He removed his Foster Grant sun glasses and caught Beth's eye.

She put on her best waitress' smile. "Welcome to the Wagonwheel. Sit yourself anywhere you like and I'll be right with you."

She turned to Ruth as if they were discussing diner business, and dropped her voice to a whisper. "I need you to go out the back door and write down his license plate number while I keep him busy."

"Why? ... Beth, what's going ...?"

"Just do it Ruth. I'll explain later."

Beth lifted the order pad out of her apron pocket and approached the new customer.

"Would you like something to drink while you look at the menu?" Beth glanced over at the kitchen door in time to see Ruth headed out to the parking lot.

"Sure. A diet cola with a wedge of lime will be fine," the man said, checking his watch.

"Coming right up. Our lunch special is the 'Thing'; an open-faced cheese burger smothered in chili con carne and topped with shredded lettuce, tomatoes, and sour cream. It'll fill you up, especially if you've been on the road a while. Where are you headed?" She asked innocently. Her eyes went to the door to the kitchen. *She's not back, yet* ... Beth thought.

"Just covering my sales territory. I was in Idaho yesterday, Helena this morning and on to Great Falls and Butte from here," he replied with a smile.

"Wow, sounds like a tough job. Where do you call home?" Beth stalled for time.

"Jackson, Wyoming. I think I'll have the Reuben sandwich, and I'm in a bit of a hurry." The conversation ended. Further inquiry would only serve to arouse suspicion.

"Sure thing. I'll be right back with your drink and some tortilla chips." Beth turned and walked behind the counter. She tore the man's order out of the pad and stuck it on an overhead turn style for Bert. Ruth nodded to her from the swinging door to the kitchen, and Beth walked over to her.

"I wrote down the plate number." Ruth handed her the slip of paper with the information written in pencil.

"Thanks, Ruth." Beth leaned close to her friend. "There's something strange about him ... probably nothing at all." Beth grabbed a plastic boat of tortilla chips and drew a cola from the fountain behind the bar.

Carl and Buck brushed down the horses after hanging their saddles and bridles in the tack room. They turned Lucy and Two-bit out into the corral to graze and drink.

"You handled yourself like an old ranch hand Buck ... impressive. So, what do you think? Is it doable?" Carl needed Buck's endorsement. The General's military background would provide for a highly accurate assessment of the operation.

"I'd need to go over your charts, but based on what you've told me, it's doable; dangerous, but doable,"

"Good ... very good." Carl released a sigh of relief. "C'mon in the house. We'll go over the charts and grab some lunch." Gifford was waiting for them when they entered the living room.

Carl noted his son's expression. He was worried about something. "How come you're not out in the barn, Giff? Is something wrong?"

"I heard from the Serbs again, Pop. I think our timeline just got a lot shorter. Take a look at this." Gifford produced a VHS video tape.

"Let's take this to the den. I don't want anyone without a need to know walking in on us." Carl led the way.

He slid the tape into the VCR and turned on the TV. The scene filling the screen was heartbreaking. Cody sat in front of the camera. As before, two masked soldiers stood by the chair. Each of the men held an AK-47 assault rifle at the Port Arms position. The young pilot's hair was matted with dried blood, his flight suit was caked with blood as well. Dark circles framed both eyes. In just over two weeks since his capture, Cody had been tortured, starved, and denied the most rudimentary care demanded by the Geneva Convention. Carl's heart sank as he imagined the squalor of Cody's living conditions.

Dad, the Serbs want me to read this statement. The camera moved into a close-up shot of Cody's brutalized face. *You are to be at the port of Portland, Maine, five days from receiving this message. You will deliver two shipping containers holding the items we require marked for delivery to pier 5. The Port Authority will be expecting you. Simply follow their directions and leave. The Czech Republic registered ship, the 'Hvezda Severu', will take the containers aboard. When the containers are in our possession your son will be guaranteed safe passage to the U.S. embassy in Prague to whom he will be released. Do nothing until you are notified by the embassy.*

"I don't like this. In five days the Serbs will be expecting delivery of the weapons at the dock in Portland, Maine. It'll take five days to make the transit; six depending on the port of entry on the other side. We've got to get Cody out of there before the ship reaches Hamburg ten days from now," Gifford observed.

"We're five days into the refit of *Annie*. The air show is in eight days. We'll need to leave here in six days in order to make Aviano in time. Giff, can you get the *Annie* ready for a shake-down flight in four days?" Carl asked. His mind raced with a flood of the things that needed to be accomplished.

"Four days? Wow, that's pushing things. The avionics are installed. We still need to field test and calibrate the IVOTACS and cannons. We're refitting the bomb-bay and installing the missile racks as we speak." Gifford paused for a few seconds while he worked out a few details in his head.

"We can save some time by not field testing the IVOTACS on the ground. We'll finish the installation and test the weapons when you and Buck shake the kinks out of the *Annie*. That means your gunners will need to do their training on the initial shakedown flight as well. If everything goes smoothly we can be ready in time."

"Okay. Giff, load the shipping containers and send them out as scheduled. We'll need to think of some way of securing them before they arrive at their destination. I figure six days for the ship to make the crossing. You've got to buy us an extra day. The extraction team has to get Cody to safety before the cargo reaches port. I'll give Mac a call and give him an update." He was about to make the call to the Agency when his phone rang.

"Hi, Bethy. What's up, sweetheart?" He was anxious to hear from her about the stranger at the diner.

"Carl, I've got the plate number from the car. The man came into the diner and ate lunch. He claimed to be a travelling salesman covering his territory, but there was something off about him. Anyway, the number is VGM three-seven-two. Also, your two friends are here. They're settling into their rooms. Do you want me to send them your way?" Beth asked.

"No, I'll come to you after I check on a couple of things first. I'll be at your place by four o'clock. Thanks, Beth." He turned his attention back to Gifford.

"Son, I want Harry and Doc familiarized with the IV-OTACS telemetry tomorrow. Can Dr. Dupree handle that part in the morning first thing?"

"I'm sure she'll be ready, Pop."

"Good. Let's go see how the re-fit's going." The three men left the house and headed toward the barn just as two cars pulled onto the gravel driveway. Carl recognized the black unmarked Crown Victoria from earlier and it bore the same plate number Beth just gave him. The other displayed the paint scheme of one of only three Cascade PD cruisers in the city's fleet of vehicles.

"Oh, brother. What now?" Carl mumbled as the men climbed out of their cars. "It's show time, Buck. We can't let them get into the barn."

"Don't worry, Carl. They won't." Buck put on his celebrity face.

The two men approached. The officer, name of Brent Stanley, held his hand out to Carl. "Howdy, Carl ... it's been a while. Quite a show you put on a couple days ago. A little low weren't you?" Brent had been Cascade's police chief for twelve years and commanded the department of six officers. "This here is Special Agent Phillip Pallin of the FBI." The agent flashed his FBI credentials.

"What can we do for you, gentlemen?" Carl asked politely. *First a salesman and now an FBI agent. This guy has CIA written all over him.* Carl figured the man to be Mac's agent from the Great Falls field office.

"For starters, Mister Bridger, we need to take a look inside the barn and your airplane." Pallin took three steps when Buck stepped in front of him.

"Put the speed brakes on there, Turbo. I can't let you go in there." Buck's smile remained warm, but the icy tone of his voice said he meant business.

"Excuse me? I wasn't asking permission." Pallin spoke evenly.

"Young man, do you know who I am?" The agent shrugged his shoulders. "I'm Brigadier General Buckminster Rogers. You two are standing on the ground of a classified United States Air

Force project."

"You're Buck Rogers the astronaut?" The chief of police was truly taken aback by the revelation. "Holy crap, Carl, I had no idea the Air Force was out here. Well, that's enough for me. C'mon, agent Pallin. Let's head back to town."

"Not so fast, Chief Stanley. Gentlemen, you are interfering with a duly sworn Federal Agent. I'm ordering you to step aside." Buck stood fast.

"I'll tell you what, agent Pallin, or whatever your name is; you come back with a warrant from a *duly sworn* Federal Judge and we'll chat again real soon. But, until such time as you do, young man, you really must get the hell off the 'Double-B'." Buck placed his fisted hands on his hips.

Pallin stood for a brief moment and glared at Buck. Buck never broke eye contact with him. The agent must have realized he wasn't going to win the battle of wits with Buck, because he spun on his heels and marched back to his car. The encounter bought the InterDyn crew at least another day.

Carl pulled into the gravel parking lot in front of the Wagonwheel and turned off the ignition. He retrieved the cell phone Mac gave him from his shirt pocket, and pressed "Call". Mac picked up on the second ring.

"Aldrin."

"Mac, I need you to run this Montana plate for me; Victor-Golf-Mike-three-seven-two. I believe it'll trace to your man in Great Falls. Check also for an FBI agent name of Phillip Pallin ... most likely a cover name."

"Give me five minutes. I'll call you back on this line.

Carl entered the diner. Harry and Doc were eating a late lunch. He walked over to their booth, grinning. "Hey, boys. You two are a sight for these old eyes. How long's it been, seven ... eight years?" Doc and Harry stood to greet their old command pilot with handshakes and back slaps aplenty.

"Not since the reunion in '85, Skipper." Doc added, resuming his seat.

"Yep ... been too long, Skipper." Harry Osborne chimed in. He slid into the booth and Carl took a seat next to him.

Picking up a fresh pot of coffee, Ruth walked over to the men. "Beth went on a grocery run. She should be right back. What can I get for you, Carl?"

"How about a slice of your famous banana-cream pie and some coffee?"

"Coming right up. Help yourselves to the coffee." Ruth placed the coffee pot on the table and walked behind the counter.

When she was out of ear shot Carl hunkered forward on the table, dropping his voice to a whisper.

"Guys, we need to talk. Let's eat then head out to the ranch. I guarantee, what I'm going to show you will absolutely blow your minds." Carl looked up to see Beth enter through the kitchen door.

"Hi there, boys. How are the rooms?" She asked with a cheerful smile.

"Comfortable, thank you. You keep a nice place, Ma'am," Doc smiled up at her.

"Now don't you 'Ma'am' me, Doc. Carl has told me all about you. I'm 'Beth' to you boys." She smiled warmly.

"Okay, 'Beth' it is." Doc laughed.

After eating, Carl eased out of the booth, walked over to the counter and sat down on a stool in front of Beth. She put a hand on his.

"It's getting close, isn't it?" Her question was more of a statement.

"Yes. Two days. I want you to come with us out to the

ranch. I need for you to know everything we're doing. It's like you said; you do better when you have all of the information." Carl covered her hand with his.

"Okay; only for a couple of hours, though. I need to get back to help with the dinner crowd." She bent across the counter and kissed Carl to the accompaniment of whistles from the booth.

As Carl, Doc Henreid, Harry Osborne and Beth walked to the barn, Doc and Harry took immediate notice of the B-25 and changed their course for the *Annie*.

"Oh, my, Harry. Look at her." Doc's eyes were as wide with surprise as those of a six-year-old boy on Christmas morning. "She's beautiful, Skipper ... and her nose; those blisters are for the 20mm cannons, right?"

"Yep. Six-thousand rounds per minute of titanium tipped armor piercing explosive rounds each," Carl said proudly.

An attractive white-coated young woman approached the men.

" He's correct, gentlemen. Each round is capable of penetrating three inches of armor plating before exploding. The inside of every round is designed to fragment like a hand grenade, sending shrapnel in a three-hundred-sixty-degree arc.

"Picture three dozen tiny steel BBs coming at you at five-hundred miles per hour. Multiplied by however many rounds are exploding almost simultaneously in a confined space, and, well, I think you've got the picture. I'm Dr. Lauren Dupree. I developed the IVOTACS system that will convert you two gentlemen into killing machines like nothing you can imagine." The scientist extended her right hand.

Doc Henreid offered his own and the two shook. "Doc Henreid, Doctor, and this skinny old gent next to me is Harry Osborne; the best damned B-25 turret gunner who ever walked the planet."

Harry took his turn shaking the scientist's hand. "Pleased to meet you, ma'am; first time I've seen such a smart brain in so beautiful a package. You remind me of my daughter."

Lauren Dupree smiled at Harry's use of the formal greeting.

"'Ma'am.' Aren't you the polite one, now? Such gentlemanly behavior is lost on the younger generation, I'm afraid. Thank you for your service ... both of you. I hope you gentlemen are up for learning some new tricks."

"Whenever you give us the word, Doctor, you'll find we are both quick learners," Doc said with a downright flirtatious joviality.

Doctor Dupree turned to get back to work. "Tomorrow morning at nine, then. Pleasure to meet you, Doc ... Harry," she said over her shoulder.

Carl had been showing Beth around the barn. In place of the familiar horse stalls, hay, and farm equipment, stood a combination of a hi-technology laboratory and an assembly line. The place buzzed with activity as the InterDyn team busily focused on getting everything ready to go for the shakedown flight of the *Annie* and the first ever live-fire test of the IVOTACS.

Beth stared in wide-eyed amazement at the flurry of activity.

"I'm impressed beyond words, Carl. Gifford must be quite the corporate boss to inspire the kind of loyalty these people obviously feel toward him."

"They're not aware of the rescue mission. For their own protection, Giff didn't want to make them party to something that might subject them to criminal prosecution for conspiring to break ... oh, I can only guess how many Federal and international laws." Carl still worried about the legal mess ahead, but managed to keep his concerns tucked in the quiet recesses of his mind, focusing instead on getting Cody back home. To him, his grandson was the only concern.

He walked Beth to her car and opened the driver's door for

her, but she put her hand on his and raised herself up on her toes. Carl wrapped his arms around her waist and lifted her to his lips in a sweet, lingering kiss.

"Be safe." she kissed his ear which sent a thrill down his spine.

"I will." They kissed again and Carl watched Beth drive away from the ranch for the Wagonwheel. When she reached the highway, he forced his attention back to the task at hand.

"Let's go inside, you guys." He led the way to the main house.

Doc, Harry, Buck and Gifford sat in Carl's den to discuss any issues the bomber's crew wanted to talk about.

"Boys," Carl began; "We take the *Annie* up day after tomorrow for a shakedown. She's a new ship. Harry, you'll man the 50cals in the tail. Doc, you and Giff will handle the cannons and the IVOTACS. There's no Plexiglas turret to look out of like back in the day. You will need to trust the IVOTACS helmets to be your eyes."

"Dr. Dupree will start our training in the morning, Skipper. I figure I'll catch on pretty fast. The medical robotics technology in the O.R. has me in the right mindset to *mind meld* with the IVOTACS. Gifford and I will be fine. We'll stay with it 'til we've made friends with her contraption."

Gifford chuckled at Doc's Star-Trek reference. "Doc's Vulcan mind-meld metaphor is an apt one. The concept of melding human cognition with technology was, until now, only theoretically possible. The IVOTACS technology is about to bring fantasy into reality."

Buck smiled at Giff and nodded in agreement. "Every time I took a plane up to test some new bit of technology designed to make a human pilot more efficient ... faster, more accurate, safer ... it required an element of trust in the technology and in the people who designed it. I *trust* the team working on the *Annie*, Carl. I *trust* Doctor Dupree, and I *trust* you, Gifford. I *trust* this mission. The strategy is sound, given the total insanity of it all. But, gentlemen we are doing this for a just cause, and the Almighty smiles on his avenging angels. It's as Don Quixote said; 'Destiny guides our fortunes more favorably than we could have expected. This is noble, righteous warfare.'"

Carl stood. "Fill your glasses gentlemen." He passed around one of his best bottles of Kentucky sour mash whiskey. "To the mission; no nobler cause exists than for one man to offer up himself in the defense of another man's life and liberty."

"To the mission!" The crew of the *Annie* shouted in unison.

Carl placed his empty glass on a coaster.

"We've had a long day, boys. I suggest we all get some sleep." He waited for everyone to leave. Harry and Doc left for town and Buck went to the guest room. Gifford headed out to the barn to be with his team. They would be working through the night as they had been doing since they arrived to get the bomber ready for her maiden flight.

Carl switched off the lights in his den and walked upstairs to his bedroom. His thoughts turned to his son. Gifford's concern for Cody didn't weaken his natural leader's instinct. If anything, Carl knew the Inter-Dyn CEO was even more focused and determined in his resolve. Like any good field commander who understands the value of standing on the front line of a battle where his men can see him; so too, Gifford understood the need to stand with his people in the midst of their hard work. Giff's presence inspired the best from his "troops." Carl could not have been more proud of his son.

The encrypted Agency phone rang in Carl's pocket. He fished the device out and pushed the talk button. "Hi, Mac. What did you find out?"

"Your instincts haven't lost their edge, Carl. There is no FBI agent name of Phillip Pallin. Can you describe the man?" Mac asked.

"Six feet ... skinny, maybe one-sixty, one-seventy, late

twenties to thirty. His hair was cut high and tight ... dark brown and thinning on top ... blue eyes." Carl waited for Mac's response.

"Sounds like Wes Steed. He's Agency out of Great Falls. The car is a rental from a company called Quality Rentals, also in Great Falls." Mac paused for a few seconds. "We've got two possibilities here, Carl. Either Steed is working on orders from Shel Macvie, which I hope is not the case, or someone in your midst is an informant and they're passing information directly to Steed, possibly on orders from Helm's office. Be careful, pal."

The next morning, Cal asked Doctor Dupree to share breakfast with him, Gifford and Buck.

"Those of us sitting at this table are the only people who know what the mission of the *Annie* is about. We've kept it quiet for obvious reasons, chief of which is to avoid leaking anything to the authorities. After talking with my friend at the CIA, I believe there's a leak from either the ranch, or at InterDyn back in Utah. We were visited yesterday by the Cascade Police and someone who introduced himself as an FBI agent. As it turns out the fed was, in fact, CIA."

"CIA? What in the world ..." Doctor Dupree was genuinely surprised.

"What I am about to tell you cannot leave this room, Doctor. I already briefed Gifford, but I think you need to be read-in as well. A friend of mine at Langley, Mac Aldrin, is doing everything he can to help us. He is providing us with regular satellite photos and intel on troop movements around Sarajevo. He's even been out to the ranch. He and I go way back to my days in the Agency." Carl paused and looked at the perplexed engineer.

"You're CIA, Carl? Gifford, what in hell is going on here?" She demanded.

"Dad's friend is Director of Covert Operations, Lauren. I've met him. He's not the problem here. Go on, Pop."

"I'm driving to Great Falls this morning to find this guy. I can warn him off. Mac Aldrin is his boss. If I tell the man he's been participating in an unauthorized operation he should back off, especially since he's been working on the QT for someone else in the Agency. Of course, Mac will find out if someone is working behind his back without authorization. Now, I need to ask both of you a question. Is there anyone on your team who is new to InterDyn, or whom you're not personally familiar with?" Carl waited for Gifford's and Dupree's response.

Lauren's eyes widened and she sat more erect in her seat. "Our lead welder, Andy Breinholt. One of his journeyman welders had to be replaced by a fellow from another project in a different building. Andy and I just assumed that he was cleared from higher up. I'll check it out. I'm sorry, Gifford. I should have checked him out myself."

"Let me know what you find out ASAP, Lauren. You should get back to the barn. Thank you, and don't worry. You didn't do anything wrong." Gifford reassured her.

Carl motioned for the scientist to stop. "Lauren, we need to be on the same page here. If word gets back to the Director of Central Intelligence, we'll all be in the stew pot. We have to stop the leak now if there is one. Mac can handle things at the Agency if we can put an end to the spy crap here."

"Understood, Carl." Lauren left the main house and headed back to the barn where Harry Osborne and Doc Henreid waited, excited to begin their training.

Twenty miles outside of Great Falls, Carl was speeding toward a showdown with Wesley Steed, aka Phillip Pallin. He wondered how far the lad would go when he was confronted. He figured the junior agent probably wouldn't risk escalating the situation by threatening Carl directly. On the other hand, Carl couldn't know how far up the chain of command the puppeteer pulling the agent's strings was; CIA, NSA, The Justice Department; perhaps even the White House. Given the possibility that the rescue mission could trigger an international situation, he worried that if word got back to the State Department of the goings-on in Montana, Mac wouldn't be able to prevent a raid on the ranch.

The thought sent a chill up Carl's spine. "The damned State Department should have done something!" Carl yelled as he slammed his fist on the steering wheel. He turned on the truck's radio and checked the traffic behind him. He almost missed the black sedan following about a half-mile back. *It's too far away to see if it's him or not,* Carl thought. He eased up on his speed a little and watched through the rear-view mirror. The black car held back and allowed two other vehicles to pass him. Carl waited until the same two cars passed him. The "tail" still hung back.

Carl patted the concealed weapon beneath his windbreaker, a Smith and Wesson 40 caliber semi-automatic pistol. A green and white traffic sign told him the Ulm Vaughn State Road exit was a quarter mile ahead. He slowed and snapped on his turn signal. After stopping at the bottom of the exit, he turned left on Ulm Vaughn toward Ulm Pishkin State Park. *Good, no traffic ahead,* Carl thought, a plan forming in his mind. He slowed until he saw the black sedan coming over the rise in the road behind him, then he sped up and headed over the next rise. The horizon of the road rose above the line of site between the two vehicles, and Carl slammed on his brakes as he simultaneously cranked the steering wheel hard to the left. In a cloud of burning tire-smoke the pickup skidded in a 180 degree arc, nearly rolling in the process. Carl jammed the accelerator to the floor and the pickup lurched forward as he swerved into the oncoming lane.

Wesley Steed drove at a steady 65 miles per hour, certain that Carl's truck would appear from the top of the rise in front of him. He wasn't disappointed. Carl's pickup rocketed straight for him on a collision course. Steed didn't have time to think and instinctively swerved on to the soft shoulder and lost control as the Crown Victoria slid sideways down into the barrow pit. The car jerked to a stop in a cloud of dirt and the agent threw open the car door and leapt out, his hand reaching under his suit jacket for the Sig Sauer 9 mm semi-automatic he carried.

"Not so fast agent Pallin." Carl used the agent's cover name for the moment. His gun was pointed at the man's torso. "Let's not make this any messier than it already is." He walked down to the young agent while keeping the boy firmly in his sights. "Put your hands on your head and turn around."

The agent complied.

"Mister Bridger, you have no idea how much trouble you've gotten yourself in to. Lay your gun down and we'll talk."

"I intend to do precisely that, agent Pallin. On your knees, do it now! Good, now ease your weapon out and toss it to your left ... slowly." The young man did as he was told. "Good boy. Stand up and turn toward me. Walk up on to the road and sit on the tailgate of my truck." The agent trudged up the embankment and onto the blacktop. He sat down as instructed.

Carl directed him to remove his handcuffs and loop one cuff around one of the tailgate chains and attach the other to his right wrist. "Good, now let's talk; you first. Why are you following me?"

"The FBI wants to know why InterDyn people are at your place and ...".

"Stop right there." He drew closer, nose-to-nose with the young agent. "Now, you see, we have a little problem here, sonny. So, if you lie to me again, I'll lay my gun up alongside your jaw.

I'll probably break it, too; your jaw, not my gun. Understood?"

The agent glared back at Carl, but didn't say a word.

"Okay, let's try again. Why are you here? Why are you following me? Who sent you?"

"I told you, my name is Phillip Pallin. I am a special agent for the FBI, and ..." A burning flare of pain caused his eyes to go out of focus as his head snapped to the right. His mouth filled with blood. The agent moved his tongue around and located a tooth which he spat out onto the ground." Carl offered him a handkerchief which he accepted with his free hand.

"I'm sorry I had to do that, agent. In our line of work, sometimes we must resort to unpleasant measures, don't we? Now, the truth this time. What is your name?" Carl asked evenly. He chambered a round and aimed the barrel of his weapon at the man. He had no intention of shooting the kid. Most often, an imagined threat is more intimidating than the real thing.

"Alright! ... alright. I'm Wesley Steed. I'm not with the FBI. I work for the CIA. This was supposed to be a simple surveillance operation to find out why a major U.S. weapons systems developer like InterDyn is moving two semi-tractor trailers of arms and equipment to your ranch. I didn't buy General Rogers' act, either. The local police chief bought it all, but not me." He paused and rubbed his jaw gingerly. "So, where do we go from here?"

"Well, I'm not going to shoot you, Wesley. Who in the Agency gave you your orders?"

"They came from the Deputy Director of Domestic Affairs office itself. My contact is Sheldon Macvie."

Helm's office, Carl thought. Steed's story rang true. Shelley MacVie had gone over Mac's head straight to the DODA. Steed would never question orders directly from Langley if he was told they came from the Director of Domestic Affairs. Sheldon Macvie was the assistant to the Director of Covert Operations, Mac Aldrin.

The young field operative would not be alert to any deception and would take his orders at face value. "Okay, Steed. I'll take the cuffs off, but first I'm going to put someone on the phone that you need to talk to." Carl punched in Mac's number on the secure cell phone.

"Mac here. How are things at the ranch, Carl? Oh, by the way, I know who's been following you." Before he could continue, Carl interrupted him.

"I already found out ... the hard way. Agent Steed is here with me. The poor lad has been misled to believe he is working under orders from Domestic Affairs. I need you to set him straight. Hold on, I'll put him on." Carl handed the phone to Wes Steed.

"Hello, who is this?" The CIA operative asked. He waited for a reply from the other end and then jumped to his feet, an expression of equal parts surprise and fear appeared on his face. Steed released a painful yelp as the steel cuff jerked hard against his wrist. "Yes, sir ... yes sir ... I understand, sir. Yes, I will do that immediately, sir. I ... uh ... yes, sir ... as soon as I hang up, sir. Good-bye, sir." Steed handed the phone back to Carl.

"Sir, I ... I must apologize to you, Mister Bridger. Mister Aldrin confirmed that General Roger's presence and the InterDyn testing at your ranch is a classified legitimate operation. I'm ordered to return to Langley for debriefing by Mister Aldrin, so there will be no further confusion over the matter." The now complacent Wesley Steed stood motionless for a moment. "So, what do we do next, Mister Bridger?"

"For starters, Wesley, we should probably call Triple-A." Carl unlocked Steed's handcuffs. He picked the pistol up from out of the dirt and removed the rounds from the magazine. "Here you go, kid. Sorry about your jaw. It's not broken, by the way. I pulled my punch."

Carl climbed into the pickup and drove back to the Interstate. He decided to stop by the Wagonwheel before returning to the ranch.

"Hi, Bethy. You got a minute to sit?" He wanted to update her on what had happened in the last hour, but mostly he had thoughts of spending the night with her.

Beth's eyes examined Carl's disheveled appearance. "You're a mess, Carl. Have you been roping steers or something?"

"Nope, more like ropin' a federal agent. Maybe we can talk over some of Ruth's banana cream pie and coffee." He felt his body begin to relax. Beth had a calming effect on him. The tension in his shoulders and neck begin to ease up.

"I'll get it. Be right back, hon." She went behind the counter and loaded a tray with a carafe of coffee and two generous slices of pie then returned to the booth. "So, what's going on, Carl? Is everything alright?"

"Right as rain, my love. Events have taken a turn for the better since this whole thing started." Carl told Beth about the encounter with Wesley Steed and of Mac's phone conversation with him as well. They talked for the next half hour and agreed Carl would meet Beth at her place after she closed the diner at nine o'-clock.

The next morning saw Gifford stretched out in a prone position on the couch, which was set up to simulate the firing position in the bomber. Buck, Lauren Dupree and Doc Henreid looked on. He grasped the joy stick in front of him and pressed a button with his thumb, activating the IVOTACS heads-up display on his visor. He and Doc had been schooled on the various features of the system. Gifford scanned the symbols and mentally noted their names and functions; decline-incline, artificial horizon, distance to target, and target acquisition reticle.

"We've simulated the targets on the HUD. A beam of light

95

will trace the trajectory to the target each time you fire. Remember what I said, Gifford. Let your eyes do the work. The computer will do the rest. All you need to do is lock on to the bogey with your eyes. Focus on the cross hairs of the reticle. When they change from red to green you can fire," Lauren Dupree instructed while Buck stood alongside her, absorbing everything she was saying.

"Yes. I'm holding on target ... I'm green to go." Gifford pressed the fire-control button on the joy stick in his right hand. A pulsing red beam shot forward and ignited the virtual target in a flare of white light. "Yes! Like shooting fish in a barrel." He removed the IVOTACS helmet and placed it on the pedestal next to his seat.

"Okay, Doc, it's your turn. Tell me when you're ready." The scientist waited for Doc to get into position.

Gifford crawled off of the couch to make room for Dupree's next student.

"We're going to check you boys out on something a little more challenging. You're going to see a formation of three predator aircraft. When they come into view, I want you to take them out. Remember, they're not stationary targets. They'll be moving across the screen from different angles as your pilot maneuvers the B-25 into firing position."

Doc Henreid pulled the helmet over his head. "I'm ready, Doctor ... er, Lauren." Doc held the joystick with a surgeon's touch. At first the Heads-Up Display was filled with a few clouds, but then something flashed in front of his eyes before drifting back into view. The cross-hairs glowed red as Doc forced his eyes to focus on one of the planes. The reticle flashed green and back to red as Doc's peripheral vision drew his eyes off target, *a light bloom from the sun,* he thought as he searched for the next opportunity. Suddenly one of the predators was in full view. He centered his eyes on the target and when the reticle flashed from red to green, he pressed the fire button without a nanosecond of hesitation. A flash of light shot forward in front of him and then the screen was clear. The next two predators were dispatched in a similar fashion. Doc removed his headset.

Lauren smiled her appreciation. "The two of you possess excellent eye-hand coordination and reaction time," she said. "I guess old skills never completely die, do they Doc? Well done, both of you."

"Thank you, Doctor. You're IVOTACS would have saved a lot of lives back in the day." Doc removed the helmet and stood next to Gifford.

"Impressive, Lauren, very impressive. Nice work Gifford ... Doc," Buck said with an approving nod. "I've gone over the flight instruments and avionics modifications. The HUD is similar to my F-16. Otherwise, the rest seems straightforward enough. I think Carl will be pleased with your redesign."

Carl overheard the conversation as he approached from the main house. "Did somebody mention my name? Hey, Giff ... Doc. How's the training going, Buck?"

Lauren fielded the question. "They're doing well, Carl. The boys worked hard all day and neither Gifford nor Doc seems to be the least bit tired. Frankly, I'm pooped," Lauren chuckled at her own joke. "Please, join us. We were on our way to the *Annie* to familiarize them with their real couches. You should probably come along, too."

"Is the *Annie* ready for a test flight, Lauren?" Carl asked.

"She's as ready as she can be. We need to do a final calibration of the IVOTACS, and she'll be good to go. All that's left is for one of my technicians to link up the helmets. The next test will be a live-fire exercise. Buck has gone over the flight modifications."

"Yes, indeed, and I think you're going to like what the InterDyn team has done," Buck affirmed.

"Let's walk over to the plane now and get you oriented, Carl. Gifford, you and Doc can get comfortable with your couches." She exited the barn and started for the *Annie* with the rest of them following along. The scientist wasted no time in taking care of business, Carl observed.

The original crew entry hatch behind the nose wheel had been moved back toward the bomb-bay. Carl stuck his head up into the belly of the refurbished B-25 and looked at the changes. "It's a tight fit with the missile racks, but we can squeeze ourselves in okay. He stepped aside to let Harry, Gifford, and Doc check it out.

"Notice where the two gunner positions are located," Doctor Dupree said. "Two twenty-four inch wide couches are mounted one above each cannon. You can sit on the couches with your feet in the walk space between them until it's time to get into attack position.

"There isn't enough headroom in the cabin for you to sit above the cannons in a forward-facing position, so you'l lie prone on top of them. Six inches of Kevlar reinforced sound-proofed padding between the couches and the guns will suppress most of the noise which will be extreme, and will insulate your bodies from the heat. The noise cancelling technology in the helmet will take care of the rest of it.

"Your radio headset, contained in the molded head-piece under your helmet, will help as well. Carl, it will be a tight fit, but you and Buck can squeeze your way forward between the couches to the flight deck. If you gentlemen are ready, the targets are in position for your test flight." Lauren nodded to the men and walked back to the barn.

"Let's do it. Buck, why don't you climb aboard while I do a walk-around? Harry you go first so you can make your way aft to the rear guns, then Buck, Giff and Doc. I'm last."

Carl's crew boarded while he checked all of the control surfaces, tires and struts. He ran his hand over the shiny, smooth aluminum bullet-shaped hub of the starboard 4-bladed propeller. Doc had confirmed the correct oil and fuel levels earlier. Satisfied with the pre-flight check, Carl climbed up the ladder through the bomb-bay and punched-in the code to close the bomb-bay on a touch-pad. He eased forward in a crouch to the flight deck.

"Just a quick note about the instruments, Buck. You're probably used to reading indicated airspeed in knots. The B-25 air-speed indicator uses miles per hour. It's no big deal. The bombsight was originally calibrated to miles per hour, so it made sense to have the pilot's Airspeed Indicator the same as the bombardier's." He buckled himself in. "Are you ready to do this, partner?"

"I am, indeed, my friend." A broad grin was plastered on his face. "This is like Christmas morning and I'm opening the last and best present."

"Okay, let's get the show on the road. Starboard ignition switch on."

Buck turned the appropriate switch to the "on" position. "Switch on," he confirmed.

"Booster pump on. Prime for two seconds, Buck. That's good. Turning one!" Carl yelled out the open side wind-screen. "Hold down the energizer, primer, and engaging switch until the engine fires up.

Buck held down all three, and the propeller began to turn with the whine of the turbine. The fuel ignited and the manifold emitted a loud cough accompanied by a blast of smoke. The big Double-Wasp engine fired up. Carl advanced the mixture to full rich and adjusted the throttle to one-thousand-two-hundred rpm. With the right engine idling smoothly, they repeated the process for the left engine.

"Turning two," Carl called out. Soon, both engines were running smoothly. Carl checked the oil pressure gauges on both sides and noted they were in the green at forty pounds each. Carl backed off the mixture a bit to compensate for the three-thousand-foot elevation. As soon as the cylinder-head temperature gauges rose to the green safety zone, Carl eased forward a bit on the throttles and the '25 started a slow roll to the end of the runway.

"Give me a notch of flaps, please, Buck. Comm. check boys. Y'all copy back there?" Carl asked.

"Harry here. You are five-by-five, Skipper."

"Doc. Loud and clear, Skipper."

"Giff, here, Pop. I copy you."

"The plane is yours, Buck. Let's go. Use a gradual but firm hand. Don't jam the throttles." Carl pulled his side wind screen closed.

Buck eased the throttles forward, saving the last inch until barely shy of take-off speed before pushing the throttles to the wall. The big eighteen-cylinder engines roared and *Annie* rotated into the air. Carl brought the gear up and, when they reached 120 mph, he raised the flaps.

"Nice, Buck. A little different from the F-16, eh?" Carl grinned.

"She's a sweet lady, Carl. What's next?"

"Lauren had some guys set up a couple of aluminum sheds off the end of the runway. We'll fly left traffic and line them up with *Annie's* nose. Giff, Doc ... Are you ready? Giff, you take the shed on the left. The right one is yours, Doc. Don't hit the little shed behind and between the two big ones. Harry, that is for you. You're going to do it the old fashioned way," Carl said.

"Roger that, Skipper. I've got the leftovers."

"I've got the aircraft, Buck," Carl announced.

"The aircraft is yours, Captain." Buck glanced at Carl and winked his approval of the pilot's natural ability to command.

The *Annie* flew a long downwind leg then banked left until she was flying into the wind at one-thousand feet relative altitude.

Carl dropped the nose and the bomber descended to two-hundred feet above the surface. He increased his speed to 250 miles per hour, accelerating to 270 as he centered *Annie's* nose between the two distant sheds now visible about a mile ahead.

Two simultaneous one-second bursts of 20mm cannon fire erupted from beneath the flight deck. Carl and Buck felt *Annie* brake a little from the recoil of the Vulcans. Two clouds of dust billowed up in front of them. Then, as they passed over the targets, Carl aimed the '25s nose skyward, angling the tail downward. The twin fifty-caliber guns breathed fire down on the third smaller shed with the Japanese rising sun battle flag painted on the roof. The structure virtually exploded in the path of Harry's gunfire.

Carl banked the plane sharply to the left and did a fly-over to assess the damage. All three sheds were obliterated. If any living thing had been inside, it would have been shredded. "Well done, boys. You have the controls, Buck. Let's head for the barn; hold your downwind speed at one-twenty and lay in one notch of flaps."

When the *Annie* flew about two thirds of the way down the runway at five-hundred feet above the surface, Buck laid in twenty-five percent of his flaps and dropped the landing gear. He allowed a descent of five-hundred feet per minute and turned on to his base leg. He held his airspeed at 120 mph and lowered the flaps to thirty degrees as he turned onto final approach. He lined up the bomber's nose and let his speed drop to 100 mph while lowering the flaps to full.

"When you're over the threshold, pull the throttles back to full idle and hold your glide angle. Don't let the nose drop. You'll feel the ground effect when you are about to touch down. Keep the nose pointed at the end of the runway and she'll land on the mains." Carl mentally critiqued Buck as he went through the approach without a hitch.

"Will do, Skipper. She's not as responsive as the F-16, but

I'm getting used to her. Reducing speed ... full flaps .. .throttles back to idle. Easy, baby, be nice to papa now." Buck raised the nose slightly and the mains thumped onto the grass strip and bounced once before settling down.

"Well done, Buck. I think we're ready."Carl keyed his mic. "Boys, debriefing in the main house in ten minutes. The bar will be open."

Carl and his crew sat down with Dr. Dupree and went over every aspect of the test flight.

"The technology of the IVOTACS worked wonderfully, Lauren. Lying on top of the cannon when I fired was something akin to lying on the world's most powerful full-body vibrator. It was positively orgasmic," Doc said, to the laughter of all.

Everyone expressed confidence in the hardware and in their mastery of it. Even Carl didn't mind the subtle difference in the handling characteristics of the airplane. The forward shift in the center of gravity resulting from the weight of the two cannons made for a slightly higher stall speed, but was nothing that couldn't be handled.

"Gentlemen, we leave at 0900 hours. Gifford ... Doctor Dupree, you have done an incredible job. I can't thank you enough for the work you and your team have done. Without you, a brave American boy would be dead. Because of you, Cody has a chance to return home to his family. Again, thank you. Your job is done. Now, ours begins."

With that, Gifford and Lauren walked out to the barn where the InterDyn team were packing up and loading everything on the trailers for shipment back to Utah. Giff would send his people home under cover of darkness five hours later.

At eight-forty-five p.m. Carl, Doc, and Harry convoyed their way to town after the debriefing. Carl left them at the motel. "Get some sleep, boys. We have a long few days ahead of us."

Beth brought a huge bowl of popcorn with sodas into the living room and placed them on the coffee table. She curled up next to Carl, who was in his stocking feet and a pair of pajama bottoms. Beth wore the top.

"You ready, hon?" She turned on the television and thumbed the "play" button on the VCR remote. The movie *Bodyguard* starring Kevin Costner and Whitney Houston came on the screen and the audience of two settled in to watch it. In the final scene where Whitney Houston ordered her plane to stop and she rushed down the steps and embraced Kevin Costner, kissing him passionately, Beth shuddered and wept. Carl held her close.

"It'll be alright, Beth. I'll come back to you. Nothing can stop us from going forward. I love you." He lifted her face and looked into her eyes and dabbed the tears from them with the edge of the blanket.

That made her cry even more and she wrapped her arms around his neck and squeezed as hard as she could, as if he would be restrained from leaving by the sheer force of her strength.

"Beth ... honey, your choking me," he gasped. The words came out sounding like *chokig be* and sounded so funny they both fell into a fit of laughter.

"I believe you, Carl. I believe that you will do everything in your power. I have to believe it. Oh, my love, my love. Make love to me."

"What ... here; now?" They rolled off the couch onto the floor and let the passion flood through and over them.

At six-thirty the alarm clock went off. Carl reached over to Beth's night stand and turned it off. The smell of bacon and freshly brewed coffee wafted into the room. His stomach growled in anticipation of breakfast, so he climbed out of bed and walked barefoot to the kitchen. Beth, still wearing Carl's pajama top, was cooking a hearty platter of eggs, hash browns and sausages.

"Sit down, lover. You deserve a major cholesterol fix after last night. I'm still all tingly."

With a coquettish smile, she wiggled her hips at him.

"Beth Thomlinson, you're outrageous!" Carl laughed.

"Here you go, hon. Eggs, hash browns, sausages, and toast with my apricot preserves, coffee and orange juice." She served them both generous helpings of everything.

They ate silently, communicating volumes with telling looks and smiles. When they finished, Beth cleared the table while Carl filled his cup with more coffee and carried the steaming mug to the sofa.

Beth joined him and snuggled close. She brushed the hair from his eyes and smiled into them. "What time do you have to leave?" She asked in a somber tone.

"I need to be at the Ranch in an hour," he said.

"Do me a favor, then?"

"Yes, of course, Bethy. Anything."

"Let me go first. I'll leave for the Wagonwheel. I want to remember you just as you are; sitting on the sofa. I want that memory to tide me over until you come back to me. Will you do that for me?" She pled with a suggestion of desperation in her voice.

"Yes ... of course." His heart ached from the pain he was bringing to her.

They kissed in one final warm, lingering embrace before she left the house and drove down the driveway and out of sight. Carl watched through the living room window until her car disappeared from view. He drew the blinds before he walked out to his truck and headed for the Double-B. He hoped ... prayed, that Beth would be in his arms again in a few days.=

CHAPTER VII

The yellow-orange edge of the morning sun peeked over the low mountains as Carl climbed out of the cab of his truck, clutching a bouquet of fresh flowers he cut from Beth's flower bed. He walked across the landscaped lawn of Cascade Memorial Park, careful to walk between the grave markers. Annie's grave was located beneath a hundred fifty year old cottonwood tree on top of a knoll at the rear of the cemetery. He removed his hat and knelt by her headstone. He replaced the limp and wilted flowers from two weeks ago with fresh chrysanthemums; her favorite. Carl ran his finger tips over the engraved words on the cold granite:

Annabeth 'Annie' Petersen Bridger
December 23rd, 1926 – June 17th, 1982
Beloved daughter, wife and mother
Until we meet again

"Hi, sweetheart. A lot has happened in the last couple of weeks and I need to ask for your blessing. First, I'm leaving this morning to go and get Cody. He's in trouble and there's only Gifford and me to save him. You remember the old B-25 I've been trying to restore? Well, she's done. Her name is *Annie* because I want you to be with me ... at least in spirit. Heck, you likely know how this is all going to turn out anyway, given where you are and all. The second thing I need to say is this: I never thought I'd feel this way for another woman, but Beth Thomlinson and I are in love."

Voicing his feelings for Beth brought forth a well of emotion and he choked back a sob. "She kind of grabbed hold of my heart. I never expected it to happen. Please understand, my love; no one will ever replace you in my heart. Anyway, Beth and I have been friends for a long time and neither one of us had a clue this was going to happen. She reminds me of you in a lot of ways, and maybe that has something to do with it. Like you, Beth is without guile toward anyone ... always thinks the best of people. She's quick to smile and offers a helping hand to anyone who needs it ... just like you, Annie ... just like you." Carl wiped his sleeve across his eyes. "Well, I'll go, now. I'll be back in a few days. So long, sweetheart." He put his fingers to his lips and touched the headstone.

Ten minutes later, at eight-thirty in the morning, he pulled up in front of the main house, clomped up the wooden steps and opened the front door. He expected to walk into an empty living room, thinking he would need to rouse the men out of bed, but was pleasantly surprised to see them all sitting and talking over coffee and cinnamon sticky-buns courtesy of Lauren Dupree, who apparently was as comfortable in the kitchen as she was in the lab.

"What's all this, guys? Lauren, I thought all the InterDyn folks would be gone by now." Carl was surprised, but pleased.

"Oh, they're gone. The trucks pulled out at five-thirty this morning. My ride is waiting to take me to the airport in about twenty minutes, but I wanted to wish all of you a successful and safe trip." Her voice became serious and quiet as her eyes brimmed with tears, revealing tenderness beneath her otherwise austere personality.

"I pray you will get your grandson back alive and well, Carl. Now, sit down to some warm sticky-buns and some coffee."

Lauren sat down between Doc and Harry. "I've gotten rather attached to all of you." She patted both of the old B-25 gunners on the knees. With a tear running down her cheek she added, "...and you must promise me you'll come back."

They ate and chatted for the next twenty minutes. Carl glanced at his watch and stood. "Boys, it's time. Let's head out to the *Annie*."

The tent had been removed along with all of the InterDyn equipment. The barn doors were closed. To look at the building, one would not have so much as a clue of the goings-on of the last week.

Carl stopped in his tracks as he noticed the logo *Annie's Raiders* emblazoned in red lettering encircling the image of a reclining lady over the olive green skin beneath the cockpit. The words were outlined in gold paint and shone brightly in the morning Montana sunlight. He smiled. "Thanks, guys. Annie would be as proud of you as I am. Let's climb aboard."

Everyone took their station inside the bomber. Doc Henreid and Gifford sat on their couches with their feet in the narrow walkway. Harry Osborne snuggled into his bucket seat in the tail-gunner position. Their flight gear was stowed and Carl closed the bomb-bay doors. The missile racks that made climbing into the '25 a tight squeeze now held two AIM radar guided shoot-and-forget air-to-air missiles.

Annie's Raiders lifted into the sky as the landing gear rose into their respective bays. At five-hundred feet above the ground, Carl banked her to the left and leveled the wings on a course of zero-eight-seven degrees for their first leg of the trip. He held the aircraft at a steady one-thousand feet per minute climb at two-hundred miles per hour.

"Settle in, boys. Aurora, Illinois is just over a thousand miles from here. It's nine-fifteen our time, so we'll get there at about three-thirty this afternoon Illinois time," Carl announced over the intercom.

"Hey, Skipper. Will the flight attendants be serving lunch today, or just the usual pretzels and chips and stuff?" Harry quipped from the rear gunner position.

"Very funny, Harry. I assume you all brought water and food. We'll stock up again in Aurora. Carl out."

He turned to Buck. "*Annie* handles like a two-year-old quarter horse in a barrel racing competition. The bigger engines and increased wing area make her as responsive as a fighter. She's a little heavy in the nose, but nothing we can't trim out. Oh, by the way, we should discuss sleeping arrangements."

"What? You mean we're not going to share the bed?" Buck regaled himself with laughter and Carl couldn't stifle his own outburst of mirth.

"Gosh, Buck, do you always preface everything with a joke? You're killing me here." The two looked at each other and the laughter started anew.

"Okay, enough already." Carl regained his composure. "Neither one of us needs to fly fatigued, so I propose we alternate three hours at the controls with three hours of sleep. What do you think?"

"Sounds right. I slept well last night, and if I don't miss my guess, you and Beth didn't get a whole lot of rest," Buck winked at Carl who couldn't withhold a nervous laugh.

"Dammit, man, there you go again. But, you're right. Wake me when we're about seventy miles out from Aurora. The aircraft is yours, Buck." Carl took his hands off the control yoke, pulled his cap over his eyes, and leaned back.

"I've got the aircraft, Captain," Buck responded.

108

Harry had already made himself comfortable. He'd packed a soft cervical pillow for neck support and a floral printed sleep mask he found among his wife's Good Will donations. Presently, he drifted into a sound sleep. This was a knack he had even back in the day when they were approaching a bombing objective. On one such occasion, Carl had to wake him when the flack started, as if bursting ack-ack rounds weren't enough to do the job.

Giff and Doc sat across from each other and traded stories. "What was it like growing up with your dad, Giff?" Doc asked.

"In a word, crazy. Mom and Dad married after the war in '46. Dad got assigned to the occupation forces in Japan and he and Mom lived in Tokyo until '47 when I was born. The CIA recruited him in 1948 and we moved to Virginia, then to D.C. for four years. In 1952 the Agency assigned Pop to the embassy in Moscow, but Mom decided to keep us in the States. She and Dad bought a cottage on the coast up in Massachusetts. By then Mom was pregnant with my sister. Her name was Martine."

"Was? You said 'was'," Doc said.

"Yes, she died a month after she was born ... 'Crib Death'. It nearly killed my mother. Dad couldn't get back home, and I was only five. But Mom was a strong woman. She started writing; a hobby at first, until the local newspaper printed one of her essays. Before long her editor assigned her a weekly human-interest column for the paper. She threw herself into the work. I think it helped her get through the heartache."

"Wow! You have to respect the woman after whom Carl's bomber is named. It sounds like the real Annie was a tough and smart woman. I would like to have known your mother."

"Indeed. She and Dad were ... are ... both brilliant. Anyway, we lived in Massachusetts where I went to school. I graduated High

School early from Milton Academy and entered undergraduate studies at M.I.T. on a full-ride scholarship. I was only fifteen and I felt overwhelmed at first, but soon fell in love with the challenges."

"M.I.T., eh? Pretty impressive." Doc wanted to learn more about the man who built InterDyn and engineered the kind of technology he'd seen back at the ranch.

"Well, as things turned out, I had an affinity for math and ended up with PhD's in Aeronautical and Mechanical engineering. After that I went on to Harvard and got an MBA. I met a girl while I was there; a third-year law student. Somehow we found the time to date and fall in love. I proposed to Alisa Finch in the Harvard yard and we got married on Christmas Eve of 1970. Our son Cody was born in November of '71 and a year later we had Rachel.

"After I finished my MBA I hired on at Lockheed-Martin where I got to work with Clarence Kelly's team on the SR-71 project. From there it seemed like the next natural step was to start my own company, so I left Lockheed in 1980 and started InterDyn in an old warehouse in Orem, Utah. Alisa is InterDyn's attorney, so we get to work together quite a bit."

Doc released a quiet whistle. "Hoo-wee! You single-handedly created one of the premier aerospace design and engineering firms in the world ... impressive!"

"Thanks, Doc. I guess we learned to build a better mouse trap. But, what about you? How did you get from being a B-25 mechanic and gunner to a surgeon?" Gifford was glad to change the subject. He wasn't given to talking about his achievements and preferred learning about the people in his life.

"I'm afraid my story is a much shorter and less interesting one. The Army trained me as a medical corpsman for the Air Corps at first, at Clark Field in the Philippines. I loved to watch the '25s take off and I enjoyed the crew chatter in the day room following a mission. I found myself wanting to be a part of that, so, I decided to study for the flight mechanic's exam and apply for crew status. Your dad lost his mechanic in a scuffle with a Jap fighter and I had just qualified, so he took me on. The rest is pretty much history; medical school after the war and doing surgery in the VA hospital network until I retired in '85. When your dad called me, I couldn't say no. I dreamed of the chance to fly with him again. Now, here we are," Doc grinned. "I wouldn't miss this for the world."

"Did you ever get married; have kids?" Gifford asked.

"Yep, Elli passed two years ago. We had four boys and two girls. They're all scattered from heck to breakfast. They come to visit every year at Christmas. My youngest daughter, Jessica, still lives close by and takes good care of her 'Papa'. She thinks I'm out in Montana visiting your dad. She'd have a conniption fit if she knew what we were up to." He laughed. Doc reached into a zippered pocket of his war surplus flight suit and pulled out a deck of cards. "You up for a little two-handed five-card stud, Giff?"

"Sure, Doc. What's the ante?"

"Tell you what. I have three rolls of nickels; picked them up at the bank just for this occasion. I'll stake you one roll, how's that?" Doc produced the wrapped coins and the two men got down to business.

Buck reached over and shook Carl's shoulder. "Wake up, Skipper, were fifty miles out."

"Huh? ... Oh, yeah, okay." Carl sat up, yawned, and looked at the GPS. They were right on course. "Let's start our descent. I've got the controls."

"The aircraft is yours." Buck let go of the yoke.

Carl throttled back a little and *Annie's Raiders* started down. Every thousand feet of elevation they lost, he adjusted the mixture and monitored the engine instruments. At thirty miles out,

Carl tuned his radio to 120.6 MHz. and keyed his mic.

> *Kilo-Alpha-Romeo-Romeo, Army four-zero-two-two-three-six is experimental type Bravo two-five. We are two five miles east at one-zero-thousand feet inbound to land full stop.*

Annie's Raiders received clearance for her descent and approach and dropped beneath the scattered cloud cover.

Ten minutes later they entered the traffic pattern for Aurora, Illinois Regional Airport and entered their downwind leg at 1,700 feet elevation. Carl began a gradual descent to the assigned runway. Buck lowered the landing gear and the bomber turned onto base leg, then on to final approach.

> *Army two-two-three-six, you are cleared to land runway niner,* the tower advised.

Annie's Raiders touched down on the center line and Carl exited on the nearest taxi way. He switched his radio to the ground frequency of 121.7 MHz. and requested directions to the fueling station. He had checked ahead to make certain all of their scheduled stops had the right AVGAS octane for the '25.

Carl pulled up to the yellow stop line and shut down the engines. He and Buck stepped down onto the tarmac followed by Gifford, Doc and Harry.

"Doc, will you supervise the refueling, please? We'll get together inside the executive terminal. We should probably grab a bite and take a potty break. We need to be back here in forty minutes. Doc, can I order something for you?"

"Sure, Skipper. A steak sandwich, onion rings and a Heineken for me will be dandy." Doc walked around to the front of the plane as the fuel truck pulled up.

While the crew of *Annie's Raiders* ate together in the cafeteria, Carl's Agency cell phone rang.

"Bridger here. What's up, Mac?"

"The DCI has gotten wind of the mission and is pushing to find out the details. Apparently Will Helms mentioned the InterDyn movement as well as my name to the boss and now he's called me in. Carl, I need to read him in on what we're doing."

Carl was concerned for Mac. A meeting with the Director of Central Intelligence could mean almost anything. "How do you think he'll react when you tell him?"

"Most likely, he'll go nuclear on me. But, the DCI is a Marine vet. He understands the 'No man left behind' rule. I'm thinking he doesn't like leaving a U.S. Navy airman in enemy hands any better than we do. I'll get back to you. Good luck pal." Mac hung up.

Forty minutes later, the crew returned to the plane only to be greeted by a dozen rubberneckers curious about the World War II bomber and its unique facelift. One suited individual introduced himself as an FAA Flight Service Station administrator.

"I noticed you've done some unusual modifications on your '25 Mister ..." The man's voice trailed off.

"Bridger. Carl Bridger. We have, indeed, sir. It's all for show, though. Those barrels you're looking at couldn't shoot as much as a spit wad. They're dummies, made of fiber glass tubing and plastic. Pretty realistic, eh? We're taking her to Aviano, Italy for the big World War II Warbird expo; should be quite a show." Carl lied jubilantly.

"Do you mind if I take a peek inside, Mister Bridger," the man pressed.

Buck approached and saw what was happening. The man was using his position with the FAA to snoop around. "That would be quite fine, mister, uh, I didn't get your name."

"Emerson Underwood, sir. I'm the FAA Flight Service Station authority at this airport." The man actually puffed out his chest. Buck strained to maintain his composure. Laughing in the man's face would not be the prudent thing to do given his status with the FAA. The bureaucrat was an observant man, and his expression changed from pomposity to awe when he added two-plus-two. First, he noted the jacket being worn by the man standing before him. The NASA logo with the Apollo 14 mission patch over the left breast pocket piqued his interest. Next, his eyes went to the U.S.A.F. command pilot wings and then the Air Force blue name tag with "B Rogers" in white letters. "Are you ...," he gulped, caught his breath, and squeaked out "... Buck Rogers, the astronaut?"

"I am, indeed, and while my friend here would be happy to show you around, I'm afraid we are on a tight schedule. Perhaps some other time." The general shook Underwood's hand firmly and flashed his brightest smile at the man.

"Of course, General Rogers. How foolish of me to presume ..."

"Not at all, Mister Underwood, not at all." Buck shook the fellow's hand again and bade him a good day. "Let's get the hell out of here before that popinjay takes it upon himself to stop us from leaving," he whispered to Carl.

"Roger that, Buck," Carl chuckled as he scampered up the ladder.

Seven minutes later, *Annie's Raiders* lifted off, bound for the next stop; Halifax, Nova Scotia. The range of the Mitchell B-25 was 1,350 miles. Halifax was just over 1,100 miles. They would be pushing the fuel reserves, but the risk was acceptable. The next and longest leg, however, would prove to be more problematic at 1,239 miles to Nuuk, Greenland.

Carl took the controls and Buck pulled his cap down over his eyes, leaned back and within a few minutes was snoring peacefully. Carl banked the bomber to the northeast and climbed to fifteen-thousand feet to clear the cloud layer. He punched in the heading, speed and altitude into the Century 68S73 auto pilot and took his hands off the yoke. *Annie's Raiders* held to the red line of the GPS heading and adjusted automatically to the magnetic heading as she flew along the preprogrammed flight path. The capability of the autopilot to make course adjustments to match the GPS heading was cutting-edge technology and, thanks to InterDyn, made this marathon trip much more manageable. Lindbergh had to fly by the seat of his pants using celestial navigation and dead reckoning. *This is a piece of cake compared to Lucky Lindy,* Carl thought.

"Guys, we have about an hour longer on this leg. I figure five and a half hours. Sorry there's no movie, but we loaded a bunch of in-flight meals: sandwiches, chips, cookies, sodas and beer. Go easy on the beer, but enjoy. The engines are humming a sweet tune, and all the gauges are in the green. The weather is below us, so relax and read a book or something. Bridger out." Carl released the talk button on his mic and settled back. The sun was above and behind him now, so there was no glare to contend with. He decided to write a note to Beth. He would send it off in an envelope when they landed.

Dearest Beth. How I miss you. We're at fifteen-thousand feet flying roughly over Niagara Falls. Buck is sleeping and the rest of the boys are playing cards back in the bomb-bay. I'm looking at the most beautiful sky right now. All of the clouds are below us and the air is smooth as silk. One day, you and I will do this together; just the two of us. I think you'd love it. I said good-bye to Annie before we left. I told her about us and asked for her blessing. I know she would be happy, Bethy. You two were good friends. More later — Carl.

He put the notepad back in his pocket, and pulled a novel out of his flight bag from behind his seat. Tom Clancy's *Patriot Games* was a geo-political thriller, and he soon found himself embedded in the intricately woven plot line. Every couple of minutes he checked the instruments and each time he was reassured to find them all solidly in the green. He read twenty more pages when he felt a slight shudder vibrate through his seat. The mild tremor stopped as fast as it started. He glanced over at Buck who still snored quietly. The General's turn at the controls was approaching, so he nudged his shoulder. "Hey, Buck. Wake up."

"My turn already, Skipper?" Buck released an opened-mouth yawn. "Okay, I'm awake. It's your turn to ..." He paused as he scanned the instrument readings. "Hey, Carl, the starboard cylinder head temperature's close to the caution line."

"Yeah, it started climbing a few minutes ago. The gauge is still in the green, but the needle's higher than the port engine. I leaned the mixture a bit and pulled back on the prop RPM a tad. I also opened the cowl flaps to full. That should cool the temp down. Just keep an eye out for any changes." Carl lay back and closed his eyes. He had barely slipped into that comfortable twilight between wakefulness and sleep when Buck nudged him.

"Skipper, we've got a problem with the number two engine. I think we need to have Doc take a peek. The cylinder head temp is in the caution range and the oil pressure has dropped a little." Buck's voice was even and calm, but he was concerned, notwithstanding.

"Roger that. I've got the controls, Buck"

He called Doc forward and the surgeon poked his head in between the two pilots. "Hmm ... interesting," he said as though he were diagnosing a patient. He squeezed in further until he had a better view of the starboard engine through the windscreen. "Aha. The exhaust flames coming from the manifolds are all burning a nice clean blue ... except one. Oil is being dumped into the cylinder and it's igniting, causing the exhaust flame to burn yellow."

Carl needed answers. His mind raced with calculations ...

fuel, airspeed, distance to the airport, altitude. "Okay, so what do we do?"

"How far until we reach Halifax?" Doc asked.

"A little over a hundred miles. About thirty minutes."

"We need to take her down to seven-thousand and slow our speed. Reduce the torque by decreasing the prop RPM as much as you can. Do the same for the port engine. You may need to lay-in some flaps. Take the strain off that cylinder, Skipper. If we lose it entirely, we may lose the whole engine." Doc thought a moment. "We may only be dealing with a fouled plug, but most likely it's a cracked piston ring. I'll check the equipment bay for the right parts."

"Thanks, Doc." Carl already had the throttles pulled back and *Annie's Raiders* started to buck in the turbulence caused by the clouds. At seven-thousand feet, Carl reduced the prop RPM to the lowest point in the green. He matched the port engine and *Annie* slowed to 150 miles per hour. Within a minute, the manifold temperature stopped rising and held steady. The oil pressure was still low but was holding in the green as well.

"Uh oh, I think the bottom just dropped out of our good fortune, Boss. We're losing oil pressure." The starboard engine began to cough, and then backfired.

"Feathering the starboard engine!" Carl started flipping switches. "Fuel off. Prop feathered. Ignition off. Increasing power to the port engine. Give me left rudder trim, Buck. Watch the air speed. We don't want to stall. Call it in." Buck pressed the transmit button:

> Mayday, mayday, mayday. Army four-zero-two-two-three-six declaring an engine out emergency. Number one engine is still operational. Request immediate priority vectors for straight in approach. Do you copy Halifax?
>
> We copy you, Army two-two-three-six. Make

straight in approach runway three-four.

Cleared straight in runway three-four. Army two-two-three-six.

Carl fought the controls to keep *Annie's Raiders* level. She wanted to slip hard to the right because of the increased drag on the starboard side. The dead engine pulled at the bomber with such force that he had to strain to stay on the glide path.

"Give me one quarter flaps and drop the gear."

The runway was in sight, but the center line was a writhing snake.

The B-25 slipped into a right quartering headwind that helped push her back to the left. The right wing ballooned upward, and the stall warning horn blared.

Carl jammed the left engine throttle all the way forward and the left landing gear touched down, then lifted off again.

He crammed the left rudder down and the plane slipped left. Just at the moment he was centered on the runway and his wings were level, he pulled the left throttle all the way back and kicked in some right rudder.

The ship settled onto the runway, and Carl slowed her to taxiing speed. He exited the runway and requested permission for a tow to the big main hangar.

He didn't realized how hard he had been gripping the controls. Every finger and every knuckle throbbed. He looked over at Buck, who looked back at him, smiled and shook his head in disbelief while he released a huge sigh of relief.

Carl taxied clear of the runway and brought the '25 to a full stop. A yellow tow truck hooked on to the nose-gear strut and towed *Annie's Raiders* to the first of two large maintenance hangars. The crew climbed down to the floor of the hangar, and Carl took Doc aside.

"Doc, we're under the gun for time. I need your diagnosis

ASAP. Can you save the engine?" Carl asked.

"Skipper, I'll need at least an hour. You see the oil spray here? I'll need to remove the cowling and replace the leaking line before I can get to the cylinder. Check with me in an hour and I'll let you know where we stand." Doc went to work.

"Okay. Make it fast, though. I don't want to lose more time than we have to." Carl walked out of the hangar toward the crew lounge.

He returned to the hangar forty-five minutes later to find Doc elbow deep in the engine.

"I found the problem, Skipper." He turned to a pair of mechanics who'd offered their assistance. "Put the cowlings back on, boys, and button her up." He climbed down the ladder and walked over to Carl, wiping oil from his hands on a dirty shop rag.

"A loose tension-coil on one of the cylinders, caused the ignition to fall out of timing. I replaced the coil and the spark plugs. It should run fine. I also tightened down the leaky oil line that had vibrated loose. Do you want to do a run-up on her, Skipper?" Doc asked.

"No. Let's get everyone aboard. The weather is closing in. We need to go now. Doc, get the rest of the guys. I'll have the plane towed out of the hangar." Carl called for the tow truck while Doc trotted toward the crew lounge.

Annie's Raiders stood in a slight drizzling rain. Visibility had dropped to two miles with a twelve-hundred foot ceiling. With the crew aboard and both engines idling smoothly, Carl called the tower:

> *Charlie Yankee Alfa Whiskey, Army four-zero-two-two-three-six requesting taxi for immediate departure to the east.*
>
> *Army two-two-three-six be advised a weather advisory is in effect to flight level one-eight-zero. PIREP reports lightening and wind-shear five-zero miles east of the airport.*

Carl acknowledged the instructions from Ground Control to taxi to the departure runway and *Annie's Raiders* began to roll down the rain-spattered tarmac toward the hold-short line. His thoughts of the Pilot Report of the weather advisory produced a worry line on his forehead. *I hope we can make it through the storm.* The thought was accompanied by a line of cold sweat running down his spine.

Carl received clearance for immediate departure. The sky was dark and overcast. The rain fell steadily now, and Carl turned on the windscreen wipers. The falling rain glistened like a million silver darts plummeting down through the glare of the landing lights. He added power and the warbird began her takeoff roll. Her engines roared, and her tires threw up spray as she picked up speed. Carl lifted *Annie's Raiders* off the runway and the bomber slipped into the night sky with only the flashing of her recognition lights to tell anyone that she was there.

Twenty minutes into the flight, the bomber approached a buildup of cumulous clouds towering above them. It was night and they would not have seen it at all if it were not for the lightning flashes in and around the looming mass of storm clouds.

"Looks like we'll have to swing to the southeast where the cloud layer is quite a bit lower." Buck turned off the automatic pilot for the time being and banked right to one-one-zero degrees. "I hope we can get around this stuff soon. We don't have much fuel reserve."

"True that, partner. Let's hope we can catch a tail wind. The last METAR report out of Nuuk indicated twenty-six mile per hour winds at a one-seven-thousand from two-niner degrees. Let's climb, Buck." Carl pressed the intercom button. "Guys, things are going to get a little bumpy, so hang onto your drinks and buckle up. We're climbing to one-seven thousand to try and catch a push from Mother Nature so put on your O2 masks for the time being. Carl out."

Eight Hours Earlier

The Director of Central Intelligence sat behind his desk waiting for Mackenzie Aldrin. He had been informed of the recent stir of activity about InterDyn and a test of some sort in Montana involving InterDyn and former CIA Budapest Station Chief Carl Bridger. He had read the transcripts of the intercepted communications which analyst Ted Van Patton had talked to his boss Will Helms about, and had discussed the matter personally with Helms who was unable to shed any light on the subject. Helms suggested he talk to Mac Aldrin, who, according to the DODA, had gone to Montana himself to look into the matter. Helms hoped Aldrin would know how the pieces of the puzzle fit together.

"Director, Mister Aldrin is here to see you." The aide held the door open for Mac, who entered the DCI's office.

"Mac, come in, please. Ellen, will you bring in some coffee for us, please?" DCI Byron Kelley waited for the aide to close the door and motioned for Mac to sit on the sofa in front of a mahogany colonial-style coffee table. Director Kelley pulled up a chair and sat across from the Director of Covert Operations, leaned forward and laced his fingers together. He looked at Mac squarely and held his gaze until Mac began to fidget in his chair.

"Mac, something is going on in Montana that's come to my attention. I just finished talking with Will Helms. He tells me you've been to Montana. I need to know what is going on that involves InterDyn, and the movement of a truck load of their technology to a ranch belonging to a former Agency Station Chief."

Mac had a decision to make. He knew he couldn't sugar coat the mission. Kelley would read any deception at all coming from him. *It's time to read the Director in on the plan and hope he doesn't order Carl's plane shot down.*

"Director, three weeks ago, a Navy F-14 was shot down over Sarajevo. There is a no-fly zone over that entire area because of the Bosnian-Serbian conflict. It is the official position in D.C. that the Navy fliers violated that air space."

"Yes, yes, I know all of that. Get to the point, Mac." The Director leaned forward, hands on his lap with fingers tightly interlaced.

Mac told his boss everything; about how he had been in on the planning of the rescue operation from the beginning, about Sheldon Macvie's activities and of the Great Falls agent's efforts to investigate the operation on Macvie's orders. He told the DCI that he'd already notified his operative inside the Serbian camp of the rescue operation.

"So this pilot, Lieutenant Bridger, is the son of Gifford Bridger, and the grandson of Carl Bridger. You're telling me that InterDyn is actively using its resources to modify a B-25 and that the President and CEO of that company is conspiring with a former CIA Station Chief to launch a rescue mission for a downed U.S. Navy flier in direct violation of orders from the Departments of State and Defense?"

The DCI stood and began to pace the floor like a caged tiger. "What kind of insanity ever gave you the idea this can turn out any other way than the international crisis of the century?" He slammed his fist down on a table, nearly knocking a large vase of flowers to the floor. "Stop it, Mac! End it now before the White House hears about it. You know that the Agency will be blamed when the President goes to the press, right?"

"The President won't hear about it until the operation is over, Director. He won't want to hear about it. If he does get wind of it, he'll just deny he knew anything about it. Like you said, he'll blame it on you and the Agency." Mac countered.

"You need to end this before it's too late. When is this asinine operation of yours supposed to get underway?" He sat behind his desk.

Mac checked his watch. "They took off about two hours ago, sir."

"Damn. We've got to stop them, Mac. Get the FAA on the line. Tell them you have information about a terrorist plot, or something. Tell the FBI to intercept the plane at their first stop." The DCI stood and paced again.

Mac stood and faced his boss. "Sir, we can't do that. There's someone on that plane whom you don't want to label a terrorist."

"I don't care, just ..." He paused and reconsidered. "Okay, who?"

"Buck Rogers, sir."

"Buck ... holy crap, this just gets better by the minute." Kelley returned to his desk, sat down, and ran both hands through his hair. "Okay, Mac, tell me the rest." He sat and clenched his fists in front of him.

Mac pulled a chair in front of the Director's desk. "Sir, there is one thing we can do that should take the Agency and the White House off the hook. Hell, we might even end up looking pretty damned patriotic after the smoke clears. First, with your permission, I'll reign in Shelley Macvie and Wesley Steed. I'll put them on such a short leash they won't be able to wipe their butts without asking me for the Charmin."

"Then what?" Kelley asked.

Mac began to lay out his plan to the CIA Director, playing to Kelley's sense of honor as a former Marine. Kelley listened and, as Mac continued, his boss actually started to buy in to it.

"Alright, Mac. I'll ride this out with you. You're authorized to proceed. I admit I never liked the idea of leaving those two young men in enemy hands. The State Department these days doesn't have the balls to stand up to our country's enemies. This had better work, though, or we'll both find ourselves in front of a Senate hearing."

The DCI walked Mac to the door.

"We're pushing the envelope, Buck. We never caught a break with the tailwind we needed. I figure we have about an hour of fuel left and we're still over two-hundred miles from Nuuk. We can make the coast of Greenland, but I don't know if we can reach the airport. I'll run the numbers again. Maybe I missed something."

He removed the manual flight computer from his flight suit and began adjusting the dial for fuel capacity, weight and moment, wind, altitude and airspeed in hopes that the new calculations might buy them a little more fuel reserve. *Annie's Raiders* had skirted the worst of the weather and was back on their flight path for Bravo-Golf-Golf-Hotel, the designation for the airport at Nuuk, Greenland. However, vectoring around the storm added an extra hundred miles onto the longest leg of the trip.

"Okay, Buck, take us down to one-three-thousand and trim for two-hundred-thirty miles per hour. We'll be running on fumes, but we might make it. I figure with the streamlining that InterDyn did by removing the top gun turret and the new skin on the nose, we at least have a chance." Buck reduced power and *Annie's Raiders* started down.

"Okay, boys, you can take off the O2 masks. We're starting our descent into Nuuk," Carl announced.

As they got closer to Nuuk, the plane entered some moderate turbulence. "Headwind! Dammit! The stars are gone, too. We need to find out the weather. I'll radio AFIS at Nuuk for an update."

Carl dialed in the Nuuk Airport Flight Information Service on 119.2 MHz. He decided to descend to a lower altitude to get beneath the fog. "I've got the controls, Buck."

Buck released the controls to Carl.

"What about it, Buck? We're at five-thousand and still flying in soup. We're eighty miles out. I'm taking us down to two-thousand. The airport is two-hundred-eighty feet above sea level." Carl knew he was pressing his luck, but when the visibility didn't improve, he decided to descend to one-thousand feet.

"Forty miles out, we've got to go lower. Turn on the landing lights, Buck. We're dropping down to the deck. Call Nuuk and get us clearance. This is going to be close."

Bravo-Golf-Golf-Hotel, Army four zero two-two-three-six is at altitude five-hundred feet, four-zero miles west. We are low on fuel. Request straight in approach VFR to runway five.

Negative, Army two-two-three-six. Nuuk is closed to VFR traffic. Divert to Tasilak.

No can do, Nuuk. Repeating: we are low on fuel. We need to land at Nuuk.

Roger, Army two-two-three-six. Remain on this frequency. Tune transponder to one-one-three point five and squawk ident.

One-one-three point five, roger, Carl confirmed.

We have you, Army two-two-three-six. Turn left to zero-eight-five degrees and climb to one-thousand-two-hundred feet.

Army two-two-three-six you are eight miles out. Turn to zero-five degrees and maintain one-thousand-two-hundred until established. Report runway in sight. Turning to zero-five degrees, Carl repeated.

Carl turned to the correct heading and kept the airplane symbol on the red GPS line. A minute later, he saw the faint glimmer of the ILS lights through the fog.

Nuuk traffic I have the runway in sight.

125

Roger, Army two-two-three-six. You are cleared to land, runway five.

The tower crew at Nuuk peered through their binoculars looking for some sign of the endangered B-25. The fog and light drizzling rain obscured the end of runway five. Beyond, nothing was visible but the runway lights showing as fuzzy dots through the thick fog.

"There she is!" One of the men shouted, pointing at a faint hazy light moving in the distance.

Carl throttled back to a hundred-thirty miles per hour and lowered his flaps and gear. He let the airspeed drop to one-hundred twenty miles per hour when the left engine sputtered and abruptly quit as the fuel tanks ran dry. The '25s nose yawed sharply to the left. "Shit!" He said to no one in particular.

"I see her landing lights," another man in the tower said in a thick Danish accent. "She's yawing badly; one wing low. I think she lost an engine."

"C'mon, *Annie*, get us down, baby!" He crammed the right engine throttle to the wall and kicked the right rudder pedal to straighten out the nose. The starboard engine sputtered as the plane settled into a flare. Carl pulled the throttle back to idle and *Annie's Raiders* touched down. Her left main wheel missed rolling off the runway by less than two feet.

"A tad left of the center line, weren't you, Boss?" Buck released a sigh of relief.

"Don't be a smart ass." Carl was trembling. He caught Buck's sympathetic expression and smiled back at him. "I'm fine, partner. I may need you to pry my fingers off the yoke, though."

"Hey, Skipper, we'll need to supersize the waste bags for the chemical toilet if you keep scaring the crap out of us back here," Harry announced nervously.

"I'll second that. Glad I packed an extra pair of shorts."

Doc chimed in.

"The worst part is over, boys. That was the longest leg of the mission. The rest should be a piece of cake. We'll tank up and leave in forty, so stretch your legs. We're half way to Aviano."

Carl taxied to the AVGAS pumps where a ground attendant waved them forward to the stop line, and crossed his illuminated batons in front of his face in the "stop" signal. Carl braked to a stop and pulled back the mixture to the starboard engine. The propeller stopped turning, and Carl set the parking brake.

The crew of *Annie's Raiders* gathered together in the crew lounge at Nuuk, Greenland and ate Danish pastries, washing the sweet confection down with cups of rich, dark coffee.

"How's everyone holding up, Doc?" Carl wanted the physician's professional opinion.

"We're good to go, Skipper. A few aches and pains from being unable to move around in such close quarters, but I think we're all doing as well as can be expected."

Carl looked at Harry. "How about you, Harry? Doing okay back in the tail?"

"Snug as a bug. It's colder than a witch's bazooms, but I've got three layers of clothes on. Actually, I have best seat in the house. The new molded seat is much more comfortable than the original. The InterDyn crew really planned well for the extended flight." Harry was always the jubilant one, a quality which hadn't faded a bit since the days when his sense of humor lifted their spirits through some tense situations while flying missions over Formosa and the Pacific theatre of World War II.

"Alright, then. We've come thirty-four-hundred miles with twenty-six-hundred more to go. It's 2:30 a.m. local time. I figure we'll reach Reykjavik by 7:00 a.m. in four-and-a-half hours. From there it's five hours to Dublin, Ireland. Dublin to Aviano is about five more, so figure landing at Aviano at around 7 p.m. tonight after allowing for time zone changes. The Air Show kicks off the next day on Saturday. We'll stay for the show and leave at first light Sunday morning. Any questions?" Carl's gaze met the eyes of each crew member in turn.

Everyone nodded their understanding. "We're with you all the way, Skipper," Doc affirmed.

"Good. Let's load up and get out of here." Carl drained his coffee cup and pushed his chair back.

CHAPTER VIII

Pier 5, Port of Portland, Maine

The day before *Annie's Raiders* left the Double-B Ranch, two shipping containers were lifted off a New Haven Railroad flatbed car and craned over to the loading dock at Pier 5. The blue containers, along with a dozen others bound for various ports in Europe waited to be loaded aboard the *Hvezda Severu*. The Port Authority signed the manifest and released the cargo to the ship's captain who handed an envelope to the man. He glanced inside the thick envelope, smiled at the captain, and stuffed the packet into the inside pocket of his pea coat. He felt no need to count the money. Any attempt to short change him would have the Coast Guard boarding the ship before she could leave U.S. waters. The captain boarded the vessel, and the cranes began lifting the containers on to the deck. Four hours later, the *Hvezda Severu* eased out of her berth and into the channel.

InterDyn Corporation, Utah

InterDyn's Chief of Security Gloria Collett sat in front of a computer screen in the basement of InterDyn. The room was cool, and she wore a light sweater to warm her. The racks of computer servers and the dozen or so terminals in the room generated a lot of heat which accounted for the cooler than normal temperature needed to cool the electronics. At the moment, Gloria was looking at a flashing red dot on a grid overlaying a topographical map of the Portland, Maine metropolitan area and the Port of Portland. The dot moved, almost imperceptibly into the harbor. Gloria picked up a phone and tapped a button. Two rings later, a voice on the other end answered.

"Dupree."

"The ship is leaving the Port of Portland, Doctor. Her itinerary has her in port at Reykjavik, Iceland in two days for a one day layover." Collett continued monitoring the *Hvezda Severu* as the red dot moved further out into the harbor. .

"Thank you, Gloria. The boss will be calling in when he lands at Reykjavik. I'll let him know. I I'm crossing my fingers that the transmitters won't be detected before the ship reaches Hamburg."

"I don't think we have to worry about that, Doctor. The devices transmit a signal to an X-band satellite, which, in turn, directs the signal back to Earth and to InterDyn. The signal is virtually undetectable by anything other than the latest radio detection instruments. Of course, there's no absolute guarantee. My team will monitor the signal twenty-four-seven until she reaches port. I'll let you know if there's any trouble." Gloria waited for Doctor Dupree to ring off, then turned her attention back to the red "blip."

Somewhere over the North Atlantic

The sky had cleared since leaving Nuuk. The horizon in front of the plane was beginning to lighten and in a few minutes, the first rays of sunlight would glisten on the surface of the water seven thousand feet beneath them.

"Mornin', Carl. It's a beautiful day outside," Buck said.

Carl stretched his arms out and rotated his neck which had stiffened. "Morning, Buck. Everything look okay?"

"In the green, Skipper. You hungry?" Buck produced two shoe-box-sized white boxes. "Not *The Cordon Bleu* by any means, but we have ham and cheese with potato chips and fruit punch with a chocolate chip cookie, or a club sandwich with all of the afore mentioned accoutrements."

"I'll take the club sandwich, thanks." Carl opened the packets of mayonnaise and mustard and squeezed them onto the turkey and ham. The lettuce was limp but edible. He took a generous bite and licked a blob of mustard from his lips while he scanned the instruments. *Good, the engine instruments are in the green. The starboard engine seems to be behaving itself.*

"Why don't you take us on in to Reykjavik, Buck? I think I'll go see how the boys are doing." He finished his sandwich and unbuckled his harness. "See you in a few," he said as he worked his way aft toward the bomb-bay.

"Hey, Skipper, what brings you to our little playpen?" Doc smiled affably.

"Just stretchin' my legs, Doc. How are you boys holding up?" He noticed that Gifford was lying on his back with his arms folded over his chest and his hat pulled down over his eyes. He reached down and lifted up the brim of the blue cap with the Inter-Dyn logo on the front. "Good morning, sunshine," the senior

Bridger said to his son.

Gifford swatted at his face as if a fly had tickled him, and he opened his eyes and sat up. "Oh, hi, Pop. Where are we?"

"Less than an hour out. We caught a little tail wind so we're running almost ten minutes ahead of schedule. Have you guys heard from Harry?"

"Yup. He was up here until about twenty minutes ago. We played a few hands of poker and then he went back to his fifty-caliber cubby hole," Doc replied.

"Good. It's important to keep the circulation going. Especially for us old farts," Carl chuckled. "How 'bout a couple of hands of penny-ante poker, boys?" Carl rubbed his hands together. "I'm feeling lucky. Wait a minute, I'll be right back." Carl stooped low and worked his way back to a white cooler that was secured to a bulkhead by a pair of bungee cords. He returned with three Heineken beers. He reachedinto the breast pocket of his jacket and produced his pipe and a pouch of sweet cherry blend tobacco. "Mind if I light up, boys?" Gifford looked at Doc and the physician shook his head …

"It's your life, Skipper.".

"Thanks. Deal em', Doc."

The three drank beer and played poker until Buck came over the intercom. "We're ten miles out, Carl." With that, Carl folded his hand and worked his way back to the flight deck.

"Do I smell pipe smoke, Carl?" The General sniffed the air.

"You do indeed, General. A smoke and a beer, and all is good with the world," Carl smiled as he strapped himself in.

Annie's Raiders touched down in Reykjavik fifteen minutes ahead of schedule. The additional ground time allowed the crew to stretch their legs, grab a bite to eat and make brief phone calls.

Inside the small terminal building, Gifford excused himself and found an alcove with three telephone kiosks. He lifted a passenger courtesy phone from its hook and punched in a series of letters and numbers. He listened to a few clicks and heard a far away ring, echoing as if coming from a world away.

"Lauren Dupree. Are you in Iceland, Boss?"

"Affirmative. Do you have a status report on the package?"

"They left port about three hours ago, Gifford. The transmitters are working fine. Hey, someone here wants to talk to you. Hold on." The phone went silent for a moment.

"Gifford, honey, it's Alisa. I miss you. How are things? How's your dad?" Her voice echoed, but was perfectly understandable.

"We're all good, sweetheart. How are you holding up?"

"Oh ... a little; anxious, I guess ... proud of you. I'm worried about Cody, of course. I know you're doing everything you can; it's just ... oh never mind, just mommy worries. I love you, my husband. Don't let anything happen to you; promise?"

"We'll be fine, Lisee. Don't worry. Cody and I'll both be home in a few days, okay? I have to go now. I love you, baby." Gifford waited for the "good-bye" and hung up.

Carl used a landline in the pilot's lounge, picked up the receiver and keyed in his credit card number. He waited for the recorded voice to tell him to enter the area code and number. A phone rang on the other end.

"Hello?" a sleepy sounding voice answered. It was 4:30 a.m. in Cascade, Montana.

"Beth, hi, it's me," Carl said.

Beth sat bolt upright in her bed and snapped on the lamp. "Carl? Oh honey, I didn't think you'd call until ... after. Are you alright?"

"I'm fine. We're all okay. I needed to hear your voice is all. How are you holding up?"

"I'm having the time of my life; NOT!" Beth laughed. "I'm really okay, Carl. I love you, hon. Come home to me, okay?"

"I will. I'll call again after the job is done. I love you, Beth. I gotta go, sweethear t... bye." He hung up and rejoined his crew.

Everybody enjoyed a hot breakfast of sausages, *Aebleskivers* (Danish pancake balls served with sweet-tart lingonberry jam and dusted with powdered sugar), and coffee. When they were done, they walked out to the tarmac.

A suited man dressed in a black overcoat was waiting by the plane. A black Mercedes sedan was parked a few yards away.

"Mister Carl Bridger?" The man asked.

"That's me. What can I do for you?" Carl noted the serious looking fellow had Agency written all over him. He clearly meant to make his identity known to Carl. *He looks like a bit player out of an old spy movie.* Carl had a picture in his mind of Bogart in "Casablanca."

"I have a dispatch for you, sir." He handed the manila envelope to Carl and promptly walked back to the Mercedes.

Carl waited until everyone was aboard before opening the envelope. He read the message and keyed the intercom. "Boys, the cat is out of the bag. Langley has been read-in on the mission. The good news is the DCI is on board. It's all being kept in-house while the Director figures out how he wants to proceed. For now, we go forward as planned. Carl out."

"That's good news, partner," Buck said.

"Yup. At least we're safe from getting shot down by our own people anytime soon. Start em' up, Buck. Let's head for Ireland."Carl tested the flight controls while Buck started the ignition sequence. A minute later the big radial engines were idling smoothly. Carl taxied out of their parking slot and followed the airport ground controller's instructions for taxiing to the departure runway. They were second in line behind a Canadian Regional jet.

Army, two-two-three-six, hold short of taxiway Bravo. Follow the aircraft on taxiway Bravo approaching from your left side.

Holding short for the aircraft on Bravo, Army two-two-three-six.

Army two-two-three-six. The Canadian Regional jet requests you switch to 121.5 MHz.

Switching to 121.5, Army two-two-six.

"I wonder what the man wants," Carl said.

Canadian Regional Jet, Army four-zero-two-two-three-six is at your service. What can I do for you, Captain?

That's one heckuva sweet looking ride you have there, Captain. I don't think I've ever seen a B-25 sporting twin cannons. Are those M61A1 Vulcans?

You know your armament, Captain. The cannons are dummies, though. We're bound for an air show at Aviano. You a 'fighter jockey?

Former F-16 jockey. Been ten years now. It's a good thing those gatlings aren't real. They'd probably tear the nose right off that sweet girl .Fly safely, Captain. Canadair two-one-two, out.

"That guy would be surprised ... if he only knew." Buck laughed.

The CRJ lined up with the center line and shot down the runway. As soon as the jet reached an altitude of five hundred feet, the tower gave the '25 permission to enter the active runway. Carl added one quarter flaps, released the brakes and started his takeoff roll.

"Next stop, the Emerald Isle, boys, about three-and-a-half-hours ahead." *Annie* lifted off and Carl banked right to one-five-zero degrees heading south-southwest down the North Sea toward Dublin, Ireland. At seven-thousand feet he trimmed the plane for level flight, adjusted the mixture and propeller RPM and set the automatic pilot. They cruised through clear smooth air at two- hundred-thirty miles per hour. "Take the controls, will you Buck? I'm going to catch some shuteye."

Carl lay back as best he could and closed his eyes. The drone of the bomber's engines was softened by his ear plugs and was mesmerizing. The vibration in the seat of his pants added to the almost hypnotic calm. He thought of Beth and the last night they spent together. She came into his mind's eye as clearly as if she were sitting beside him. He glanced to his right as if to confirm that she was not really there. *Nope, just Alex.* His mind told him as he drifted deeper into a peaceful sleep.

"Hey, Skipper, you daydreamin'? We're almost at the I.P," Alexandre Chekov said. Carl was the pilot in command of Red-Two flying behind Red-Leader Major Billy Carpenter who commanded the six bombers of Red-Group.

"I've got the controls, Alex. Red-Leader should be banking inland now." The coast of Formosa was five hundred feet below them. Carl banked left behind the lead plane in his squadron, and headed inland. The lead squadron of six B-25Js stayed on course due north. He saw the six B-25s of Blue-Group continue on a northerly heading along the coast of Formosa. "What the hell are they doing? We need to get into attack formation."

Red-Group was supposed to follow a second flight of attack B-25J's, designated Blue-Group, which was expected to lead the attack in the first of two waves.

"Red-Group, Red-Group. This is Red-Leader. It looks like

Blue-Group has missed the intercept point. We need to hit the Jap troop encampment. Move into line-abreast formation, Red-Group. We're going to have to do this the hard way ... by ourselves."

Carl accelerated and drew alongside the lead plane. Soon four other '25s joined them.

"Open the bomb-bay doors. Gunners, charge your guns." Seconds later gun fire erupted from the forward .50 caliber guns and the .30-cals in the side blisters. Carl heard Harry's top turret fire off a few rounds. "Be sharp, boys." The lead plane peeled away and dropped to tree-top level. Carl was right behind him. The Six B-25s arrowed in a staggered line toward the objective which lay just beyond the bend in the river ahead. "There's our marker, boys, dead ahead," Red-leader announced from the lead plane

As if on cue, the bombers added full power and toggled the water injection to keep the engines cool during the use of military power. The airspeed rose to nearly three hundred miles per hour. The encampment was dead ahead.

"Steady ... steady," Carl coaxed. "Fire! Fire! Fire!" The twin fifties and all eight .30 cals breathed fire down on the encampment while simultaneous cargos of parafrags spewed down from the bomb-bays. Each of dozens of the 23-pound bombs dropped from the bomb-bays of the B-25s deployed tiny drag parachutes to cause them to fall to earth far behind the bomber. When the bombs struck the ground, they burst into one-inch fragments, saturating a ½ mile long zone with a carpet of high velocity metal shards that tore into structures, vehicles, and enemy soldiers. A line of explosions erupted as the bombers roared a hundred feet above the enemy stronghold. Fuel storage facilities and ammunition dumps exploded in billowing red clouds of flame and smoke.

"Red-Group, veer right!" Red-Leader yelled over Carl's headset. He didn't have to be told twice. Dead ahead Blue-Group was converging, closing at a combined speed of six hundred miles per hour. As the six B-25s of Red-Group banked sharp right, Blue-Group raked the enemy encampment from the opposite direction. The Jap stronghold was decimated.

"Blue-Group, what in hell was that?" Red-Leader demanded.

"Sorry, Red-Leader, we missed the nav point and ended up having to turn around and come down from the north."

"Well, hell, fellas. Somebody ought to write this strategy up and put it in the manual."

The twelve bombers of the 823rd bomb group turned for Clark Field on Luzon Island and headed home.

"Skipper, we have company. I count two ... no, three flights of zero's above and behind us at nine o'clock high," Harry Osborne said as he swung the top turret around and charged his thirty cals.

"Stay close, Red-Group. Close in tight, boys," Red-Leader coaxed. "We should pick up our escort soon." A squadron of P-47 Thunderbolts out of Mindanao was five minutes away.

The first wave of zero's angled down out of the sun. All twelve '25 gunners opened fire as the Jap fighters cut through the formation like butter. Carl could hear the 20 mm rounds tear into the fuselage. Harry waited for the next wave. He focused on the lead plane and squeezed the firing grips of his twin .30-cals. The tracers told him he had found his mark. The lead zero disintegrated. He swung around to catch another flight of zeros coming at the left side of the bomber. The fighter's 20 mm cannons blinked their death fire at the same time he held the zero in his sites. Again, his aim was on the money. The zero veered off and spiraled down out of sight trailing black smoke.

Finally, the Thunderbolts shot out of the clouds like rain, tearinginto the zeros. The bombers were forgotten as the P-47s engaged the enemy, scattering the attacking Jap fighters. The bombers were safe; almost. One lone fighter had sneaked in behind the formation. He raked Carl's right wingman with cannon fire and flame erupted from the bomber's right engine. Red-three began a steep descent, falling out of formation. The zero decided to follow the wounded American plane, getting into position for the kill.

"Harry, let's splash that zero." Carl dived on the fighter with full military power. The zero cameinto his sites and Carl pressed the .50 caliber nose guns. The zero waggled his wings as if taken by surprise and was unsure of what to do. That brief hesitation allowed Carl's plane to shoot past the enemy's left side as Harry opened fire from the turret. A line of holes traced the zero from the engine, through the zero's cockpit and blew off the vertical stabilizer. The fighter wobbled oddly and spun away out of control.

Carl pulled back on the throttles. At almost three hundred miles per hour, he had to use every ounce of his strength to pull the bomber out of the power dive. "Come on, baby ... come on. Climb, dammit!" he yelled. The nose started to lift toward the horizon. The bomber leveled off and screamed over the ocean's surface a mere fifty feet above the whitecaps. Ocean spray spattered the windshield.

"Carl. Carl! Wake up. You're having a nightmare." Buck shook Carl hard. "We don't need to climb. We're doing fine."

"Huh? What. Oh ... okay, I'm awake. Geez, I haven't had one of those dreams in a long time." His heart raced like a jackhammer, and it took a minute for him to calm down.

"What were you dreaming about? You sounded pretty desperate." Buck was concerned about his new Montana cowboy friend. "You seemed to be chasing some demons there, my friend."

"Our last mission during the war, when Harry saved our butts by splashing three zeroes off the coast of Formosa. We damned near didn't make it back. I guess flying *Annie* into this mission brought back some things. Don't worry, I'm fine, Buck.

You can stop looking like you think I'm a nutcase." He laughed nervously.

"What, me ... worry?" Buck gave Carl his goofiest Alfred E. Newman cockeyed grin. Carl cracked up and they both had a good laugh.

"Whoa! What do we have here?" Carl exclaimed, surprised to see two Grumman F-14A fighters; one on each wing. They sported the orange, green, and white roundel of the Irish Air Force emblazoned on the fuselage. "One of them is signaling: one...two...one...dot... five...two...five. He wants us to tune our comm to his frequency.

Buck dialed 121.525 MHz into comm1 and keyed his mic.

Army four-zero-two-two-three-six. Do you copy, fighter jets?

Copy you loud and clear, mate. We are flying coastal patrol and came across a fine looking old American warbird. Where might you lads be bound for if I may inquire?

Belfast City Airport for a brief lay over, and we'll be on our way. You should have our flight-plan.

Checking ... right, we have you. You're flying to Aviano, Italy for the air show.

That's affirmative, sir. We'll be taking on fuel, then we'll be on our way.

We shall provide escort to Echo-Golf-Alpha-Alpha. Belfast city airport is closed. It seems as though a rather large sink-hole has forced their runway to close. Follow us, mate, and welcome to The Republic of Ireland, Army two-two-three-six.

The two fighters banked left, and five minutes later the coast of Ireland came into view.

"Echo-Golf-Alpha-Alpha is Belfast Aldergrove according

to the chart. There are two runways, seven and two-five. I'll set comm2 to one-two-zero point nine for approach control." Buck adjusted the radio setting as well as the GPS Destination Airport.

They were vectored for a left traffic approach to runway 25 which had a paved 9,081 foot long surface.

"I didn't really want to land at a large airport; too many lookey-loo's. We need to find a hanger to get *Annie* under cover."

The two F-14s peeled away when the B-25 turned on final approach. Buck lowered the landing gear and the rest of the flaps.

Annie touched down and Carl ordered the flaps raised. He followed the taxi instructions to the general aviation hangar.

The crew lounge sported laundry and shower facilities. To a number, the crew of *Annie's Raider's* availed themselves of a shower, shave and change of underwear. Refreshed and re-energized, they sat in the cafeteria and ordered up a traditional meal of Irish stew made of mutton neck with generous wedges of onions, potatoes and carrots in a light broth, and served with a thick piece of boxty; an Irish potato bread. The meal was washed down with pints of Guinness.

"If we can push ourselves away from the table, boys, it's time to shove off. We're running about an hour behind schedule, but it was worth the added rest. Is everyone ready?" Carl asked.

"We're good to go, Skipper," Doc spoke for the crew and they all stood up. Harry released a healthy belch of contentment and swallowed the dregs of his glass.

They walked out of the building and across the tarmac toward a weather-worn old World War II era hangar that concealed the B-25. The previous tenant was a PT-17 Stearman bi-plane. The owner was glad to move his plane for the twenty pounds sterling he was paid.

Fueled and ready, the engines were started and the bomber taxied out into a rare sunny late afternoon Irish day.

The Last Raider

B-25 Cockpit

CHAPTER IX

The commander of the Serbian encampment, Stefan Radic, sat behind his grey steel desk dining on a plate pljeskavica (a spicy hamburger), and a chunk of a peasant flat bread called lapinja. The man was the same individual who had ordered the brutal torture of Cody and murdered Lieutenant JG Perry Judd.

He dabbed his mouth with a clean linen napkin and smiled as his door opened.

"Come in, come in, my young American friend. Please, sit down. May I offer you some vodka and nourishment?" His thin attempt at politeness failed to cover his disdain for the American.

"No," Cody answered evenly. The brutish guards manhandled himinto a steel chair. He barely kept his balance, as he tried to keep his weight off his splinted leg which throbbed painfully.

He felt as though the fracture was healing; a good sign for the plan he had in mind to escape. He needed to find the right opportunity ... identify the enemy's weakness and exploit it.

"Oh, come now, Lieutenant Bridger. The time for the unpleasantness of war is past. Please, eat some food," the commander offered again.

Cody saw the man's feigning of affable reassurance for what it was; a ruse.

"No. I'd rather starve than take food from your murdering hand. Why am I here? I've done everything you've demanded of me. What else do you want?" Cody asked in a defeated tone. He was tired and sick from the filthy conditions of his internment. He had developed a chronic cough which he suspected was pneumonia and was losing weight at an alarming rate. The muscles of his former athletic body had atrophied to the point where his posture had taken on the slouch of a much older man.

"Very well, have it your way. Let us speak of business, shall we?" Radic dabbed his lips with a linen napkin. "You are to be moved to other accommodations; a farmhouse nearby where you will be able to regain your strength and clean yourself up. You see, Lieutenant, I am not without compassion," Radic smiled.

"My father is paying the ransom, isn't he? What is it ... money, weapons; what?" Cody demanded.

"The details are not for you to know; but, yes, your father is doing exactly as directed. You Americans are weak. Take away your riches and expensive cars and you are all the same; nothing more than lazy, glutinous capitalists who give into the slightest threat of losing what you care about most ... your money. Soon, you will be released. I want your countrymen to understand that we Serbians are a reasonable and compassionate people. It is in your best interest, and ours, to recover your health and energy, lieutenant." Radic stood and walked around his desk to sit face-to-face in front of Cody.

"Until your release, then, take this time to regain your strength. Remove him," he ordered and the two Serbian guards took him away.

Cody wondered how long it would be before Radic put a bullet in his head. *If Dad is paying a ransom, I have at least until it's delivered to escape. How long, though ... a day ... a week?*

Small farms dotted the landscape around Sarajevo. Most had been abandoned and their owners forced to flee the war-stricken area. A few continued to be worked. Those farmers and their families, mostly Bosnian, provided the food for the Serbian Army who occupied the area and continued to lay siege to the city which once hosted the international winter Olympic Games. What the Serbs didn't take, the farmers were allowed to keep, which provided barely enough to subsist on. It was to one of those farms where Cody was taken by his captors.

Native Yugoslavians Tihana and Radovan Pavlovic had been caught up in the war between the Bosnian and Serbian factions looking to take control of the former Soviet satellite country. They and their children, Marija and Borislav, sat in the kitchen which also served as the living room of the three room farmhouse, with two Serbian soldiers when Cody and his escorts entered. One of the men shoved Cody hard with the butt of his rifle and he stumbled into the room. He tried to maintain his balance by reaching for a chair, but ended up sprawling on the floor instead. Radovan and Borislav helped him into the chair. The armed men left without a word.

One of the two remaining soldiers motioned to Tihana.

"брига за њега," he ordered. Tihana and Marija helped Cody to his feet and took him into a bedroom where they gently laid him on a bed.

"We are ordered to care for you. You are American?" Radovan asked.

"Yes. I am sorry that the soldiers are in your home," Cody responded while he massaged his injured leg gingerly.

"I am in America when I was boy. I like," the farmer smiled. "You no worry. Tihana take good care, American." Radovan and his wife left.

Several minutes later, Tihana and Marija entered the room carrying cloths and a basin of warm water heated by the fire in the fireplace which served as both a cook stove and heat source for the house.

Tihana helped Cody sit up. Marija began to unzip his flight suit when Cody grabbed her hand. She gently took hold of his hand and placed it on the covers, and then continued to remove his flight suit and shirt. She winced at the deep bruises, welts and oozing lacerations on his back from the torturing at the encampment and involuntarily released a gasp of horror. To her credit, she didn't turn away, but gently attended to his wounds. Once cleaned, she dressed the worst of the cuts with the meager supplies they kept in a cabinet in the bedroom. Injuries came all too often in the harsh environment of farming without modern implements and machinery. It was prudent to have a store of first aid supplies in such cases. When they finished, the women left the room with all of his clothing. Cody could only lie beneath the blankets, but soon his body and mind succumbed to the inviting softness and warmth of the downy mattress and reassuring weight of the blankets. Feeling warm and comfortable for the first time since his capture more than two weeks earlier, Cody succumbed to the gentle mercies of the Pavlovic family, and he slept.

"American, you wake up now." Marija's voice came to him through the fog of sleep and his mind fought its way back to consciousness. "You eat ... is good." She lifted his head and put an

146

extra thin pillow behind him. She offered him a spoonful of some kind of soup which he accepted.

"Is called corba od jecuma i sociva, how you say, soup made from lentils and barley. My English is good, no?" She smiled.

"Your English is very good. Thank you." Marija fed him the rest of the soup. He even managed to chew a piece of lepinja which was still warm from the oven. The aroma took him back to his grandma Annie's homemade breads during the Thanksgivings of his childhood. Her kitchen was always redolent with the alluring scent of breads, rolls, pies, and cookies.

As late afternoon turned to dusk, one of the Serbian soldiers entered the room and tossed him his underwear, socks and flight suit. They smelled of lye soap and were wrinkled and still showed some of the deeper stains, but they were clean.

"You dress now." The man waited until Cody tied his boots. "You come." He grabbed Cody under one arm and lifted him to his feet. Nudging him in the back with his rifle, he pushed Cody into the main room where Tihana sat at the small family table with her hands in her lap.

"Sit, please." Tihana motioned with one hand toward the fireplace. "You sleep in bed by fire, yes?"

"Yes. You want me to sleep out here. Thank you." Cody felt himself humbled and full of gratitude toward this family who seemed happy to share their simple means with him. Their home had been invaded by these brutal men, yet they maintained their dignity and were helping him as they would have any stranger who had endured so much of what they themselves had been subjected to at the hands of the cruel Serbian invaders.

The two soldiers left the house, but maintained constant vigilance by patrolling around the building, guns ever at the ready. They locked the family and Cody inside the farmhouse by barring both the front and rear doors from the outside. The windows had been nailed shut the day before in preparation for Cody's transfer.

Night time settled over the region and bright stars soon peppered the clear velvet sky. A truck pulled up to the front door, and the two guards were replaced by two others. Cody lay in his cot by the fire while the Pavlovic family slept peacefully in the other rooms. The flickering flames relaxed him and his eyelids soon became heavy.

The sound of a faint scratching at the back door brought him back to full wakefulness. He dismissed the sound thinking one of the sheep dogs he had seen when he arrived at the farm wanted to be let in. The scratching came again ... louder. Cody gingerly eased out of his bed and, bracing himself against the wall, worked his way to the back door. In the faint glow of the fireplace lay a scrap of paper on the floor in front of the door. He bent to pick up the slip of paper and almost didn't have the strength to stand back up, barely managing to shuffle back to his bed. He lay facing toward the fireplace, careful to turn away from the window. He opened the folded piece of paper and read:

I am CIA. Rescue is coming. Burn this.

His heart jumped in his chest as his pulse quickened. Hope entered his mind for the first time since his friend had been murdered before his eyes. Cody read the note several more times before tossing it into the fire. He wondered what was being planned and by whom. *Had the Navy finally decided to act?* Questions cascaded through his mind, none of which offered any answers. He could only wait for the next note. For the next hour he lay on his bed staring at the shadows dancing across the ceiling in the flickering firelight until sleep finally overtook him.

The next morning came early for Cody. He added more wood to the fire, coaxed the glowing embers into a warm flame and returned to his cot.

The Pavlovic family rose and dressed for the day as first light crept over the eastern slope of Mt. Bjelasnica and cast a golden crown upon the Igman polje, a high plateau which served as the venue for the cross-country and Nordic events of the '84 winter Olympic games.

The morning shift of Serbian guards lifted the heavy wooden bar from the door and entered the small cottage as if they owned the place.

"You cook now, woman," one man said in a gruff voice.

This was easy duty for these men. They got to enjoy the good farm food that Tihana prepared, not the gruel that other troops had to put up with. Only the commanders ate as well. They understood this and knew not to antagonize the farmer and his family. The men ate their meal of sausages, fried squash and bread. Tin cups were filled with cold goat's milk to wash down the meal. After the table was cleared, Radovan and Borislav left the house to go about their farm chores of caring for their sheep, pigs and goats. Tihana and Marija tended the small garden on the south side of the house.

Cody sat at the table, alone in the house. He walked to the window and saw a guard standing by the door. The other soldier stood by the back door. *They're being casual, but not careless,* he thought. He found himself wondering when he would hear from the mysterious CIA operative again. Once more the questions of the previous night played through his mind; *if a rescue is coming, who is it?...the Navy? ... How will I know? ... When will I know? ... Who is the man with the note?* The boredom was almost as maddening as the questions. He decided he had to do something. He started exercising again, trying to get his body backinto some semblance of shape. If a rescue was, in fact, imminent, he wanted to be physically ready.

Two hours later, Radovan Pavlovic entered the house through the back door. He carried two carved planks of wood. Approaching Cody, the peasant farmer knelt in front of him. Without speaking, he lifted up the trousers from Cody's fractured right leg. The purple bruising which was deep, but beginning to yellow around the edges, brought a compassionate expression to the old man's face.

"You are healing, da?"

"Yes. I think so. Thank you."

Radovan gently lifted his leg and placed one of the pieces of wood over the calf. The plank had been carved out and molded to the approximate shape of Cody's calf, sanded and lined with lambskin. Eight holes were drilled along the length of the plank. He placed the second polished and sculpted plank over the top of Cody's leg covering the shin from below the knee to just above the ankle. Radovan threaded eight foot-long lengths of raw hide through the holes in the wood and tied the planks together. The soft lambskin pulled tight against his leg. It felt remarkably comfortable.

"You stand now," the farmer said.

Cody stood. The pain in his leg was significantly reduced, so he decided to take a couple of steps. A slight jab of discomfort shot up his leg when he bore down on his right foot, but it was tolerable. He walked few more steps without the aid of a crutch. He limped, but could bear full weight on the splinted limb.

"Thank you. Thank you, Radovan." Cody was touched by the farmer's compassion. It must have taken many hours away from his daily chores to fashion the splint.

"I go now." Radovan smiled at Cody and left.

Cody lay on the floor and flexed his knees until his feet were flat on the wooden planks. He folded his arms across his chest and began performing sit-ups. After completing twenty repetitions, he broke a sweat and decided to strip down to his boxers. He didn't hear Marija enter from the back door. He turned toward the creaking of a floor board and gasped in surprise to see her standing in the middle of the room.

"I'm sorry, Marija, I didn't see you." He blushed sheepishly.

"I am ... sorry to disturb. My mother tell me, go and feed the American. He too skinny," she smiled. "She is right. You must eat." Marija smiled at Cody and began to prepare slices of bread and goat cheese with goat butter and goat milk. She sliced some slabs of smoked bacon and placed everything on the table. Marija turned to walk out, when Cody stopped her.

"Please, stay ... please?" Cody stood and pulled another chair out from the table.

"I stay, but I must go soon." She sat across from Cody.

"Please, eat, Marija." He slid the plate of cheese over to her.

She took a small slice and nibbled at it. "The soldiers; they hurt you?" She asked.

Cody's heart filled with sorrow at the sadness in her eyes. "Yes, some."

"No, more than 'some'. They hurt you much, I think." Again her eyes showed sadness; and something else, Cody noticed ... *pain*.

"Marija, they hurt you, too. Didn't they?" Cody asked quietly and with much sympathy.

Marija's eyes teared up. Cody placed his hand on hers. She pulled back as if frightened. Then, she relaxed and held out her hand, which Cody took in his.

"Yes. They hurt many women ... the young ones. They make Papa and Boris watch." She lowered her head and tears rolled silently down her cheeks. "And my mama, they ... hurt her, too. The officers; they hurt me and mama. Another soldier tried to hurt me and ... and an officer heard me scream. He shoot the man." Her voice trembled as she related the story of what happened to so many women when the Serbs attacked the peaceful villages around

151

Sarajevo. Fortunately for the Pavlovic family the raping had been discontinued after the initial invasion. The Serbs had their hands full fighting off the better organized and better supplied Bosnians.

"Marija, I promise you; I will not let any harm come to your family while I am here. I promise," Cody said.

"What you're name ... what *is* your name, please?" She asked.

"I am Cody; Cody Bridger," he answered.

"You are very ..." Marija searched for the right word "... kind, Cody Bridger." She stood and walked back out to the garden.

Night time came quickly in the mountain village of Lukomir. A thick layer of clouds made for an early and spectacular sunset.

A single horse drawn cart laden with kegs of goat's milk, many loaves of bread and smoked bacon rattled its way toward the besieged city of Sarajevo. The people in the city needed food and medical supplies. Many were starving. The old man driving the cart made twice weekly trips to Sarajevo. The soldiers at the Serbian guard station on the road just beyond the city seldom inspected his cart which was as familiar to them as the mountain from which he came, Mount Bjelasnica.

Between Lukomir and Sarajevo lay a Serbian army encampment. The old merchant continued on the road until he was clear from view of the guard station. He glanced behind him to confirm no one followed before turning onto a goat path which led to the farms outside the Serbian camp. Drawing within view of the camp, he stopped and knelt at the base of a fence post. The perimeter was thinly manned and the patrols never ventured this far beyond the barbed wire enclosure of the Serbian stronghold.

The overcast sky made the dark night even darker, obscuring the old man and his cart from detection. The fence had fallen into disrepair, but once was part of a network of fences that enclosed thousands of sheep and other livestock belonging to the local farmers. Most of them had left, taking what animals with them they could manage. There was no longer any need for fences. The man removed a leather pouch from his tunic and placed it beneath a flat stone at the base of a fence post. Satisfied, the merchant, a Bosnian by birth and a Christian by choice, continued his journey of compassionate service to relieve a small portion of the suffering inside the city walls.

Under cover of darkness, a lone man, dressed in the ragtag uniform of a Serbian soldier, recovered the pouch, the fourth such communiqué delivered to him since the capture of the American fliers. He placed a quickly written response containing precise latitudinal and longitudinal coordinates of both the Pavlovic farm and the Serbian encampment, inside the pouch. The old merchant would retrieve the intel on his return trip to Lukomir. The soldier returned to the encampment in time to catch the truck that would take him and another soldier to the Pavlovic farm to relieve the guards there.

Cody looked through the window at the military vehicle that pulled up in front of the farmhouse. He checked the ornate old spring wound clock on the wall. *One o'clock a.m. Right on time,* he noted. He wondered if he would find another message, and so he waited, laying on his cot for over an hour. Just as he was about to give up on the idea, the familiar scratching sound brought him bolt upright. He limped over to the door and picked up a folded piece of paper.

Two days. 2030 hours extract. Veliko Polje. Plane waiting. Be ready at 1930.

At 5:30 a.m. Friday morning, the Pavlovics were up and ready to start their day. They fed the guards and waited for them to take their places outside near the front and back doors. When the family and Cody were alone, Tihana and Marija cooked breakfast for all of them. As was the family's routine, when the cleanup from the meal was completed they went about their farm chores.

Cody needed to talk to Marija and devised an excuse to go outside. He banged on the barred back door, and the guard immediately lifted the bar and opened it, the muzzle of his AK-47 aimed at Cody's chest.

"Toilet," Cody said and pointed at the shed which held the two-seater out-house. The guard walked with him to the latrine without so much as a word; his rifle pointed at Cody the entire time. When Cody completed his chore the guard led him back to the house. Marija looked at the American. *Good,* he thought and nodded in the direction of the back door. She returned an affirmative nod.

Twenty minutes later, Marija entered and began to prepare an afternoon meal for Cody. She brought a plate, fork and cloth napkin to him and bent close as she set the table. "What is it that you want, Cody?" She whispered.

"What does this word mean?" He showed her the word *Veliko Polje*. He hid the rest of the note from her.

"Veliko Polje is high up on the mountain we call Bjelasnica. Is where ski walking ... um, what you call 'croos-the-country' people did when was winter games here before war."

"*Cross* country? The Olympic cross-country venue?" He asked.

"Yes; cross country. Why you ask about Veliko Polje, Cody?" Marija asked.

"I heard the guards talking about something and the words

'Veliko Polje' were mentioned many times. They must have been talking about the games. It isn't important." *Now I know. Veliko Polje will be the LZ.*

Langley

Mac stood before SOG Team Alpha. The ten man team was just one of six elite teams made up of Army Special Operations Detachment-Delta (Delta Force), and the Navy Special Warfare Development Group (SEALS). The CIA regularly recruited from the Army and Navy for its Special Operations Group. Skilled in anti-terrorism insertion, The SOG teams conduct covert disruption of terrorist plots, elimination of known terrorists, intelligence gathering, and hostage recovery to name a few.

"Gentlemen, in four days you will be airdropped from high altitude over Serbian occupied territory near Sarajevo. The exact coordinates and mission details are in your 'Go' orders. In a nut shell this is a snatch-and-go operation; strictly quiet. You will be extracting American U.S. Navy pilot Lieutenant Cody Bridger. Our intel has him being held in a farmhouse three klicks from the main Serbian encampment. You will escort Lieutenant Bridger to the extraction point two klicks from the farmhouse where an aircraft will land on the old cross country trail used for the '84 Olympics; a location called Veliko Polje. The Agency has a deep cover agent, code named Snake Charmer, inside the Serbian camp. Following the extraction, Snake Charmer will direct you out of the war zone after the op."

"Can we expect any help from the locals, Mr. Aldrin?" One of the team members asked.

"Negative. This is a *dark* operation. We can't risk detection. You'll need to travel cross-country, avoiding well-travelled roads. There are roadblocks everywhere. You will proceed west to the coastal city of Makarska where an Italian freighter, the *Abitante*, will take you aboard. Major Pierce is your team leader. He'll answer any other questions. Good luck, gentlemen. Wheels-up in six hours." Mac returned to his office.

The plans for the operation had already been given to Snake Charmer by his handler at a predetermined drop location near where Cody was being held. There was nothing left for the CIA Director of Covert Operations to do except confirm the op with Carl at Aviano.

CHAPTER X

"Turning one," Carl called out through the side wind screen. The left engine caught hold and settledinto a rhythmic idle. "Turning two." The starboard propeller started to turn, but when the engine failed to fire up after a few seconds, Carl shut it down.

"Okay, one more time." He and Buck repeated the engine-start procedure. This time the engine sputtered, but didn't catch. "Come on, baby!" he coaxed, pulling back the mixture, and easing the lever forward again. The engine blew out a wet, dark blast of smoke which turned the desirable blue-white before disappearing altogether, and smoothed into a steady purr.

"I hope we're not going to have trouble with the starboard engine again."

"Naw, it's nothing, Buck; probably some condensation in the carburetor. All the gauges are in the green. Radio ground control and let's get out of here."

Carl wasn't as confident about the right engine as he let on. The beginning of a worry-knot grew in his gut telling him that Buck's concern may have been premonitory.

He released the parking brake and rolled the bomber out to the taxiway, stopping at the hold-short line. Ground control cleared them for departure and *Annie* taxied onto the active runway. He lined up her nose with the center line and briskly moved the throttles forward. The engines roared, increasing in pitch as *Annie* accelerated down the runway.

The B-25 lifted off and Carl banked to a heading of 124 degrees toward the coast of France. After reaching 15,500 feet, he turned the controls over to Buck. "I'm going back to check on the boys, Buck. I'll be back in a few. Keep a close eye on the starboard engine."

"You've got it, Boss."

Carl hunched down and wiggled his way between the bulkheads to the bomb-bay where Harry, Doc and Gifford sat hunched together in a three-handed game of draw-poker. Their cards rested on a makeshift table consisting of a slab of cardboard resting on their knees.

"Hey, boys; you need a fourth for a game like that. Mind if I join you?" He pulled the cooler up and sat down.

"We'll be in Aviano in about four-and-a-half hours. We're staying overnight, so we'll get some much needed rest. Everybody holding up okay?" He arranged the hand he was dealt. *Nothing promising here,* he thought, scanning his cards.

"Right as rain, Boss. A bit bored, but otherwise everything is copasetic," Harry remarked.

"I hear that. Remember back in the day, Harry ... Doc, at Clark Field with the 823rd? We used to get so damned sick of the boredom ... always waiting for the next mission, and when the fight came, we prayed to God we'd make it back to the boredom. The war was like that, half mind-numbing boredom and half fearing for our lives." Carl checked his cards. He discarded two of them. Gifford dealt him two more. Carl was hoping to fill a straight, but came up with nothing.

"I envy you guys," Gifford said. "You got to defend our country against two powerful enemies. There was never a greater cause. Even Korea and Vietnam, as bloody as they got, were regional conflicts. You guys, though, that was the real thing; Pearl Harbor in the Pacific. I remember reading about the Normandy invasion. It still stands as the biggest sea-based invasion force in the history of warfare. You guys truly are the greatest generation." Gifford smiled at his dad and patted his knee.

"Don't kid yourself, youngster. When you're in a fight, you're not thinking about God and Country. You're trying to cover your own ass and all of the other asses up there with you." Doc paused for the reaction to his quip.

"Gee, thanks, Doc...," Harry put in. "...and all this time I thought you were looking at my ass cuz you thought it was cute." The retort was classic Harry. Everyone cracked up.

"Seriously though, Gifford. If not for you and a lot of folks like you, this would be a different world; and not in a good way. You help keep the peace with the work you do. Every GI, every sailor and every pilot who uses your technology does so with gratitude for YOUR service." Doc smiled warmly at Gifford.

Gifford blushed. "I'll start the bidding at three nickels."

"I'll see that and raise you another three," Carl responded.

"I'll reciprocate and bump the pot a quarter-dollar." Doc grinned over the top of his cards.

"You're either bluffing or you have all the marbles. I fold." Harry laid down a dry hole of a hand showing not so much as a pair.

"Okay then, back to me. I'll match your two-bits and call. Dad, are you in?"

Carl checked his cards and shook his head. "It's too rich for me. I fold." He laid down a pair of fives.

159

"Read em' and weep, boys." Doc laid down a pair of eights and a pair of jacks.

"Good hand, Doc, really good." Something in Gifford's voice told Carl he wasn't finished .

Just as Doc was reaching for the pot, Gifford smiled. Carl knew what was coming.

"But, not good enough." Gifford laid down a queen-high straight.

"Aw, Gifford, you take after your old man. I could never bluff him, either" Doc chuckled and ruffled Gifford's hair like his dad used to do when he was a boy.

The four of them played more poker and talked for the next hour about everything but the mission. They laughed at each other's jokes to relieve the tension that hovered over them like the leading edge of an approaching storm. Carl's ear caught a slight change in the sound of the engines; an almost imperceptible alteration in the pitch of the right engine. Like two vocalists singing the melody in a duet, the engines were distinguishable, one from the other, but they held the same tone...the same pitch, when they were running smoothly. The right engine sounded a trifle flat to Carl's sense of perfect pitch.

"Gotta go, boys. Time to give Buck a break." Carl stood and a bolt of pain shot from his buttock down his right leg. He massaged his aching lumbar spine. His orthopedist said he'd eventually have to do something about L-4 and L-5.

Carl maneuvered his way back to the flight deck where he found Buck adjusting the trim and prop RPM. The auto pilot was off for the time being.

"What's wrong, Buck?" Carl was worried. They were still over two hours from Aviano. They couldn't afford a forced landing in France to say nothing of crashing in the French Alps.

"The oil temperature is running high normal again. I'm reducing the stress on the engine as much as I can. Oil pressure's good, though, but the temp is going up. The cylinder head temp is up a bit, too. I've opened the cowl flaps and reduced the prop RPM to cool down the engine. I also trimmed the plane to compensate for the yaw problem. We're holding at two-hundred-fifteen miles per hour indicated airspeed and almost two-thirty, thanks to a tail-wind." Buck checked the instrument panel again.

"Thanks, Buck. The engine doesn't seem to be getting any worse. Temperatures are settling back down. Let's keep our fingers crossed. Why don't you catch a nap? I've got the controls." Carl checked the heading and altitude. He re-engaged the A/P and breathed a sigh of relief as he sat back and allowed the stress of the moment to ease off a little along with his back discomfort. For now, at least, *Annie* was minding her P-s and Q-s.

Their course would take them over the French Alps to Zurich and down into Italy north of Venice to Aviano.

When they exited Switzerland and turned southeast into Italy, Carl smiled at Buck, who smiled back and gave him a thumbs-up "everything is hunky-dory" sign. Just as the knot in his stomach began to relax, he noticed a thin line of smoke streaming back from the right engine nacelle.

"Buck, we've got trouble." Carl's urgency brought Buck bolt upright in his seat. His eyes went straight to the right engine.

"Yep, we've got trouble right here in River City. There's oil spray on the engine. RPM is dropping off ... so's the oil pressure. Do I feather it, Carl?" Buck asked.

"No, were too far out. Keep an eye on the gauges. Reduce airspeed to two-ten and open the cowl flaps to full. When we're forty miles out, we'll feather the prop. We need to maintain altitude just in case. It'll make for a steep descent and final approach, so things could get dicey."

"Roger that." Buck made the adjustments. "Oil temperature

is holding in the yellow caution zone; cylinder head temp, too. RPM is stable." His eyes were all over the instruments.

"Feel that vibration on the right, Buck? My bet is we've lost at least one cylinder." Carl looked at the oil spray and the faint trail of white smoke from the engine. *Good, it's no worse.* He keyed his mic to the intercom.

"Doc, come on up here. The rest of you buckle up. We're about to lose the starboard engine...again. We're farther out this time, but..." He was interrupted by a loud "whang!" The white smoke had turned to black. He released the mic button.

"Feather the engine, Buck." Before Buck could react, flames gushed from beneath the cowl flaps and the RPM needle plummeted. Carl pulled the fire bottle to the damaged engine and a thick cloud of white smoke trailed behind the bomber. The fire was out, but smoke was still visible. "Call it in, Buck...engine out mayday."

Buck brought up 120.125MHz on comm1.

Aviano approach, Army four-zero-two-two-three-six is type Bravo two-five, declaring engine-out emergency. We are at one-five-thousand on a heading of one-seven-four degrees, six-five miles north of Lima-India-Papa-Alpha. Request vectors for straight-in approach.

Army two-two-three-six, roger. You are cleared VFR approach. Make straight-in runway five. Emergency vehicles are standing by.

Make straight-in runway five, Army two-two-three-six.

"Okay, here we go. I don't like the smoke that's still coming from the engine. If the fire starts up again it could reach the fuel tanks." Sweat stung his eyes and the muscles in his neck tensed painfully.

"I've switched off the fuel feed. There's nothing left to burn...I hope. The engine is covered with oil, though, and that's what's smoking." Buck's voice was calm, but he was as fidgety as a cat in a dog kennel.

The B-25 descended to 3,500 feet. A line of low mountains loomed ahead. Carl brought the bomber's left engine to full power and leveled off. The airspeed dropped to one-hundred-fifty miles per hour. They skimmed over the mountains, clearing them by two-hundred feet and entered the Po Valley. Normally, Carl would lay in one-quarter flaps, but he didn't want to add additional drag to the plane. Maintaining airspeed and altitude was critical.

"We're five miles out, Buck. Lower the gear. We'll go to full flaps just before we reach the runway."

"Gear down and locked," Buck confirmed.

Army two-two-three-six. You are cleared to land runway five. Good luck, Captain.

Cleared runway five. Roger. Army two-two-three-six, Carl confirmed.

As he slowed to a hundred and ten miles per hour, *Annie* began to yaw to the right and the nose drifted off the centerline. Carl kicked the left rudder pedal and straightened the plane out. He added in some left aileron to bring the right wing up. Compared to Iceland it was a no-sweat landing. The main gear touched down and the nose wheel settled onto the runway only a foot or less from the centerline. Carl slowed the B-25 to taxi speed and exited the runway behind a yellow emergency vehicle with a tow rig. Once clear of the runway, Carl shut down the left engine and the tow truck hooked onto the front strut and gently started the plane rolling toward one of the hangers reserved for the World War II warbird exhibit. *Annie's Raiders* was expected and the truck towed the bomber to her assigned place inside a large hanger housing two other planes: an F-4U Corsair, and a P-47 Thunderbolt.

He removed his headset and draped it over the control yolk. Buck did the same and followed Carl into the bomb-bay. The other men were already standing on the hanger deck.

Carl got right down to business. "Doc, can you round up a couple of good mechanics? I need you to tear down the starboard engine and see what we need. The rest of you, give Doc a hand. Buck, you and I need to go to the registration building, get *Annie* officially registered and get our billeting squared away. We'll be right back, guys."

As they walked toward the registration building, Carl couldn't suppress his fear and concern any longer.

"Buck, if *Annie's* engine can't be fixed and ready to go by 5 p.m. tomorrow my grandson will be dead by Monday. When the Serbs find out their shipment isn't going to reach them, the bastards will kill him!" His voice trembled with despair.

Buck gave Carl a friendly back-slap. "Don't you worry, my friend. One thing I've learned from the many times my butt has been pulled out of the fire is, when things are at their worst, it's usually because I haven't thought of all the options. The answer is always somewhere in the wind. You may need to look harder to find it is all. That's why I'm still here, old man."

"I'm not so sure, Buck. I used to think that, too. Annie still died in spite of everything I tried to do to save her. Sometimes, nothing you do will make a difference. I don't want to fail my family again."

They walked the rest of the way in silence.

A half-hour later they left the registration building. Carl's cell phone rang. He flipped open the phone Mac gave him in Montana.

"Bridger," he answered.

"Mac here. Are you in Aviano?"

"We're here. Got in about an hour ago. What's the news, Mac?" Carl asked.

"A courier will meet you in one hour at Base Operations. Your password is *Last Hope.* He'll hand you a locked briefcase.

The combination is the date you and I took *Annie* up for her maiden flight. You will find all the details of the operation inside: GPS coordinates, time table, everything. Get yourself to the LZ on time, Carl. Timing is critical. The SOG team and Cody will be waiting. My team will leave ten minutes after the scheduled extraction whether you're on the ground or not. Good luck, Partner." Mac hung up.

Carl hadn't told Mac about the problems with the '25. Somehow, he felt if he put a voice to his doubts, he'd be giving them life and the mission would be doomed. *Stop it! Stop it, you idiot!* He thought to himself. "If this mission can't go on, it won't be for lack of trying, dammit!" He said in a too loud voice. His sudden outburst drew a concerned look from Buck. "Whoa, where did that come from?"

"Let's get back to the hangar, Buck. I'm afraid we're not going to get a whole lot of sleep tonight."

"I think I've found the problem." Doc called out. He was standing on a ladder, bent over one of the cylinders on the rear bank of nine cylinders.

"Crap! Hand me a rag, somebody. I need to wipe away some gunk so I can see what's going on here." Someone handed up a clean shop rag and Doc began wiping away the burned-on oil from around the cooling fins of the suspect cylinder. He pulled the spark plug caked with black sludge.

"What'd you find, Doc?" Gifford asked.

"I want to check something just to be sure. Give me a couple of minutes. I need two strong men to pull the prop through a quarter of a turn." Doc removed the valve cover and unbolted the cylinder head, exposing the piston. "Now, boys. Pull it through."

Two men grabbed hold of one of the four prop blades and

pushed. The blade moved a few inches, then a few more.

"Okay, stop!" Doc climbed down off the ladder as Carl and Buck walk into the hangar. "Hey, Carl...Buck," he said while wiping his hands with the shop rag.

"Did you find anything out, Doc?" Carl asked

"We pulled the prop through. One piston didn't budge because the connecting rod has broken loose." Doc shook his head sadly.

"Can you make the repair?" Carl hoped more than anything that the problem was minor.

"I could if we had a replacement master rod and bearing. But, we have a more serious problem." Doc fell silent.

"What problem ?" Carl knew Doc well enough to read the old mechanic's affect. *This may be a deal breaker.* He braced himself for the fall of the other shoe.

"Alright, Doc, tell us the rest of it," Buck said.

"Okay. The aluminum block is thinnest around the cylinders because of the cooling fins. The cylinder overheated and the expansion caused a crack between two of the fins. I suspect the whole thing started when a master bearing failed."

"So the engine is fried; right?" Carl said in a bitter tone.

"I'm afraid so, Skipper. The engine can't be fixed. Without a new one *Annie's Raiders* is grounded." Doc presented the diagnosis in the same calm manner used by the doctor who diagnosed Annie's breast cancer and gave Annie and Carl the news; only this time, it wasn't Annie who was given a death sentence, it was Cody.

Then, Carl remembered Buck's words: *When things are at their worst, it's usually because I haven't thought of all the options ... the answer is always in the wind.*

"The hell she is, Doc! I refuse to believe this is over." Carl looked at Buck, who grinned back at him. "Pull that useless piece of junk off and get ready to install a new engine!"

"But where ... how?"

"Just do it, Doc ... please! Gifford and Harry, you guys start talking to every warbird owner on this base; especially the P-47 and F-4U owners. There's a Double-Wasp engine somewhere and I mean to have it. Buck, I need you to go back to the air-show people. They may give us a lead. I'm due over at Base Operations. I'll join you as soon as I can. Let's get busy."

Carl turned and walked out of the hangar. He hailed a base shuttle bus which slowed to a stop. The driver opened the door.

"Base Operations, please." Carl found an unoccupied bench seat and sat. Five minutes later, he stepped off the shuttle in front of the 31st Fighter Wing Base Operations building. He walked up to the Air Policeman who was standing guard at the entrance.

"What can I do for you today, sir?" the Air Force E-5 asked.

"I'm supposed to meet someone here."

"Sir, do you know whom you're supposed to meet?"

"No, I don't, but he is *my last hope.*" The guard's analytical gaze spoke of neither amusement nor friendship. Carl returned the expression in kind.

The Air Police Staff Sergeant pressed the talk button on the radio attached to a clip on his shoulder.

"Sir, your visitor is here." After a brief pause, he opened the gate and Carl entered. "Sir, please enter by the door in front of you. Immediately to your left you will see the Duty Officers' office. Enter that room. Do not walk beyond that point."

"I've got it. Thank you, Sergeant." Carl did exactly as he was told. He found himself sitting in a black vinyl covered padded steel framed chair in front of a grey steel desk with a blue name plate bearing the words "Capt. A. Young." A few moments later, Captain Young entered, walked behind the desk and sat down.

"I'm Alan Young, Mister Bridger. Welcome to Aviano." He extended his hand which Carl shook firmly. The Captain grinned.

He reached into a drawer and pulled out a metal case about the size of a valise. "Before I turn this over to you, sir, I will need your driver's license and passport."

"Certainly." Carl learned years earlier to always keep his identification on his person when travelling abroad. He handed the requested documents to the duty officer.

Captain Young keyed some information into his computer and compared Carl's I.D. to whatever showed on the monitor. Satisfied, he handed the briefcase to Carl.

"Do you need me to sign for this?"

"No, sir. Enjoy your stay at Aviano. If there is anything you need ... anything at all, please call me. Here's my number." The duty officer handed Carl a business card with the 31ˢᵗ Fighter Wing logo, his name, rank, and contact information.

"Thank you, Captain. I don't need a thing unless you have an extra Pratt and Whitney R-2800 engine hanging around," Carl quipped.

"I'm afraid I haven't. Good day, sir." The Duty Officer picked up some papers from his desk and began perusing them. Carl left and caught a shuttle back to the hangar.

While Carl was meeting with Captain Young, Buck, Gifford and Harry scoured every hanger, talking to pilots and mechanics that had anything to do with World War II warbirds; specifically the F-4U Corsair and P-47 Thunder Bolts. Those two planes were powered by the Double-Wasp engine. Buck had his eye on a pair of planes hangered with the B-25. He tracked down the name of the pilot of the Corsair and learned he was at the "O" club tossing back shots with his chief mechanic.

Giff, you and Harry head back to the hangar. I'm going to

check out the Officer's Club. Maybe I can shake the tree and see what falls out."

The Officer's Club had opened its doors to the owners and pilots of the warbirds for the duration of the air show which started the previous day and would end on Monday with a fly-over of every plane represented in the show.

"What can I get for you, mister ... uh," the bar-tender waited for a reply.

"Rogers. Get me a double-bourbon, neat. I'm looking for a Mr. Goodfellow. Do you know him?"

The waiter scanned the room. "I do, actually ... just served him a beer. He's across the room ... blue baseball hat."

"Thanks, son." Buck slipped the man a ten dollar tip, picked up his drink and walked over to the blue cap.

"Excuse me." He began. "I don't want to disturb you boys, but I'm looking for the owner of a sweet F-4U Corsair, name of Goodfellow."

"I'm Bo Goodfellow. What can the Confederate Air Force do ya for?" The 30-ish man in the blue cap smiled up at him.

The General did a quick but thorough visual assessment of the young man. Tall and lean, Goodfellow was movie-star handsome. Over-the-ears black wavy hair and aquamarine eyes framed a ruler-straight nose. His smile was broad and glistening with white, even teeth. Most important, Buck judged him to be straightforward and unpretentious.

"Do you mind if I join you?" Without waiting for an answer, Buck pulled up a chair and sat down. "My friends and I flew in a couple of hours ago in a modified B-25. We lost an engine on the way in. My mechanic said we cracked the block between the cooling fins. I'll spare you the details. The bottom line is we need a new Double-Wasp of the type powering your Corsair. Your name was given to me by the-air show people"

169

"Slow down a sec, Hos. Are you saying you want me to sell you the engine in my Corsair? Now I'm all for Southern hospitality, but, ah...NO."

Buck chuckled at Goodfellow's humorous manner. "No sir, of course not. I was hoping that you, or somebody you're acquainted with, might own a backup engine they'd be willing to sell."

"Sorry, I don't. I know most all of the Corsair owners, and don't believe any of them have an extra engine hangin' 'round. Sorry... can't help. Hey, y'all own a mighty fine lookin' '25. You did some crazy modifications on her."

"Thank you. If you catch wind of anything, give me a call, will you? It's a matter of considerable urgency." Buck stood and handed the young CAF pilot his card, tipped his blue worn-out hat sporting the NASA logo, turned and left. Before he made it half way across the room, Goodfellow stopped him.

"Hey, Mister Rogers. Your card says you're retired Air Force General Buckminster Rogers. Are you *that* Buck Rogers?"

"I am, sir. Good day," Buck smiled back, turned and took a few more steps, but was stopped again by the commotion erupting behind him.

He turned to see what all the fuss was about only to find Goodfellow and his friends, and everyone within six tables of them standing at attention. To a man, every one of them held a salute. He stood at attention and snapped a return salute. They all respected his privacy, and Buck left the Officers Club without further fanfare and with a grin on his face.

Giff and Harry were all the way to the end of the flight line reserved for the air show when they found the hangar they were looking for. Three planes were parked inside: two P-51Ds and a P-

47 Thunderbolt with a U.S. Navy World War II paint scheme.

Gifford caught sight of a middle-aged fifty-something man approaching them.

"Gentlemen, are you looking for somebody?" The man asked.

Gifford noticed he wore the preferred pilot's attire of an AOPA, (Aircraft Owners and Pilots Association), hat which shaded his electric blue eyes. A brown leather bomber jacket and blue jeans over black Doc Marten boots completed the outfit. Giff judged him to be one of the warbird owners.

"Well, sir, we are beggars in search of an engine. We lost our starboard engine, and we need a replacement if we are to participate in the air show." Gifford explained.

"Sorry, guys. I've only seen one engine; a Merlin-Rolls-Royce vee-twelve, belongs to a 51D two hangars down. You might check a couple of hangars up the line for a fellow with an Invader who may be some help," the man said.

"Thanks, we'll do that." Gifford and Harry left and headed back up hangar row. They found the sleek, black A-26 Invader parked in the hangar next door to *Annie's Raiders*. The hangar door had been closed when they started their search and they hadn't noticed the '26.

"Giff, I think we've struck gold!"

Gifford followed Harry's pointed finger to the corner of the hangar. There, mounted on a wheeled stand and covered in plastic was a Pratt and Whitney R-2800 Double-Wasp engine. They approached the engine to get a closer look.

A door slammed behind them.

"Who are you? What are you doing in my hangar?" A large bear of a man asked in a less-than friendly tone of voice.

"Howdy, mister," Gifford began. "We didn't mean to intrude. It's just; well, to be frank, we need an engine to replace the one we burned up getting here. I'd be most thankful if you'd be willing to part with your Double-Wasp. It's a matter of great urgency for us."

"It isn't for sale. Do you know how hard those engines are to come by? They stopped making them in 1960."

"Please, mister. We're in dire straits here. I'll pay you anything," Gifford offered.

"Anything?" The man considered the offer. "One hundred grand. You can take delivery of the engine after the show on Monday."

"Thank you, but we need it now ... right now." Gifford sensed he was getting nowhere fast with the A-26 owner and decided to up the ante. "I'll pay you one-fifty. That's three times the top price in the states." Gifford was feeling a trifle irritated by the smirk on the man's face and Harry squeezed his arm.

"I told you. Monday, after the air show and that's that. Take it or leave it. I don't need your money, so don't insult me by offering more." The man turned and walked away.

Harry watched him until he disappeared through a door at the rear of the hangar. He turned to Gifford. "Well, that was just plain rude."

"Let's get back to the guys, Harry. Maybe Buck or Carl had better luck." The two men left and headed for their hangar.

Bo Goodfellow and his friends were still talking together over beers twenty minutes after Buck Rogers left the Officers Club.

"That was incredible," he said. "What would bring a world-class celebrity like Buck Rogers to Aviano? Is he here for the air show?"

"I don't know, but if he was on the program you'd think his face would have been plastered all over the promotional media. He'd be a major draw." Alf Farnsworth was a P-51D jockey who had competed in the National Air Race finals at Stead Field outside of Reno the previous year.

"Hey, you guys. What was all that about Buck Rogers looking for an engine?" The question came from someone two tables away.

Someone else said, "We ought to go out and get him one. It's the least we can do for an American hero." This brought cheers from around the room and before he knew it, Bo Goodfellow found himself in the middle of a rising tide of half drunk, big hearted patriotic zeal.

Goodfellow stood on his chair so he could be heard over the din of forty or so voices.

"Quiet down! Quiet, everybody! Okay, now listen up. If y'all really want to do this, yell out a good old rebel 'Yee-haw!'" He wasn't disappointed. The yell almost blew the roof off the "O" Club.

"Alright then, this is how we're gonna do it. I need three teams. I'll take one. Alf you take one. Who made the suggestion to go huntin' engines?" A young man in his twenties raised his hand. "What's your name, sir?"

"Paxton; Tom Paxton. I'm active duty with the 31st Fighter Wing ... F-16 jockey."

"Proud to know you, Tom. You take the third team. My team will start with the hangars in the commercial aircraft area on the other side of the base. Tom, you take your team down to the military flight line. They'll probably ask for I.D. so you'll be able to gain access. Alf, you work the air-show hangars and general aviation. I'm going to write my cell phone number and give it to Alf and Tom. If you find anything, call me immediately. I'll notify the other teams and we'll rally at the location of the engine, if we're lucky enough to find one. Any questions?" There were no questions. "Let's get it done boys."

The time was getting late. At 10:30 p.m., The "O" Club teams had been searching for two hours. Every hangar and every building within a hundred yards of an airplane had been blanketed by one team or another. Alf Farnsworth and his guys came up dry as did everyone else. His cell phone rang. He pulled it from his jacket pocket, extended the antenna, and answered;

"Alf here. Who's this?"

"Bo, Alf. I'm about ready to call everybody back to the Officers Club for a final round. We'll start again in the morning. What do you think?"

"Twenty minutes and we'll call it quits. There's one more place I want to check first." Alf had spotted an old C-54 parked in front of a hangar set away from the rest of the commercial aircraft in the area. The lights shone from inside and the door stood open.

"So, how 'bout it, boys? Whoever that is, looks like they've been doin' business around here for several years. Maybe they've got some ideas about where to look for our engine." Alf said.

Everyone agreed that twenty minutes more couldn't hurt, and they headed toward the hangar.

Harold Womak was the owner and chief pilot of Swiss/Italia Air Cargo. An American, and former commercial airline pilot, Hank liked to booze and preferred being left alone. He had tried marriage ... twice, (different states and separate ceremonies within a year of each other). Both women dumped him. Rather than risk arrest for bigamy, Harold fled the country with all of his savings and started the small air- cargo company. He was a private contractor who did work for the military, commercial airlines, civilian business; anyone who needed a custom cargo delivered to a place not on the usual commercial routes. S/I Air occasionally even carried cargo on a don't-ask-don't-tell basis to and from airports in Austria, Bulgaria, Romania, and Croatia. As lucrative as they were, he only flew those kinds of jobs when his bank account needed an immediate infusion of cash.

On this particular day Womak sat in his unkempt office inside his hangar waiting for one of his pilots to bring a load of engine parts from Zurich to the German Air Force NATO contingent based at Aviano. When he glanced out the window across the tarmac, walking into the light of the halogen lamps which illuminated the area in front of S/I Air, marched a group of eight or ten men. *Uh oh,* he thought. *Whoever they are, they ain't government types.* He decided he didn't need the pistol he kept in his desk drawer. Instead, he walked out of his office toward the men. Two of his mechanics fell in alongside him.

"Hello, gentlemen. What brings you to Swiss/Italia at such a late hour?" Womak asked.

"Hello, sir," Alf Farnsworth replied. "We're sorry to bother you, but we're on a kind of unusual quest and when we noticed your lights we thought it wouldn't hurt none to drop by here."

"Well, hell, boy you sound like a rebel if ever there was one. What part of the South you come from? Womak is my name; Harold Womak. Y'all call me Hank."

"Alf Farnsworth, Mister ... er ... I mean, Hank. I'm from just outside of Nashville. Me and these boys are here for the airshow. Most of us are with the CAF."

"Well, Alf, I'm a Georgia boy myself. Now, why don't y'all come on in my office and grab your selves a cup of coffee. I'd like to hear about this quest of yours." Hank led the men back to a disheveled room with a war surplus steel desk against one wall. A worn vinyl sofa and three chairs occupied the remaining space not already reserved for various boxes of engine parts and sundry items.

He asked one of his mechanics to bring in a few more folding chairs. Soon, all the men held cups of black hot coffee laced with a jigger each of Kentucky sour-mash whiskey.

"Hoo-wee! Now that's a good cup of coffee," Alf evoked a round of laughter from everyone in the crowded room.

Hank Womack freshened his drink, scratched his head, and got down to business. "Now, tell me boys. What is so danged important that's got y'all walking around Aviano at this hour?"

Alf fielded the question. "Hank, do you recall an astronaut back in the Apollo years name of Buck Rogers?"

"Hell, yes, I remember. He was a test pilot until he retired from the Air Force ... ranks right up there with Chuck Yeager in my book. He tested the prototypes of some of the jets you see on this very base: the F-16 and the Navy F-14 to name two."

"Well, he and a crew flew in for the air show. They lost their right engine and need one. He seemed kinda desperate when he talked to us at the officer's club. Anyway, a bunch of us have been looking from heck to breakfast for an engine for Buck, and we've had no luck. I was hopin' that you might have a handle on what we need," Alf concluded.

"So, you boys are lookin' to do a good deed for old Buck Rogers and his crew; is that about right ? What kind of bird did they fly in on?"

"A modified B-25. He says she's one of the original Doolittle Raiders," one of the other guys in the group answered. It was Sherman Grant, a mechanic for the CAF Corsair and Thunderbolt. "They're needing a Pratt and Whitney R-2800 Double-Wasp."

"Hmm. The B-25 uses the Wright 2600 engine, not the R-2800 Double-Wasp," Hank Womack said.

"She's a modified '25, Hank. All I know is they need the R-2800," Sherman replied.

"Hmm ... let's say I might be able to find what you're looking for. How much is Buck lookin' to pay for it?"

"He seemed pretty desperate, Hank. More than you might think. I'd guess he'd pay pretty much anything," Alf offered.

"Now here's a coincidence; my C-54's run the R-2800. I like to have a spare and a passel of parts. I think I'd like to meet old Buck and his crew. You boys come on back in the hangar, and let's take a gander at what's in there." Harold Womak led Alf, Sherman and the rest into the hangar.

A grease-stained tarpaulin was draped over some kind of wheeled frame. Womak pulled the tarp off and revealed a sparkling R-2800. "This here is the R-2800-59 engine variant. Which variant is Buck using?"

Alf appeared stumped. "I don't know, exactly."

"Well, hell, son, I need to find out if we have a match. The wrong model could mean the difference between can and can't. Let's get this puppy over to Buck's hangar, and we'll go from there." Womak directed the others to wheel the heavy frame out to his one-ton 1986 Ford pickup.

The crew of the '25 gathered in the hangar. Harry had supervised the removal of the crippled engine. A mass of tubes and wires protruded from the mounts where an engine used to be. The faring around the engine was lying on the concrete alongside the ruined engine.

Carl sat on a wooden crate and shaking his head.

"Well, boys, we've done all we can do for now. I guess we can only hope someone will call us. Listen, the air show people have us set up in a hotel off base. The place is called the Hotel Bella Fanciuna. Why don't you guys grab a taxi and hit the sack. I'll be along shortly." Carl handed them their check-in packets. "Let's plan to meet back here at eight in the morning."

"What about you, Skipper? Aren't you coming?" Harry asked.

"No. I'm hanging around here in case somebody calls. Keep your phones handy. I might need you back here in a hurry with a little luck."

Gifford shook his head adamantly. "Pop, if you're staying, then I am, too." Carl began to object, but Gifford cut him off. "No arguing, Pop. I'm staying."

Before Carl could object to Gifford's stubborn resistance, they were interrupted by the sound of ... singing.

"What in hell is that?" Buck called out. He was standing just outside the hanger looking at something. In the distance the voices of men singing; *Bless em' all, bless em'all, the long the short and the tall...*filled the night air.

Carl and the others joined Buck. A truck approached from hangar row. Men hung on everywhere: to the flatbed, sitting on the hood and the roof. Two guys were sitting on something being towed by the truck. The odd entourage pulled to a stop in front of the hangar.

Alf climbed down off the hood of the truck and walked over to Buck. "General Rogers? I'm Alf Farnsworth. Me and these here boys met you at the Officers Club."

"Of course, Mister Farnsworth. This is Carl Bridger and his son Gifford. Those two with them are Harry Osborne and Doc Henreid. To what do we owe the pleasure, Alf?"

"Well sir, I brought somebody I want you to meet. Come on over here Hank." Hank stepped forward and removed his grease stained hat. "Harold Womak, I want you to meet Buck Rogers and his crew." Alf stepped aside and Harold extended his hand.

"I am honored, sir ... absolutely honored," Harold beamed.

"I'm pleased to meet you, Mister Womak. Is that what I think it is?" Buck walked toward the rear of the truck. The other men opened a space so Buck could pull away the tarp from the engine. "Holy flaming cow! Carl, Doc, is this what we need?"

Doc held a flashlight and walked around the engine. "You've got the G.E./Bendix ignition system with the tubular harness, mister Womack. What is this, the fifty-nine variant?"

"You know your engines, sir. She's a fifty-nine, alright. I told these boys the model number might make the whole difference. What are you runnin' on the '25?"

"The fifty-one variant, identical to your fifty-nine except for the ignition system. The fifty-nine variant puts out a bit more horsepower, but that can be adjusted for. The turbocharger is a different one, too, but ... yeah, we can make this work, Skipper."

"Mister Womak, how much do you want for your engine, sir?" Carl was scarcely able to contain his excitement.

"Now, before we discuss the money, something's been itching at me all the time we were driving over here. Why the urgency? An air show can't get you boys all this riled up. I'm curious about why General Rogers is a part of this. Something's goin' on, and I need to scratch that itch." Womak chuckled and waited for the answer.

Carl turned to Gifford and put his hand behind his son's head and pulled him close so he could whisper.

"It's up to you, son. We need the engine, but it looks like we'll have to let the cat out of the bag to get it."

Gifford stepped forward.

"I'm Gifford Bridger, Mister Womak. My son is Cody Bridger, a Navy pilot shot down over Serbian airspace almost a month ago. The Serbs are holding him for ransom. When they don't get what they want ... well, by this time tomorrow they'll kill my son. Please, Mister Womak. No one can know about this. None of you can say a word about what I just told you ... please."

"You mean to tell me you're going to rescue your son in a B-25? Boys, you are out of your minds." Womak laughed, looking at Gifford. He shook his head and extended his arms. "I reckon I've heard everything, boys ... I love it!"

"Come on over here, Mister Womak. In fact, all of you gather around." Carl said. He and Gifford took the men on the grand tour. They described the refit in detail. Gifford explained the IVOTACS and how it tied in with the 20mm cannons.

"Hoo-wee! That is some serious hardware," Womak whistled out loud.

"So, Mister Womak, what do you say? How much for the engine?" Carl needed to wrap-up the deal and move forward.

Harold Womak removed his hat and simply shook his head in admiration. "Boys, I figured on chargin' an even one hundred large."

"A hundred thousand? That's a lot of money, but...you've made a sale, Mister Womak," Gifford said with an edge of excitement to his voice.

"Now put the brakes on, Turbo. I said I *was* going to make you pay the hundred G's." He turned to Buck. " Look ... Mister Rogers. May I call you Buck?"

Buck smiled and nodded.

Harold continued."Here we have a bunch of guys, mostly old ones. From the way Doc knows his way around the Double-Wasp I'd guess he learned it back in the war. Am I right?"

Doc chuckled. "Well, Harold you got us figured out. Harry and I were on Carl's B-25 crew in the Phillipines right at the end of the war."

Womak slapped his thigh with his hat.

"Now I've been privy to some yarns in my time, but yours beats em' all. Damned if that's not the grandest story I ever heard!" Womak placed his shop-worn hat on his head and took on a serious expression.

"Fellas, I'd give anything to go on this adventure with you.

But, I can't. So I'll tell you what. Just knowin' my engine is going to carry you on your way and that I had a small part in makin' it happen is plenty payment. She's all yours, boys. I'd like to hang around and help with the install. Maybe I can teach Doc a couple of things about the fifty-nine. And no more 'Mister' Womak. I'm Hank to y'all."

"Welcome aboard, Hank. We can use all the help we can get. I can't thank you enough." Carl shook Womak's hand warmly with a grin on his face put there by a renewed sense of hope.

Doc and Hank Womak examined the new engine and came up with a plan to make it compatible with *Annie's Raiders* remaining good engine.

"Both the fifty-one and fifty-nine variants are essentially the same engine. The turbocharger mounts are the same, so we'll remove the newer one from your engine and put the one on from the old engine. What do you think, Hank?"

"My mechanic's the man to ask, but seems to me it should work. Is the ignition system going to be a problem?"

Doc shook his head. "I don't think so. The power needed to fire up the engine may be a bit different. If the G.E./Bendix ignition on the new engine pulls too many amps, we would only need to install a higher capacity fuse to handle the load. I think the electrical system is the same, otherwise."

"We're going to need some welding equipment and a drill press. Probably a grinder as well. I'll tell you what; I've got a shop over at my hangar. I'll bring my chief mechanic back with me, too. Why don't you do what you can here while I'm gone? I shouldn't be more than an hour. Can you think of anything else you might need, Doc?"

"Some tools for pulling off the turbocharger would come

in handy; also some gasket material and a pair of snips. Tell your mechanic what we're doing. He'll bring what we need."

Gifford walked up to Doc and Hank Womak. "I can probably help with the schematics you need. Let me do some measurements and crunch a few numbers."

He went to work measuring, drawing sketches, punching numbers into his calculator and drawing more sketches. Finally, he handed Doc and Hank a three-dimensional schematic drawing of the drill holes for bolting on the finished parts.

"We'll need gaskets cut to these exact dimensions, Hank." Gifford handed over the drawings.

"Man, I would have taken all day trying to figure this out. We'll be back as soon as we can." With Gifford's schematic in hand, Hank walked back to his truck. He had his phone to his ear talking to his chief mechanic.

Doc busied himself removing the turbocharger from Womak's engine as well as the one from *Annie's* blown engine. He disconnected and removed the water cooling pipes and the compressed-air supply line while thoroughly cleaning the openings. An hour later, he stepped away and looked at the chore awaiting him.

"Skipper, we just need to wait for Hank to get back. Can I ask you about something that's been bothering me?"

"Sure, Doc, anything; what's on your mind?" Carl gave his old friend his full attention.

"I'm thinking that letting the cat out of the bag to all those boys might not have been your smartest decision. There are now ten more people who know the real reason why we're here and what the mission is. The more people we tell, the harder it's going to be to keep everything from leaking out."

Carl nodded his head. "I share your concern, Doc, but those fellas have saved this mission and, most likely, Cody's life as well. They deserve to know the fullest extent of the value of their gift. I don't believe there's a man among them who would deliberately leak this to the authorities. Anyway, in about sixteen hours, we'll be on our way. It won't matter what anyone says once we're outside Italian airspace."

"I hope you're right, Skipper. We're all taking a mighty big chance on trusting those boys to keep their mouths shut." Doc turned his attention back to the engine.

Hank pulled up to his hangar at S/I Air and climbed out of his truck. He jogged over to his office where he found his chief mechanic, Enrico Francelli, asleep on the sofa. Hank nudged him. "Wake up, Ricky ... time to go to work. You can sleep tomorrow."

Enrico sat up, yawned and rubbed his eyes. "*Tusei un pazzo copo. Sognavo mia Bella Sophia.*" He sat up and looked at Hank. "I sorry, boss. I am having dream of my beautiful Sophia."

Hank handed his mechanic the schematics and explained what they were doing. "Yes, and I didn't miss the part about me being a crazy man, either; *pazzo copo,* eh?" Hank laughed. "I need these parts in one hour, Ricky. Capire?"

"Si. I start now. You will help?" He asked.

"*Si. Insieme facciono parte.* See, Ricky, my Italian is good, no?" They both laughed and went to work.

An hour later Hank and his mechanic loaded up the tools and materials they needed and climbed into the cab of Hanks truck. The time was 1:15 a.m.

At 1:30 in the morning, Hank and Enrico pulled up to Carl's hangar. "Let's get started, boys. Times a-wastin'," Hank called out as the two men climbed out of the truck. "We got us some gear in the back. You want to lend a hand?"

Enrico had everything: a heavy-duty drill and bits to create the pilot holes in the aluminum engine block, gasket material to cut new gaskets for the turbocharger, aircraft quality bolts to anchor the new engine to the mounts, and tools to adjust the stroke and timing for each cylinder.

The mechanic eyeballed the engine mounts. "Si! Is good. No problem."

Enrico and Doc bent to the task of preparing the new engine for installation. The turbocharger was removed and the one from the damaged engine was installed in its place. They worked through the night at a fever pitch until, at five forty-five in the first faint glow of the new day, Doc called out —

"Bring the crane over!"

Carl and Buck hand-trucked the motorized Ruger crane over to the engine. Doc and Enrico secured the straps around the big R-2800 engine. "Take up the slack, Skipper," Doc ordered. "Good. Now, raise the arm up about two inches. Good ... Okay, the crane's ready. Let's swing the arm around to the plane."

Harry, Gifford, Buck, and Carl manipulated the crane into position so the engine was exactly beneath the right engine nacelle. Doc and Enrico stabilized the load to prevent it swinging too much. It wouldn't take much lateral movement for the 2300 pound engine to pull the crane over.

"That's good, Skipper. Now start lifting slowly. That's good ... a little more ... stop! I need you to swing the arm about two inches to the left ... your left, not mine."

Carl tapped another toggle and the arm moved, bringing the engine into alignment with the mounts.

"Good. We're lined up. Enrico, get started on wiring in all of the electrical while I work on the engine mounts." Doc inserted the first bolt into the pilot hole. It lined-up perfectly.

Enrico began connecting all of the electronics that linked the engine to the controls on the flight deck. Dock and Gifford finished securing the engine to the engine mounts under Doc's scrutiny. The oil and fuel lines were installed and the connections carefully inspected.

"We're ready for the prop, Skipper," Doc directed. The four-bladed propeller was craned over to the engine and attached to the hub.

Half-an-hour later, the moment of truth arrived.

"Skipper, we need to push her out onto the tarmac. We're ready to run her up."

"Okay, Doc. Guys. Let's push *Annie* out," Carl ordered.

The B-25 emerged into the early morning glow of a not-yet risen sun. Carl and Buck climbed aboard. "This is scary as hell, Buck. I hope it works. Let's run through the pre-start sequence."

"Ignition switch on?" Carl began.

"Switch on," Buck confirmed.

"Booster on?"

"Booster on."

Carl primed the engine for two seconds.

"Check fuel pressure."

"Fuel pressure is in the green."

"Here we go. Hold down the energizer, primer and engaging switch on my command,"

"Clear! Turning two!" The prop should have begun to turn, but remained lifeless.

"Damn!" Carl stuck his head out the open side wind screen and yelled. "Doc, what's happening? She's dead as yesterday's fish dinner."

"Stay there, Skipper. I'll check it out." Doc pushed the wheeled ladder up to the engine and began to examine it from one side while Enrico checked the other side. Doc trusted his own and Enrico's ability, and hoped it was a minor glitch. His confidence was rewarded.

"*Dio sia lodato!* God be praised! The battery, she is a'no connected. I fix." Enrico attached the battery lead to the starter. "You try again, signore Carl."

Enrico and Doc pulled the ladders away and stood clear while Carl and Buck ran through the prestart sequence again.

"Clear! Turning two!" Carl called out again. The turbine whined and picked up pitch as the propeller began to turn. The engine coughed once and emitted a puff of white smoke. Carl worked the mixture and throttle, coaxing the big 18-cylindar Double-Wasp to life. It coughed again and then awakened with a roar. The smoke thinned as the engine settled into an even idle.

The men in the hangar leaped into the air and Doc shouted, "YES! THERE SHE GOES! WE DID IT!"

Inside the cockpit, Carl and Buck simultaneously cheered, "YES!" Carl pounded Buck on the back. "Thank God, Buck. We're back on schedule!"

"We've had more excitement than Mission Control had when Armstrong announced 'The Eagle has landed'," Buck quipped. They both laughed until tears of joy and relief rolled down their cheeks.

Carl and Buck ran the new engine through a thorough run-up, checking the instruments at various throttle settings and adjusting the prop rpm. Satisfied, they shut the engine down. Two grinning men climbed down to the tarmac.

"Let's tow her into the hangar and get the fairings back on. You all performed a miracle, Doc; you, too, Enrico. You are two of the best aircraft engine mechanics on the planet. Thank you." Carl hugged them both.

"Easy, Skipper, you're losing your image as a hard-ass," Doc chided.

"Okay, okay." Carl turned to Hank Womak. "Hank, we

probably won't see you again. A mere 'thank you' can't possibly express the gratitude that I ... *we* ... feel. You have saved this mission and have given my grandson a chance to live and come home." Carl extended his hand.

"You get your grandson back, Carl. I'd like to read your story in the paper when all the smoke clears." Harold Womak, ex-patriot, rascal, and owner of the biggest heart in Italy, walked away with a final wave and a rebel yell, "Yeee-Haaa!"

The B-25 crew watched Hank and his chief mechanic drive away.

"Who was that masked man, Kemo Sabe?"

Carl smiled at his old friend. "A heckuva decent man. I hope we'll get a chance to meet up with him again, Harry."

Carl turned to his crew. It was time to move on. He felt what all of them were feeling – a need to rest.

"Okay, boys ... into the hanger. We're going to do a briefing on how this day is going to go, and then I'm ordering six hours of sleep for everyone."

They gathered around a workbench and Carl laid out a map.

"This is our route. We'll fly from here, down the east coast of the Adriatic Sea to this point." Carl drew a red line from Aviano to a point west of Zadar. "We'll turn inland at Zadar and fly straight to these coordinates just outside Sarajevo. The total distance is two-hundred thirty-four miles. We need to reach our rendezvous point at exactly twenty-thirty hours. That's when an SOG extraction team will hit the farm where Cody is being held. It's fifteen minutes from there to the LZ on foot. That's how much time we'll have to lay down cover fire to discourage the Serbs from going after Cody and the SOG team. I figure our flight time to the LZ will be one-hour-and-twenty minutes. We're scheduled to take part in a small fly-over for the air show starting at seventeen-thirty hours. After that, we'll land back here. Wheels up will be at nineteen-fifteen hours.

187

Once we reach Zadar, we'll drop to the deck until we reach our objective. Any questions?" Carl began refolding the map.

"Skipper, why not fly straight at them? We'll save time in the air and the Serbs will have less warning to scramble any fast movers to intercept us," Doc offered.

"We can fly as far as Zadar inside the commercial air lanes. Any radar operators will think we're another small commuter plane. It's the best camouflage we could hope for. When we turn toward Sarajevo, we'll have to keep an eye out for MiGs from Croatia, Bosnia, and Serbia. We'll stay in the mountain valleys at tree-top level so hopefully our radar returns will be sporadic, and they won't get a fix on us."

"Sounds about right, Carl." Buck nodded affirmitively.

Everybody agreed to the plan.

"Alright then, we're good to go. It's off to the *Bella Fanciulla* and sleep. I'll have the shuttle pick us up from the hotel at sixteen-thirty hours." Carl put the maps and mission plans in the aluminum briefcase, and the crew climbed aboard the shuttle bus.

CHAPTER XI

Beth lay staring at the ceiling fan above her bed, hoping the turning blades and the faint *hum* would lull her to sleep. After counting a hundred and twelve revolutions she gave up, slid her feet into a pair of sheepskin slippers, and pulled her bathrobe on. She started out to the kitchen, then she thought, *maybe he'll call.* She turned back and retrieved her cordless phone from the nightstand.

"Hell, Beth, he said he'd call when they're all safe. Stop fretting like a school girl," she said to the empty room.

She poured milk into a ceramic microwaveable teapot and stirred in some powdered hot chocolate mix. The clock on the microwave oven read 3:00 a.m.

Sitting at the table she pulled the phone out of her pocket, resisting the urge to throw the darned thing across the room, and set it on the table instead. The microwave oven let out three annoying beeps and Beth removed the teapot, poured herself a steaming cup of cocoa and sat back down at the kitchen table. *3:00 a.m. here. What's the time in Italy ... seven hours later? This is the day. Only a few hours until...*

"Enough!" She yelled; rebuking herself for her impatience. She took a sip of hot chocolate. The sweet, creamy liquid warmed her stomach. Not wanting to go back to bed, Beth walked into the living room, picked up the T.V. remote and searched for some early morning news.

"Too early for any news of note," she muttered and walked back to the kitchen.

After pacing a circuit through the kitchen and into the living room and back for another ten minutes, Beth felt relaxed enough to go back to bed and add up a few more revolutions of the ceiling fan. She just started to doze off when her land-line rang. She sat bolt upright lifted the phone from its charger base.

"Hello. Carl, is that you?"

"This is National Express Banking. You have been selected to qualify for a limited time offer of a seven-percent low interest automobile loan. If ..." Beth slammed the receiver down on the cradle. "Crap recordings," she said and lay on her bed staring at the ceiling fan.

Carl was asleep in his hotel room when he was awakened by the ringtone on one of the two phones that on the table next to the bed. He flipped open the nearest phone and answered. The ringing continued. "What the...," he muttered and fumbled for the other cell phone.

"Bridger," he announced in a gruff voice.

"Mac here. The operation has started on my end, and the extraction team is on its way. They'll be aboard the Theodore Roosevelt in two hours. They're scheduled to drop over the LZ at twenty-thirty hours. That's when you need to hit the Serb encampment. Do you want to go through with this, Carl? I can still call off the op if you want me to."

"No, Mac. We're all good to go. We lost an engine coming into Aviano, but we found a replacement. We did a run-up on the new one this morning early and we're back on track. Let's do this thing," Carl said.

"Okay, buddy. I'll tell the team they've got a green light. Mac out." The connection clicked off. Carl checked his Timex which read 11 a.m. He returned both phones to the table.

It was too early to wake the guys and Mac's call had stolen Carl's need for sleep by replacing it with an adrenaline rush and a flood of thoughts: *The SOG team is on its way ... it's almost time. What's waiting for us past Zadar? Please, God, protect us and Cody.* He pulled the covers over his head and forced himself to relax. Ten minutes later he fell back to sleep.

The phone rang again. He picked up on the third ring.

"What now, Mac?" He said in a perturbed voice. He waited for a response, but heard only the faint hiss of the transatlantic connection. Carl looked at the phone in his hand; it was his personal phone.

"This is Carl. Who is this?

"Carl, honey ... it's me."

"Beth? Oh, sweetheart, I ... I thought Mac was calling again. He called me a couple of minutes ago." Carl checked the time. His watch read 3:00 p.m. "Oh crap! I ... I mean, Beth it's later than I realized, honey. I need to get the boys up."

"Get them up? Hon, it's three in the afternoon in Italy. Where are you?"

"We're at the hotel in Aviano. We lost an engine yesterday and worked all night to ... oh never mind. That's not important. Beth, how are you holding up?"

"I'm dressed and leaving for the diner. I'm a little tired, but I'm fine. I'm sorry I called when you're in the middle of everything. I just needed to hear your voice,"

Carl noticed a tone of sadness in her voice which pulled at his heart. He longed to be back in her arms.

"That's alright. I wanted to call you earlier, but things got crazy busy last night. Beth, please know I love you, sweetheart.

More than anything I want to be home with you. In a few more hours this will all be behind us. With any luck, I'll be back home in two days." Carl's eyes teared up, and he wiped them on the corner of his bed sheet.

"Sweetheart, I've got to get the boys moving. I'll talk to you in the next twelve hours when we're all safe and sound, okay?"

"I love you, Bridge. Fresh banana cream pie is on the house when you get home. Bye." Beth hung up.

Showered, shaved and dressed in jeans, cowboy boots, leather bomber jacket and his working hat (the sweat-stained Stetson he used for his work on the double-B), Carl left his room with his duffel bag slung over his shoulder.

He reached Harry's and Doc's room and pounded on the door which opened in mid-pound.

"Hey, Skipper, come on in, join us for some cappuccino and cannolis." Harry appeared alert and raring to go.

Carl looked on the table. The flaky cream-stuffed pastries had a dusting of powdered sugar on them. The plate still held several, and Gifford poured his father a fresh cup of cappuccino.

"Morning, Pop. Sit down. Breakfast ... actually lunch, I guess, is on its way. Danged if my head isn't screwed up by the time-zone changes." Gifford put two cannolis on a saucer and handed it to him with the cappuccino.

"What got you boys goin' so early? I figured you'd still be sacked out, and I'd need to pry you out of your racks." Carl chuckled.

Buck spoke up between sips. "I've always been an early riser, Carl. Something about sleeping in broad daylight just doesn't settle in my brain well. I thought I'd get everyone started. I was going to give you a wake-up, too...would have if you hadn't beat me to it."

"He's right, Skipper," Doc jumped in. "I was sawing logs when old Buck started beating on my door. After a cup of a cappuccino, though, I feel like my supercharger just got a shot of hundred-thirty octane Avgas." Everyone enjoyed a good laugh.

A knock sounded, and Doc answered the door. A cart loaded with Panini and pork sandwiches, pizza, and an assortment of fruits was wheeled into the room by a handsome young Italian lad dressed in a white shirt and black tie. Authentic Gelato with more cappuccino rounded out the meal. At 4:25 p.m., the crew of *Annie's Raiders* stepped out into the afternoon sunlight in front of the hotel *Bella Fanciulla*. Five minutes later the shuttle bus for the air base pulled up exactly on time.

Gloria Collett had been spending most of her time the last three days in her InterDyn Security office receiving and analyzing updates on the location of the *Hvezda Severu* and her precious cargo of weaponry. The ship was seven hours out from making her destination port of Hamburg, Germany. The Security Chief planned to call Gifford to give him an update when an incoming call beat her to the punch. Her private encrypted phone rang its unique *beep-beep* tone. She figured it must be Gifford. Only a small select group of people had the number.

"Collett," she answered simply.

"Miss Collett, this is McKenzie Aldrin. We are speaking on a secure encrypted line. I need for you to listen carefully. We know about the InterDyn shipment, about the *Hvesda Severu* and about your boss's involvement in a rescue operation. You are tracking the location of the ship, and you're in need of a plan to stop the shipment. Am I correct?"

Doris was caught completely off guard by the call, and her mental red-flag warning went off. *Careful, Doris. This guy could be anyone,* she thought.

"Mister Aldrin, I have no idea who you are or how you got this number, so before we continue this conversation, I need for you to tell me where you came up with this preposterous story and who you're working for." Gloria wasn't about to let anything leak to this guy—no matter how much he already knew.

"Of course, I am the Director of Covert Operations for the Central Intelligence Agency. Now, what I need to tell you is this: shut down your radio transmitter in the shipping containers. We have intercepted the signal, and it's only a matter of time before the powers that be on the other side discover the transmission and location as well. Trust me when I tell you, Miss Collett, the shipment will never make port. Can I rely on you to comply with my instructions?" Mac asked.

"I ... I don't..." Gloria was at a loss for how to respond. *The CIA? What the hell?*

"Gloria ... may I call you Gloria? I am a friend to your employer. I know him very well, indeed. He is much like his father, Carl. Call Gifford. Tell him of our conversation. He will calm your suspicions. Please, act fast. Good day, Gloria." Mac Aldrin hung up.

The shuttle bus from the *Bella Fanciulli* approached the main gate to Aviano Air Base when Gifford's phone rang. He pulled the cell phone from his jacket pocket.

"Hello, this is Gifford Bridger."

"Mister Bridger, this is Gloria Collett," Gloria's voice echoed faintly.

"Gloria, why are you calling? Is everything alright with the shipment?"

"I got a call a few minutes ago from a McKenzie Aldrin. He appears to be read in on the operation and claims to be with the

Central Intelligence Agency. He says he's your friend."

Gifford relaxed a little. The shipment was still underway, and the tracking bug was, as yet, undetected.

"He's legitimate, Gloria. I met Mac Aldrin at Dad's ranch last week. What did he want?"

"He asked me to turn off the transmitters in the shipping containers. He says the CIA is tracking them and that a plan is in place to intercept the shipment before the cargo reaches Hamburg."

"Do what he says, Gloria. If the CIA can detect the tracking signals, it won't be long before the Serbs figure it out as well." Gifford thought a moment. "By the way, has Lauren Dupree spoken to you about a possible leak inside InterDyn?"

"Yes, she briefed me when she got back from Montana. I'm running checks on every employee who has hired on in the past month. So far, everyone checks out fine."

"Good ... uh, Gloria, another call is coming in. Good work." Gifford tapped the call-waiting icon. "Hello, this is Gifford Bridger."

"Giff, honey, this is Alisa. Are you in Aviano?"

"Hi, sweetheart. We're on a bus. We just passed through the main gate. I was planning on calling you a little later, but I'm glad you called. How are things at home, Lisee? You holding up okay?"

"As well as could be expected under the circumstances. Oh, guess who walked through the door about a half-hour ago?" Alisa's voice brightened.

"Well, let's see ... uh, I bet she has long red hair down to her waist, and she's the prettiest girl this side of heaven ... er, besides her mother, of course," Giff chuckled.

Alisa laughed. "I can't put anything over on you, can I? Oh, and Mom and Dad pulled in last night. They're all here."

Gifford was unaware that Alisa had told her parents about

the operation. They told Rachel, of course, but Harrison and Paula Finch had been kept in the dark; partly for security reasons, but mostly because Gifford didn't want them getting their hopes up in the event the mission failed.

"Did you tell your parents about what we're doing, Lisee?"

"I'm sorry, Giff, honey. I told Mom yesterday. I just couldn't let them continue to mourn as though Cody was already dead. You should have seen their faces light up when I told them you and your dad were going to get him. It's the first time I've seen them smile since Cody's plane went down. I hope I didn't do anything wrong."

"It's alright, Lisee. It'll all be over in a few hours anyway. I'm glad they're with you. I would expect in about five hours, it'll be all over the news. Oh, hey...put Rachel on, will you? Lisee, I love you. I always have and always will." He waited for Rachel to come on the line.

"Daddy? Are you okay? How much longer before...?" Rachel's voice trailed off.

"I'm fine, sweetheart. Shouldn't you be in classes today?"

"Yes, but I can make them up any time before the end of the semester. All the professors at the "Y" are flexible about working around family emergencies."

"Rachel, you didn't tell anyone about what's going on, did you?" Gifford asked with an edge of concern in his voice.

"No, Daddy, of course not. I just told them you were out of the country on business and that mom had come down with a flu bug or something, and I needed to be home with her."

"Good. Well, Rach' I need to go, sweetheart I'll be calling tonight your time, maybe around 10:00 p.m. I love you all. Bye."

"Love you too, Daddy. Bye." Gifford returned the cell phone to his jacket pocket.

"How's everything at home, son?" Carl asked.

"Lisee and Rachel are doing okay. The Finch's are up from Cedar City. I told them I'd call later after we get Cody back."

"Good. What about Gloria; is she going to let the Agency handle the weapons shipment from there?"

"Yes. She needed to know that Mac was who he said he was. Everything is good back at InterDyn, Pop." Gifford's reassurance brought a perceptible sigh of relief from his father.

The shuttle bus took the men straight to their hangar where three civilians were standing in front of the closed hangar door, clearly awaiting their arrival. Carl and the boys stepped off the bus and walked over to the two men and the woman. Carl recognized her from the air- show registration office.

"Good afternoon, gentlemen ... ma'am. I'm Carl Bridger. What can I do for you?"

"Mister Bridger, I'm retired Colonel Mike Kelly. I'm with the air show. This is Martin Heimlich and Claudia Rushton of the air-show committee."

"Mister Heimlich, Ms Rushton. What brings you folks over here? Is there a concern?" Carl had enough concerns the last couple of days to fill a hangar.

"No, no concerns at all. Actually, we were wondering if perhaps you might help us with a little situation that came up this morning." Kelly cleared his throat.

"As you are aware, the program calls for a live-fire demonstration by a P-51D. Well, the aircraft was performing a mock dogfight with an ME-109 earlier this morning, when his ADI injection failed. Rather than aborting the demonstration, the pilot continued flying at high rpm's. His engine overheated and forced the '51 down in a trail of smoke. It made for good drama. The spectators thought it was all part of the demonstration. Hell, the '109 even

performed a victory roll which brought cheers from the audience."
He chuckled.

Claudia Rushton got right to the point. "Mister Bridger. We
heard from a fellow over at the Officers Club that your B-25 has
operational weapons on board. He described them in remarkable
detail. Let me ask, if I may. Are those guns on your plane real?"

Buck jumped right in, as was his custom. "Ms Rushton,
gentlemen. Are you asking us to take the place of the P-51 in the
live-fire demonstration?"

Colonel Kelly fielded the question. "In a word ... yes; provided, of course, you possess the capability."

Carl considered the request. "You all seem to be awfully
casual about knowing we're carrying real guns with live ammo.
Why haven't you reported us to the military police?"

"To be honest with you, Mister Bridger, I was going to do
just that," Colonel Kelly replied. "Then a certain Bo Goodfellow
asked me to sit with him over a drink. He told me a most remarkable story; a story of heroism and of justice. I got to thinking of
our own disappointment with the live-fire demonstration having to
be cancelled. So, I thought perhaps we might solve each other's
problem; mine with the air show and yours with the authorities."

"What time is the demonstration scheduled for?"

"At eighteen-thirty. You would make two passes at a group
of small makeshift buildings, and return to the exhibition area,"
Mike Kelly explained.

"We are scheduled for the fly-by at seventeen thirty..." Carl
checked the time on his chronometer. "...in about forty minutes. I
need to be briefed on the traffic pattern I'll be flying and the location of the targets. We won't have the time to participate in the fly-
by if we do this," Carl said.

"Of course, you would not be expected to be in the fly-by,
Mister Bridger," Martin Heimlich offered.

"Can you push the demonstration back to say, nineteen hundred?" Carl was calculating in his mind, looking for an opportunity that would help the mission.

"That should not be a problem, Mister Bridger. I have all of the information with me to brief you. Can we step inside the hangar and get started?" Mike Kelly turned to lead the way.

"One moment, Colonel. I need to confer with my crew."

Carl pulled his friends aside and lowered his voice to a whisper.

"Boys, providence has blessed us yet again. The new engine hasn't been tested, and we could use another dry run over a real target. We wouldn't even need to land back at the base. We can simply request tower clearance to depart straight out and be on our way. What do you say?"

Gifford was the first to speak. "I like it, Pop."

"Let's do it, Skipper," Doc said. Buck and Harry added to the unanimous vote and the decision was made.

"You have a deal, gentlemen, ma'am," Carl announced.

The committee and the crew of *Annie's Raiders* entered the hanger to go over the plan for the live-fire demonstration. At 5:30 p.m. (1730 hrs. military time), the men left the hangar. The crew had an hour before boarding the bomber. Carl figured one last beer at the Officers Club would not be out of order, and five minutes later the shuttle bus dropped them off at the club.

A young Italian waitress took their orders, and soon two pitchers of beer and five schooners were served.

Buck stood at the table. "Gentlemen, fill your glasses. To quote from Beowulf, *Fate saves the living when they drive away death by themselves ... Let whoever can, win glory and claim the victory.* To glory and victory!"

"To glory and victory," everyone said in concert.

It was Carl's turn to offer a toast. He stood and cleared his throat. "Boys, I don't know what to say. Two of you, Harry and Doc, fought together with me in the Pacific in '45. I have never met braver men than you. Our loyalty extends beyond just being crew mates. We are truly brothers. Buck, you have become one of us. You act out of conscience. You never knew any of us until that day at the ranch. Yet, here you are, laying your life on the line for the cause of righteousness. And Gifford; you and I alone share a common bond for the only victim in this morality play ... Cody. To Cody!"

Finally, Gifford stood.

"Oh Lordy, not another Bridger. We gotta leave sometime before midnight, fellas," Harry blurted. This brought a round of laughter from everyone.

Gifford remained standing. "Thank you ... Pop, and thank you, my friends. To friendship and loyalty!"

"To friendship and loyalty!" Everyone repeated.

"That about does it, boys. Now let's drain these pitchers," Doc laughed.

They all lightened the ballast in their bladders before leaving the "O" club.

Carl waved down a shuttle, and they were soon on their way back to the hangar.

The hangar door rose up on its tracks. *Annie's Raiders* was ready to go. The faring around her new engine was secure, and she looked as beautiful as a bride on her wedding day. Her olive green skin shone brightly. The three white battle stripes on her fuselage announced that she was a lady ready for a fight. Her twin 20mm Gatling guns warned any potential threat that her words spoke death.

The vintage bomber was towed out of the hanger. She looked proud and ready under the late afternoon sun.

Carl and Buck did an outside pre-flight check before boarding.

"All aboard, boys," Carl ordered. He waited for everybody to climb in, then pulled himself up through the bomb-bay.

"Close the bomb-bay doors, Buck," He said as he worked his way into the left seat."

"Bomb-bay doors closed."

Carl began the engine start sequence. Both engines started without any problems and were idling smoothly.

"Radio check, boys. Call it back," Carl said.

"Loud and clear in the tail, Skipper," Harry announced.

"Five by five, Pop."

"Doc copies, Skipper."

"Let's get this bird in the air, my friend," Carl said jovially to Buck.

The bomber taxied to the departure runway as per directions from Aviano ground control.

Army four-zero-two-two-three-six switch to tower frequency one-two-zero point one-five-five.

One-two-zero point one-five-five for Army-two-two-three-six.

Carl switched to comm2 which already had the tower frequency dialed in.

Aviano departure, Army two-two-three-six ready for departure, remaining in the Air show live-fire area for low-altitude straffing demonstration.

Army-two-two-three-six, roger. The airspace is cleared for live-fire exercise. Depart at your discretion, Captain.

Carl added 25 percent flaps. The rumbling idle of the twin Double-Wasp engines changed to a roar which rose in pitch until he had the throttles pushed all of the way forward. At one-hundred miles per hour, he lifted the nose wheel off the runway center line. As *Annie's* speed increased she lifted smoothly off the runway.

"Wheels up, Buck," Carl directed.

"Wheels up and locked."

"Flaps up?"

"Flaps up, Captain," Buck confirmed..

Carl looked across at his co-pilot and noticed a smile on Buck's face. He had come to know Buck well enough and accurately surmised the former astronaut and test pilot was in his element and enjoying every second.

At eight-hundred feet above the ground, Carl banked the plane to the left and headed out to a flat clear space designated on his knee board as the live-fire demonstration area. He performed a fly-over to check the wind sock for wind speed and direction. The orange sock hung limp and motionless.

"Good. No wind. Okay boys, ready the cannons. We have two passes to take out four targets. Let's do this exactly like we planned in our briefing. Three of the buildings are staggered in a rough line. The fourth is off to the side. We'll take out the three ducks on the first pass with the cannons. Harry, we'll do a low pass over the last building. When we pull up, *Annie's* tail will put the shed in your sights. Let's show the folks a good time. Giff, you're the fire-control officer for the Vulcans. I'll line up the nose however you want."

"Roger that, Pop. Doc, put your IVOTACS helmet on now. I'll take the right side of the buildings, you're on the left. We'll have barely enough time for two quick bursts each, so let's make them count. Remember, the cannon will go where your eyes lead it. When the reticle on your visor flashes green, you're ready to fire."

"My helmet is on and powered up, Giff. I'm good to go."

"Harry, you've got the HUD. Otherwise, it'll be just like the old days. You call your own shot back there, pal. All set?" Carl's excitement grew with each command.

"Roger that, Skipper. Just like back at the double-B," Harry added a chuckle. "Hey, Skipper, this is fun!"

"I hear you, Harry. Okay, I'm turning to line up the target.

No chatter unless it's business. Carl out."

He banked left and the targets cameinto view. He scanned the length of the range and took note of what must have been in excess of two-thousand spectators lined up behind a chain-linked fence. All of their faces were turned toward *Annie's Raiders*. It bothered Carl that they were so close to the line of fire; no more than a hundred yards. Debris could conceivably go into the crowd.

Carl put the nose of the bomber in line with the irregular row of three small buildings. He nosed down and increased his airspeed to two-hundred-eighty miles per hour, centering the cross hairs of his Heads-Up-Display on the middle building. The articulated cradles holding the cannons would allow Gifford and Doc to fire low at the first building then cast from left to right, raking all three structures with a devastating rain of fire as *Annie's Raiders* passed overhead at a mere one-hundred feet above ground level.

"Coming up on target," Carl said.

"Bring us left a bit, Pop," Giff said.

Carl added some left rudder.

"You're on target. Hold her steady," Gifford directed. "Okay, Doc, at your discretion," he said. The reticles on both visors glowed green.

Two one-second bursts of fire erupted from the 20mm cannons in concert, followed by an encore a half-second later. The B-25 slowed slightly from the recoil. The noise in the cockpit was deafening. Carl and Buck felt the vibrations through their padded seats.

Carl pulled the throttles back and took the plane into a steep climb, banking left to go around for another pass. He looked down on the damage. Doc and Gifford were spot on target. The three buildings were obliterated. Not a single wall stud or piece of wall was left standing. In fact, other than a blanket of metal and wood shards there was no evidence that any of the three structures had been there. A few bales of hay survived, but that's all. The hay was intended to absorb the explosive rounds.

"Buckle up tight boys. We're going to put *Annie* to the test on this run. Grab your barf bags if you need 'em," Carl advised.

"Okay, Harry...your turn."

"I'm locked and loaded, Skipper. Ready when you are."

"I'm starting our run now." This time, Carl brought *Annie* in low; not more than fifty feet off the ground. Fifty yards before he reached the third building he pulled back sharply on the yoke. The bomber's tail angled down. Harry anticipated perfectly the precise moment the building would pass in front of his .50 caliber gun sights. He squeezed the firing levers in both hands and a twin row of tracer bullets trailed out behind the B-25 and settled on the small building. The makeshift shack blew apart and disintegrated.

At maximum power, Carl took the aircraft into a steep two-thousand feet per minute climb and applied full right aileron with enough right rudder to perform a victory roll for the crowd below. He leveled out and turned back around for a fly-by in front of the grand stands, waggling his wings as the last of the Doolittle Raiders roared by at two-hundred-sixty miles per hour.

Carl turned away from Aviano air base onto a course of one-hundred-fifty degrees.

Aviano traffic, Army four-zero-two-two-three-six is departing to the southeast, VFR to Zadar. Thanks for the fun, Aviano.

Roger, Army two-two-three-six. Be advised of military operations east of Zadar. Stay clear of Serbian airspace, Captain and watch for possible hostiles. Tune Lima-Delta-Zulu-Delta tower on one-two-zero point seven-zero.

Carl confirmed the frequency change:

One-two-zero point seven-zero for Army two-two-three six.

He punched the intercom button.

"Listen up guys. We're cleared VFR to Zadar. We have about an hour before things start to get dicey. Grab a bite to eat and relax. Buck, please take the controls. I'm climbing into the back for a few minutes."

The Last Raider

CHAPTER XII

The USS Theodore Roosevelt Carrier Group orbited on-station in the Mediterranean as part of the Atlantic 3rd Fleet under command of Vice Admiral Allen C. Richards. The Captain of CVN-71 ordered the carrier's bow turned into the wind in preparation for landing an LRC-30A Provider. The twin engine U.S. Navy variant of the Grumman C-2A was used to transport mail, supplies, equipment and personnel to the Theodore Roosevelt's compliment of 3,200 crew members. This particular aircraft was painted a non-reflective black and the usual Navy insignia had been painted over to make its identification by an enemy more difficult.

At the moment "Thunder five-zero" was carrying a cadre of six members of a Special Operations Group of elite warriors trained in covert incursion and, as in this case, the extraction of friendly "assets" from enemy hands. The aircraft was three-quarters of a mile out on its final approach.

Thunder five-zero, call the ball, the Landing Signal Officer announced.

Thunder five-zero, ball, four-point–two. The pilot positioned the airplane and checked the green hook-down light one more time. The LSO signaled clearance for landing.

The Provider's tail hook caught the first arresting cable and decelerated from 120 knots to a standstill in less than two seconds.

"Grab your gear, boys," Pierce shouted to his team when the loading ramp at the rear of the plane dropped down. The six men de-planed and headed toward the "island" — the vertical structure on the starboard side of a carrier from which flight operations are directed.

SOG team Alfa was escorted below decks to their quarters.

"Jake, you and I'll bunk here. The rest of you guys choose your roomies. Be ready to meet in five minutes." Lieutenant Commander Frank Pierce tossed his duffel bag on the top bunk of the cramped quarters, and his second in command, Gunnery Sergeant Jacob "Night" Shade, took the lower bunk.

Army Technical Sergeant Guillermo "Gus" Sanchez and Army Sergeant 1st class Padington "Paddy" North shared the adjoining room. Petty Officer 1st class Michael "Flipper" Dufner and Marine Lance Corporal Zedekiah "Zed" DeLuka, the newest recruit to the CIA's Special Operations group, shared the quarters directly across from the team leader.

A loud rap on the steel door to Commander Pierce's room announced the presence of the team's personal watch dog, a large and very fit Marine sergeant. "Enter!" Frank said loudly.

The door opened and the sergeant, clad in Marine khakis and blue trousers with red stripes on the side stepped into the small room.

"Sir, You are invited to Admiral Richards's quarters."

The team leader received no explanation of the purpose of the appointment, but he understood that one does not put off the Commander of Naval Air Forces of the 3rd Fleet, or COMNAVAIRFOR as he was called in Navy shorthand.

"Thank you, Sergeant. Lead the way." Frank dropped the remaining items yet to be stowed onto his bunk and followed his escort to the Admiral's quarters. A smile crept into his countenance as he thought that "door" would be a fitting nickname for the man whose size kept him in his shadow.

Upon reaching Admiral Richards' quarters, Frank waited to be announced. As soon as the big Marine stepped aside, he entered and closed the door behind him. He snapped a sharp salute and held it until the Admiral returned it.

"You wanted to see me, sir?"

"Yes, Commander. Please, sit down." He held a file folder stamped "CLASSIFIED" in red letters. Frank had a good idea of its contents.

"Lieutenant Commander Frank Pierce, third in your class at Annapolis in 1981. Entered Submarine warfare training and assigned to the U.S.S. Greyback in February, '82 where you served with distinction until the Greyback was decommissioned in '84. You were transferred to SSN-712, the U.S.S. Atlanta, shortly afterward. You hold black belts in Karate, Taekwando and Kung Fu, and you're fluent in Russian and French. In '86 you completed SEAL training and in 1988 left the Navy to work for the CIA. Currently you are team leader for one of the Agency's Special Operations teams." The Admiral laid the dossier on his desk.

Frank Pierce raised a concerned eyebrow. "Sir, that last part is classified info..."

The Admiral cut him off with a raise of his hand.

"I tell you these things by way of informing you I've been read-in about your operation. I'm the only one who knows what your objective is. A few people are aware of a black ops team being dropped into Serbia, but not why. Commander, you have the support of the Theodore Roosevelt and her resources. We stand ready to support your mission in whatever way we can without directly injecting the United States into the regional conflict in Bosnia. I will be monitoring your progress closely. When and *if* the opportunity presents itself for the Theodore Roosevelt to conduct an 'air exercise' near Serbian-controlled airspace, under the auspices of NATO, of course, we will. When are you scheduled to depart?"

"In a little over two hours, sir. The team needs to grab some chow and a little rest first."

"Very well, Commander. I suggest you do the same. I'm going to give you a radio frequency to use if your team gets into trouble. It is a secure dedicated line linked to my satellite phone. Use it only in case of a dire emergency; understood?"

"Yes, sir." Frank was impressed with the Admiral's hands-on approach, and felt more at ease knowing he had his support.

"Good luck, then." The Admiral stood and extended his hand which Frank shook warmly. "Get our pilot back to us, son."

"We will, sir." As he returned to his room, his thoughts shifted to briefing his men.

The six-man SOG team met in the mess hall for a briefing. The dining hall sat mostly empty and the team found a table where they talked quietly. Frank Pierce placed a map on the table with their insertion path marked by a red line from the drop zone to the farmhouse. Another line showed the path from the farmhouse to the extraction point. A third line, drawn in yellow, showed the path they would take back into Croatia to the sea-port of Makarska.

"Each of you has the same map. Comm. will be handled by Zed. This is your first op, Zed, so stay by me and you'll be fine." Frank searched for signs of hesitancy in the young man's eyes and found only steady, focused determination. The kid was cool as a cucumber.

"Roger that," Zedekiah responded.

"As usual, Gunny, you handle the long rifle. Our jump point is here, over an area called Veliko Polje. This will be a HALO (High Altitude Low Opening) jump from twenty-five-thousand feet. Full oxygen will be used. Make sure your O2 gear is operational.

"The farmhouse is here," he said, pointing to a red dot on the map, "about two-klicks from our LZ. Our approach to the house will be from the tree line here. There's about a hundred yards of low grass to cover before we get to the objective.

"Gunny, you'll have to cover our *'six'* if any Serbs start moving like they've spotted us."

"Roger that, boss. I'll hang back in the trees." Jake had earned the nickname "Night" for his almost preternatural ability to find a target in the black of night.

"You've all been briefed on the location of the LZ. If there are no questions, grab your gear and let's head top-side. Hoo-ah?" He raised his fisted right hand.

"Hoo-ah!" everyone repeated back.

Seventeen minutes later the six men sat harnessed in their seats aboard the Provider LRC-30A. The pilot of *Thunder five-zero* brought the throttles to full military power, and their plane was catapulted off the deck of the Theodore Roosevelt somewhere in the Adriatic Sea.

Flying east of Aviano Air Base another airplane turned on a heading toward the same place.

Cody checked the clock — 4:15 p.m. In a little more than four hours all hell would break loose and he paced the floor, adrenaline pushing his body into an elevated fight-or-flight level of awareness. His mind raced as it played out scenario after scenario. Always, one variable repeated itself every time ... *The Pavlovics stand a good chance of getting caught in the cross-fire if a fight breaks out.* That thought forced him to make the only decision he could ... *I have to tell them,* he decided. The idea that another person he cared for might die so he could go on living was unbearable.

I'll wait until I'm alone with the family.

After being fed their evening meal, the guards barred the door and resumed their duties of patrolling the farm.

Tihana and Marija began cleaning up after feeding the Serbian guards, and Cody sat on his bed by the fireplace with a pencil and a piece of brown wrapping paper that had been used at one time to wrap a slab of smoked bacon. He scribbled a quick note to Marija.

Marija – I must leave you. American soldiers are coming. In about an hour they will be here. It is important that you and your family remain in your room near a wall. The walls will protect you. You must move quickly when I tell you. I will not let anyone harm you. – Cody

The table was set and the Pavlovic family and Cody sat down to eat their dinner. Cody reached across under the table to Marija and dropped the note on her lap. Before she could react, Cody spoke, "May I have some water, please?"

Marija stood and walked over to the water urn on a small table across the room. She unfolded the note and read it, returning the folded paper to the pocket of her apron. She turned, engaging Cody in a wide-eyed stare. Cody read her fear and smiled reassuringly, nodding his understanding. She returned to her seat and placed the tin pitcher of water on the table, her hand visibly trembling.

The family spoke of the day's events. Radovan recounted the daily routine of mending fences and caring for the sheep in the field. He'd completed the final shearing of the season the day before Cody's captors brought him to the farm. While Radovan spoke, Cody was looking at Marija whose expression of worry and fear hadn't changed. He held her hand under the table to reassure her.

Radovan noted Marija's worried expression. "What is

wrong daughter? Why are you so quiet?" He asked in their native tongue.

"It is nothing, Papa," she answered.

"No, Marija, you are troubled," he insisted.

Marija glanced toward Cody. Cody looked at her, then at Ratovan and Tihana, and finally at Borislav. They all focused their attention on him. He nodded at Marija.

"Tell them," Cody said. He was no longer concerned about his own life. He had seen his best friend executed before his eyes while he survived. If he had to die to save these good people from harm, then so be it. "Tell them everything, Marija."

Marija read Cody's note to her family. Radovan turned to Tihana. More discussion ensued, this time spoken in rapid phrases with much gesturing. Cody didn't understand the details, but the intensity of the exchange told him they were making plans. Finally, Radovan nodded to Marija, giving her permission to speak to Cody.

"My papa say...you no worry. Under house is tunnel to barn. Tunnel was built by my...how you say...Granpapa? Germans would come and Granpapa hide my papa and family from soldiers. We hide in tunnel when is time."

"Good. After you are all in the tunnel I will hide the trap door from sight of the soldiers," Cody said. "You tell your family?" He waited for her to relay the message.

Something surprising happened as Radovan stood, walked around the table and pulled Cody to his feet. He smiled at Cody and wrapped his arms around him in a bear hug.

"You are good American boy. We like; da?" Radovan laughed. Tihana, Borislav and Marija joined in the hug-fest. Cody's eyes brimmed with tears, his heart flooding with love and gratitude.

Carl worked his way back to where Gifford and Doc were sitting. The two were munching on sandwiches.

"Hi, Pop. Grab a bite to eat. We probably won't get another for a while." Gifford handed Carl an in-flight boxed meal of a turkey, ham and cheese sandwich, a bag of potato chips and a granola bar. A boxed tropical-fruit punch drink topped off the bland meal. Carl layered on some mustard and mayonnaise from the squeeze packets included in the box.

"How're you holding up?" Carl asked, taking a large bite of his sandwich.

"Honestly? Scared as hell. I miss Alisa and Rachel. I can't wait to get Cody … all of us … out of harm's way and get back home to Utah. I'm ready for this, though. Having a son in enemy hands is a powerful motivator."

"I'm sorry, son. I understand how you feel. I visited your mother's grave before we left. I promised her we'd bring Cody home. I miss her. Weeks ... even months can go by without thinking much about her passing, but every so often I get hit with this incredible ache in my heart. Those are the times when I miss your mother the most."

"I miss Mom, too. What about Beth, though? She's a nice lady. Are you two getting serious?" Gifford took a swallow of cola.

"Well…yes, I suppose we are. While I visited your mother's grave I told her about Beth and me. I think she would approve. She and Beth were good friends back in the day." Carl paused for a moment. "She...your mother...told me before she passed that she didn't want me to spend the rest of my life alone. I reckon she understood me pretty well."

"I'm happy for you, Pop." Gifford reached over and patted his father's shoulder.

"So, how's the ammo situation?" Carl asked. "The demonstration used some up."

"We've got plenty, Skipper," Doc answered. "Man, we could have made good use of this equipment in the Pacific. The Japs wouldn't have known what hit them,"

"I hear that. If we'd had the armament we have now, there wouldn't have been a need for 'Fat Boy'." The reference to the Hiroshima bomb, though apt, brought a chill to the men in the bomb-bay of *Annie's Raiders*.

"Eat up boys. Oh, did Harry get something to eat?"

"Yea, he took it back to the tail," Doc replied.

"Okay. Check your gear and stow any stuff you won't be using. We'll be flying low and fast. It's going to get pretty rough, so we don't need loose items crashing around back here." With that, Carl grabbed an extra boxed lunch and worked his way back to the cockpit.

"Take a break, Buck," Carl said and handed the in-flight meal to him. "I've got the controls."

"Thanks. I'll sit right here and eat this. I want to be in the cockpit when we reached Zadar. There's no telling what the Croats might do when they notice us veering away from our VFR flight plan in the direction of Serbian airspace."

Fifteen minutes later Carl pressed the intercom button. "The Croatian coast is dead ahead about ten minutes out, guys. I'm dropping down to three thousand. We're going to come in just north of Zadar so as not to interfere with normal air traffic."

He felt a familiar surge of pre-battle excitement/fear wash over him. He knew that Doc and Harry were feeling it, too. All of his senses were on alert. *Here we go, boys. God help us.*

CHAPTER XIII

Zagreb Air Base - Zagreb, Croatia

One-hundred-seventy-seven miles north of Zadar, at the Croatian Air Force Base in Zagreb, Colonel Ljudo Babic sat at his desk in the 91st Fighter Wing Command Center. He was going over a stack of reports, mostly logistical in nature, when his telephone rang. He reached for the receiver.

"Colonel Babic," he announced gruffly.

"Comrade Colonel. This is Colonel Damir Vukoyic at Zadar. Our radar has picked up an inbound aircraft. The pilot has not attempted to contact the control tower at Zadar and does not respond to our attempts to make radio contact on any of the standard frequencies. It is approaching Zadar at approximately two-hundred-eighty kilometers per hour. At present the aircraft is thirty kilometers from the coast." Colonel Vukoyic spoke fast and with

217

precision. Babic took his tone to be serious and urgent. *Most likely some civilian commuter pilot who has forgotten to radio-in his location. But, best to follow protocol,* he thought.

"I will scramble one of our fighters to intercept the aircraft. Thank you, Colonel." Babic made a mental note of Colonel Vukoyic's use of the formal title *comrade.* The man was old guard like himself; and one deserving of respect. He rang the duty officer in charge of the 21st fighter squadron. A young lieutenant answered and immediately snapped to attention when Babic gave him the order to scramble one of the MiG-21's to intercept the bogey.

When the claxon sounded the scramble order, Captain Antun Knezevic leapt to his feet. He rushed to the operations center next door to the pilots lounge. His orders and the latest known coordinates of the intruder were handed to him, and he dashed through the door across the hall to the hangar where his MiG-21 SMT was prepped for takeoff. He climbed the ladder to the cockpit and pulled his helmet over his head. A ground crewman removed the ladder while two more men pulled out the chocks from in front of the wheels. The MiG's turbine whined as jet fuel ignited. The fighter taxied out onto the tarmac.

Less than six minutes had elapsed from the time of Colonel Babic's scramble order to the MiG's after burner lifting the fighter into the sky.

Knezevic took his fighter to five-thousand feet and slowed to four-hundred knots. Within minutes the outer edge of his radar screen picked up a *blip* traveling in a straight line approaching the coast off Zadar. No other aircraft flew that far north of the controlled airspace around Zadar airport. "Whoever you are, I have you now," he said to himself.

"Keep your eye on the radar, Buck. Call out if you spot any fast movers coming our way." Carl's eyes were in constant motion, scanning the sky from left to right and above him.

Part of the InterDyn re-fit included Active Electronically Scanned Array (AESA) radar with Infrared Search and Track (IRST). The new generation 4.5 radar tracking and target acquisition technology existed in only a handful of modern U.S. fighter jets. The system was linked to the missiles in the bomb-bay of the B-25. Once fired, the SRAAM would lock onto the heat signature of an enemy and track it down.

Buck glanced at the RWR (Radar Warning Receiver). A *blip* was moving toward them.

"Uh oh, I think we've got company. I'm reading a bogey about thirty miles out ... coming in fast," Buck announced.

"We're over land now. The Dinaric Alps are straight ahead. Find us a valley or gorge, Buck. I'm dropping us down to the tree tops." Carl eased back slightly on the throttles and held his speed steady at two- hundred-fifty miles per hour as he descended to two-hundred feet above ground level. He keyed his intercom mic.

"Bogey inbound! Harry, charge your guns. Strap-in, all of you."

Five seconds later a half-second burst of Harry's fifty-caliber machine-gun fire vibrated through the plane. He was locked and loaded. Buck poured over the topographical maps around Zadar and found what he was searching for.

"Here!"He pointed to a cleft in the mountains. "That should be the Velika Paklenica Gorge. It runs clear through the Paklenica National Park. Head there and I'll plan a route the rest of the way."

Carl set *Annie's* nose toward the Gorge. "Where's our bogey, Buck?" His temples pounded and he could hear the blood rushing in his veins. *Calm down, Bridger ... think!* He took a couple of deep cleansing breaths, exhaling through his nose. His heart-rate slowed a trifle.

The Russian-made radar aboard the MiG-21 was early generation-two. Knezevic knew he would have to stay close to the American before the clutter caused by other objects in the line-of-sight of the radar signal made the readings unreliable. Fog, rain, and snow also create a clutter effect which could mask the target. In this case, he knew the course and altitude of his target and had little difficulty in maintaining a reading. At ten miles from the target, he tried once again to raise the aircraft on the general aviation frequency, but got no reply. At two miles out, he acquired a visual description of the target.

"What is this?" He said out loud. He couldn't believe what was before his eyes. He drew to within a mile of the plane. Knezevic pressed the transmit button to talk to his commander at Zagreb.

Zagreb, base, this is Captain Knezevic. I have a bogey at two kilometers in front of me. It is an American B-25 and she is showing guns in the tail...requesting orders.

"Captain, this is Babic. Do not engage the target. Line up on his left wing and signal for him to land. Did you say an American B-25?"

"Confirmed, an American World War II B-25. I am approaching his left wing.

He eased the MiG into position alongside *Annie's Raiders*.

"Well, Buck, it's time to play dumb." Carl waited for the Croation fighter pilot to signal him to land.

When he matched speed with the American bomber, Knezevic lowered his landing-gear and looked at Carl. He pointed down, ordering the plane to land.

Carl smiled back at the MiG pilot and waved. He needed

one more minute to reach the Gorge. The fighter pilot raised his gear and climbed to position himself for an attack run.

"Zagreb base, the aircraft is not going to land, request initiate Intruder Protocol."

Colonel Babic responded immediately.

"Intruder Protocol is authorized, Captain. Babic out."

The MiG roared down on the B-25, and lined up to fire a burst of cannon-fire as a warning to the American.

"Whoa! He's shooting at us, Buck!" Tracer bullets flashed in front of the '25's wind screen. "We're at the Gorge."

Carl entered the gorge at tree-top level. A paved highway wound through the narrow cleft of the popular National Park. Several cars were on the road filled with families enjoying the fall colors of the dense surrounding forest. The drivers must have been startled at the sight of a World War II American bomber flying toward them no more than fifty feet above their heads. If that wasn't enough, a Croation Air Force MiG- 21 was in pursuit a hundred-fifty yards behind. The pilots of both airplanes didn't see the pileup of cars left in their wake. A half-dozen cars caromed off the wooden guard rails while others had to slam on their brakes to avoid hitting them. Within seconds twenty or more cars, all turned askew in every direction, blocked off the road completely.

Carl banked sharply left, then right. He slowed to one-hundred-thirty miles per hour. "full flaps, Buck."

Buck anticipated the command and the flaps dropped. Carl banked hard left, bringing his wings almost vertical while kicking in hard right rudder to keep *Annie's* nose up. The stall warning horn blared as his airspeed dropped dangerously low. Buck pushed the throttles to full and the twin two-thousand horsepower engines screamed. The '25's belly brushed the top of a tree as *Annie* picked up speed. The gorge widened enough to allow Carl to level off and get into position for the next turn.

Captain Knezevic toggled up the "ARM" switch to his arsenal of six AAM missiles. The LED display on his primary weapons screen turned from green to red. He didn't dare fire a missile with so many people in the area. *The American is smart;* he thought to himself. He would wait until the terrain forced the B-25 to climb out of the gorge.

The fighter pilot failed to anticipate the sharp turn ahead, believing the bomber would climb above the cliff in front of him. Instead, the vintage B-25 banked hard left and disappeared from sight behind a mountain. Knezevic was forced into flying straight toward the cliff wall. He jammed his throttle to military power, and the afterburner lit up. He pulled sharply back on the controls, putting his plane into a near vertical climb. The G-forces pushed the blood from his brain and he began to black out. The Croatian strained his core muscles as if he were having the mother of all bowel movements in an effort to force blood back up to his brain. The jet flashed over the peak of the mountain, and he was clear. *Thank you, Holy Mother,* the devout Catholic thought.

Carl took his plane through two more turns, and found himself flying toward the mountains rising in front of him at the end of the gorge. He went to full throttle and climbed.

"Harry, is he behind us?" Carl asked over the intercom.

"I don't have a visual, Skipper. We probably lost him on that last tight turn. By the way, I think I saw a squirrel lose his nuts when he flew out of the tree we kissed." The ensuing round of laughter calmed the tension of the moment.

"This guy is a fighter jockey. He knows military tactics," Buck interjected. "He's likely to come at us out of the setting sun above and behind us. He's going to fall back a ways and then set us up for a missile. Our radar will tell us when he locks on. When he fires, I'll call FLARES. Harry, that's your job. We have three flares. You have the fire button. Punch one time, and a blossom of magnesium will erupt behind us."

"Yea, yea, Buck I know the drill. Hey, Giff, the flares are a nice add-on. I think they're going to come in handy," Harry said.

"Okay, you guys, cut the chatter. Gifford and Doc, I need you to stay strapped into your couches. I may have to fire a SRAAM, so when the bomb-bay doors open, I don't want to lose one of you. The air blast will be intense." Carl was all business — focused and alert. His brain was in hyper-drive as scenario after scenario played through his mind.

"He's here, Carl," Buck said calmly. "He's coming in high and fast. He'll drop to our altitude and fire."

The MiG dropped out of the clouds behind the B-25.

"He's got a missile lock!" Buck yelled.

A trail of smoked spewed forth in front of the MiG's right wing as an air-to-air missile shot ahead toward *Annie's Raiders*.

"FLARES!" Buck ordered. Harry lit up the sky behind them with an array of white-hot magnesium flares. A second later, Carl took *Annie* into a steep climb. He leveled off and pulled the throttles all of the way back.

"What are you doing?" Buck shouted in a panic.

"Watch this ... an old World War II trick," Carl said. "Harry, let him have it!"

The MiG pilot didn't anticipate the sudden slowing of the B-25. Before he could react he found himself coming up fast on the bomber's tail.

Harry squeezed life into the twin .50 calibers in the tail and sent a line of tracers at the jet. His aim was dead-on target. The bullets tore into the skin of the MiG's right wing and along the length of the fuselage.

The fighter pulled up and away and sped ahead of the B-25 banking sharply around, setting up for a head-on attack in an attempt to force the American into altering his course away from the Serbian border which approached less than four miles ahead of the bomber. The Croatian pilot headed straight at *Annie's Raiders* in a high-speed game of chicken.

Carl pulled the throttles back and slowed the bomber.

"Open the bomb-bay doors!"

"Bomb-bay doors open." Buck confirmed as the bomb-bay door light flashed red.

Carl armed the two SRAAMs. The racks dropped beneath the belly of the plane. Carl pressed the firing button once, waited one second and pressed it again. The missiles shot forward. Carl banked *Annie* sharply away from the on-coming fighter.

Knevic pulled his plane into a steep climb and released his flares. The first missile went for the flares, but before he could fire more of them, the second missile was on him. His ailerons had been damaged by Harry's .50-cals, causing the MiG to be sluggish and unable to avoid taking the missile hit just behind its engine. A hard jolt shook the young captain. Alarms blared and his fighter began to yaw out of control. He pulled the canopy release lever, and then, with both hands, pulled up sharply on the seat ejection lever between his legs. In a scorching trail of flame, Knezevic rocketed up and away from the crippled plane. Three seconds later his seat separated from him, and his parachute deployed. The pilot was stunned, but alive. His eyes followed the fighter as it spiraled down. A boiling ball of flame erupted in the trees marking the point of impact. Captain Knezevic would live to one day tell his children of his battle with an American World War II bomber.

"You got him, Skipper. Hey, there's his chute. Lord I hope he makes it," Harry said in a near whisper.

"Me, too, Harry...me too," Carl replied while he brought *Annie's Raiders* back on course for Velico Polje, which lay twenty minutes ahead.

The B-25 stayed low, seeking cover from the mountains and hills of the Dinaric Alps. *Annie's Raiders* flew a zigzag pattern so any sporadic radar blips would not show a specific heading or destination. She passed out of Croatian airspace into Serbian-held territory.

"Watch for bogeys. We're in Serbian airspace. Call out if you see any aircraft at all." Carl figured fighter jets would be sent to intercept them.

"Hopefully, by the time we're spotted the fight will be over and Cody will be safely aboard. That's the plan, anyway."

Buck laughed nervously. "I love your optimism, Boss. The best made plans of mice and men …"

"Yeah, I know the rest of the saying. We can only hope. How are you guys doing back there? Call in. Harry?"

"A-Okay, Skipper."

"Giff?"

"I'm good, Pop."

"How ya doin', Doc?"

"A little air-sick, but fine otherwise, Skipper."

"Stay sharp, guys, and keep strapped in. Carl out."

The '25 flew low over a road that wound between the hills toward Lake Ramsko. Small towns and villages dotted the shoreline.

One particular town, Ripci, held a large contingent of heavily armed Serbian rebels known to frequently ransack nearby towns for supplies, and anything else they had a notion of doing. They had a penchant for targeting Christian churches and families for harassment and abuses. Killings, rape, burning of homes, and other atrocities kept townspeople in a constant state of fear.

Matija Stankic, former Colonel of the Yugoslavian Army before the dissolution of the USSR, was ruthless in his stranglehold over the village of Ripci. He ruled his men in similar fashion, occasionally flogging a man in front of others under his command for some minor infraction.

At the moment, Colonel Stankic sat at a table drinking a bottle of a Serbian-brewed dark beer called Niksicko Tamno, when his radioman entered the room.

"Colonel, please forgive the intrusion. I have received a radio intercept between a Croatian fighter plane and his base at Zagreb. An old American warplane is coming toward us at low altitude, destination unknown. He has fired on the fighter plane."

Colonel Stankic leapt to his feet and ran into the street.

"All of you men, come to me! You, get the SA-7 launcher, Quickly!" He snapped at a soldier. The man ran in to a building and emerged with the Russian-made shoulder-launched surface-to-air heat-seeking missile. He handed it to Stankic.

"All of you listen! A low flying American plane is coming! Take aim and fire on my command!" A dozen men locked-and-loaded their automatic weapons and formed a line across the stone street in the courtyard. Civilians disappeared from the street.

"There! The American! Prepare to fire." He waited for the old bomber to get within range. "Fire!" he screamed. A barrage of gun fire erupted from the street. The bomber flew overhead above the buildings to the right of the Serbian troops.

Stankic waited for the plane to pass overhead and squeezed the trigger of the launcher. The missile arched toward the B-25 leaving behind a trail of white smoke.

Carl sat at the controls and dropped his eyes to the instrument panel to check the readings. Everything was functioning fine.

"Carl! Heads up!" Buck yelled. Carl jerked his head up in time to see a line of armed soldiers in the street open fire on the plane. In the three seconds or so that the B-25 was in the line of fire, at least a dozen or more automatic rifle rounds sounded a metallic staccato drum-beat on *Annie's* fuselage, raking her from nose to tail.

"Incoming!" Buck yelled again. "Flares! Flares!" He yelled. Less than a second after Harry released the flares the force of the exploding missile violently rocked *Annie's Raiders*. Shrapnel struck the left vertical stabilizer and rudder as well as the Plexiglas bubble of the tail gunner's enclosure. One panel of the clear protective bubble shattered as if a window had been struck by a rock thrown by a vandal. The impact left a twelve-inch square hole to the right of Harry's head and a spider's web of cracks spread across nearly half of the protective enclosure. *Annie's* tail lifted from the force of the missile strike, forcing the nose down. Carl reacted instinctively and brought the nose back up in time to miss a barn by a hair's breadth.

"Damage report!" Carl ordered

"Gifford is good, Pop."

"Doc is A-okay, Skipper."

A few seconds passed. Harry hadn't called in. Carl pressed his mic button.

"Harry, report in, buddy." He waited...nothing.

"Harry, you talk to me, now!" Still, there was no response.

"Doc, get back there and check on Harry. I'm on my way." Carl unbuckled himself. "Buck, take the controls." He lifted himself out of his seat and climbed down into the bomb-bay.

The first thing Carl noticed was the sound of the wind coming from the rear gunner's position. Doc was already helping Harry out of his chair, and Gifford pulled the old gunner into the bomb-bay. Harry lay unmoving on the deck. Blood covered his face and stained his shirt and jacket. Both hands were red with his blood.

"Doc, is he...?" Carl started to ask, choking back a sob.

"Not now, Carl. Give me a minute," Doc said. "Hand me some cloth...anything. Giff, bring me the first aid kit, the one marked "Surgical Field Pack." Doc checked for breath sounds and pulse. "He's alive." He cleaned away the bulk of the blood from Harry's face and head. A deep scalp wound about four inches long was bleeding badly. He applied a cloth compress. "Carl, hold this in place." Carl placed his hand on the compress. Harry began to stir and groaned. His right hand went to his head.

"Easy, Harry. Lay still, buddy. We've got you," Carl said.

"Wha...what happened? Did we crash, Skipper?" Harry's eyes swam into focus then widened. "Crap, you guys, who's bleeding? You're all a bloody mess." He tried to sit up.

"Lay still, dammit, Harry. You've got a gash on your noggin. I'll have you fixed up in a minute. You're going to feel a couple of little pinches." Doc drew some Lidocaine into a small syringe and injected the contents around the laceration before threading a suture with Polyglactin, a synthetic absorbable thread. Working in layers from the deepest point to the final surface closure, Doc finished the job by reinforcing the stitches with Steri-Strips. He placed three four-by-four sterile bandages over the wound and wrapped Harry's head with a roll of cotton gauze. "Good as new, Harry. Now, you need to rest easy."

"Rest easy, hell. What about my guns? Did they get damaged?" Harry pulled himself into a sitting position.

"Now you just sit here for a minute, Harry. Let me check

you out," Doc said. "Look at me and keep your eyes open." Doc flashed a small penlight into Harry's eyes. "Now, cover your left eye. Without moving your head follow my finger." Harry's right eye followed Doc's finger.

"Who's the President of the United States?" Doc asked in a serious tone.

"Franklin D. Roosevelt, Doc. Now, can I get back to my guns?" Harry's expression of sarcasm was met with a loud laugh from Doc Henreid.

When Doc was finished examining Harry, he sat back and shook his head. "If you aren't the toughest old fart I've ever seen, Harry Osborne, I'll be damned."

"What about it Skipper? I want to get back to my babies," as Harry referred to his fifty-cals.

"Doc? It's up to you," Carl said.

"I didn't find anything else wrong. His eyes are both reactive. Cognitive functions are sharp and clear, at least for Harry." Doc winked at his friend. "Heart and respiration are good. I guess he can sit back there as easily as he can be up here bothering Giff and me."

"Alright...Harry I want you to check the guns. If they're still operational, you can stay back in the tail. It's going to be cold, so bundle up," Carl said and patted his old friend on the shoulder.

"Yes, Mother. I promise," Harry joked. He headed back to the tail as if nothing had happened.

"He's feeling the Lidocaine, but in an hour or so he'll be in for a whopping headache." Doc shook his head at his friend's stubborn tenacity.

"I'm just mighty glad you're here, Doc. Carl patted his friend's shoulder then worked his way back to cockpit.

"How're we doing Buck?" He eased himself into the left seat and pulled tight his harness straps.

"No sign of any more hostiles. The rudders are a little sluggish, though. They probably took some damage from the missile strike. They're still functional as long as we don't have to fly down any narrow canyons. We're about seven minutes out from our target. How's Harry?" Buck's voice was quiet.

"He's fine; a little scalp wound is all. Man, if he hadn't released those flares when he did, we'd all be sleeping in the trees tonight," Carl said flatly. He switched to the intercom. "Harry, how are you doing?"

"Fine, Skipper. It's noisy as hell with the wind, though. I'm ready to test the guns."

"Roger that. Fire when ready, Harry. Carl out." Carl thumbed the off switch to his mic.

A few seconds later, a burst of .50 caliber gunfire confirmed that Harry's "babies" were awake and crying to be fed.

Colonel Stankic picked up his phone. "Get me Colonel Radic at the Forward Command Post," he ordered his communication sergeant.

The field phone on Radic's desk buzzed.

"This is Radic," Cody's interrogator answered.

"Stefan, Matija Stankic here. An enemy aircraft is approaching you. Unless he changes course, he is headed straight for you. He is an American B-25," Stankic said.

"Did you say he is a B-25, Comrade? Is this a joke, Matija?"

Stankic spoke in a tone that could not be mistaken for humor. "I assure you, comrade. I fired a missile at him myself. I believe the tail of the aircraft received some damage."

As the sun sank farther below the horizon, the sky darkened into dusk. A black, twin-engine Grumman LRC-30 droned high overhead approaching Sarajevo. Its navigation and position lights were off. The six men inside the cargo bay were dressed in identical black HAPPS gear (High Altitude Precision Parachute System) including full-cover helmets and O2 masks. They were linked by radio so they could hear and talk to each other. Each of the men carried an M-14 .223 automatic rifle and a Heckler and Koch .40 caliber semi-automatic pistol.

The jump would be a high-altitude (25,000 feet), low-opening insertion to a predetermined LZ two kilometers from the farmhouse where Cody was being held. The team would cover that distance in less than fifteen minutes with plans to reach the objective at precisely 2030 hours.

"Stand up!" shouted team leader Frank Pierce. The men stood in perfect unison.

"Face the door!" Pierce commanded and everyone faced the door two-abreast.

The door of the cargo plane lowered. Frank waited for the red light in the cargo bay to change to green, indicating their position over the drop zone. The light flashed and Pierce ordered, "Go! Go! Go!"

In pairs of two, Special Operations Group Team Alpha took to the air and soon reached a terminal velocity speed of just over one-hundred-ten miles per hour.

The only sound was the rushing wind buffeting Frank Pierce's body as he plummeted through the night sky. Only a faint line of light could be seen on the western horizon. Above him the stars shone like diamonds on black velvet. When his altimeter reached four-thousand feet, he deployed his parachute. Five other chutes blossomed around him at the same time.

Sarajevo lay below them at two-thousand feet elevation,

leaving only two thousand feet between the men and the ground. Their objective was a pasture below and to the right of them about a hundred meters away. The men guided their chutes toward a point where the pasture bordered the edge of the woods.

They released straps holding their field gear and radio equipment. The equipment containers dropped, dangling eight-feet beneath their boots. The men landed within a fifteen-yard diameter area. They silently gathered their chutes and folded them into the duffels they each carried. Frank motioned to the tree line and the team made their way to cover.

"Gather around," Frank ordered. He opened his plastic covered mission map and shined a tiny, hooded penlight on the surface. "We're here; right on target." He pointed to the map. "I'll take point. Zed, you're with me. I don't expect any trouble until we reach the farmhouse, but keep alert for activity of any kind. Let's move."

The team jogged at a brisk pace with weapons held at the ready. Every man's head scanned from left to right, alert to any movement. Beneath the cloud layer the night sky provided perfect cover with the absence of moonlight to cast any revealing twilight glow on the fields of grass. The men moved, silent as ghosts, to the edge of the forest.

Their path took them across the high country, often times above the tree line, enabling them to make good time. Suddenly, Frank raised his right fist, and squatted low. Everyone stopped and dropped to a crouch. The team leader headed into some bushes for cover, and the team followed suit, silently and without a word.

Ahead of them, approaching on foot, four men approached— soldiers by the look of them, and they were armed with rifles. It would have been easy to take them out quickly and silently but not without revealing their own presence. So, they hunkered down and waited.

The four Serbian soldiers chose that moment to take a

smoke break. One of the men stood no more than six feet away from Gus Sanchez. The former Army Special Forces non-com moved his hand to the butt of his K-bar. If he had to, he would slit the man's throat before he could make a sound. The Serb flipped open his Zippo lighter and lit up a cigarette. He stood with his back to Gus, otherwise he wouldn't have missed the out-of-place black mass crouched virtually at his feet. The men talked and laughed in their Serb dialect. After no more than five minutes, they moved on. When their voices faded in the distance, Frank stood and motioned his team forward.

They were minutes behind schedule and they quickened their pace. Up ahead, a flashlight blinked on the path ahead. Frank stopped, and the team stopped behind him … waiting. He returned the signal with two flashes from his hooded flashlight, and the source of the signal approached. Frank squeezed his eyes closed to allow his pupils to dilate. He opened them and his night vision allowed him to identify a lone man leading a donkey which pulled a cart. The man approached Frank.

"You are American, yes?" He asked.

"Who are you, old man?" Frank asked.

"'Snake Charmer' is waiting. You walk twenty-meters, take path to right into woods. Where woods end, you will be near farm. Soldiers patrol around farm. Be careful. May God go with you." The old man continued down the road.

"Jake, you're on point." Frank whispered. 'Flipper' you're next, then Paddy and Gus. Zed and I will bring up the rear. Put on your NVG's now. Hoo-Rah?"

"Hoo-Rah," the team confirmed and fell into position with Jake Shade on point with his long rifle. Their new AN/PVS-7B Night Vision Goggles were third-generation technology that wouldn't be released for Army field trials for more than a year. They provided 20/20 to 20/40 visual acuity for up to two-hundred yards. Beyond that distance acuity would begin to lose definition. The only drawback was the short battery life. The NVG's were good for about two hours before needing to be recharged.

Jake "Night" Shade reached the edge of the woods. He raised his fist and dropped to one knee. Frank eased quietly up to Jake's side. He checked his chronometer. It read 2025 hours; just five minutes more.

"There's our target, Buck. That group of lights up ahead. The coordinates match up exactly," Buck said.

"I need to be sure. I don't want to kill any civilians." As if to answer his concerns, four powerful search lights came on and lit up the sky. They converged on the B-25.

"They must have known we were coming. Here we go. Man your guns boys! We're going in!" Carl ordered over his mic.

"We're dialed in, Skipper," Doc confirmed.

Carl dropped *Annie's* nose and let his airspeed climb to three-hundred miles per hour, pushing the bomber to the red line.

"We're lit-up like a Broadway marquee. We need take out those lights."

"They're all yours, son!" Carl shouted.

"Hold her steady, Pop. We've got this." Gifford and Doc fired the M61A1's in a two second burst, raking the compound. Buildings disintegrated. One guard tower with a search light mounted on top had its supports blown from beneath it. It toppled into the compound. *Annie's Raiders* pulled up and banked hard right to approach from an oblique direction to their previous pass.

"I'm going to line you up for those storage tanks and the trucks parked by them," Carl said.

"Roger, Skipper," Doc said.

They came in fast and low. Once more the Vulcans breathed fire. Two thundering explosions erupted as the fuel storage tanks

ruptured and ignited, lighting up the entire compound in a surreal-
istic orange light resembling something out of the movie "Apoca-
lypse Now." Another tower toppled into the conflagration.

Men scattered all over the place. Some found vehicles and
scurried to get away from the holocaust. Flashes of gunfire glinted
from below, but were sporadic and ineffectual.

"Check out those trucks getting away from the compound,
Skipper," Harry said from the tail.

"Okay, Harry. I'll make my next pass in line with the road.
When the cannons do their work, I'll line you up so you can take
out the trucks with the .50-cals," Carl said.

Annie banked back around for another run. Gifford and Doc
swept the cannons in narrow arcs, taking out the radio antenna and
the communications shed— Cody's torture room. Carl pulled the
'25's nose up, and the two trucks carrying Serb soldiers rose up
into Harry's sights. He squeezed the firing levers of the AN/M3
twin .50s, and a barrage of .50 caliber steel jacketed bullets tore
into the trucks at one-thousand-two-hundred rounds per minute
each. Both vehicles stopped dead in their tracks.

What was once a regional stronghold of Serbian dominance
was now nothing more than a twisted, scattered, burning mass of
disorganized wire, metal and wood. Carl did another fly-by to
check for signs of life. There were none.

"Time to pick up our boy, Giff," Carl announced. He turned
Annie's Raiders toward the coordinates for Velika Polje and the old
1984 Winter Olympic Cross-Country venue.

Jake Shade scanned the open grass field between the team
and the farmhouse. He pointed first to his left and raised two fingers indicating two soldiers patrolling the tree line approaching
from a hundred yards off. Frank had eyes on them as well. Another

soldier walked in a parallel path to the other two from the opposite direction and twenty yards closer to the farmhouse.

Frank pointed to "Flipper" Dufner and Gus Sanchez. The other three, Jake, Zed, and Paddy would stay behind to cover their *six* while they worked their way to the farmhouse. Frank motioned for Dufner and Sanchez to maneuver their way toward a wagon which stood in the middle of the field.

They dropped to their bellies. The grass was almost two feet tall and hid them from view. They crawled slowly and steadily forward to within fifteen feet of the wagon. A sheep-dog emerged from beneath the wagon and perked up his ears and released a *huff!* The sound was not a full-on bark, but it was enough to get the attention of the patrolling Serbian soldier.

He was about thirty yards from the wagon approaching from Jake's right when he stopped. He brought his AK-47 to the ready and took a few cautious steps toward the wagon.

Jake had the Serb in his sights. Frank must have seen him as well, because the three team members lay stock still and flattened themselves out as much as was possible. Jake thumbed the safety lever down exposing the red "fire" dot. He placed the tip of his forefinger on the trigger of his McMillan M87R sniper rifle, slowed his breathing...and waited. He would fire only if the soldier raised his weapon into firing position. The man would be dead before he could pull the trigger. Instead, the soldier slung his rifle over his shoulder and whistled. He called out some unintelligible words and the sheep dog ran from behind the wagon to the soldier. The guard played with the dog and laughed. A few moments later, he stood, trotted past the wagon and resumed his patrol.

Jake safetied his weapon and lowered the muzzle.

When Frank, "Flipper" and Gus reached the gate at the rear of the house, Frank motioned for Gus to circle to the left around the farmhouse. He tapped "Flipper" Dufner on the shoulder and pointed to the right. Together, the two would neutralize the guard at the front door. Frank would take care of the guard at the back door. The three team members moved silently and fast.

"It's time, Marija. Take your family to the tunnel," Cody said. He doused the fire in the fireplace. Radovan removed two oil lamps from their hooks and gave one to Borislav. Tihana extinguished the remaining lamp.

Radovan and Borislav lifted the bed away from the wall and pulled back the rug covering the trap door. Borislav lifted the door up. The hinges squealed, as the door swung open. Radovan and Tihana Pavlovec dropped down into the tunnel first, followed by Borislav. Marija turned toward Cody and placed the palm of her hand on his face.

"Go with God, Cody," she said, then turned and dropped down to join her parents. Radovan and Borislav each held an oil lamp to light the way to the barn.

Working fast, Cody pulled the rug over the trap door and lifted the bed back in place. *There's nothing to do now but wait*, he thought. He put on the coat that Radovan gave him and sat at the table, alone and in the dark.

Gus peeked around the corner of the house and immediately pulled his head back. A guard stood in front of the door. He knew "Flipper" was in position around the other side of the house. Gus tapped the barrel of his assault rifle on the wall.

"Who is there?" the guard said in his Serb dialect. He started toward the location of the *thunk!* He'd heard. Gus stepped into view, and the Serbian corporal started to raise his rifle. "Flipper's" left hand reached around him from behind and covered his mouth while he plunged his knife into the man's side with a lightning fast upward thrust. It severed his aorta on its way in to his heart. Without a sound, "Flipper" lowered the body to the wooden porch.

Frank Pierce put the barrel of his pistol to the neck of the guard at the back of the house. "Say your name," he said, thumbing back the hammer of the H&K .40 caliber semi-automatic.

"Snake Charmer, don't shoot," the native Croat said. Frank turned the man toward him with his free hand.

"Alek, is that you?" Frank lowered his gun immediately. "My God, I haven't seen you since we were at the 'Farm'. What's it been, three, four years now?"

"It is I, Frank. Hurry, we must leave quickly."

Cody heard the scuffle on the front porch. A moment later, both the front and rear doors opened. Three men dressed in black, and the guard who was at the back door, entered.

"Let's go, Lieutenant — you ready?" Frank asked.

"Hell yes." He stood and limped to the front door.

"Whoa! What's wrong with your leg?" Frank studied the splint.

"They broke my leg when I wouldn't answer their questions. C'mon let's get out of here." Cody took a couple of more steps.

"Gus, you and Flipper, one on each side. He can't move fast enough on his own." Frank opened the front door and started toward the wagon. From their left, two Serbian soldiers approached at a run. One of them fell to the ground courtesy of one of Shade's sniper rounds. The other stopped to take aim, but before he could fire his AK-47 his head snapped to his right and he, too, fell to the ground. Meanwhile, the team leader and his men reached the wagon in time to take cover as a third soldier opened up on them. The automatic fire sent shards of wood everywhere. The Serb began to work his way around the side of the wagon for better angle. A sniper bullet found its mark, and the last patrolling soldier at the farm fell limp to the ground.

"C'mon, we need to get to the tree line." Frank started off in a running crouch.

Thirty seconds later they were in the trees and back with the rest of the team.

"Guys, meet Lieutenant Cody Bridger, United States Navy. Lieutenant, I'm Frank Pierce. The two men carrying you are 'Flipper' and Gus. The sharp shooter there is "Night" Shade. That's Paddy and the youngster with the radio is Zed. We need to get to the extraction point in ten minutes. Let's haul ass."

Alpha team headed back up to the dirt road where they'd met the old man with the cart. From there they would cut across open fields to Veliko Polje, one-and-a-half kilometers distant.

At the dirt road, the team stopped to catch their breath. A bloom of orange lit up the sky to the west followed two seconds later by the deep "crump!" of an explosion.

"That's our air cover, right on time. Let's go," Frank ordered.

The team started running. This time, Drasko Aleksic and Paddy North carried Cody. Soon the men were huffing and panting, but they never slowed down. The going was easy on the paved pot-holed road leading to the '84 Olympic cross-country venue.

Cody's feet never touched the ground while the SOG team pressed onward. Five minutes later the clearing at the LZ coordinates lay only a hundred yards ahead.

"Drop down!" Frank called. Everyone headed for the deep grass at the side of the road and crouched low. Two sets of headlights approached and stopped thirty yards from the extraction team. A dozen men leapt from the vehicles and started toward them with rifles at the ready.

"Damn! We've been made. Pick your targets boys." Frank fired first followed by the rest of the team. Two of the oncoming soldiers dropped. Frank motioned for "Snake Charmer" and Paddy to continue on to the LZ with Cody. He directed Gus, Zed, and Jake to circle around the side of the enemy troops in a flanking maneuver.

With a man on each side of him, Cody was carried away from the fire-fight toward the LZ.

The Serbians were in the deep grass, but were not being careful about seeking cover. Frank's NVG goggles revealed three of the enemy advancing toward him with weapons at the ready. He raked the three men with automatic fire from his M-14. None of them got up. The remaining soldiers fired back at the muzzle flash from Frank's weapon. They were right on target. Sprays of dirt and grass flew up where Frank had been crouching. He took aim twenty feet to the left of his previous spot and fired two bursts at the men. Gus, Zed, and Jake opened fire at the same time.

One of the men ran for the trees. No one else was left alive.

"Should I go after him, boss?" Gus asked as he and the other two joined Frank.

"No time," Frank said. They started for the LZ at a run. The landing lights of a plane flashed on overhead.

Seeing the landing lights of the plane, Paddy North fired a flare, momentarily illuminating the grassy strip. The plane banked and started down.

"Gear down, Buck. I wish we had more light." Carl lowered the flaps.

He pulled the throttles back and let the airspeed drop to one- hundred miles per hour as another flare lit up the night sky. He banked *Annie's Raiders* around and lined up as best he could on the old cross-country-ski trail.

As if answering Carl's wish, six flares burst into incandescent jewels all in a line. The old ski trail lit up like a carnival. Carl gave the B-25 a little left rudder and lined up *Annie's* nose. Just as he reached the edge of the clearing at about twenty feet off the ground, he pulled the throttles to idle.

The bomber dropped suddenly and he compensated by adding power and pulling back slightly on the yoke. Three things happened almost simultaneously: *Annie's* nose came up, the stall warning horn blared and the main gear landed firmly on the ground with a jolt. Carl Held the yoke back to keep weight off the nose strut as much as possible. Soft field landings were notoriously hard on tricycle landing gear. He prayed the nose wheel wouldn't bury itself in a rut.

The last of the Doolittle Raiders slowed to taxi speed a hundred feet from the trees. Carl stood on the right brake and added power to the left engine. *Annie* swung to the right until her nose was pointed in the opposite direction. He left both engines idling and lowered the bomb- bay doors.

"Giff, go get our boy. The rest of us need to stay aboard. We have to get airborne ASAP." Carl wiped sweat from his brow..

"What in the hell am I looking at?" Frank Pierce couldn't believe his eyes. "That's a B-25. I guess the liberals in D.C. must have cut the Agency's budget." He shook his head in wonder.

"I would know that plane anywhere. Grandpa!" Cody yelled and half-limped-ran toward the bomber.

Gifford was the first to drop down to the ground. As soon as he was clear of the plane Cody fell into his arms.

"Pop! Oh, Pop!" Cody cried as he clung to his father.

"Let's get you aboard. C'mon." Giff helped his son toward the bomber.

SOG Team Alpha had formed a perimeter around the bomber. It wouldn't be long before they had company. Serbs soldiers were scattered all around the region and Frank figured they had no more than five minutes before some of them would show up. The flares would mark the exact spot where the enemy would attempt to rally toward.

Suddenly, automatic gun fire sounded from the edge of the woods.

A lone figure charged into the clearing...firing and screaming, "American! I will kill you! I will kill all of you!"

Cody and his father ducked low when a couple of rounds ricocheted off *Annie's* fuselage.

The man emptied his AK-47 at the men standing in front of the B-25 until his magazine was empty. Colonel Stefan Radic threw down the useless rifle, and pulled his pistol from his holster; the same pistol he had put to Cody's head. He charged forward, firing.

Cody pulled away from his father and limped/ran to the nearest M-14 carrying SOG team member.

"Give me that!" He tore the M-14 rifle from the hands of a surprised Gus Sanchez and limped toward his torturer.

"Here I am, Radic! This is for Perry!" Cody squeezed off five rounds. Four of them found their mark. Radic fell back, dead. Cody handed the weapon back to Gus. "Thanks, man. Thank you all."

Lieutenant Cody Bridger returned to his waiting father who helped him up into the plane. Gifford climbed up behind him and closed the bomb-bay doors.

"They're aboard and secure, Skipper. Let's get this lady rolling," Doc said as Gifford laid his son down on his gunnery couch and strapped him in.

"Roger that, Doc. Buck, lower the flaps all the way. I'm going to stand on the brakes until the engines reach full power. You handle the throttles, gear, and flaps. Ready?" Carl asked.

"On your command, Carl," Buck responded and lowered the flaps to their full down position.

"Now!" Carl said, and Buck pushed the throttles forward.

The extraction team stood back as the B-25's engines roared

into life. The deafening sound of the twin Double-Wasp engines increased to a screaming pitch as they strained to pull *Annie's Raiders* forward. Carl released the brakes, and her tires began to roll.

Blue flames licked at the nacelles as the engines strained to pull the aircraft through the grass that wanted to hold her tires down.

The bomber picked up speed. At fifty-miles-per-hour, Carl pulled back on the control yoke to lift the nose wheel out of the grass. "We've only got about two-hundred-fifty yards to get airborne and clear those trees ahead of us."

The trees seemed to march toward them like an army of not-so-jolly green giants. *Annie's* nose lifted up and her tail skid dropped to six inches above the ground. Carl could feel the main gear cutting through the grass more smoothly. *Oh, God, I don't think we're going to make it!* His mind screamed. At ninety-miles-per-hour, her mains lifted off and Buck Immediately pulled up the landing-gear lever. Carl pointed the bomber's nose to a point just barely above the tops of the trees.

"C'mon, *Annie*! Sprout wings, angel!" The stall-warning horn sounded, quit, and sounded again as the plane threatened to stall. Carl dropped the nose slightly to keep *Annie* from stalling, and the fuselage brushed the uppermost branches of the trees. As their airspeed climbed to a hundred-twenty mph, *Annie* settledinto a smooth climb.

Frank Pierce watched the B-25 rise above the trees and then called his men together to begin their journey west to Makarska.

Soldiers of the Republika Sprska walked into the clearing seven minutes later. Other than *Annie's* wheel depressions and the burnt leftovers of a few flares, all was calm.

CHAPTER XIV

"Gear up!" Carl released a rush of pent-up air.

Buck raised the landing gear followed by the flaps.

"Gear up and locked, Captain. Flaps up." Buck slapped Carl's back.

"That was too close. For a second there, I really didn't think we'd clear those trees." The General uttered a nervous "Whew!"

Annie's Raiders banked to a southwesterly heading, back into Croatian airspace.

"Plot me a course to Albania, Buck. Find an airport with AVGAS. We've got to find some way to hangar *Annie* so we can repair the rudder, she's really sluggish, and I don't want to lose rudder control when we're over the Adriatic. Montenegro is closer, but they're loyal to Serbia. We'll need to go further south."

Buck poured over the aeronautical charts for several minutes. He found what he was looking for: a small airport with run-

245

way lights, a tower, and available fuel.

"Here, at Tirana. They take general aviation and regional commuter planes. Call sign is Lima-Alpha-Papa-India. It's two-hundred -forty-nine miles, thereabouts, from Sarajevo."

Carl thought through Buck's recommendation.

"Albania is an independent democratic republic. Politically, they're about as close to Switzerland as they can be. They shouldn't have a problem with an American private plane landing there. Program Tirana into the GPS."

Buck set up the GPS for LAPI as the destination airport. A red line appeared on the screen and he set the Automatic Pilot to fly by the GPS heading.

"You've got the plane, Buck. I'll be in the back. Let me know when we're thirty miles out." Carl unbuckled his harness. His heart ached to embrace his grandson.

Cody was lying on his back talking to Giff and Doc. Harry sat on the other Gatling firing couch while Doc examined Cody's leg.

"How is he, Doc?" Carl asked, kneeling next to Cody's head. He kissed his grandson's forehead and rested his hand on his brow.

"I'm fine, Grandpa. Don't worry." Cody gently removed Carl's hand from his head.

Carl looked at Doc with concern.

"His leg seems to be healing. His toes are pink and warm, so circulation is good. That homemade splint may have saved his leg. I need to examine the rest of his body, but I can tell you he's had a tough time of it."

Carl nodded, relieved. "Can you stand a bite to eat?"

"Roger that, Grandpa! I could gnaw the paint off the fuselage. I don't suppose there's anything stronger than water to drink." He smiled up at Carl.

"Grandpa, I...I can't find the right words. When the B-25 came in low over the trees I knew it had to be you. I couldn't make sense of it at first. I thought I was hallucinating; it was all so...surreal. How did you ...?"

Carl smiled down at him. "Well, your dad and these guys made the whole thing possible. Doc here was my flight mechanic in the Pacific. Harry, the guy with the turban wrapped around his noggin was my gunner and radio man back in the day. Your father brought all of the resources of his company out to the Double-B and refitted *Annie* into one hell of a fighting machine. My co-pilot...well, you won't believe this...is General 'Buck' Rogers, the former astronaut."

"But why YOU, Grandpa? Why did any of you risk your lives?" You must have known you were more likely to get yourselves killed than pull off such a...an insane plan." His lip trembled and he turned his face away.

Carl realized that his grandson was still in shock from his ordeal, as well as mourning the loss of his friend.

"You get some rest, Cody. We'll talk later."

"No, it's okay ... I need to sit up." Cody wiped his eyes with the sleeve of his flight-suit. He visibly winced as Carl helped him sit up. "How about that chow?" He managed a sheepish grin.

Gifford handed Cody one of the last in-flight lunches they had stocked up on back at Aviano. He included a cold beer from the cooler.

Cody took a long swallow of beer and belched. "Oh, man! I think I've died and gone to heaven. Thanks, Pop." he grinned at his father, and took a huge bite of the club sandwich.

Carl turned toward the flight deck. "Well, I need to get back to the cockpit. We're landing in Albania, so let's get everything buttoned up back here. Doc, as soon as we find a hangar I need for you and Giff to look at the rudders and come up with some sort of fix. We'll stay there, get some fuel, and high tail it at first light." Carl worked his way back to the flight deck and strapped himself in.

Buck was relaxing. The auto-pilot was doing its job and all of the gauges were in the green.

"How's your grandson doing, Carl?"

"He'll be okay. Doc says he took quite a beating in that Serbian camp. He's got bruises all over and lacerations on his back. He's lost a lot of weight, too. The poor kid's been through hell. On top of that his best friend was murdered in front of his eyes. He's tough, though. I think he'll get through this in time." Carl glanced over the instruments and then looked at Buck. "How're you doing, partner? Ya need a break?"

"No, I'm fine. I think I'll kick back here with you, if you don't mind. I've got to tell you, old man; I've never been through anything that scary in my life. You, sir are one hell of a pilot."

Buck sat quietly watching the blue flames of the exhaust coming from the right engine and at the stars shining like jewels against the black night sky.

"What's next, Carl? Tomorrow we leave Albania and head out over the Adriatic Sea; then what?"

"That's the million-dollar question, my friend. We'll need to land and get Cody some medical attention. We could be in trouble with the Albanians or the Italians. Hell, we might still get shot down or intercepted and forced to land somewhere. I'm sure by morning the international press will have gotten wind of the mission. I don't know, Buck." Carl sighed. "We'll just wait and see what tomorrow brings."

As much as he was relieved that the immediate threat was over, the knot in his gut gave him a twist as he contemplated the risks that lie ahead. *I need Beth ... and home.* He fell quiet as his mind sought refuge in the safety and peace of the Double-B … and Beth.

They flew on for another fifteen minutes until they were thirty- miles from Tirana. Buck set the radio transmitter on Comm. 1 to the tower frequency at LAPI and pressed the talk button.

Lima-Alpha-Papa-India, Experimental four-zero-two-two-three-six is a twin engine type Bravo two-five. We are two seven miles north at seven-thousand inbound to land full stop.

Experimental two-two-three-six, this is Tirana tower. You are cleared VFR to land runway two-seven. Make left traffic and notify when a-beam the tower.

Make left traffic for runway two-seven. Will notify when a-beam the tower, experimental two-two-three-six, Carl read back the directions.

Annie's Raiders descended to one-thousand-five-hundred hundred feet. Through a thin haze of fog, the runway lights appeared as a line of diffused spots not much brighter than the ground-fog. Carl dropped to pattern altitude and flew parallel to the runway on a heading of ninety-degrees. He notified Air Traffic Control when the control tower appeared off his left wing. After completing her downwind leg *Annie* banked onto the base leg followed by another turn to line up her nose on the center-line for the final approach.

"Full flaps and lower the landing gear, Buck."

"Flaps full." He waited for the flaps to deploy before pulling the landing gear lever down. Two green lights flashed on.

"Gear down and locked."

The landing lights lit up the yellow-striped apron as Carl descended to twenty-feet over the runway. He pulled the throttles back to idle and let the bomber settle onto the surface. The main wheels touched down with a *squeak* and the nose wheel dropped onto the centerline.

He requested taxi instructions to general aviation for fuel and maintenance. Tirana Ground Control directed them to the All Albania Air hanger for maintenance and refueling.

When the plane rolled up to the hangar door, Carl and Buck shut down the engines. The crew and Cody climbed down to the tarmac and headed over to the hanger. Cody's arm was over his father's shoulder for support.

At 11 p.m. local time most activity at the airport had ceased for the day.

The door of the hangar rose up on its tracks. Activity in the hangar at that hour caused the crew to be wary. Carl motioned for the men to stay close to the plane in the event a hasty retreat was called for. A man, dressed in overalls, approached Carl and Buck. He held his hand out and smiled.

"I am Dren Hoxha. English is not so good. You are American, yes?" He spoke with a pleasant tone. "I hear on the radio. We listen to traffic. Welcome 'All Albania Air'. How I can help you, please?"

Doc stepped forward. "We need welding equipment, Mister Hoxha, perhaps some cable and aluminum skin. I will have to examine the damage to our airplane."

Dren Hoxha walked around the B-25 inspecting the bullet holes, the shattered Plexiglas on the rear gunner's enclosure, and the damaged rudder.

"You have been shot at, Americans. Your aircraft has been in a battle, yes? I must inform police of this."

"No, no, please don't do that." Carl moved closer to the man. "Dren, are you a friend to the Serbians?"

"No, I no like. Why you ask?"

"Because, a Serbian jet shot at us for flying over their borders. We did not know we were in their airspace until we were fired on. Please, do not report us to your police. We will be gone as soon as the sun rises in the morning. I promise." He waited for the man's response.

"No. I call police. They arrest me if I no call." He turned and walked quickly toward the hangar. Gifford walked after him. The rest of the crew followed along. Buck helped Cody toward the hangar.

Inside the hangar, a door led to an office. Over the door a sign read "All Albania Air" in blue letters. A red jet airliner between three broken red lines ran beneath the words. Dren walked to the desk to pick up the phone. Gifford stepped up behind him and put his hand on the phone. His other hand held a Sig Sauer 9mm. semi-automatic pistol.

"Sit down, Mister Hoxha," Gifford ordered. The Albanian did as he was told.

"Giff, what are you doing?" Carl was stunned.

"We have to tie him up, Pop. He was going to call the police."

Carl scanned the room and made a mental inventory of its contents. A cot with a pillow and blanket stood against one wall. He wondered if this man might be the night watchman or mechanic and if he was the only one scheduled to be here.

"Alright. Keep him still while I get something to tie him up with." He walked out into the hangar.

"What's up, Skipper?" Buck had helped Cody down onto an old office sofa while Doc was inspecting the damage to the '25.

"We've got trouble. Get *Annie* inside and close the big door." Carl frantically rummaged through some equipment on the shelves and workbenches until he found what he wanted: a roll of duct tape, and a coil of lightweight nylon rope. He gathered the items together and then hurried back to the office.

"Put him on the cot," Carl unraveled the rope .

Gifford directed Dren Hoxha with the barrel of his gun and the man sat down on the cot. Carl tied his feet together and ordered the complacent man to turn on to his side. He pulled Hoxha's feet up behind him and hog-tied them to his hands. He examined the mechanic's hands to be certain they were getting good blood flow.

Carl spoke in a calm, low voice. He needed the man to believe he was in no danger.

"Mister Hoxha, you are going to go stay on your bed until we are gone in the morning. I suggest you sleep as much as you can. Time will pass more quickly. When we are ready to leave, I will untie you and let you go. We only want to repair our airplane and leave. Do you understand?"

"Yes, I understand," he replied without protest.

The crew muscled the B-25 into the hangar with help from an electric-powered tow-tractor. Buck lowered the door while Doc finished assessing the damage.

Tying up the innocent mechanic left Carl with a sick feeling in his gut as though he had committed a criminal act. He left Gifford behind to watch after the man and joined Doc at the tail section where his old friend was examining the left rudder.

"Skipper, I think I can patch her up. The missile didn't cause any structural damage other than a twisted trim-tab. Quite a bit of the damaged fabric on the rudder was torn away by the wind but the frame is intact. I noticed a paint shop in the back of the hangar. I should be able to find some mercerized cotton and some dope. I can remove the trim tab and hammer out the dings. The spars are undamaged, so I'm sure I can reattach the trim-tab. It won't be pretty, but the aerodynamics of the rudder should be fine."

"Thanks Doc. Let's check out that paint shop." The two of them headed toward the rear of the hangar. Carl fumbled up and down the wall inside the door and found the light switch. Doc hurried over to a workbench. Hanging above was a roll of fabric.

"Look at this, Skipper! We just struck the mother lode! I found a roll of Ceconate and some dope and spray equipment, too." Doc laid the fabric out on the work bench and began measuring and cutting the desired amount of fabric for the rudder.

"I've got three heat lamps over here, Doc," Carl announced from across the room. "Let's get started. I'll ask Buck to give you a hand and get Gifford out here to help. You think the three of you can have *Annie* ready by daybreak?"

"We'll need a good four hours for the Ceconate to cure enough under the heat lamps to make it airworthy, but...sure, we can be ready to go by then."

"That's the best news I've heard since we landed." Carl headed toward the office.

"Cody, I need for you to keep an eye on the Albanian so your dad can help Doc and Buck." Carl walked over to the tied-up Albanian.

"Mister Hoxha...Dren. We need fuel. What is the octane rating of your AVGAS?" Carl asked.

"Fuel tanks are holding one-hundred and one-hundred-fifteen octane," Hoxha answered flatly.

"Good. Now, where is the key to the fuel truck parked next to the hangar?"

"You will not take fuel," Hoxha answered defiantly.

Carl pulled up a chair and sat down next to the Albanian. He leaned close and stared into his eyes with an intense expression.

"Understand, Mister Hoxha; we are not your enemy. We will pay you handsomely for everything we use to repair our aircraft, as well as for the fuel. If you would only help us, we will be gone before the sun rises. But with or without your help, we will take what we need. Now...please, Mr. Hoxha, where are the keys to the fuel truck and the pumps?"

The mechanic paused briefly. Carl hoped he would understand they meant him no harm. After a few moments he nodded.

"You untie and I help."

Hoxha's eyes revealed no deception. Carl had no choice but to trust him. The only alternative would be to coerce the man's

253

help, and he didn't want things to come to that point.

"Alright. I am going to untie you. But, one of my men will be with you at all times. Do you understand?" Carl nodded at Cody. The young man would be the designated baby sitter until *Annie's Raiders* was ready to go.

"I understand, American." He rolled on to his side so Carl could access his restraints. Once free he stretched and rubbed his wrists. He reached into an overall pocket and pulled out a large key ring with several keys attached. He showed Carl both the key to the fuel truck's ignition and the one to the pumps. "You show me what need you...what you need. Dren help."

"What octane fuel is in the truck's tank?" Carl asked, aware that mixing octanes of AVGAS could cause serious engine problems.

"The last time truck was filled was four days. It has half-full one-hundred-fifteen AVGAS. This is good?"

Carl nodded affirmatively. "This is very good. Come with me." He took Dren into the hangar. Doc had the trim tab on the bench, working it backinto shape with a small block of wood and a hammer.

"Doc, I have another pair of hands for you," Carl said. "Meet Mister Dren Hoxha. Mr. Hoxha, this is Doc."

Doc got right down to business. "Do you know how to re-cover the rudder with the Ceconate I saw in your shop, Mr. Hoxha?"

"Of course. I am master mechanic; most trusted for All Albania Air," he smiled, seemingly happy to have something to do.

"Good, then, you are my shop foreman." Doc explained what he needed and the Albanian went to work. With Gifford's help, they removed the damaged rudder panel and carried it to the paint shop where they stripped off the remains of the old olive-green fabric, removed all of the hardened glue and smoothed the edges of the spars which formed the skeleton of the rudder panel.

They used the panel as a template and cut the Ceconate to size. Hoxha applied glue to the spars of the rudder panel, and he and Doc carefully laid on the new fabric, brushing out the wrinkles as they stretched the fabric tight. They coated the fabric with dope, a plasticized lacquer which would stiffen the fabric and makes it airtight.

They hung heat lamps over the finished section for an hour and then flipped it over to repeat the process on the opposite side.

At 4:00 a.m.. the panel had cured enough to receive a coat of paint. At this, Hoxha was a master. He mixed yellow, blue, red paint to come up with a near perfect match for the olive green. He and Gifford hung the rudder panel by clamps tied to a line of rope. He sprayed on the paint mixture and did the same for the repaired trim tab.

Carl and Buck started the old '76 American built GMC with its five-thousand-gallon capacity fuel tank.

Buck put the truck in gear with much grinding of the transmission. Finally, he got the vehicle rolling and pulled up to the pumps. While Carl fiddled with the lock to the pump handle, Buck climbed onto the top of the truck's storage tank.

Carl pulled the lock free and handed the nozzle up to Buck who shoved it into the port on top of the tank. Carl attached the ground wire, lifted the supply lever and began transferring 115 octane aircraft fuel to the truck's tank. With the tank topped off, they secured the pump and headed back to the hangar.

Annie's Raiders received another bonus: A damaged Plexiglas windscreen to an All Albanian Air DeHaviland Beaver sat on the floor against a wall of the hangar. Upon examination, Doc did some measuring and determined enough of the windscreen was undamaged that he could cut a section of it out and shape it to replace the shattered section of the tail gunner's enclosure.

While the newly painted rudder dried under the heat lamps, Doc and Dren Hoxha fabricated the replacement Plexiglas panel and installed it into the aluminum frame where the busted panel used to be. Doc drilled some pilot holes for the original flathead bolts which he tightened down. The new panel was a serviceable match; ever so slightly more rounded on the surface than the old one, but a good match all things considered.

At 6:20 a.m. the repaired rudder panel and trim tab were reattached to the vertical stabilizer. The control cables were reconnected and Buck climbed into the cockpit to test the rudder with the foot pedals. He used the trim handle to adjust the rudder trim to the proper setting and then climbed down to the ground through the bomb-bay.

Carl sat at the desk in the AAA office with his "other" cell phone. He punched the call button, and the phone sent a signal via communications satellite to Mac Aldrin's phone. Mac picked up immediately.

"Mac here. Where the hell are you, Carl? Do you have the package?"

"Sorry I didn't call sooner, Mac. We've been a little busy here. Affirmative on the package. The perishable item is good. We are at Tirana airport in Albania. The time here is zero-six-twenty. Wheels up in ten minutes. We've stirred up a bit of a hornets' nest. We're going to need a safe escort home. Can you get us some air cover?"

"I'll do what I can. For now, you're on your own. Let me get busy pulling some strings. Mac out."

Carl pocketed the phone and walked out the door into the hanger. He didn't want to be on the ground when the business day began.

Buck was about to tell Carl that the plane was ready to go when the outside service door opened.

Abdyl Leka, the owner of All Albania Air liked to start his day early. At 5:30 a.m. he eased out of bed quietly so as not to disturb his wife Marina and shuffled to the bathroom of their cottage, a little less than two kilometers from Tirana Airport. He shaved, slapped on some expensive grass-oil scented after-shave lotion and dressed in a grey suit with grey and black striped tie. He kissed Marina on the forehead and walked out to his recently purchased Peugeot. He enjoyed the smell of the new saddle-colored leather seats. Looking into the rear view mirror, he straightened his tie, and backed down the dirt drive through the open gate.

While he drove, he turned on the radio to listen to the government news from AlbPress Informon for all of the latest propaganda. One news item caught his interest: The radio journalist reported that both Croatia and Serbia had registered separate complaints with NATO and the American Embassy in Belgrade that an unidentified vintage American aircraft, a B-25, had attacked a Croatian fighter-jet and a Serbian Army installation early the previous evening. Investigation revealed that the aircraft had been fired upon by the Croatian pilot and by the Serbian forces as well. The present location of the American aircraft remained unknown. The International Police (INTERPOL) would be investigating the incident. Abdyl thought: *Such an insane world we live in.*

He parked the Peugeot in his usual spot in front of the office to All Albania Air and climbed out of the car. He clicked the "lock" button on his key fob and smiled at the satisfying *chirp-chirp!* of the locking mechanism. The lights were on inside, but Dren was nowhere to be seen. He heard noises coming from the interior of the hangar and the sound of voices as well.

A man in a grey suit stood inside the door. He froze still as a statue. His face showed an expression of surprise at first, as his brain tried to reconcile what his eyes were telling him. Then, his expression changed. His eyebrows drew downward into a scowl and the shape of his mouth changed from an expression of wonder to one of grim determination...a lion protecting his territory. His eyes fell upon the vintage American B-25 and understanding changed his expression yet again.

"Dren, what in God's name is happening here? Who are these men? Why are they in my hangar? Call the police at once!" He yelled.

Leka marched toward Carl and the rest of the crew, his gaze settling on Cody and his blood stained U.S. Navy flight suit. The owner of All Albania Air puffed out his chest until it extended over his substantial belly and roared.

"You men are all under arrest! You are not allowed to leave here until the authorities arrive. You are the Americans who are sought by INTERPOL."

He actually believed that the crew of *Annie's Raiders* would stand by and patiently wait to be thrown into an Albanian prison. He fully intended to rush to his office and call the police. However, he was treated to an early nap courtesy of a lightning fast right cross from Cody.

Petty Officer Raymond Hill sat at his console in the communication center aboard CVN 72 when he received a "Flash" encrypted message from SECNAV (Secretary of the Navy). He quickly ran it through the decoding algorithm and removed the plain text printout. The message was coded "Eyes Only" for Vice Admiral Richard, C. Allen, COMNAVAIR, U.S. Navy 3rd Fleet. He placed the "SECRET" flagged message in a classified document folder and sealed it with "SECRET" stamped tape. When the message was ready for delivery, he called for the on duty Officer In Charge, Lieutenant William Needham.

"Lieutenant! I have a Flash priority message for the Admiral. It's 'Eyes Only', sir,"

Three minutes later, the Lieutenant stood in front of Admiral Allen on the Bridge of the Theodore Roosevelt. "Sir, we just received this 'Flash' message; your eyes only, sir."

"Thank you, Lieutenant. You're dismissed." Admiral Allen returned the young officer's salute and opened the sealed folder. The message was brief, urgent, and direct: "Launch support CIA Covert Ops extraction: Lt. C. Bridger. Location Lima, Alpha Papa India – Tirana. Aircraft is B-25. Pilot in Command is Carl Bridger. ETD from Tirana is 0630hrs."

The Admiral turned to the C.O. of the carrier, Captain Jason Phillips. "Jay, ready two Tomcats. Their destination is Tirana, Albania. I'll give you the details."

Captain Phillips turned to his counterpart, Captain Karl Messner, Commanding CVW-3, the Air Group currently deployed aboard the Theodore Roosevelt. Five minutes later, two F-14 Tomcats of Strike Fighter Squadron 49 catapulted from the deck and banked toward the Albanian coast.

"Let's get this door open and push her out boys. We've got to get out of Dodge before the posse gets here," Carl ordered.

Buck punched the button to the hangar door opener and joined the rest of the crew in pushing the bomber out to the tarmac. Dren Hoxha helped as well. Less than five minutes later they had the '25 out of the hangar and turned toward the taxiway.

Gifford tore a blank check from his check-book and scribbled All Albania Air on it. He filled in the payment amount for $10,000.00 and signed it.

Hoxha took the check, and looked at it.

"Ten-thousand American dollars? Mr. Leka will be most

259

happy. Is also good for Dren." He smiled, stuffed the check into the pocket of his overalls, and knelt by his unconscious boss.

"Climb aboard, boys. He's going to call the cops as soon as he wakes up." Carl looked at Abdyl Leka. He was stirring while Hoxha helped him up to a sitting position.

"Oh crap!" he exclaimed. "Buck, start the engines. I'm right behind you." Everyone scrambled aboard and Carl joined Buck in the cockpit. He raised the bomb-bay doors behind him.

"Turning one!" Buck called out. The left engine fired up with a cloud of white smoke.

"Turning two!" He yelled once again. The right engine started, and Buck matched the RPM settings for both engines.

Carl stuck his head out the opened sliding Plexiglas panel next to him and looked back toward the hangar. Both of the Albanian men were gone. Carl slid the panel closed. "I've got the controls, Buck."

"You have the controls, Captain." Buck read out the engine instruments to Carl: "Oil temp is in the green, manifold pressure and cylinder-head temp are green."

Carl eased the throttles forward and *Annie* started to roll.

"We're not calling the tower for clearance this time. We probably wouldn't get it, anyway. By now they've called the tower and the police."

The B-25 turned off one taxi way to another and headed toward the end of the runway at thirty miles per hour. Carl had to apply firm breaking power to make the turn toward the hold-short line. He brought the plane to a stop.

"Check right, Buck." Carl checked for traffic to the left. There were no aircraft in the traffic pattern, but at least a dozen blue flashing police lights off to the side at the end of the runway spelled trouble. "Damn! We have company."

"You're clear on the right, Carl. Let's get this bird off the ground."

Annie's Raiders rolled onto the active runway, and Carl turned her nose toward the blue flashing lights which were no longer off to the side of the runway. They were assembling themselves three abreast. The line of police cars started toward them as Carl added power.

"Give me full flaps, Buck. Here they come!" Carl added power and moved the throttles all of the way forward. *Annie's* nose lifted slightly and she started her takeoff roll.

"Flaps full, captain."

The B-25 accelerated to fifty, then sixty-miles-per-hour. The police cars accelerated in a suicidal game of chicken. *Annie's Raiders* was committed. She couldn't stop now if Carl wanted her to.

Seventy-miles-per-hour and the airspeed indicator climbed...eighty.

At eighty-five-miles-per hour with full flaps and the police cars coming straight at them, there was only one thing they could do:

"Rotate!" Carl yelled as he pulled back on the yoke. *Annie's* nose lifted off the runway. The lead police cars slammed on their brakes and skidded sideways as *Annie's* main landing gear lifted off. The last Doolittle Raider was clear, missing the cars by no more than four feet.

Sitting in the tail-gunners enclosure, Harry got an up-close view of several frightened faces staring up at *Annie's Raiders* as she roared over their heads.

Annie increased her speed to a positive rate and Buck raised the gear followed by the flaps. Carl toggled down the landing light switches.

"That's about four near heart attacks for me, Carl; how about you?" Buck released a sigh of relief.

"I'm not sure we're out of the woods yet." He banked *Annie* west toward the coast of Albania.

"Ten minutes and we'll be clear of their airspace. Then, I

261

guess we'll find out if the Italians are friendlier than the Serbs. If INTERPOL is hunting for us, I don't think any place is safe. We're likely not to get home for quite a while...if ever." *Please, God ...* he prayed silently ... *help us to safety.*

Buck looked across at Carl with an expression of resignation.

"Well, this has been one hell of a ride, partner. I'm glad you let me come along." He managed a faint smile.

"All we can do is fly the plane, Buck. Our fate is in some-one else's hands now. To quote the wisdom of Yogi Berra, 'It ain't over 'til it's over.'" He smiled back at Buck.

Carl turned his mic switch to the intercom. "Mic check boys. How's everyone doing?"

"Doc here, Skipper. Still kickin'."

"Giff and Cody are good, Pop."

"Harry is snug as a bug, Skipper. The patch is holding. I can see the rudder from here and it's holding up fine, too."

"Copy that, Harry. Hey, how's the old football doing?"

"Doing good. No worries. Oh, guess what, Skipper?

"What, Harry?"

"I got a close-up look at the faces of the police back there. I've never seen such a scared bunch of rabbits in my life. I even gave them a good-bye wave." He laughed.

Carl and Buck laughed, their spirits momentarily lifted.

"Good man, Harry. Boys, the tanks are full, so we can make it all of the way, and ..."

Carl was interrupted by two old swept-wing Russian built MiG-17s, bearing the red and black roundel of the Albanian Air Force, easing up on either side of the B-25.

American aircraft. Turn around immediately and return to Tirana, the pilot on Carl's side demanded.

Negative, Albanian Fighter. No can do, Carl replied.

American Aircraft, turn around immediately or you will be fired on.

The pilot of the Albanian jet fired a warning burst of 37mm cannon fire to emphasize his point.

The 1960s era fighters dropped back to get into firing position. Before they could roll into attack formation, two other jets approached dead ahead and flashed by the B-25.

Buck craned his neck. "Holy crap, Carl. Did you get a look at them?"

"Only a glimpse. Couldn't tell whose they were." Carl held *Annie* steady.

Bravo two-five. This is Lieutenant Commander Thomas Boyd, United States Navy. Can we be of service?

Affirmative, Commander. You are a welcome sight! A pair of Albanian bogeys wants to splash us into the Adriatic, Carl explained.

We're here to keep that from happening, sir. Stay on this frequency, and enjoy the show. There was a short pause followed by Commander Boyd's voice:

Albanian fighter planes, we are two United State Navy F-14s. Would you like to engage? Over. The Albanian pilots didn't respond, and the MiGs remained in formation.

Albanian fighters, break off now unless you want to dance. We are carrying a pair of Sidewinders waiting to make your acquaintance. Over.

The two Albanian jets turned back toward Tirana without further ado.

Captain, the bogeys are heading for home. I'm coming up off your left wing, sir.

A Navy F-14 Tomcat eased up alongside *Annie's Raiders.* His wingman performed a similar movement on Buck's side.

Captain, I'm Lieutenant Morgan Mills on your right wing. Congratulations on your successful recovery of Lieutenant Bridger. How's he doing?

He's well, albeit banged up a bit. I'm his grandfather, Carl Bridger. Lieutenant Bridger's father Gifford Bridger is also aboard, Carl announced.

Wait one, please Captain, Commander Boyd said. A minute later he came on the comm. again.

Captain, can you patch Lieutenant Bridger in...and the rest of your crew as well? Boyd requested.

Done, you're live and on the air, Commander, Carl affirmed.

Cody, Tom Boyd. How are you, Lieutenant?

I'm good to go, Commander. I'm glad to hear your voice, sir. Cody was all smiles.

Okay. Here's what we're going to do: We want to take you all aboard the Theodore Roosevelt. You need to be in the right seat to set Captain Bridger up for the approach. Do you think you're up for this?

I think so, Commander. From what I've seen my grandpa...er, I mean Captain Bridger is one hell of a pilot, sir.

Roger that. Captain Bridger do you think you can manage a carrier landing in that old bucket? Tom Boyd asked.

I sure as hell am willing to give it a shot, Commander. Can you give me seven hundred feet?

Affirmative. We've cleared the deck for you, Captain. You're going to have one of our best carrier pilots next to you. Just trust what he tells you, sir, and you'll be fine. Take your position, Lieutenant and follow us.

Buck moved back to the bomb-bay, and Cody tried to lift his splinted right leg over and around the throttle quadrant, but got stuck.

"Damn! Grandpa, give my foot a shove to the right, will you?"

Carl lifted Cody's foot into the rudder pedal well and the younger Bridger managed the rest of the way. After much grunting and an "ouch" or two, he fastened himself into the right seat.

Carl noticed Cody's grim expression. *He's hurting more than he's letting on,* he thought.

"How's the gimpy leg doin', kiddo?"

"Ache's a little, but okay otherwise. Doc says the bones are lined up fine and I should get back full function." Cody smiled at his grandfather.

"Don't worry about me, Grandpa. I'm good to go."

"Boy, you are one of the toughest men I've ever known, and that includes the guys in this plane."

"Thanks. That means more to me than you'll ever know." Cody smiled.

"Okay, Grandpa, I'm going to give you a crash course on carrier landing. Well, maybe *'crash'* isn't the best word," Cody chuckled at his own joke, and then his expression became more serious.

"I still can't believe I'm sitting here with you. Yesterday at this time I was sitting in the Pavlovec cottage." Cody patted Carl's knee. "I love you, Grandpa. I wish Grandma Annie could see us all up here."

"She does, Cody...she does," Carl whispered. He smiled at his grandson . "All right, let's figure out how to get this plane on the deck of an aircraft carrier."

"Right. First, it's all done by a system of lights called the Optical Landing system. As we line up on our approach, a row of green DATUM lights will appear toward the front of the deck. They're your reference point showing your relative position to the glide slope. Think of them as you would the horizon line on your attitude indicator. The most important lights, nicknamed the 'Meatball' or simply 'Ball' will drift above the green lights if your approach is high, and will drop beneath the green lights if your approach is below the glide slope. If your glide slope is good, the ball lights won't be visible. Are we good so far?" Cody paused.

"Yeah, we're good; green lights for the glide slope and yellow ball lights for our position above or below the glide slope. Keep going." Carl's mind was processing a visual image of the approach.

"Okay. The Landing Signal Officer will guide us in until we are about three quarters of a mile out. If we are on the glide slope he will say something like: 'B-25, call the ball.' I'll say, 'Ball, B-25.' At that point the LSO will not talk. It's all us from there. Oh, by the way; if something happens to throw us off the glide slope, the LSO will turn the yellow lights to red. That's your sign to add full power and go around. You can't hesitate. When the LSO says *Wave-off!* You have to go around," Cody paused again.

"Wave-off...red lights. I've got it...I think." Carl's stress level shot up at the thought of trying to land on the short, pitching deck of an aircraft carrier.

Captain, we are one-five miles out. Please turn your comm. to one-two-seven-point-two-five now and squawk ident, Commander Boyd directed.

Carl dialed 127.25 on comm.2 and pushed the "ident" button. Aboard the Theodore Roosevelt, a blip on the LSO's radar screen brightened.

Army B-25, this is the Theodore Roosevelt. We have you one-zero-point-four miles out. Descend and maintain six- hundred-fifty-feet and turn to heading two-niner-five degrees.

Descending to six-five-zero feet. Turning to two-niner-five degrees. Army B-25.

Carl dropped to the assigned altitude and reduced his speed to one-hundred-twenty mph and lowered *Annie's* flaps to one quarter.

Army B-25, do not acknowledge from this point. I

*am your LSO. Please comply with my orders forthwith. You
are below the glide path.*

Carl checked his altimeter. It had dropped to six-hundred-
feet. He added power and brought the bomber's nose up slightly.
The deck of the carrier swayed to and fro ahead of him and he
played the rudder pedals to keep the ship centered at the bottom of
the wind screen.

*You're left. You are on glide slope. Come right,
Captain...Good. You're on the glide slope.*

The green DATUM lights showed him on the correct glide
path with two miles to go. He laid in full flaps and set his final approach speed to one-hundred-ten miles per hour.

*You're a little high, drop your nose; good. You are
on the glide slope,* the LSO coaxed the B-25.

At three-quarters of a mile out, *Annie's Raiders* was lined
up for landing.

Three-quarters of a mile. Call the ball.

Ball, Army Bravo two-five! Cody affirmed.

"Hold it steady...steady...almost there," Cody said.

A sudden gust of wind pushed the bomber right, toward the
Theodore Roosevelt's island.

Wave-off! Wave-off! The Landing Signal Officer ordered.

Cody jammed the throttles to full power and Carl banked
hard left. The B-25 skimmed over the deck with engines screaming.
Carl held her in a left bank and entered a cross wind leg for another
approach. He climbed to one-thousand feet and turned downwind
parallel to CVN-71.

*Army B-25, welcome to carrier landing school. You
handled the wave-off like a pro. The people on the bridge
got quite a thrill.*

The LSO had a way of settling a pilot's frazzled nerves.

Wave- offs happen frequently as any carrier pilot

The Last Raider

can attest to, Captain, but they are always a nerve-racking experience.

We're going to try this again, Captain. Are you game? The LSO quipped.

Hell yes, I'm game. I'm not gonna let a little chocolate in my shorts bother me.

Alright, then turn to two-niner-zero degrees. Descend and maintain six-five-zero feet. Do not acknowledge any further transmissions.

Carl set his approach speed at 110 mph and dropped his landing gear. He laid in full flaps and lined up on the carrier.

You are on the glide slope. You're doing fine. On glide slope. Three-quarter mile, call the ball.Ball, Army bravo two-five, Cody confirmed.

Carl lined up on the center line of the eleven hundred foot deck of CVN-71. The wave-off had left him shaken, and his heart was beating like a jackhammer in his chest. *Annie* was holding at one-hundred mph when her nose reached the deck. *Get it right...get it right* he admonished himself as he pulled the throttles back to idle and the main gear touched down. Carl immediately applied brakes and brought the old Doolittle Raider to a full stop fifty-feet from the end of the deck.

Captain, please follow the signalman to parking and remain in the aircraft until given permission to deplane. Well done, Captain and welcome aboard the Theodore Roosevelt

The B-25 was directed to a parking stall off to the right side of the deck just in front of the ship's island. Carl killed the engines and glanced out his windscreen.

"Hey, Cody, some folks are forming a welcome home committee for you."

Indeed, hundreds of officers and enlisted men began assembling in organized columns in front of the island. A few senior officers stepped on deck adorned in their Navy dress whites.

Captain, you have permission to deplane, the LSO announced.

Doc was the first to set his feet on the deck of the Theodore Roosevelt, followed by Harry, and Buck.

Giff helped Cody down the ladder to the deck, and as soon as Cody stepped from under *Annie's Raiders* into full view of the men and officers of CVN-71, the assembled ship's band began to play the Navy hymn "Eternal Father, Strong to Save."

Carl was the last man to leave the B-25. He walked behind the rest of his crew. He was not a man given to accolades; preferring instead to stand in the shadows.

The crew of *Annie's Raiders* stopped walking and watched Cody as he let go of his father and limped toward Admiral Allen and the Air Group Commander, Captain Messner.

Cody snapped a smart salute. "Sir, Lieutenant Bridger requests permission to come aboard."

"Welcome aboard, Lieutenant," a smiling Vice Admiral Allen returned the salute.

"Son, you should go below and clean up. This corpsman will help you." He nodded to a Petty Officer standing by the hatch. "Be on deck in thirty-minutes in your whites," Captain Messner ordered. "Welcome home, Lieutenant."

Admiral Allen whispered something to Captain Phillips, the Commanding Officer of the carrier. The Captain stepped to the microphone.

"Ship's company! At ease!" The assembled ship's crew relaxed their stance and waited, talking quietly among themselves. The Admiral motioned for the B-25s crew to join him and the ship's senior officers at the review stand.

"Crew of the Theodore Roosevelt," Captain Phillips began.

"These men standing before you represent the finest traditions of honor among brothers and patriotism toward and for The United States of America. Where others failed to act, they took action to rescue from the hands of a vicious oppressor one of our own airmen, Lieutenant Cody Carl Bridger. I would like to introduce them to you now." Gifford stepped forward. Captain Phillips shook his hand. "Mister Gifford Bridger, Lieutenant Bridger's father. Standing next to him is someone everyone in this company will recognize, Former Apollo astronaut and retired Air Force Brigadier General Buckminster 'Buck' Rogers."

A cheer rose from the deck as over a thousand men and women shouted and whistled their respect for Buck.

"These next two men, Harry Osborne; Harry come on over here, and Edward 'Doc' Henreid are former B-25 crew members of World War II. Both of these men saw action in Formosa, the Philippines and much of Southeast Asia. They volunteered their services to be a part of this daring rescue because of a simple phone call from an old friend; their former skipper and pilot, Mister Carl Bridger, Lieutenant Bridger's grandfather.

"It was Mister Bridger who first conceived the rescue operation and who, with the rest of his magnificent crew, and against all odds, carried off one of the most heroic rescue operations in the history of modern aviation. Mister Bridger, I'm sure that the entire crew would like to hear from you."

Carl stepped in front of the microphone. He cleared his throat.

"Uh...Um...Well, I guess we wouldn't be here if it wasn't for all of you...thank you." He cleared his throat again.

"I would like to thank Admiral Allen and the Navy Department for bringing us all home safely. Most of all, I...we all, thank you men and women, every one of you who breathe life into this vessel. Without you, the Theodore Roosevelt wouldn't be the symbol of freedom that she is in the north Atlantic and throughout Europe. Thank you all."

Carl's final "thank you" brought another roar of cheers and whistles.

Admiral Allen was on a roll as he filled time while Cody was changinginto his whites.

"Finally, I will ask General Rogers to say a few words, but before he begins, I'd like to ask him; how on earth does a former astronaut and retired Brigadier General get himself tangled up with these rascals and set out to break countless international laws all for the sake of saving the life of someone he doesn't even know?" The Admiral relinquished the microphone to the General.

Buck stood silent for a moment as his eyes panned the sailors in front of him .

"It was the right thing to do." He paused and waited for the cheers and applause to settle down before he continued.

"Hell, I never knew any of these boys before two weeks ago except Gifford Bridger. Now that I do know them, I feel most fortunate, indeed, to call them my friends. As for doing what we did...why hell, Admiral, that's what friends do for each other, isn't it?" Buck stepped back from the microphone, and the ship's band struck up a rendition of the Air Force song "Wild Blue Yonder."

Cody walked on deck sporting a set of crutches. Gifford and Carl looked at him; hearts swollen with pride and tears in their eyes. Buck, Doc, and Harry also had broad grins on their faces. Doc began clapping his hands, and he was soon joined by the rest of the crew of *Annie's Raiders.*

The sailors joined in the applause and the whistles and cheers turnedinto a stadium sized roar of approval. Admiral Allen waited until the noise subsided before motioning to Captain Phillips to call the crew to order.

"Attention on deck. Ah-ten-hut! Attention to orders. Lieutenant Cody Carl Bridger, step forward, please." Cody stepped forward and saluted his superior officers while he held the crutches with his free hand.

Captain Phillips removed the microphone from the podium and held it for Admiral Allen as the Chief of Naval Air Operations, U.S. Navy 3rd Fleet got down to the business at hand.

"Lieutenant Bridger, with gallantry and heroism before an enemy, you put yourself in harm's way to protect your friend and fellow officer Lieutenant JG Perry Judd from the severe beating and torture that you willingly and courageously endured. You acted with bravery and valor in the finest traditions of the United States Navy. It is my most sincere honor to present you with this third highest medal for valor that any sailor can receive; the Navy and Marine Corps Medal."

Admiral Allen pinned the blue, red, and gold ribbon with its gold octagon-shaped medal on Cody's chest. He then stepped back and saluted the young Navy pilot.

CHAPTER XV

Mac Aldrin sat across from the Secretary of the Navy H. William Memmot. He spoke to Carl from Tirana earlier, and called the Secretary's aide immediately after to inform him that he was on his way to Memmot's office to discuss a high security matter. He hung up before the aide could do what he did best; make excuses and lie to avoid inconveniencing his boss.

"Mister Secretary, thank you for taking time from your busy schedule to see me, sir," Mac began. He felt little love for most D.C. bureaucrats, but Memmot was former Navy himself. As SECNAV, he had a record for pushing hard to continue funding of the Navy at its current level during a time when downsizing the military was high on the agenda of both the President and Congress. As a result, he had the respect of every man who wore the uniform.

"Is this concerning our missing Navy flier?" The SECNAV asked.

"Yes sir, it is. He is safe. Sir we need to act fast to stop the ship carrying the ransom shipment to the Serbians from reaching port. She is only a few hours away from Hamburg," Mac said.

"I'm aware. We've been tracking her since you told me of

your plan to rescue the Lieutenant. The U.S.S. Greenville's on-station. Hold one second."

Mac waited as the SECNAV picked up his phone to the Pentagon. Admiral Peter Kensington, the commander of the Navy's Atlantic submarine fleet (COMSUBLANT) picked up after two rings.

"Admiral Kensington here, Mister Secretary. How are you doing this morning, sir?"

"I'm fine, thanks. Pete, Is the Greenville still in international waters?"

"Yes, but she's hugging the border."

"Good. She needs to make herself visible and turn the *Hvesda Severu* around. Our officer is out of danger."

"Aye, aye, Sir. I'll issue the order to the Greenville forthwith. Goodbye, Mister Secretary."

The Navy Secretary placed his phone on the hook and looked stoically at Mac.

"A United States attack submarine is about to surface somewhere in the North Atlantic and force a civilian foreign registered cargo ship to heave-to while she is boarded by United States Navy personnel, whereupon she will be diverted to a port other than her planned port of call. Mac, you and I are going to take a ride over to the White House where you will have the pleasure of briefing the President. I figure we have about twenty minutes before the first word reaches the press."

Mac nodded, stood and offered his hand to the Secretary of the Navy. "Mister Secretary, I know, as you are well aware, sometimes it's easier to do the right thing first and then ask for forgiveness later. In this case, I think the President will recognize this as an opportunity to improve his ratings in the polls. I can see the headlines: 'U.S. President risks international ridicule to save downed American airman.' The West Wing is going to grab on to

this as 'manna from heaven' goinginto an off-year election." …
and I hope to hell I'm right. Mac swallowed back the sour taste of
bile that had risen in his throat from the stress and worry of the last
few days.

The SECNAV chuckled. "Agreed. Never underestimate a
politician's nose for a press opportunity. Let's get going."

Beth Thomlinson rolled over and looked at the clock on her
nightstand. "Five-thirty. May as well get up, Beth. You can worry
about him over a cup of coffee," she said to herself. She hadn't had
more than three hours of sleep, knowing that Carl and his friends
were in the thick of things. The aroma of the freshly-brewed coffee
awakened her appetite as she poured herself a cup-full and checked
the time on the clock by the kitchen table. "It must be eleven thirty
where you are, Carl. Why haven't you called?" Only the kitchen
walls heard her frustrated plea.

Beth picked up the T.V. remote and turned to the Great Falls
Fox news affiliate. A peppy twenty-something brunette was doing
her best to sound like a meteorologist while striking her Miss Montana pose for the camera. As a weather girl she was okay, but Beth
decided she probably wouldn't be sitting at the network anchor
desk anytime soon. With a final toothy grin, she turned the time
over to the talking heads.

*Dan, this strange story is just in from the Eastern
Mediterranean. N.A.T.O authorities and the American Embassy in Belgrade have received reports that an American
World War II era warplane has shot down a Croatian
fighter jet and attacked a Serbian stronghold outside Sarajevo. Details are unclear as to the accuracy of the report
or the reason for the bizarre attack. We'll keep you informed as we receive updates. Again, an American...*

Beth's heart seemed to stop in her chest. "Oh, dear Lord! Carl!" She searched some other channels for more information, but got nothing new. The rest of the news was the usual local fare, but Beth mentally tuned out all of the community interest stuff that dominated the local news media.

Pacing the kitchen, her mind was frantic with worry. *Where are you, Carl, honey. Are you alive? Please...please; I've got to know.* The incessant thoughts were maddening.

A glance at the clock told her it was time to shower and get dressed for the day. Relieved to have something to take her mind off the news broadcast, she looked forward to the diner where the routine of taking orders and talking to the locals was better than wringing her hands and contending with the knot or worry that had formed in her stomach. She walked back to her bedroom and un-plugged her cordless phone charger, carried the phone to the bath-room and plugged in the charger next to the vanity, so she wouldn't miss any calls while she was in the shower.

She opened the shower door and turned on the water just as her phone jingled its familiar ring tone. She ran to the phone and reached for it. Her hand paused. *What if it's bad news?* She swallowed, drew in a deep breath, and lifted the phone to her ear.

"Hello, this is Beth," she answered, trying to sound calm.

"Beth, sweetheart, it's me." The voice had a faint echo and came to her over a steady background flow of static, but she im-mediately recognized Carl's voice

"Oh Carl, thank God it's you! Are you alright? Where are you? Are you in jail somewhere? Oh, sweetheart, are you hurt?" Her mind was awash with questions and pent-up worry.

"Beth...honey...Beth, calm down. I'm fine. Everybody's fine. We got him, Beth. We got Cody. He's here with us. We're all safe. Beth, listen to me. I 'm only allowed two minutes on this call. I'm at sea aboard a U.S. Navy aircraft carrier. I'm coming home, sweetheart. I love you, Beth. I'll call again when I have more information."

"I'm...I'm so happy. I don't know if I can talk without crying, Carl. Just hurry home, darling. Ruth's banana cream pie is waiting for you, sweetheart. Bye."

Beth hung up and sat down. She remained motionless, on the edge of the bed, trying to catch her breath. A tremor shook her body, and she brought her hands to her face and wept. Sobs of joy and released tension flooded over her. She wept until she could weep no more.

Finally, she wiped her eyes and stepped in front of the bathroom mirror. She dabbed at her tear-stained cheeks with a face cloth. A grin forced its way onto her face. She folded her right hand into a fist and pumped it high into the air and yelled..."YES!"

Carl hung up the phone, thanked the Petty Officer who handled the satellite connection, and left the communications center to return to his quarters. The officer's berth he was assigned to was the same one previously occupied by CIA SOG Team Alpha leader Frank Pierce. Harry and Doc bunked next door to Carl. Gifford shared the room with his father, but the InterDyn CEO was in a meeting with the brass; presumably having to do with the two shipping containers.

As for Buck, Carl assumed he was sharing stories with Vice Admiral Allen. He lay back on his bunk and indulged himself with a rare few minutes of rest and introspection. His thoughts turned to Beth. Hearing her voice on the phone had lifted his spirits and caused his heart to yearn for home. He dozed off and found himself dreaming about being with Beth at her place in front of the fireplace when a loud knock at his door awakened him. He opened the door to find a Marine Corps MP filling the narrow space.

"Excuse the interruption, sir. The Admiral and Captain Phillips would like for you and your crew to join them in the Captain's mess for lunch," the MP said in a cordial tone. I'll show you the way, sir."

"Thank you, Lance Corporal. I'll get the men," he said sleepily. He yawned and shook himself awake.

"No need, sir. They're already there," the MP smiled in a way that made Carl think the corporal knew something he didn't.

Hel followed the Marine to the Captain's mess. The Marine rapped on the door and Captain Phillips opened it.

"Mister Bridger! Come in sir. Come in." He stepped aside and Carl entered the room. Everyone was there, including Admiral Allen and Cody. He couldn't help but wonder why he was the last to be summoned.

Everyone in the room stood and began to sing; *Happy Birthday to you. Happy Birthday to you...*Carl was dumbfounded. The men before him stepped aside to reveal a cake with a hastily iced replica of a B-25 and the words *Happy 70th* scrolled on it.

"Gifford told us your birthday was two days ago, but we thought, as long as we're celebrating your successful rescue mission...well, why not make a birthday party of it as well. Happy birthday, sir," Captain Phillips said, and shook Carl's hand.

Everyone sat around the table, while the ship's kitchen staff started bringing in food. Lunch began with a savory New England Clam Chowder followed by brazed salmon with asparagus. White wine and beer were offered. For dessert—Carl's birthday cake; a moist white cake with raspberry filling and a powdered sugar icing with a hint of lemon flavoring.

After the impromptu birthday lunch, the table was cleared and Admiral Allen tapped his beer bottle.

"Gentlemen, the smoking lamp is lit." He lit up a cigar, sat back and blew a perfect smoke ring into the air.

"Now, then; we need to get down to the business of keeping the Atlantic third fleet from running afoul of someone's fishing boat out here, so let's discuss getting you boys home. Captain Phillips?"

The Commanding Officer of CVN-71 cleared his throat.

"Gentlemen, the 'Big Stick'was deployed to the Red Sea in support of Operation Southern Watch. Two days ago we were diverted to the Adriatic ostensibly to provide increased U.S. presence in support of the U.N. no-fly zone under 'Operation Deny Flight.' We also took aboard a special team of CIA Special Ops people. You've already experienced firsthand the nature of their role in the safe extraction of Lieutenant Bridger.

"We need to keep you safe and in American hands until you're back on U.S. soil. The Theodore Roosevelt is under orders to return to the Red Sea. So, let me ask you, Mister Bridger...Carl. How would you like to perform another carrier landing, this time on the Navy's newest Nimitz class carrier, the U.S.S. John Stennis?"

"Another carrier landing? I never would have tried a landing here if not for Cody. That's about the scariest thing I've ever done." Carl spoke with hesitation.

"I understand. Lieutenant Bridger is on sixty-day recuperative leave as of now. We want him to fly with you and your crew to the John Stennis. She's undergoing sea trials right now in the Atlantic. The plan is to get you within range to launch *Annie's Raiders*. We will reach the Straits of Gibraltar in two days. You will launch from there. The John Stennis will be on station south of the U.K. not more than one-thousand miles away, well within the fuel range of your aircraft."

"Whew! This must be the craziest sea operation in the history of the Navy." Carl looked at Harry, Doc, Gifford, and finally Buck. "Are you guys up for this?"

"Hell yes, Skipper; no sense breaking up a team that's

worked for almost fifty years." Harry chuckled.

Doc smiled his approval. "I'm in."

"You owe me another ride on Lucy, pal. I'm with you all the way to the Double-B," Buck said.

Carl smiled at his friends, nodded his approval and gratitude and turned to Gifford. "Gifford...Cody, let's go home boys."

A group of eight seamen towed the bomber to the end of the flight deck and pointed her nose upwind. The crew boarded, and Buck raised the bomb-bay doors.

Carl opened the sliding Plexiglas panel, leaned his head out the opening and called, "turning one!" The left engine fired up and settled into a warm-up idle.

"Turning two!" he yelled. With both engines warming up, he turned his eyes toward the ship's island. Standing beneath the huge white "CVN-71" insignia, Admiral Allen stood watching. Carl threw him a salute and held it. Admiral Allen stood at attention and snapped a return salute. Carl slid the panel closed.

"Fifty-percent flaps, Buck," he said. "Taking off should be easier than landing...no pitching deck to worry about."

"One-half flaps. Roger that, my friend. My fighter is used to long cement runways. I don't know how these Navy jet jockeys do this every day." The whine of the flap servos lasted for about five seconds and then stopped.

"Brakes on?"

"Brakes on."

Carl eased the throttles open to full and called out, "Release brakes."

Buck released the brakes, and the B-25 started her takeoff roll. The last time old 40-2236 took off from the deck of an aircraft carrier was forty-eight years earlier when she and sixteen others of her kind lifted off the U.S.S. Hornet to bomb military targets in Tokyo.

At ninety miles-per-hour, Carl lifted *Annie's* nose, dropping the tail skid almost to the deck. With plenty of room to spare, the B-25s main wheels rotated in-to the warm blue Mediterranean sky.

"Set a course for the Straits of Gibraltar, Buck. The Roosevelt was nice enough to stock the cooler with beer and sandwiches. Do you want one?"

"Sure. Why don't you sit and I'll get the goodies." Buck worked his way back to the bomb-bay where he found Doc, Gifford and Cody sitting down to a card game.

"Could you use a fourth, fellas?" Buck asked.

"Sure thing, General. Take a seat." Doc scooted over to make room for Buck.

"How's Harry doing, Doc?" Buck sat on the edge of the firing couch.

"Oh, Harry's fine. He's back there in his cubby hole reading a novel. I'll check on him again in about an hour."

He looked at Cody as Gifford dealt each player five cards. Cody met Buck's eyes. The youngest Bridger's eyes were clear and steady. But, Buck saw something deep behind them that spoke of pain and sorrow. His was the gaze of one who had lived the hell of war and returned out of the cold clutches of death to live again; to grieve, to love, to weep, to laugh. That he wanted to return to flight status and continue to defend his country as a U.S. Navy aviator, Buck realized, was a testament to his courage, to his patriotism, and to his honor. The General respected the young pilot's strength.

"How are you feeling, son?" He asked.

"Fine. A lot cleaner than I was the last time I was in here with you guys," he smiled back at Buck. "I still can't believe that you all signed on with Dad and Grandpa to come and get me. I only wish..." Cody tried to focus on his cards. His eyes teared-up, notwithstanding.

"You wish we could have gotten to you before they killed your friend?" Buck finished Cody's thought.

Cody nodded his head and brushed the back of his hand over his eyes. "Perry would have liked you guys.Well, let's play some poker; what do you say?" He smiled weakly.

Half an hour later, Buck joined Carl in the cockpit. He handed him a beer and a sandwich and buckled himself into his harness.

"That's a fine grandson you have there, Carl. I see a lot of you in him."

Four-and-a-half hours later, *Annie's Raiders* skimmed over the calm waters of the Atlantic a hundred-fifty miles south of the Dingle Peninsula and the Cliffs of Moher which make up the geography of Ireland's southern coast. If everything was in order, the U.S.S. John Stennis should be steaming toward them. Buck turned the frequency dial of comm.1 to CVN-74's air operation's frequency 119.25MHz.

November-Juliet-Charlie-Sierra, Army four-zero-two-two-three-six. Do you copy?

Carl waited for a moment, but got no response.

November-Juliet-Charlie-Sierra this is Army four-zero-two-two-three-six, we are one-zero-zero miles south at four- thousand. Heading three-five-zero degrees. Do you copy, over?

Still, no answer.

"Buck, double-check the frequency will you? We can't be more than ninety miles out."

"I read one-one-niner point-two-five," Buck confirmed.

"We must be on the wrong frequency. They should..." Before Carl could finish, the John Stennis responded.

Army two-two-three-six, this is the John Stennis. Do

you copy; over?

Roger, John Stennis, Army four-zero-two-two-three-six. You are five-by-five.

Army two-two-three-six, Roger. Captain you are on the main communications channel. Please turn to one-one-niner-point-two-seven-five for flight operations.

Buck dialed comm. 2 to the assigned frequency, and Carl called in:

November-Juliet-Charlie-Sierra, this is Army two-two-three-six, over.

Army two-two-three-six we read you now. Turn transponder to two-four zero-two and ident.

Buck dialed the numbers into the transponder and pressed the "ident" button.

We have you on radar, captain. Descend and maintain two-thousand, and turn to heading three-three-zero degrees.

Turn to three-three-zero degrees, descend and maintain two-thousand, Carl confirmed.

Captain, I understand Lieutenant Cody Bridger is aboard?

Roger that. Lieutenant Bridger is aboard.

Very good. Please direct him to take the right seat. Captain, this is going to be a repeat of what you did on the Theodore Roosevelt. The John Stennis' flight deck is configured exactly the same. The seas are calm and there are no cross winds. This should be a piece of cake. My name is Commander Ed Horsely, and I will be your Landing Signal Officer.

I'm Carl Bridger, Commander Horsely.

Buck unbuckled and scrambled back to the bomb-bay.

"You're on deck, Cody. The John Stennis is vectoring us in as we speak."

Cody squeezed between the Gatlings and the missile racks onto the flight deck and, with Carl's help, wiggled into the right seat.

"Hi, Grandpa. Are you ready to do this one more time?" Cody looked over at Carl, who flashed him a smile and a wink.

"I'm ready. The John Stennis is reporting calm seas and no cross winds. You've got the radio. Just guide us in."

"Roger that." Cody keyed his transmit button.

November-Juliet-Charlie-Sierra, this is Lieutenant Bridger, over.

Roger, Lieutenant. This is the LSO. Captain, you are three-five miles out. Descend and maintain seven-hundred, and turn to heading three-five-five degrees. Do not acknowledge any further communication.

Carl made the course correction and waited for the Landing Signal Officer to respond.

I show you on the glide slope. Slow to landing speed, Commander Horsely directed.

Carl pulled back the throttles and set his props to one-hundred-percent pitch. He adjusted the fuel mixture for the lower altitude and let *Annie* ease into a gentle descent. At seven-hundred feet he leveled off and added three-quarters flaps as he reduced his airspeed to one-hundred-ten mph. He noticed the amber "ball" lights above the green DATUM lights and pulled back on the throttles a tad.

You're looking good, Captain. You're right on glide slope...you're drifting right. Correct left. Good...you're back on the glide slope.

Carl's eyes moved in rapid succession between the green DATUM lights and the center line of the deck. Two amber "ball" lights appeared beneath the green lights, and he eased the throttles slightly forward, bringing *Annie's* nose up until the lights disappeared.

Three-quarter mile. Call the ball! The LSO said.

Ball. Bravo two-five, Cody said.

"Bring your nose up a tad more," Cody coaxed.

Carl added a little power and laid in full flaps. At ninety mph *Annie's* nose passed over the deck. Her wheels were only ten feet above the surface. Carl pulled the throttles to full idle, and the main wheels dropped to the deck. He applied brakes and brought the B-25 to a stop. A yellow-jacketed plane handler directed Carl to a parking stall just forward of the island. Carl shut down the avionics followed by the engines and three crewmen chocked the tires.

"Wow, Grandpa! That was a perfect landing. I didn't need to help much at all this time."

"Thanks, Cody. I don't know how you guys do this every day. I don't think my heart could take it," Carl said with a nervous tremor in his voice as he unbuckled his harness.

The crew climbed down to the deck and waited for Carl and Cody. Standing clear of the plane, Carl punched in the five digit code on the hand-held remote for the bomb-bay doors, and the servos pulled the doors closed. The men walked toward the island as a khaki uniformed officer wearing a navy-blue ball cap with CVN-74 emblazoned in gold letters on it, appeared through the hatch. Judging from the gold "scrambled eggs" on the bill of the hat and the insignia on his collar, Carl judged the man to be a senior officer. Cody came to attention and saluted him.

The officer returned Cody's salute as he approached the crew. "Which one of you men is Captain of that magnificent aircraft?"

"Carl Bridger, Captain. Let me introduce the rest of my friends." Carl introduced everyone. The skipper of the John Stennis seemed to know them already.

"I'm Captain Charles Yarborough, Skipper of the John Stennis. Welcome aboard, gentlemen. I've been talking to Captain Phillips and Admiral Richards aboard the Theodore Roosevelt. I'm familiar with your operation. Let's get inside out of this twenty-knot wind." The captain led the crew through the hatch to the interior of the floating city.

Two minutes later, they entered the officer's mess. A grey-haired black-suited man sat at the head of the table. He was flanked by two Marine MP's. The suit stood and immediately smiled at the rag-tag assemblage of senior citizens standing before him.

"Gentlemen...," Captain Yarborough began. "Allow me to introduce Secretary of the Navy, William H. Memmot. Mister Secretary, the crew of *Annie's Raiders.*" Yarborough introduced them individually, and when he got to Cody, the SECNAV held up his hand.

"There's no need to introduce this young man. Welcome home, Lieutenant Bridger. It's an honor for me to meet you and this group of men who did what our government could not do; bring you back home." Secretary Memmot shook the hand of each man. Carl was pleasantly surprised to see the SECNAV's eyes brimming with pride and sincere joy.

"Now then, gentlemen; as much as I would like for this to be a pleasure cruise for all of us, I'm afraid there's some business to take care of; a matter of State, if you will." The SECNAV looked at the men before him.

"Let me preface my remarks by bringing you up to date on the White House position on the hornet's nest you all stirred up in the hive of foreign relations. First, you acted in opposition to State's hands-off policy for launching a rescue mission. Second, you came very close to undoing the NATO peace plan for ending the Bosnian/Serbian war. In fact, by shooting down that Croatian fighter...a helluva feat, I might add...you nearly started a regional conflict of much greater proportions.

"All of this and we haven't even begun to talk about the numerous international laws you gentlemen shredded during your...*excursion*. You're all wanted by INTERPOL, by the way, which is why you are sitting here instead of in a Croatian jail. Anyway, that's the worst of it. Now for the flip side:

"The United States is the chief member of NATO. We provide the muscle NATO needs to maintain order throughout Europe. American money pays for the lion's share of maintaining a ready force: ground, sea, and air, to prevent rogue fascist states like The Republika Sprska from practicing ethnic cleansing and political and religious genocide. The international community, including Croatia, is willing to turn a blind eye to your little adventure. Simply put, your actions against a principle Serbian military outpost had the unintended consequence of significantly weakening the Serbian stranglehold on Sarajevo and bringing both parties closer to a negotiated peace accord.

"Where peace in the region was still two, maybe three years away, it now looks like hostilities will cease within the year. So much for the international situation: The political climate at home is simpler, but involves your willingness to do one thing." The SECNAV paused.

"What 'simple' thing, Mister Secretary?" Carl asked. He could sense the other shoe about to fall.

"The White House is going to release a statement to the Press Corps stating the rescue of Lieutenant Bridger was a CIA covert operation from the beginning. That's partially true, actually. Your friend Mister Mckenzie Aldrin, convinced the Director to support your rescue mission.

"The CIA does not want to widen the rift between the Agency and the White House, so Mister Aldrin and I met with the President and brokered a deal. The deal is this: you all agree to say nothing to the press or to any other person EVER about the operation except that you were part of the CIA and White House combined strategy to extract two Naval aviators from Serbian hands. In return for your cooperation, the President will instruct the Justice Department to file no charges." Memmott looked at the men.

Carl looked at the Navy Secretary. "So, the President intends to go before the American people and take credit for the daring rescue of Lieutenant Bridger under the deep moral commitment to leave no man behind. Is that about it, Mister Secretary?"

"Yeah, that's about it. A ceremony is already being planned at the Arlington Cemetery for Lieutenant JG Perry Judd with full military honors. His body was recovered by the SOG team and successfully returned into friendly hands. The President himself will be in attendance."

Carl looked at each of his crew. He didn't like the cover-up. He also recognized that his going public with the true story would only bring hardship to his crew and to himself. It was their decision as much as it was his. Harry nodded an affirmative vote, as did Doc. Buck, who Carl knew understood the politics of situations like this, also nodded affirmatively.

"What about you, Giff? The decision belongs to all of us."

Gifford looked at Cody, and then nodded at Carl. "We got my son back thanks to you, Pop. It's time to go home and get back to our lives."

"Mister Secretary, we are agreed. Do you need us to sign anything, like a statement under oath?" Carl asked with a note of sarcasm.

The SECNAV dropped his eyes. "Mister Bridger, if it were up to me, I'd say your word is good enough; better than any printed document. But, yes, Washington wants each of you to sign a non-disclosure agreement under oath, the violation of which is punishable by law."

The Secretary of the Navy opened a metal case and extracted the documents which had been prepared ahead of time. Each crew member of '*Annie's Raiders* signed the agreement.

"Gentlemen, now that the unpleasant business of State is concluded, will you join Captain Yarborough and me for dinner? I promise you, the John Stennis' chef is among the best."

CHAPTER XVI

Four days after landing on the deck of CVN-74, the carrier was fifty-miles off the coast of Norfolk, Virginia. Carl and Buck were busy performing a pre-flight check of the B-25.

"Climb aboard and lower the flaps, will you Buck?" Carl checked the struts on the landing gear. There was a normal amount of hydraulic fluid on all three struts and they showed good height between the cylinders and sleeves. A walk-around of the engines and inspection of the propellers also indicated normal wear. The bomber had logged over forty hours since she left the Double-B Ranch. Carl knew that she would be due for a thorough mechanical check from a certified mechanic in Great Falls.

With the flaps dropped down, Carl checked the cable linkages to all of the control surfaces. His visual inspection revealed no anomalies. *Annie* had held up remarkably well. He ran his hand along the bullet holes which pocked the length of the fuselage. The riveted panels of aluminum alloy were solidly in place. The damage would not adversely affect the aerodynamics of the aircraft. The repaired right rudder assembly was in excellent condition. Carl smiled and patted the *Annie's Raiders* logo. His mind raced with memories of the fourteen missions he flew in the Pacific with Harry and Doc. His eyes brimmed, and his heart swelled with love for his "brothers."

"We're good down here, Buck. Raise the flaps and climb on down." Carl reflected on all of the good fortune he had experienced, that they *all* had experienced, because of General Buckminster Rogers. The former astronaut had endeared himself to Carl and forged a bond of heartfelt friendship.

"The men in blue were kind enough to top off our tanks. I'll tell you; these sailors don't waste time. I watched them fuel the plane. Every movement was a dance, like every motion had been choreographed. Anyway; I think we're ready to go, my friend." Buck joined Carl and the two walked toward the John Stennis' island.

"Alrighty, then. Let's get everybody together and go over the flight plan."

The officer's mess was mostly empty. The first shift of the evening meal was still two-hours away. A pair of Junior-Grade officers were chatting quietly at a table while they sipped from white ceramic cups of steaming coffee. When the crew of the old bomber entered the dining hall, they both stood up as a show of respect. Everyone on board had heard the story of *Annie's Raiders* and the young officers saluted them for their heroic rescue of one of their own.

"As you were, gentlemen. Thank you," Buck said. The two men smiled and resumed their conversation.

"It's almost time for us to take off, you guys. We'll go wheels up in an hour when we are about twelve miles out of Norfolk. Captain Yarborough has us approved for VFR through the military restricted airspace around Norfolk Naval Airbase. From there, we head for Green Bay, Wisconsin for refueling and a layover until dawn. At first light tomorrow we'll head for the Double-

B." Carl looked at each man. "Suggestions, anyone?"

"Dad, Cody and I are going to stay aboard until we dock. I've arranged for the company jet to meet us tonight at Norfolk International Airport. We're going to fly straight to Provo where the rest of the family is waiting," Gifford said.

"Well, I can't say I wouldn't do the same thing. What about the rest of you? Any special requests?"

"We're with you all the way, Skipper." Doc grinned.

"Hell yes, we are. I haven't had this much excitement since '45." Harry agreed.

Buck smiled. "You know me, Carl. I'm ready for a day of ridin' the Double-B range before I get back to work. That is, if you can put up with me for a couple of more days."

"Lord, you have no idea how much I'm looking forward to trading the cockpit for a saddle." Carl pushed his chair back and stood.

"Wheels up in one hour, boys. Doc, will you see if the galley can provide us with some chow to take along with us?"

"Roger that, Skipper." Doc answered, and headed for the galley.

Gifford and Cody stayed behind with Carl as the rest of the men left the mess hall. "Pop, I wanted to talk to you alone." Gifford sat back down next to Cody.

Carl took a seat.

"What's up, Giff?"

"Well, first and foremost, I want to tell you how much I love you, Dad. What you did for our family...well, no value can be placed on it. You saved Cody's life. You brought him back home. Thank you...from the bottom of my heart." Gifford cleared his throat. "The second thing I wanted to say is, whatever damage was done to *Annie's Raiders* InterDyn will repair. I want to restore her to her original condition. All of the modifications will be reversed and the cannons and IVOTACS equipment will be removed. She deserves to be returned to her World War II mint condition."

Carl looked lovingly at his son and grandson.

"You two are my family. You know that. What we did, you and I, came as naturally as morning coffee to me. There was no way I could stand back and let Cody suffer the same fate as his friend. You don't owe me anything, son. As for *Annie*, I accept your offer to fix her up. Neither of us is ready to be grounded, yet.

"Now give your old man a hug so we can get out of here. Oh, and one more thing. You have to promise to bring Alisa and Rachel to the ranch, preferably before Cody has to report back to the Theodore Roosevelt."

"You've got it Pop." The three generations of Bridgers embraced each other. "We'll see you stateside."

"Thanks again, Grandpa," Cody said and stepped back.

Carl turned and walked out of the mess hall toward his quarters. Saying goodbye to Cody and Gifford marked this stage of the mission with a sense of finality. Up to this point, they'd all been a family, protected by the wings of an angel...*Annie*. The sudden realization that he … all of them …were safe, hit home, and left him with a lump of gratitude swelling in his chest. He leaned against the hatch to his quarters and barely managed to stifle a sob.

Having regained his composure, Carl closed the hatch behind him and breathed a deep sigh of relief. He stuffed his belongings into a duffel bag and headed topside, but was stopped by a very large Marine Lance Corporal. *I wonder if the Marines grow these young men especially large for sea duty.* He chuckled whimsically at his own joke.

"Sir...?" the MP asked.

"Nothing...it's nothing. What can I do for you, Lance Corporal?"Carl grinned.

"Captain Yarborough requests the pleasure of your company, Mister Bridger, and your crew as well; if you'll follow me, sir?" the Marine MP said, turning on his heel.

Carl slung his duffel-bag over his shoulder and followed the man to the Captain's wardroom. When he entered, he found everyone gathered there. They all stood, and the C.O. of the John Stennis addressed the assembled men.

"Attention to orders. Carl Bridger, for meritorious service and for having demonstrated superior flying skills under unique circumstances, not the least of which includes completing two carrier landings, it is with pride that I award you your Navy Pilot Wings with Carrier Certification. Lieutenant Bridger; if you will."

Cody stepped in front of his grandfather and opened a navy-blue case. Inside the case were the gold aviator wings of a Navy pilot. Cody removed the wings and handed the box to Gifford. He pinned the wings on Carl's worn leather bomber jacket then stepped back and came to attention. He and Captain Yarborough saluted sharply. Carl returned the salute, and Buck led a round of "Hip-hip-hoorah!"

Carl stood before those in the room, speechless. He opened his mouth to speak, but knew only meaningless jabber would escape his lips. He looked at his friends, feeling like a helpless child. Finally, Buck spoke in his behalf.

"What my educated friend is trying to say is: he is grateful for this honor and for the respect shown to him and the crew of *Annie's Raiders* by the men and women of the John Stennis and the Theodore Roosevelt. He is proud of Cody, as are we all, and we wish for Lieutenant Bridger a long and successful career in the service of his country."

"Thank you, General. Let me bid you all a safe journey home. I believe the plane handlers have your aircraft ready for your inspection, Carl. Good luck, gentlemen." The captain led the way to the flight deck and waved a final farewell as the crew of the old

B-25 climbed aboard.

Carl turned and through a salute to Yarborough, then climbed up through the bomb-bay, and worked his way forward to the cockpit. After buckling his harness, Carl looked over at Buck and smiled.

"Let's go, Buck. Time's a-wastin' .You have the controls on this one."

Buck flashed Carl a surprised expression. Without a moment's hesitation, he replied. "Roger that, Skipper. Give me one-half flaps."

"Fifty-percent flaps, Captain," Carl affirmed.

Army two-two-three-six requesting permission to depart, Carl announced over the radio.

Army two-two-three-six you are cleared for departure. Good luck, Captain.

A plane handler stood off to the side and saluted the old bomber. Buck returned the salute then closed and latched the sliding Plexiglas panel. He eased the throttles forward all the way. "Release the brakes."

Carl released the parking brakes, and the B-25 started forward. At full power *Annie* shot down the deck until she reached takeoff speed. The main gear lifted off and the plane climbed into the sky.

"Positive rate, gear up."

"Gear up," Carl announced as he noted the two green *Gear Up* lights flash on.

"Flaps up."

"Flaps up, Captain," Carl confirmed.

Buck took the liberty of flying up-wind for a couple of miles and then banked back toward the John Stennis. Dropping the vintage plane to nearly deck level, he waggled the '25s wings as they passed low and to the side of the Nimitz-class carrier. The few men remaining on deck waved at the old bomber as *Annie's Raiders* flew past and banked west toward the Virginia coast with the rising sun at her back.

Carl pressed the talk button on his microphone.

"Boys, here's the plan: We'll fly north to Pennsylvania and west from there to St. Paul. We'll layover in the twin cities for some chow and rest. Tomorrow morning we'll head for Cascade and the Double-B. I figure we should be home by 11 a.m. Montana time."

"Roger that, Skipper. Hey, with Cody and Gifford gone, Doc and I have the whole bomb-bay to ourselves. We're cozy back here," Harry announced.

"How's your head doing, Harry?" Buck asked.

"Oh, it's fine. The Navy Doc checked me out and said whoever stitched me up did a fine job," Harry winked at Doc. "They didn't know the other man in the room was a surgeon."

"Well, you boys just make yourselves comfortable back there. If you don't mind, Harry, Carl and I could use a cold brew up here."

"Got you covered, General. I'll be right up." The old gunner worked his way forward and handed the beers to Buck.

Six hours later, the sun hung high overhead. Carl turned *Annie* toward the northwest. As they passed through and around each area of controlled airspace, Carl notified every airport along his flight path of their location, direction of flight, and altitude. At the moment, they were approaching PHL, the designation for Philadelphia International Airport.

Papa Hotel Lima, Army four-zero-two-two-three-six is type Bravo two-five. We are three five miles southeast at niner- thousand. Request transition to the northwest.

Roger Army two-two-three-six. Did you say you are

a Bravo two-five?

Affirmative Philly Traffic. We're headed back home to Montana.

Roger, Captain Bridger. You're fame precedes you, sir. News of Annie's Raiders is flooding the airwaves. You are cleared for transition. Turn to one-two-five point two-one-five and squawk ident.

Annie's Raiders passed through Philly's Class B airspace and pointed her nose toward Reading seven hours after they lifted off the deck of CVN-74.

Buck was taking a break in the back with Doc and Harry. Carl had the auto-pilot set to the GPS heading and was chewing on a pastrami and provolone on rye sandwich when he glanced out the left side of his windscreen just as a shiny red-tailed P-51D Mustang eased up off his wing. The pilot signed the numbers 1-2-5-point-5-5. Carl turned comm. 2 to 125.55.

Well, hellooo, beautiful! Uh...I mean the plane, not you. Carl Bridger is my name. Who might you be? he asked.

Name's Phil Shaw, Carl. We've been listening to you boys over the Ham radio network ever since you left Norfolk. You fellas are national celebrities.

The '51 pilot pointed for Carl to look out over his right wing. A P-47 Thunderbolt was cruising alongside.

That's Pat Finney in the Thunderbolt, Carl. Say howdy, Pat.

Howdy, Carl. It's a pleasure to make your acquaintance, Pat said with a deep Tennessee drawl.

Anyhow, as I was saying about you being a celebrity, it's been all over the news about your rescue of a Navy pilot in Serbia. Even the President called you a hero.

We haven't had a chance to catch up on the news,

Phil. We've been flying for the last several hours and at sea for four days more.

Let me tell you something: Us boys at the Air Museum in Reading are connected with warbird enthusiasts by ham radio all around the country. Anyhow, me and Pat would be honored if you'd let us fly escort with you for a few minutes, Carl.

Carl chuckled. *We could have used you fellas as an escort over Croatia. Sure, we'd be glad for the company.*

Pat noticed the bullet holes on the right side of the '25s fuselage.

Hey, Carl, are those real bullet holes I'm looking at? Whoo-wee! It's like you came up through time from Doublya Doublya Two.

Sort of feels like it, too. I'd like to not talk about the last couple of days, if you don't mind. If I told you the whole story, I'd have to shoot you boys down. Carl laughed.

Roger that, Carl, Phil said. *Hey, word has it that Buck Rogers is on board.*

You heard right. I'll put him on the comm. and you can say howdy.

Carl put them all on the intercom. "Buck, come on up here. A couple of boys off our wing would like to meet you."

Buck stuck his head between the two seats. He glanced left and then right. "Well, I'll be." He put his headset on.

Hello, gentlemen. Now where did you come by those two fine looking birds?

He climbed into the right seat.

Hey, General Rogers. We're honored to meet you, sir...kinda weird circumstances, though. Phil Shaw laughed.

Like I was telling Mister Bridger, Pat and I are part of an air museum in Reading. The whole bunch of us are in the business of restoring as many of these old warbirds as we can in honor of those guys who flew them in the war. We started in nineteen-eighty. Hey, would you be interested in joining our group?

Oh, I don't know, Phil. I'm busy running a ranch up in Montana. Not much time for other things, Carl said.

Yea, I know what you're saying. Well, we'd sure like to invite you to our fly-in next month. Your '25 would be a real highlight. You'll find us on the internet. Well, listen, fellas, we hafta go. By the way, one of our boys has been flying chase with a camera while we've been talking. He's been filming our formation as part of our ad campaign. I'd like your permission to use the footage. If it's okay with you, can I mail you a release form? Phil asked.

You go ahead and use the film, Phil. I have no objection. But, you can reach me at P.O. Box 12, Cascade, Montana. Maybe I'll come to your fly-in, Carl offered.

The honor would be ours, Carl. We'll break off now, my friend.

Phil peeled away. Carl got a glimpse of the chase plane, a sleek P-38 Lightning.

"Wow, Buck, those are some gorgeous wings those boys are flying. I wouldn't mind seeing their whole museum."

"We can plan on it, partner. My dance card is pretty free these days."

Three hours and seven hundred miles later, Carl dialed in Comm.2 to 124.475MHz to the ATIS frequency for Crystal Airport (call letters MIC) Northwest of St. Paul, Minnesota. The recording announced winds at twelve knots from 065 degrees, active runway was 24 Right, visibility six miles, ATIS information was Charlie, Tower frequency was 120.70 MHz, and Ground on 121.60 MHz. Carl wrote all of the information down as Buck tuned Comm.1 to the tower frequency and Comm.2 to the ground control frequency. The Airport Traffic Information System told Carl everything he needed to know.

Mike, India, Charlie, Army four-zero-two-two-three-six is a warbird type Bravo Two-Five, three-five miles east at niner- thousand-five-hundred inbound to land runway two-four right with Charlie.

Roger, Army four-zero-two-two-three-six. You are cleared straight-in approach for runway two-four right. Be advised of microbursts on the runway. A Skyhawk had to go missed approach about three zero minutes ago, but landed on his second approach. Shouldn't be a problem for your bomber, Captain.

Roger, Crystal Tower. Cleared straight in to runway two-four right for Army four-zero-two-two-three-six.

Carl had *Annie* lined up on the centerline of the runway about seven miles ahead. Each time they passed over one of the countless small lakes, the cool air bounced the plane up, and then the '25s nose would drop back down as they flew into warmer air over dry land. The buffeting and the gentle yaw back and forth were all perfectly manageable.

With wheels and flaps down, Carl pulled the throttles back, and the B-25 settled into ground effect. Then, as if pushed upward by some giant invisible hand, the nose violently angled up and the stall warning horn blared. Buck, who had his hands on the throttles, jammed them forward to the stops. The engines revved up to a scream as Carl dropped the nose back into a landing attitude. Buck pulled the throttles back, and the main wheels squeaked on to the tarmac.

Outstanding recovery, Captain. Exit the runway as soon as possible and contact ground on one-two-one point six-zero.

One-two-one point six-zero, roger. Thank you, tower.

Annie's nose wheel rolled slowly along the yellow line and stopped on the painted crossbar of the parking stall adjacent to a hanger. Carl turned off the avionics and then Buck pulled the mixture all of the way back on first one engine followed by the other. Carl shut down the rest of the electronics and placed his headset on the control yolk in front of him.

"That was some pretty quick thinking back there, Buck. That microburst really got my blood flowing!" Carl shook his head. "It's a good thing you already had your hand on the throttles."

"We right-seat guys are here to serve, my friend." Buck slapped Carl's back as they, along with Harry and Doc, walked toward the opened hanger.

They located a mechanic in the big hangar, and Carl asked the man to do a quick once over of the plane. He also asked for all of the fluid levels to be checked and topped off. Doc remained behind to brief the mechanic on the specifics for the B-25. The enthusiastic young man immediately set to work as Doc turned toward the terminal building to join the others for some chow in the cafeteria. He got as far as the hangar door when a wave of vertigo forced him to stop and lean up against the door-track for a moment until the dizziness abated. His head cleared and he walked on. The momentary fugue, he told himself, was nothing more than the result of too much excitement and not enough sleep.

Carl, Buck, Doc, and Harry sat at a booth drinking coffee and waiting for their food.

"I think the first order of business is to get us some rooms and settle in for a good night's sleep." Carl was exhausted and he figured the others were as well.

"Agreed. I'm ready for a comfortable bed and no engine noise." Buck punctuated his point with a wide-mouthed yawn.

"Yeah, I hereby prescribe sleep forthwith before our final journey's end back at Carl's place," Doc said tiredly as he massaged his left arm.

Carl took notice of Doc's sallow complexion and grew suddenly concerned. "You okay, Doc? Your arm hurting?"

"Huh? Oh, I'm fine; a little arthritis in my shoulder is all," Doc smiled wanly.

The waitress brought their orders and the men dug in. For the time being, at least, conversation stopped in favor of satisfying the more urgent need for food.

"Can I get you boys anything else?" The friendly waitress asked. She looked to be college age and was quite attractive with her red hair pulled back in a pony tail. Her blue-green eyes sparkled behind wire rimmed glasses. Her name tag spelled out "Fiona" in gold letters over a blue field.

"No thanks, Fiona. Oh, by the way, can you recommend a decent hotel where four tired boys can check in for the night?" Carl asked.

Fiona smiled, seeming happy to be of service. "Oh, yes. The Sun's Inn is about a half mile east on Airport Road. Would you like me to call them for you while you eat? I'm happy to do that. I don't have any other customers at my tables. It's been a pretty slow night."

"I'll tell you what, Fiona; you take this credit card and give the Sun's Inn a call. Set us up with four rooms and..." Harry interrupted.

"Three rooms will be fine, Skipper. I think Doc and I will share a double." Harry had an expression of concern...concern for Doc shared by Carl and Buck. Doc didn't argue with Harry's suggestion.

"Make it two singles and a double. Wait a second, Fiona." Carl fished his wallet out and withdrew a ten and a twenty. "This is for you." He put the cash in Fiona's apron pocket.

"Oh, my! Thank you, sir. That's very generous. I'll get right to work on those rooms." She turned, walked toward the kitchen and disappeared through the swinging door.

Ten minutes later, she reappeared.

"You're all set. Just check at the desk when you get there. Your rooms are reserved under your name, Mister Bridger. Can I get you all some dessert?"

"Oh, I don't think so, thanks. You've been a huge help...oh, one more thing; is there a car rental or ground transportation available?"

"I already arranged for the Sun's Inn shuttle to meet you in front just outside the doors you came in through. They're only about ten minutes away. Here's your credit card and the bill, Mister Bridger. Excuse me, I see some new customers." She walked over to the newly arrived diners.

The four friends finished their meal, and Carl left another ten dollar tip for Fiona. He signed the restaurant's receipt and they left to wait for the shuttle outside.

The Sun's Inn was one of those cookie-stamped hotel/motels like every other "motel row" lodging facility in any city across the country. The only unique characteristic was the sign telling which conglomerate owned the building. Generally, they were clean enough and the crew didn't much care one way or the other. They were all exhausted and wanted only to hit the sack. After sleeping on the narrow mattresses in the confined space of on-board housing on the two carriers, the motel rooms seemed like luxury suites.

Carl dropped his duffel bag on the floor, threw back the

comforter of the king-sized bed and undressed. He wanted to be comfortably tucked in before he called Beth. He needed to hear her voice before going to sleep.

The analog alarm clock on the nightstand read 10:15 p.m. *nine fifteen, Montana time. Good. I'll call Beth after I unpack and take a shower,* he thought.

He showered, shaved, brushed his teeth and slipped between the cool sheets. *Oh, this is nice,* he thought as he pulled the covers over his aching body. *Now I know why war is left to the younger men,* he reflected and smiled. "Yep, Carl, you're assignment to the ranks of the old fart command is official," he said aloud. He yawned broadly and lay back. *I'll close my eyes and enjoy this just for a second ... call Beth in ... a minute.*

He dreamed he lay in his own bed at the ranch. He and Beth had retired early for some cuddle time. The mission was in the distant past and he and Beth had been married for what seemed like several years. The dream was one of those that came once in a blue-moon these days; rare and poignant, but with one major difference: instead of Annie lying next to him, it was Beth, whose arm lay across his chest.

Someone began banging on their bedroom door.

Bam! Bam! Bam! "Carl, answer the door, dammit! It's Doc!" Harry pulled Carl from his dream. Carl bolted out of bed and pulled open the door to face a distressed Harry; his face filled with fear and worry.

"Harry, what's wrong? You were screaming about Doc. Has something happened?" Carl's mind was fully alert now and adrenalin coursed through his veins.

"Come on. Now!" The old gunner said. He pulled at Carl's arm.

"He's having a heart attack or something, Skipper."

As soon as Carl entered the room he knew Doc was in trouble. Carl's mind raced to take inventory of the situation; *face:...pale and ashen...lips: cyanotic and blue.* Doc lay motionless, his eyes staring and void of life.

"Call 9-1-1, Harry." Acting quickly, Carl placed pillows under Doc's feet and put his first two fingers on his friend's neck and pressed on the carotid artery. "No pulse," he said, and began chest compressions. He used to be CPR certified and recalled the correct procedure: five compressions to one breath into Doc's mouth. On the second set of compressions he felt one of Doc's ribs break. He noted the "pop" in Doc's chest, but frantically continued as Harry finished the 9-1-1 call. "C'mon, Doc, breathe, dammit!" he cried.

"Harry, get Buck in here, and call the desk. Ask them if they have emergency oxygen." Harry ran out of the room.

Carl continued the CPR. He stopped to check for a pulse and signs of breathing...*nothing.* He kept working on his friend despite the burning in his shoulders and aching arms. Sweat trickled down between his shoulder blades as his mind calculated the time since he began the compressions. *Five...six minutes?*

Buck and Harry entered the room. Buck saw what was needed and relieved Carl, expertly beginning chest compressions while Carl did the CPR breathing technique: clear the airway, tilt the head back, close off the nasal passage and perform mouth-to-mouth breathing.

Five minutes later, the sound of a siren, close by...the EMT's had arrived. In less than a minute they were running down the hall toward Harry's beckoning wave.

"In here. He's in here. Hurry!" Harry sobbed, leading the way. Carl noticed Harry was wearing only white boxers and a T-shirt.

The EMT's went to work. One of them, a woman, bagged Doc and began to squeeze air into Doc's lungs. The other medic, a man, scissored off Doc's T-shirt and charged the defibrillator. "Clear!" he yelled. Doc's body jumped with the shock. The medic checked for a heartbeat. Twenty minutes had elapsed since Carl first started compressions. The EMT tried to shock Doc's heart several times, increasing the power to 400 jewels, but to no avail.

The EMT's looked at each other. The man shook his head and stood. "I'm sorry, sir. He's gone. We'll take him to Holy Trinity. You're welcome to follow in your car if you'd like. I'm very sorry for the loss of your friend."

They placed Doc's body in a black body bag and took him out on a gurney. Harry, Carl, and Buck sat down. They sat silently, unable to speak, their minds reeling beneath the storm of their heartbreak. Finally, Buck, who had known Doc the least, spoke.

"We need to call his family. His wife passed a few years ago, didn't she?" Buck asked.

Carl patted Harry's back. "That's right. His daughter, Jessica, has been keeping an eye on him. I'll check his belongings for a number. I'll take care of it, Harry, don't you worry."

He stood and walked to the closet. He found Doc's wallet and an emergency contact card with an AARP logo on it. On the reverse side were three names with phone numbers. He recognized the name of Jessica Wilkins.

"Guys, I'll be right back. Give me a few minutes." He returned to his room, picked up the phone from the nightstand, and punched in the number for Doc's youngest child. He drew in a deep breath and released it with a shudder.

"Hello, this is Jessica," the voice on the other end answered. Carl opened his mouth but couldn't speak. He wasn't ready for this.

"Hello...is someone there?" Jessica asked.

"Yes...yes, I'm here, Misses Wilkins," Carl choked out.

"This is Carl Bridger, Jessica. I'm a friend of your father."

"Yes, Mister Bridger I know who you are. Dad speaks often of you. Why are you calling? It's 2:00 a.m. here. Is this about Dad? Is he alright?" Jessica Wilkins' voice took on a tone of concern and fear.

Carl spent the next twenty minutes talking to Doc's daughter, pausing between her uncontrollable sobs of grief. Fortunately, her husband was with her. She had put her phone on speaker, and Carl could hear him comforting his wife. A few moments later, he took the phone from her.

Martin Wilkins spoke in a calm, pleasant voice.

"Mister Bridger, thank you for your call. We'll contact the hospital and take care of the arrangements to have Dad brought home. Will you please give me your contact information? I'm sure we'll need to speak again soon." Carl gave him the information and ended the call.

That's it? The measure of one man's existence is summed up with a simple phone call? "Dear God, I hate this!" Carl buried his face in his hands and wept. All of the memories, especially of the last couple of weeks cascaded through the corridors of his mind, some opening doors of long forgotten decades of past events. "Doc. I'm so sorry...so sorry."

Carl walked back across the hall where Harry and Buck were talking. The two men stood when Carl came into the room.

"Hi, Skipper. By the looks of you, you must have talked to Doc's daughter." Harry had put on some pants.

"Yes, yes I did. They'll take care of all the arrangements for Doc to be sent home. The poor girl was devastated." Carl looked at his two friends. "I guess there's nothing we can do now, but get some rest and fly out of here at first light."

"Oh yea, like sleep is going to happen...not!" Harry said." I need a beer or three. What do you say we raid the mini fridge and see what's there?"

"Sounds about right, Harry. Let's drink a toast or four to Doc," Buck said. "I only knew him for a short time, but he is...was, one helluva man on all counts."

For the next two hours, the remaining three crew members of *Annie's Raiders,* drank and talked, reminisced and laughed and drank some more.

Seven-thirty a.m. came with unwanted sunlight streaming into the room and the three old aviators waking to whopping hangovers. Harry, Buck, and Carl awoke with arms and legs entangled on the same bed.

Buck rose and rolled off the bed onto the floor. His head hit the carpet, eliciting an "ouch!"He covered his eyes against the sunlight streaming in through the unshaded window.

"Get up, you guys. Oh, man...coffee! We must all have coffee, forthwith; and acetoniphoneminofin, er, acetamino...LOTS of Tylenol." He ran his tongue over his teeth. "My mouth tastes like I slept with my shorts over my head."

Carl and Harry sat up.

"I was dreaming of Beth. We had our arms wrapped around each other." Carl rubbed the grit out of his eyes.

Harry grinned at Carl. "That was me, Skipper." He laughed.

For a moment, at least, the laughter had pushed back the pain of the loss of their friend.

"Oh, yuck!" Carl threw a pillow at Harry's face. "I'm going across the hall. What do you say we take advantage of the free continental breakfast? Downstairs in half-an-hour?"

"Roger that, Skipper. Out, you two, I need to hit the shower," Harry ordered. Buck and Carl left Harry for their own rooms.

Harry showered, shaved, and brushed his teeth. Dressed in

a clean shirt and tan Dockers, he packed up his duffel bag and turned toward the clothing rack where Doc's clothes hung on hangars. Harry laid out all of Doc's things and packed them carefully.

"I'm sorry, Doc," he spoke aloud. "Sleep well." He slung his duffel over his shoulder and carried Doc's in his hand. Pocketing the room key, the old gunner headed down to the dining area where the smells of breakfast wafted through the lobby.

Carl and Buck were already there, but barely. They looked as though their heads were still reeling from the night before. They both wore their aviator sunglasses and moved noticeably slower.

The three men loaded their plates with sausage gravy over biscuits, scrambled eggs and bacon. They carried their meals to a table and sat down. They drank coffee and tossed in a couple of ibuprofen each then dug in.

Twenty minutes later, with full stomachs and feeling much less hung over, they walked over to the reception desk where Carl paid their bill. The clerk was a portly middle-aged man. His gold-tone name tag said he was the hotel manager.

"We'd like to take the shuttle to the airport, please," Carl requested.

"He's about ready to leave right now. If you hurry you can still catch him." The manager smiled pointing toward the door.

The men hurried through the main entrance as the shuttle driver closed the sliding door on the van.

"Hey, wait up!" Buck called out.

"Good morning, gentlemen. Perfect timing eh?" The young man said.

They climbed in and relaxed in their seats for the ten-minute ride to the airport.

"Thanks for packing all of Doc's stuff, Harry. I'm sorry I didn't think of it or I would have helped," Carl said.

"Happy to do it, Skipper." Harry turned his head to watch the scenery pass by. His expression told Carl that further conversation about Doc was unwanted, at least for now.

The shuttle pulled up in front of the hangar. Carl, Harry, and Buck climbed out and headed for the door. Stepping in to the small lobby of *Great Lakes Aviation*, they looked around for someone who might be running the place. No one was in the office, so Carl stepped in to the main hangar where the B-25 was parked. A ladder stood next to the right engine and a mechanic, dressed in denim overalls with a Great Lakes Aviation logo over the breast pocket, climbed down to the ground.

"Mister Bridger?" The mechanic wiped his hands on a stained shop rag. Carl nodded affirmatively. "I'm Johnny Bidwell, chief mechanic and bottle washer, sir. She's a fine looking aircraft...kinda strange modifications, though. Are those for real?" Johnny pointed at the cannons protruding from the "blisters" on the side of the fuselage.

"Nope, only for show. The bullet holes, too. She's going to be in a movie being filmed out west," Carl lied. He hoped that Johnny Bidwell had not been watching the news. Paparrazi and reporters were not on their dance card today. "How about the '25...problems?"

"Oh, no sir; a little too much oil spray, so I checked all of the fittings and tightened them down. The oil levels were a trifle low on both sides...normal if you've been flying very far. Where you in from, if I might ask?" the mechanic inquired.

"To tell you the truth, Mister Bidwell, we flew off a carrier out in the Atlantic about eleven hundred miles east of here. You ever hear of the Doolittle Raiders? Well, this is one of them." Carl smiled. In this case, the truth was far better than fiction.

The mechanic gave Carl an incredulous look. "Okay, okay, I got it. You're a funny guy, Mister Bridger," Johnny chuckled.

"Well, sir. The tanks are topped off with a hundred-fifteen octane. Oil is topped off and you are good to go. If you'll come into the office, I'll work up your bill."

Carl paid the bill and scribbled some instructions on a blank piece of paper. He folded the paper and handed it to the inquisitive young mechanic.

"I'd be grateful if you'd call this number after we take off. She'll understand why I didn't call myself. I'm much obliged for your good work, Johnny. I've left you some money for the long-distance call and for your trouble." Carl turned to walk away and stopped. "By the way, Johnny, if you watch the network news tonight, you may learn something about old *Annie's Raiders.*" With a wink and a smile, Carl joined Harry and Buck.

Twenty minutes later, *Annie's Raiders* sat outside the hangar on the tarmac. Her engines were idling, and she was ready for the last leg of her adventure. Carl had received taxi instructions.

Roger, Crystal ground. Taxiing to runway two-four right via Alpha-two to Bravo-one. Hold short is active. Switching to tower frequency one-two-seven-point-five-seven-five.

Carl taxied the bomber to the hold short line, switched to comm..2 on the tower frequency and requested permission to depart.

Army two-two-three-six you are cleared for departure.

"Set flaps one-quarter, Buck," Carl requested.

"Flaps at one-quarter."

"Let's go home." Carl smiled at his friend and pushed the throttles forward gradually but firmly. The bomber picked up speed and thundered down the runway. *Annie* lifted off the runway, and Carl maintained runway heading until they reached five-hundred feet above the ground. It didn't escape any of them that they were leaving one of their own behind. Carl waggled *Annie's* wings in a farewell wave to their late friend.

CHAPTER XVII

"Gear up, Buck."

"Gear up," the astronaut/co-pilot repeated.

Buck raised the flaps and Carl banked right to three-zero-zero degrees.

"Set the GPS destination airport to Kilo Golf Tango Foxtrot and set the auto pilot to the GPS heading at altitude twelve-thou-sand-five-hundred, please Buck. We'll let *Annie* fly herself straight to Great Falls, and we'll fly visual from there to the ranch."

Buck programmed the call letters for Great Falls Regional Airport into the GPS. The B-25 would make automatic course corrections as they flew the portion of the great arc between Minnesota and Montana, a distance of nine-hundred-eighty-six miles. At their current airspeed of two-hundred-twenty mph they would land at the Double-B in about four-and-a-half hours.

"We should be home in time for a late lunch." Carl checked his watch. "It's 9:30 in Minnesota...only 8:30 in Montana. We should be on the ground by 1:00 p.m. Montana time."

"Sounds good, partner. Do you mind if I go in the back and spend some time with Harry?"

Carl nodded. This was not a good time for Harry to be

alone. The bond of shared war-time battle and ensuing decades of friendship was as strong for Carl as it was for Harry. Carl's heart was broken, and he figured that Harry's would be as well. Buck's ineffable sense of humor would help to salve the grief they all shared over the loss of Doc. "I've got the controls."

Beth and Ruth busied themselves with the breakfast crowd when the phone by the cashier's stand rang. Ruth was handling the calls and cashier duties, and picked up the phone.

"It's for you, Beth," Ruth called out.

Beth put down the damp cloth she used to wipe down the countertop and walked from behind the diner's main counter.

"Hello." She hoped Carl would be on the other end of the line. He hadn't spoken to her for almost two days. She figured he was busy with trying to get back home and she knew, as well, he couldn't call when he was in the air.

"Am I speaking to Beth Thomlinson?" Johnny Bidwell asked.

"Yes, this is she. Who is this?"

"Ma'am, My name is Johnny Bidwell. I'm an airplane mechanic here at Crystal municipal airport in Minnesota, ma'am. Mister Carl Bridger asked me to call you and to give you a message."

"Carl asked you to call? Is he alright? Why didn't he call me himself? What message?" Beth's anxiety level shot up off the charts. Ruth even turned to look at her, as did the two customers she was serving. Her voice had a definite edge of panic to it.

"Mister Bridger is fine, ma'am. He regrets not calling you himself. He said you'd understand if I told you that they lost Doc last night. He's gone, and..." Beth cut him off in mid sentence.

"Gone? Doc's gone? Oh, no...no. Did Carl say what happened?" she asked. Her voice became quiet. *Doc gone...dead? Oh, my poor Carl.*

"No, ma'am. He said he will be home by one o'clock your time, and he will explain everything when he sees you. That's all he said." Before hanging up, Johnny added, "I'm sorry if I've given you bad news, ma'am."

"No...no, Mister Bidwell. Thank you for calling. Good bye." Beth replaced the receiver on its cradle. She returned to finish wiping down the counter then removed her apron.

"Ruth, can you and Burt handle things until Janelle comes in at eleven?" A local kid, Janelle Franks hired on so Beth would have more time to run the business end of the Wagonwheel Hotel and Restaurant.

"Sure, kiddo. We'll be fine. Why don't you grab a banana cream pie from the fridge. You should take it with you." She smiled at Beth.

"Good idea, thanks." Beth slipped into the kitchen, took the pie and left out the back door. She needed to pick up some groceries and then head out to the Double-B. Her mind raced with a flood of conflicting thoughts: joy at the thought of being in Carl's arms in a few hours, and sorrow at the loss of Doc. *Loss ... Doc, dead? Probably a stroke or heart-attack. Poor Carl, what must he be going through?* Beth's heart ached at the thought.

The rolling hills and flatlands of the Midwest gave way to the east slope of the Rocky Mountains. Carl recognized the Missouri River where it turned southwest toward Fort Benton. He banked *Annie* and aimed her nose at a break between the Lewis Range and the Big Belt Mountains ... and the Double-B.

I'm almost home, Beth. God, how I need you. His mind and heart ached for her embrace. The last time he flew over this exact place, he and the boys were enroute to rescue his grandson. Carl remembered his heart being torn between the mission and the pull to turn back toward home...to Beth. He didn't have any expectation of returning; figuring, instead, that if the Serbs didn't kill them he would most likely be locked up for the rest of his life. Yet, here he sat; cradled inside *Annie* high above the carpeted farmlands of his beloved Montana. They had lost a friend; a price that the gods of fate charged for the life of Carl's grandson.

On the other side of the ledger was Beth...Beth; who had reawakened his heart to the hope and promise of rediscovered love, who had opened a joyous new chapter in his life.

Love had died for Carl twelve years ago. Cancer had burned it from his heart when it stole Annie from him. Then, the miracle of Beth changed all of that. She used her own love for Carl to rekindle long dead feelings within himself that brought with them happiness and a promise of peace he thought had died with Annie. He forced the pining thoughts from his mind. Home lay just over the approaching hills.

"Hey, Buck, I need you up here, buddy. We're fifteen minutes out." Carl called over the intercom.

"On my way. Buckle in, Harry. We're almost home." Buck patted Harry's knee and smiled at the old gunner. "You did good, old man ... really good. You, Doc, and Carl must have dominated the skies over the South Pacific back in the day."

Harry grinned back at Buck. "We were a team, alright ... and don't worry about me, rookie. I've got a wife waiting for me, and I can't wait to get back home. Now, go on back up front."

Buck joined Carl on the flight deck. Carl had already descended to five-thousand feet. Cascade's elevation of three-thousand-four-hundred feet above sea level allowed *Annie's Raiders* enough height to pass between the mountains and vector in for a landing at the Double-B.

"I think I see the town up ahead, Carl." Buck pointed down at a cluster of small buildings and houses which made up the town

314

of Cascade, Montana, population one-thousand-eight-hundred-fifty. The Double-B Ranch was positioned beyond the center of town to their right. Carl banked in that direction.

"Yep we're home. The Double-B is just beyond that hill to the right. I think we'll do a fly over." Carl dropped *Annie's* nose and headed up the Missouri River where it parallels the I-15 and passes through Cascade.

Annie's Raiders came in low over the Wagonwheel Hotel and Restaurant, banked around, and did another pass, waggling her wings as she flew overhead.

"I think we got their attention." Buck laughed. "Your girl-friend will likely be heading up to the ranch. She couldn't help but know that was us."

"True enough. Let's head for the barn." Carl turned the '25 toward the ranch.

The main house, the barn and silo, the corral and tack shack lay beneath them. As they flew over the house to align the plane with the runway, Carl saw his pickup truck parked in front of the main house where he had left it. Another vehicle sat parked along-side the truck.

"That's Beth's Explorer, Buck. Johnny Bidwell must have called her." *Good boy, Johhny,* Carl thought.

"There's Beth! I can see her!" Beth waved up at them and Carl waved *Annie's* wings in response.

Beth heard the B-25s engines as she stood at the stove cooking. A standing rib roast sizzled in the oven with another forty-five minutes left on the timer. She wiped her hands on a dish towel, and hurried to the front door and walked out into the yard. As the '25 flew over on her downwind leg, Beth could see Carl sitting at the controls. She waved. A thrill shot through her when the bomber's wings waved back. She watched, clutching her hands to her breast...her heart swollen with joy.

"Gear down, and give me one-quarter flaps."

"Gear down...one quarter flaps." Buck lowered the landing gear and flaps.

Carl flew downwind and throttled back to 110 mph. "Flaps to one-half."

"Flaps one-half."

"Full flaps," Carl directed and Buck lowered the flaps the rest of the way

"Full flaps."

Annie's Raiders came in low, her nose lined up with the grass strip. She slowed as she was buoyed up by the warm air rising from the ground. Her main wheels touched down as her nose wheel skimmed over the top of the grass for a moment before setting down. Carl let *Annie* slow herself to about five-miles-per-hour before he turned the old bomber's nose toward the barn

Carl and Buck completed the after-landing checklist and lowered the bomb-bay doors. Harry's boots were the first to hit the ground. Beth was on him with a rib-squeaking hug.

"Easy on an old man's ribs, Beth." Harry laughed and kissed her cheek.

"Your head...what happened, Harry?" She touched the bandage on Harry's head.

"I'll tell you all about it, but I think there's someone you've been waiting for." Harry turned toward the plane as first Buck, and then Carl appeared from beneath the bomb-bay.

Beth ran to Carl and threw her arms around his neck. Her body shook as sobs of joy exploded in a cascade of tears. "My love ... my love. You're home," she sobbed.

"I'm home, Beth. From here on in, it's just you and me. I

don't want to ever be away from you again. Marry me, Beth, and give this old man his heart back." Carl pushed Beth's hair away from her eyes. "I love you, Bethy."

"I love you, too, Carl; and yes, YES! I'll marry you." She was all tears and laughter again as the cheerleader and the football star embraced, their hearts pounding in unison as if they had just won the homecoming game.

"Okay you two, this old war horse needs his hug too. C'mere, Beth." Buck held out his arms and grinned broadly. The General had a heart as big as his smile. Beth complied and hugged him long and hard.

"Thank you for bringing him back to me, Buck." She stood on her toes and kissed Buck's cheek. "Now, inside, you three. Dinner's about ready. There's banana cream pie for dessert."

"And tomorrow, you and I are going for that ride, partner." Buck clapped his hand on Carl's shoulder.

"You got that right. What about you, Harry? You like ridin'?"

"Nope. If it ain't got wings, it's just me, my sweetheart, and my recliner. I'll head for Helena in the morning and catch a flight out for home."

The four of them walked toward the main house. Carl held Beth's hand. It felt good. *Really, REALLY good!* He smiled.

317

The Last Raider

EPILOGUE

Christmas, 1996

A cheerful fire blazed in the fireplace. Carl and Beth cuddled on the leather sofa in front of the flames and sipped on mugs of hot chocolate. The Christmas tree, a seven foot tall spruce harvested from the northeast corner of the Double-B, standing in multi-colored tinseled splendor, presided over the cheerily decorated living room in the main house while a December snow storm blanketed the landscape outside.

Two years of marriage had deepened the adoration Carl and Beth felt for each other. Following a two-week honeymoon in Paris and the Italian countryside, where Beth spent considerable time sketching the rich landscapes of the Tuscany wine country, the couple had returned to the Double-B and settled into their lives together.

"I can't wait for Gifford and everybody to get here. This is going to be the best Christmas ever." Beth snuggled closer to Carl.

"I agree. Two years is too long. I can't wait to see Cody, again. He made Lieutenant Commander last month. I wonder if he'll go back to sea-duty, or get a state-side assignment."

The sound of a car's horn blared from the front yard.

"It's them!" Beth threw off the blanket and hurried to the door. She opened it to the smiling faces of Gifford, Alisa, Rachel, Cody and his fiancé, whom Carl and Beth had not yet met. "Hi, you guys. Come in out of the storm." Beth hugged each of them.

"Who do we have here, Cody?" Carl asked from where he stood in front of the sofa.

Cody introduced his bride to be. "Grandpa, this is Katherine Kirk, my fiancé."

"Please, call me Kate." She hugged Carl and Beth warmly. "I've heard so much about you two; the rescue mission, and *Annie's Raiders*. I would sure like to the plane see her before we leave. Is that possible?"

"I think that can be arranged, Kate. Well, come, sit down. Why don't you two boys take the bags upstairs? Your rooms are ready for you."

Gifford and Cody took the bags upstairs while Beth, Alisa, Rachel, and Kate busied themselves with dinner preparations.

The men returned and joined Carl in his den where they talked for the next hour, catching up on the events of the last two years.

Gifford's company, InterDyn was booming and Rachel was in her second year of law school at Stanford.

"What about you, Cody? That gold leaf on your collar feels pretty good, I'll bet."

"It does, Grandpa. I have some news, though, that you need to here." He cleared his throat. "Kate and I will be settling in Virginia for a while."

Carl's curiosity was peaked. He sat forward in his chair, and fixed a steady gaze on Cody.

"Do I need to guess what it is you will be doing in Virginia?"

"No, I guess not." Cody chuckled. "I'll enter training in two weeks at the Intelligence Analysis School in Reston, Virginia."

"The CIA? What about the Navy?" Carl asked.

"I retired from active flight status last week. I'll retain my commission in the Navy, but for all intents and purposes I'll belong to the CIA and Navy Intelligence, at least for the foreseeable future. Kate has accepted a PCS transfer to the Navy JAG office in Norfolk."

"Wow! Changes abound in the Bridger family," Carl said, and lifted his cup of wassail: "A toast, then. To Cody and Kate. May your future be bright and filled with joy!"

Carl looked at his son and grandson. Pride and love filled his heart.

"I'm sorry we haven't had an opportunity to catch you up on the family, Pop. We've all been pretty busy. How are things going with the ranch?" Giff asked.

"The Plunkett boys, Jake and Clete, pretty much handle the wrangling and heavy lifting. Beth and I take care of the business end. Beth still runs the Wagonwheel."

He turned to Cody. How about you two? How did you and Kate get together?"

"Kate was the JAG officer aboard the Theodore Roosevelt in '94. She was actually on board when you were there, Grandpa. We didn't start getting serious until after I returned to full duty. In November the ship got reassigned to Norfolk for refitting and carrier training operations."

Kate overheard the men talking . Walking over to the sofa, she sat next to Cody, and picked up the conversation.

"I got assigned to the JAG office at Norfolk, and Cody and I were able to see a lot of each other over the next couple of months. We hit it off and, well, as the saying goes, the rest is history. You know, the most thrilling part of meeting you is remembering the day you guys launched from the deck of "The Big Stick". That was such a thrill. I'm truly honored to be here."

"Well, Kate, we're just country folks. We're glad that you and Cody could take leave time to be here with us," Carl said.

Gifford cleared his throat. "Pop, I've been meaning to ask you something. What about the '25? Are you done flying her?"

"Yea, for the most part I am. I manage to get a couple of hours in once in a while. Why?" Carl asked.

"Do you still have your license?" Gifford had a curious twinkle in his eye.

"Yes, as a matter of fact I do. Giff, what are you leading up to, son?" His curiosity was peaked.

"How would you like to take *Annie's Raiders* up for one last mission?" Gifford smiled. He placed a brief case on the coffee table and removed a folder with the logo of the Smithsonian Institute emblazoned on it. "Read this, Pop."

The folder contained two documents: an official entry certificate from the Smithsonian Air and Space Museum to include *Annie's Raiders* as a charter exhibit in the new Steven F. Udvar-Hazy annex of the Museum to be located at Dulles International Airport. Second, was an official invitation to the annual award ceremony for the John Safer Trophy which is awarded annually to an individual or team who has exhibited distinguished service to aviation history and/or technology.

"Dad, they want the last of the Doolittle Raiders. She's an historical aviation icon. They also want your story of how you found her in the Chinese countryside and of how you restored her and flew her again on the mission two years ago. Pop, she and you are a part of aviation history." Gifford paused to let the news sink in.

"How...?" Carl's mouth could not form words.

"How did all of this happen? Well, a certain friend of yours started the ball rolling in the spring of '95. He met with several senators and Pentagon people. Hell, he even got NASA to put in a pitch for you. Anyway, when things began to fall into place, Buck called me last month. We flew to D.C. and met with the Smithsonian. They reviewed the proposal and approved it. The Safer Trophy was their idea."

"You have a deal on one condition; Beth and I will fly *Annie* to Dulles. I'll need a copilot. I want Buck."

May, 1997

Memorial Day weekend brought with it parades, military ceremonies, the laying of the wreath on the tomb of the unknown soldier, and one of the busiest weekends of the year at the Air and Space Museum in Washington, D.C.

A huge crowd of spectators and dignitaries gathered in front of the executive terminal at Dulles International Airport awaiting the arrival of a vintage World War II B-25, the last raider of the historic Doolittle raid on Tokyo in April of 1942. Old 40-2236 was the last bomber to fly off the deck of the U.S.S. Hornet. As the only existing participant, *Annie's Raiders* had earned her place in history.

THE END

About the Author

Spencer Anderson is a former pilot and retired Air Force veteran whose passion for aviation is seen clearly in his writing. He is an outspoken advocate of general aviation and a student of aviation history. He lives in St. George, Utah with his wife Carole. The couple enjoys day trips in and around the Southern Utah national parks, and fishing the local lakes and reservoirs.